Anonymous

Transactions of the Obstetrical Society of London

Vol. IV

SALZWASSER
VERLAG

Anonymous

Transactions of the Obstetrical Society of London

Vol. IV

Reprint of the original, first published in 1863.

1st Edition 2022 | ISBN: 978-3-37500-333-3

Verlag (Publisher): Salzwasser Verlag GmbH, Zeilweg 44, 60439 Frankfurt, Deutschland
Vertretungsberechtigt (Authorized to represent): E. Roepke, Zeilweg 44, 60439 Frankfurt, Deutschland
Druck (Print): Books on Demand GmbH, In de Tarpen 42, 22848 Norderstedt, Deutschland

OBSTETRICAL TRANSACTIONS.

VOL. IV.

TRANSACTIONS

OF THE

OBSTETRICAL SOCIETY

OF

LONDON.

VOL. IV.

FOR THE YEAR 1862.

LONDON:

1863.

OBSTETRICAL SOCIETY OF LONDON.

OFFICERS FOR 1863.

ELECTED JANUARY 7TH, 1863.

HONORARY PRESIDENT.	SIR CHARLES LOCOCK, Bart., M.D.
PRESIDENT.	HENRY OLDHAM, M.D.
VICE-PRESIDENTS.	J. HALL DAVIS, M.D. ROBERT DRUITT, M.R.C.P. WILLIAM FERGUSSON, Esq., F.R.C.S., F.R.S. ROBERT HARDEY, Esq., Hull. JOSEPH G. SWAYNE, M.D., Bristol. THOMAS H. TANNER, M.D.
TREASURER.	ROBERT BARNES, M.D.
HONORARY SECRETARIES.	GRAILY HEWITT, M.D. JOHN BRAXTON HICKS, M.D., F.R.S.
OTHER MEMBERS OF COUNCIL.	HENRY W. BAILEY, Esq., F.R.C.S., Thetford. CHARLES CLAY, M.D., Manchester. WILLIAM FREDERICK CLEVELAND, Esq. CHARLES DRAGE, M.D., Hatfield. GEORGE THOMPSON GREAM, M.D. ROBERT GREENHALGH, M.D. FRANCIS SEYMOUR HADEN, Esq., F.R.C.S. GEORGE HARLEY, M.D. ISAAC HARRINSON, Esq., F.R.C.S., Reading. HENRY JAMES, Esq., F.R.C.S. J. C. LANGMORE, M.B. ALFRED MEADOWS, M.D. HENRY MADGE, M.D. JOSEPH THOMAS MITCHELL, Esq., F.R.C.S. WILLIAM TYLER SMITH, M.D. FREDERICK SYMONDS, Esq., F.R.C.S., Oxford. ALFRED JOSEPH TAPSON, M.B. JAMES GEORGE WILSON, M.D., Glasgow.

LIST OF PRESIDENTS.

1859 EDWARD RIGBY, M.D.
1861 WILLIAM TYLER SMITH, M.D.
1863 HENRY OLDHAM, M.D.

REFEREES OF PAPERS FOR THE YEAR 1863,

APPOINTED BY THE COUNCIL.

T. HERBERT BARKER, M.D., Bedford.
SAMUEL BERRY, Esq., F.R.C.S.E., Birmingham.
W. H. BRACE, Esq., Bath.
CHARLES CLAY, M.D., Manchester.
ROBERT DRUITT, M.R.C.P.
WILLIAM DRUITT, Esq., F.R.C.S.E., Wimborne, Dorset.
FRANCIS ELKINGTON, M.D., Birmingham.
WILLIAM TILBURY FOX, M.D.
HENRY GERVIS, M.D.
THOMAS F. GRIMSDALE, Esq., Liverpool.
ALFRED HALL, M.D., Brighton.
FRANCIS HIRD, Esq., F.R.C.S.E.
DRAPER MACKINDER, M.D., Gainsborough.
HENRY MADGE, M.D.
SAMUEL W. J. MERRIMAN, M.D.
GUSTAVUS C. P. MURRAY, M.D.
THOMAS W. NUNN, Esq., F.R.C.S.E.
WILLIAM O. PRIESTLEY, M.D.
THOMAS RADFORD, M.D., Manchester.
CHARLES H. F. ROUTH, M.D.
EDWARD JOHN TILT, M.D.
T. SPENCER WELLS, Esq., F.R.C.S.E.
JAMES WHITEHEAD, M.D., Manchester.
JAMES GEORGE WILSON, M.D., Glasgow.

HONORARY LOCAL SECRETARIES.

William Henry Brace, Esq., F.R.C.S. Edin. ...... Bath.
Samuel Berry, Esq., F.R.C.S.E. .... Birmingham.
Alfred Hall, M.D. .... Brighton.
Joseph Griffiths Swayne, M.D. .... Bristol.
Thomas Herbert Barker, M.D. .... Bedford.
Robert James Wilson, L.R.C.P. Ed....Hastings and St. Leonards.
Robert Hardey, Esq. .... Hull.
James Fenn Clark, Esq. .... Leamington.
Samuel Smith, Esq., F.R.C.S.E. .... Leeds.
Thomas Skinner, M.D., &c. .... Liverpool.
David Lloyd Roberts, M.D., &c. .... Manchester.
Frederick Symonds, Esq., F.R.C.S.E. .... Oxford.
John R. Kealy, Esq. .... Portsmouth.
Isaac Harrinson, Esq., F.R.C.S.E. .... Reading.
Charles Robertson, L.R.C.P. Ed. .... Scarborough.
James H. Aveling, M.D. .... Sheffield.
James Allen, Esq. .... York.
Thomas C. S. Corry, M.D. .... Belfast.
E. W. Pritchard, M.D. .... Glasgow.
David John Williams, M.D., F.R.C.S.......Victoria, Australia.

OBSTETRICAL SOCIETY OF LONDON.

HONORARY FELLOWS.

BRITISH SUBJECTS.

Fleetwood Churchill, M.D., Professor of Midwifery, King's and Queen's College of Physicians, Ireland, 15, Stephen's green north, Dublin.

Alfred H. McClintock, M.D., late Master of the Lying-in Hospital, 21, Merrion square north, Dublin.

James Matthews Duncan, M.D., A.M., Lecturer on Midwifery and Diseases of Women and Children, Surgeon's Hall, 30, Charlotte square, Edinburgh.

Archibald Hall, M.D., Professor of Midwifery, University of McGill College, Montreal, Canada.

James Y. Simpson, M.D., Professor of Midwifery, University of Edinburgh, Physician-Accoucheur to the Queen in Scotland, 52, Queen street, Edinburgh.

FOREIGN SUBJECTS.

Walter Channing, M.D., late Professor of Midwifery in the University of Cambridge, Boston, U.S.

Baron Paul Dubois, Professor of Clinical Midwifery in the Faculty of Medicine, Paris.

Charles D. Meigs, M.D., late Professor of Obstetrics, &c., in the Jefferson Medical College, Philadelphia, U.S.

F. W. Scanzoni, M.D., Professor of Midwifery, Würzburg.

Rudolf Virchow, M.D., Professor of Pathological Anatomy in the University of Berlin.

ORDINARY FELLOWS.

Those marked * have paid the Composition Fee in lieu of further Annual Subscriptions.

Elected

1859 ALDERSEY, WILLIAM HUGH, M.B. Lond., Buntingford, Herts.

1861 ALDRIDGE, JOHN PETTY, M.D., Shirley House, Dorchester.

1859 ALFORD, HENRY, F.R.C.S., Consulting Surgeon to the Taunton and Somerset Hospital; The Mount, Taunton, Somerset.

1859 ALLEN, GEORGE, M.D., 14A, Dean street, Soho, W.

1859 ALLEN, JAMES, Lecturer on Midwifery at the York School of Medicine; 16, Petergate, York. *Council*, 1859-60. *Hon. Loc. Sec.*

1859 AMSDEN, GEORGE JOHN, M.D., 5, Gloucester terrace, St. John's Hoxton, N.

1859 ANDREWS, JAMES, M.D., 8, Cornwall crescent, Camden road, N.W.

1861 APPLETON, JOHN GRIGG, Luton, Bedfordshire.

1859 ARCHER, JOHN, F.R.C.S., Surgeon to the Birmingham Lying-in Hospital; Deritend, Birmingham.

1859 ARDEN, ARTHUR OCTAVIUS, Surgeon to the Hull Lying-in Charity; 29, Nile street, Hull.

1861 ARMSTRONG, JOHN, M.D., Gravesend, Kent.

1860 ASHBURNER, JAMES, M.D., Surgeon in Ordinary to St. Mary's Hospital, Manchester; Broad street, Pendleton, Manchester.

1859 ASPINALL, THOMAS, Belgrave square, Over Darwen, Lancashire.

1861 ATHERLEY, JOSEPH, Mountsorrel, Leicestershire.

1859 AVELING, JAMES H., M.D., 5, Howard street, Sheffield. *Hon. Loc. Sec.*

1859 AYLING, WILLIAM HENRY, 103, Great Portland street, W.

1859 BADGLEY, FRANCIS, M.D., Holyrood House, Great Malvern.

Elected

1860 Bailey, Geo. Hewlett, 25, Charles street, Middlesex Hospital, W.

1859 Bailey, Henry Woodruffe, F.R.C.S., Thetford, Norfolk. *Council*, 1863.

1859 Baker, John Wright, 102, Friar Gate, Derby.

1859 Ball, Ancell, L.R.C.P. Ed., Spalding, Lincolnshire.

1859 Ballard, Thomas, M.D., 10, Southwick place, Hyde Park, W.

1859 Bannister, John Henry, 436, Oxford street, W.

1859 Barker, Thomas Herbert, M.D., Harpur place, Bedford. *Hon. Loc. Sec.*

1859 Barker, Samuel, M.D., St. George's House, 18, Eaton place, Brighton.

1859 Barnes, Robert, M.D., F.R.C.P., Lecturer on Midwifery at St. Thomas's Hospital; Physician to the Royal Maternity Charity, and Assistant Physician-Accoucheur to the London Hospital; 12, Finsbury square, E.C. *Vice-Pres.* 1859-60. *Council*, 1861-62. *Treas.* 1863.

1860 Barnes, Thomas Buxton, Thaxted, Essex.

1859 Barnett, Lysander Hooker, 72, Fore st., Limehouse, E.

1859 Barnett, Thos. W., 72, Fore street, Limehouse, E.

1859 Barron, George B., M.D., Surgeon to the Southport Hospital; Southport, Lancashire.

1861* Bartrum, John S., Surgeon to the Bath General Hospital; 41, Gay street, Bath.

1861 Bate, Henry Francis, 1, Clifton terrace, Maida hill, W.

1859 Bateman, Henry, F.R.C.S., 32, Compton terrace, Upper street, Islington, N.

1859 Batty, Edward, Lecturer on Midwifery and Diseases of Women and Children to the Liverpool School of Medicine; 34, Stafford street, Liverpool. *Council*, 1859-60.

1859 Battye, Richard F., L.R.C.P. Ed., 77, Warwick street, Pimlico, S.W.

1859 Beardsley, Amos, Bay Villa Grange, Newton-in-Cartmel, Lancashire.

1859 Beck, T. Snow, M.D., F.R.S., 9a, Langham place, W.

1860 Bell, John Pearson, M.D., Senior Surgeon to the Lying-in Charity; Waverley House, Hull.

Elected

1859 BELL, RICHARD PENROSE, L.F.P. and S., Glasg., Goole, Yorkshire.

1861 BENNETT, FRANCIS, Surgeon to the Gateshead Dispensary; Gateshead, Durham.

1859 BERRY, SAMUEL, F.R.C.S., Surgeon-Accoucheur to the Queen's Hospital, and Professor of Midwifery and the Diseases of Women and Children in the Queen's College; 11, New Hall street, Birmingham. *Vice-Pres.* 1859. *Hon. Loc. Sec.*

1861 BEST, FREDERICK WARNINGHAM, L.F.P.S., Glasg., Stanningley, near Leeds.

1859 BILLINGHURST, HENRY, M.D., 5, Church row, Islington, N.

1859 BIRD, FREDERIC, M.D., Lecturer on Midwifery and Diseases of Women in the Westminster Hospital School of Medicine, Senior Physician to the Westminster Maternity Charity; 62, Park street, Grosvenor square, W. *Council*, 1859.

1859 BLACKSTONE, JOSEPH, Park House, Gloucester road, Regent's Park, N.W.

1859 BLAKE, VALENTINE W., F.R.C.S., Surgeon to the Birmingham and Midland Counties Lying-in Hospital, Lecturer on Midwifery at the Sydenham College; 6, Old square, Birmingham.

1861* BLAKE, THOMAS WILLIAM, Hurstbourne Tarrant, Andover, Hants.

1859 BLENKINSOP, HENRY, F.R.C.S., Senior Surgeon to the Warwick Dispensary; Jury street, Warwick.

1860 BLOOD, MICHAEL, The Terrace, St. Helier's, Jersey.

1859 BLOXAM, W., M.D., Lecturer on Midwifery at the Grosvenor Place School of Medicine; 28, Duke street, Grosvenor square, W. *Council*, 1860-62.

1859 BLOXAM, W., Jun., 21, Mount street, Grosvenor square, W.

1861 BLUNDELL, THOMAS LEIGH, M.D., 12, Warrior square, St. Leonard's-on-Sea.

1859 BOTTOMLEY, GEORGE, F.R.C.S., Surgeon to the Carshalton Hospital; Croydon, Surrey.

Elected

1859 BRACE, WILLIAM HENRY, Surgeon to the Bath United Hospital and Lying-in Charity; 1, Gay street, Bath. *Hon. Loc. Sec.*

1862 BRAITHWAITE, WILLIAM, M.D., Lecturer on Midwifery, Leeds School of Medicine; Clarendon House, Leeds.

1859 BRICKWELL, JAMES, 17, Finsbury circus, E.C.

1862 BRICKWELL, JOHN, Sawbridgeworth, Herts.

1860 BRITTON, WILLIAM SAMUEL, 1, Eaton villas, Acacia road, St. John's wood, N.W.

1859 BROADBENT, WILLIAM HENRY, M.B. Lond., Assistant-Physician to the London Fever Hospital; 23, Upper Seymour street, Portman square, W.

1862 BROOKS, THOMAS THORNELEY, St. Mary's Hospital, Paddington, W.

1859 BROOKS, ARTHUR D'OYLEY, Henley-on-Thames, Oxon.

1859 BROWN, I. BAKER, F.R.C.S., Senior Surgeon to the London Home for Surgical Diseases of Women; 17, Connaught square, Hyde park, W. *Council*, 1859.

1859 BROWN, RICHARD, M.D., Adelaide Lodge, Cliftonville, Brighton.

1861 BROWN, SAMUEL WILLIAM, F.R.C.S., Lewisham, Kent, S.E.

1859 BROWNING, CHARLES, M.D., 52, Portsdown road, Maida hill, W.

1859 BRYANT, WALTER JOHN, F.R.C.S., L.R.C.P. Edinb., 7, Bathurst street, Hyde park gardens, W. *Council*, 1859.

1861 BUNNY, JOSEPH, M.D., Hon. Surgeon to the Newbury Dispensary; Newbury, Berks.

1859 BURFORD, ROBERT WILLIAM, 31, Bayham terrace, Camden town, N.W.

1859 BURKE, PATRICK, 13, Upper Montagu street, Montagu square, W.

1862 BURKE, STEPHEN JOHN, Sydney, New South Wales.

1862 BURTON, JOHN MOULDEN, F.R.C.S., Lee park, Lee, Kent, S.E.

Elected

1859 Buzzard, Thomas, M.B., late Staff Surgeon to Omer Pasha in the Crimea and Asia Minor; 41, Great Marlborough street, W.

1862 Campbell, Charles, M.D., Kingston, Jamaica.

1861 Candlish, Henry, M.D., The Infirmary, Alnwick, Northumberland.

1861 Candy, John, M.D., Alstonefield, near Ashbourne, Derbyshire.

1862 Carpenter, Robert Henry Spencer, Carr villa, Durham.

1861 Carter, Albert Pleydell, 34, London road, Gloucester.

1860 Cayzer, Thomas, Mayfield, Aigburth, Liverpool.

1859 Chance, Edward John, F.R.C.S., Surgeon to the Metropolitan Free Hospital and City Orthopædic Hospital; 59, Old Broad street, City, E.C.

1862 Chapman, Walter, F.R.C.S., Lower Tooting, Surrey.

1859 Cholmondeley, Joseph, Surgeon-Accoucheur to Queen Charlotte's Lying-in Hospital; 3, Nottingham place, Marylebone road, W. *Council*, 1859-60-61.

1859 Chowne, William Dingle, M.D., Physician to Charing Cross Hospital, and Lecturer on the Principles and Practice of Medicine and Obstetrics at Charing Cross Hospital; 8, Connaught place west, Hyde park, W. *Council*, 1860-62.

1861 Church, William John, F.R.C.S., 22, Circus, Bath.

1859 Claremont, Claude Clarke, 1, Thorney-place, Oakley square, N.W.

1859 Clark, James Fenn, 18, York terrace, Leamington. *Hon. Loc. Sec.*

1861 Clark, James, M.D., 4, Penton street, Pentonville, N.

1862 Clarke, John, Lynton, North Devon.

1859 Clarkson, Josiah, 85, New Hall street, Birmingham.

1859 Clay, Charles, M.D., late Medical Officer in Ordinary and Lecturer on Midwifery and Clinical Medicine in St. Mary's Hospital; 101, Piccadilly, Manchester. *Council*, 1863.

1859 Clay, John, Surgeon-Accoucheur to the Queen's Hospital; 64, Moseley street, Birmingham.

1859 Clayton, Oscar, F.R.C.S., 87, Harley street, W.

Elected

1859 CLEVELAND, WILLIAM FREDERICK, 23, Beaufoy terrace, Maida vale, W. *Council*, 1863.

1861 CLIFFORD, HERBERT WILLIAM, Tivoli villa, Cheltenham.

1861 CLOGG, STEPHEN, East Looe, Cornwall.

1860 COCKELL, EDGAR, Holly Lodge, Queen's road, Dalston, N.E.

1859 COCKELL, FREDERICK EDGAR, 1, Alma villas, Dalston, N.E.

1861 COCKER, JOHN, M.D., Bank Hey, Blackpool, near Preston, Lancashire.

1861 COGAN, JOSEPH, M.D., Wheatley, Oxon.

1859 COLLENETTE, BENJAMIN, L.R.C.P. Ed., Surgeon to the Guernsey Hospital; Plaiderie place, Guernsey.

1861 COLLINGWOOD, WILLIAM, Ampthill, Beds.

1859 COLLINS, CHAMBERS, F.R.C.S., Maryport, Cumberland.

1861 COLLINSON, ALFRED, M.D., 19, Oxford terrace, Hyde park, W.

1859 COLLUM, ROBERT, M.D., Physician to the Western General Dispensary; 1, Chester place, Hyde park square, W.

1861 COOPER, JOHN, L.R.C.P. Edinb., Clapham Rise, S.

1860 CORRY, THOMAS CHARLES STEUART, M.D., L.R.C.P. Ed., Surgeon to the Belfast General Dispensary; 1. Victoria street, Belfast. *Hon. Loc. Sec.*

1859 CORY, FREDERIC CHARLES, M.D., 8, Nassau place, Commercial road east, E.

1862 COTTERELL, PETER AMBROSE, M.D., West Bromwich, Staffordshire.

1859 COULSON, WILLIAM, F.R.C.S., Senior Surgeon to and Lecturer on Surgery in St. Mary's Hospital, Consulting Surgeon to the City of London Lying-in Hospital; 1, Chester terrace, Regent's park, N.W.

1859 CROFT, J. MCGREGOR A. T., M.D., late Senior Surgeon to H.M. Ceylon Rifles; 8, Abbey road, St. John's Wood, N.W.

1861 CROSKERY, HUGH, L.R.C.S. Ireland; Chapelton, Jamaica.

1860 CROSS, RICHARD, M.D., Queen street, Scarborough, Yorkshire.

1859 CULPEPER, WILLIAM MOE, 1, Brunswick terrace, Palace gardens, Kensington, W.

1861 CUMPSTONE, W., Market Rasen, Lincolnshire.

Elected

1862 Cumberbatch, Laurence Trent, 25, Cadogan place, Belgrave square, S.W.

1859 Curgenven, J. Brendon, 11, Craven Hill gardens, Bayswater, W.

1862 Curry, William, East Rainton, Fence Houses, Durham.

1859 Davies, John, M.D., Coleshill, Warwickshire.

1859 Davis, John Hall, M.D., Physician to the Royal Maternity Charity, and to the St. George's and St. James's Dispensary, Consulting Physician to the St. Pancras Infirmary; 11, Harley street, Cavendish square, W. *Council*, 1859. *Vice-Pres.* 1861-63.

1859 Day, William Henry, M.D., 3, Park terrace, Newmarket.

1861 De La Motte, Henry D. C., Swanage, Dorset.

1859 Denny, John, 1, Sumner terrace, Onslow square, Brompton, S.W.

1860 Dickinson, John, F.R.C.S., Surgeon to the Wrexham Infirmary; Wrexham, Denbighshire.

1859 Dickson, Joseph, M.D., 56, Bath street, Jersey.

1859 Diplock, Thomas Bramah, M.D., 1, Sydney street, Chelsea, S.W.

1859 Dixon, John, M.D., 20, Prospect row, Bermondsey, S.E.

1859 Dixon, Thomas G., M.D., Northwich, Cheshire.

1859 Dixon, William, L.R.C.P. Edin., Tickhill, Yorkshire.

1861 Down, Henry Wilcox, Glastonbury, Somerset.

1859 Drage, Charles, M.D., Hatfield, Herts. *Council*, 1861-63.

1859 Druitt, Robert, M.R.C.P., Medical Officer of Health for St. George's Hanover square; 37, Hertford street, Mayfair, W. *Council*, 1859-60. *Vice-Pres.* 1862-63.

1859 Druitt, William, F.R.C.S., Wimborne, Dorset.

1859 Dufty, Fred., Stoney Stratford, Bucks.

1859 Duncan, James, M.B., 8, Henrietta street, Covent garden, W.C.

1859 Duncan, Peter Charles, M.D., 46, Great Marlborough street, W.

1862 Dunn, Joseph Thos. Holt, L.R.C.P. Edin. (exam.), 7, Carlton place, Westbourne park, W.

1859 Dunn, Robert, F.R.C.S., 31, Norfolk street, Strand, W.C. *Council*, 1860. *Vice-Pres.* 1861-62.

Elected

1861 EARLE, JAMES L., Resident Surgeon-Accoucheur to the Birmingham General Dispensary.

1859* EASSON, JAMES, 23, Princes street, Cavendish square, W.

1861 EASTLAKE, HENRY E., M.D., Medical Officer to the British Lying-in Hospital, and Accoucheur to the St. Marylebone General Dispensary; 48, Welbeck street, W.

1861 EDWARDS, THOMAS EDWIN, L.R.C.P. Lond., 98, Gloucester crescent, Hyde park, W.

1859 ELKINGTON, FRANCIS, M.D., Consulting Accoucheur to the Birmingham and Midland Counties Lying-in Hospital, and Lecturer on Midwifery at Sydenham College; 92½, New Hall street, Birmingham. *Council*, 1859. *Vice-Pres.* 1860-61.

1862 ELLAM, JOHN, L.R.C.P., Sneinton place, Nottingham.

1859 ELLIOTT, ROBERT, F.R.C.S. Edin., Senior Surgeon to the Chichester Infirmary; North street, Chichester.

1862 ELLIS, EDWARD, M.D., 8, Fitzroy street, W.

1861 ELLIS, ROBERT, Obstetric Surgeon to the Chelsea, Brompton, and Belgrave Dispensary; 63, Sloane street, S.W.

1862 ELLISON, JAMES, M.D., 14, High street, Windsor, Berks.

1861 ESSERY, THOMAS AUBREY, F.R.C.S., Senior Surgeon to the Swansea Infirmary; Melbourne House, Swansea.

1859 EVANS, GRIFFITH FRANCIS DORSETT, M.D., Trewern Lodge, 43, Addison road, Kensington, W.

1859 EVANS, THOMAS ROBERT, M.D., Coltishall, Norfolk.

1861 EVANS, GUSTAVUS, M.D., 16, Lowther street, Carlisle.

1859 EVERSHED, THOMAS EVANS, Billinghurst, Sussex.

1861 EWEN, HENRY, F.R.C.S., Long Sutton, Lincolnshire.

1859 FAIRCLOTH, RICHARD, F.R.C.S., Newmarket, Cambridgeshire.

1861 FARR, GEO. F., L.R.C.P. Edin., 171, Union street, Southwark, S.E.

1862 FENDER, THOMAS, Bondgate street within, Alnwick, Northumberland.

Elected

1859 FERGUSSON, WILLIAM, F.R.C.S., F.R.S., Surgeon Extraordinary to H.M. the Queen, Professor of Surgery in King's College and Surgeon to King's College Hospital, Consulting Surgeon to the Samaritan Free Hospital; 16, George street, Hanover square, W. *Vice-Pres.* 1862-3.

1861 FETHERSTON, GERALD H. M.D., Resident Accoucheur, Melbourne Lying-in Hospital, Australia.

1859 FISHER, ALDER, 15, John street, Bedford row, W.C.

1860 FOX, WILLIAM TILBURY, M.D., Kensington Gardens square, Hyde park, W.

1862 FRAIN, JOSEPH, M.D., Senior Surgeon to the South Shields Dispensary, Frederick street, South Shields.

1862 FRAMPTON, DECIMUS NELSON, L.R.C.P. Edin., 28, Lower Belgrave street, S.W.

1861 FRANKLAND, THOMAS THRUSH, Ripon, Yorkshire.

1861 FREEMAN, HENRY LANKESTER, Saxmundham, Suffolk.

1861 FRENCH, WILLIAM JOHN BLAKE, Wilton, Wiltshire.

1860 GARLAND, EDWARD CHARLES, Silver street, Yeovil, Somerset.

1859 GARTY, FRANCIS BOYLE, Loughborough road, North Brixton.

1859 GASKOIN, GEORGE, 3, Westbourne park, W.

1862 GAYTON, WILLIAM, 85, Brick lane, Spitalfields, N.E.

1859 GERVIS, HENRY, M.D., Assistant Obstetric Physician to St. Thomas's Hospital; 12, St. Thomas's street, Southwark, S.E.

1859 GIBB, GEORGE DUNCAN, M.D., Physician to the West London Hospital, 22, Portman street, Portman square, W. *Council*, 1859-60-61.

1860 GILL, SAMUEL L., M.D., L.R.C,P. Edin., 4, Campbell terrace, Bow road, E.

1860 GILLIBRAND, WILLIAM, L.R.C.P. Edin., Francis street, Blackburn, Lancashire.

1859 GODDARD, SAMUEL PALMER, M.D., Longton, Staffordshire Potteries.

1861 GOSS, SAMUEL DAY, L.R.C.P. Edin., 24, Newington place, Kennington park, S.

Elected

1859 Gould, Henry Merton, Wateringbury, Kent.

1859 Goulstone, John G., M.D., Knighton, Radnorshire.

1859 Granville, Augustus Bozzi, M.D., F.R.S., Consulting Physician-Accoucheur to the Westminster General Dispensary, 7, Wilton place, Belgrave square, S.W. *Vice-Pres.* 1859-61.

1861 Gream, George Thompson, M.D., 2, Upper Brook street, Grosvenor square, W. *Council*, 1862-63.

1859 Greenhalgh, Robert, M.D., Physician-Accoucheur and Lecturer on Midwifery to St. Bartholomew's Hospital, Physician-Accoucheur to the Samaritan Free Hospital, Consulting Physician-Accoucheur to the St. John's Wood and Portland Town Dispensary; 76, Grosvenor street, W. *Council*, 1863.

1859 Griffith, Thomas Taylor, F.R.C.S., Consulting Surgeon to the Wrexham Infirmary; Wrexham, Denbighshire.

1859 Grimsdale, Thos. F., Surgeon to the Lying-in Hospital, and Lecturer on Diseases of Children at the Royal Infirmary School of Medicine; 12, Rodney street, Liverpool. *Council*, 1861-62.

1859 Guest, Edmund, F.R.C.S., L.R.C.P. Edin.; 20, Halsey street, Chelsea, S.W.

1859 Gunn, Theophilus Miller, F.R.C.S., 40, York place, Baker street, W.

1859 Guy, Henry, 1, Dorset square, N.W.

1859 Haden, Francis Seymour, F.R.C.S., Hon. Surgeon to the Government School of Science and Art; 62, Sloane street, S.W. *Council*, 1861-63.

1859 Hall, Alfred, M.D., Senior Physician to the Brighton Dispensary; 30, Old Steyne, Brighton. *Hon. Loc. Sec.*

1859 Hall, Frederick, 1, Jermyn street, St. James's, S.W.

1862 Hall, William, Lecturer on Botany, Leeds School of Medicine; North street, Leeds.

1860 Hardey, Key, Surgeon to the West City Dispensary; 2, Earl street, Blackfriars, E.C.

1859 Hardey, Robert, late Lecturer on Obstetrics, Hull and East Riding School of Medicine; 3, Charlotte street, Hull. *Council*, 1860-62. *Vice-Pres.* 1863. *Hon. Loc. Sec.*

Elected

1859 HARLEY, GEORGE, M.D., Professor of Medical Jurisprudence, University College, and Physician to the Northern Dispensary; 77, Harley street, Cavendish square, W. *Council*, 1861-63.

1859 HARPER, PHILIP H., F.R.C.S., Assistant-Surgeon to the London Home for Surgical Diseases of Women; 30, Cambridge street, Hyde park, W.

1859 HARRINSON, ISAAC, F.R.C.S., Castle street, Reading, Berks. *Council*, 1862-63. *Hon. Loc. Sec.*

1859 HARRIS, ABRAHAM, L.R.C.P. Edin., Commercial square, Camborne, Cornwall.

1862 HARRIS, CHARLES, M.D., Northiam, Sussex.

1861 HARRIS, HERBERT ROBEY, Union square, Bury, Lancashire.

1861 HARRIS, WILLIAM JOHN, 4, Terrace, Worthing.

1859 HARVEY, WILLIAM, 48, Lonsdale square, Islington, N.

1860 HATHERLEY, N. COLLINS, M.D., Stonehouse, Plymouth.

1861 HAVILAND, EDWARD SAVAGE, M.D., 13, Lyon terrace, Maida Hill, W.

1859 HAWTHORNE, ARTHUR NEVILLE, F.R.C.S., Eccleshall, Staffordshire.

1862 HAYMAN, CHARLES CHRISTOPHER, M.D., Eastbourne, Sussex.

1859 HEMSTED, HENRY, Hurstborne Tarrant, Andover, Hants.

1859 HENLEY, THOMAS LEAMAN, 38, Church street, Croydon, Surrey.

1859 HERAPATH, WILLIAM BIRD, M.D., F.R.S., 32, Old Market street, Bristol.

1860 HESS, AUGUSTUS, M.D., Physician to the Jews' Hospital, Mile End; 14, City road, Finsbury square, E.C.

1859 HEWITT, GRAILY, M.D., Physician to the British Lying-in Hospital, Lecturer on Midwifery and Diseases of Women and Children at St. Mary's Hospital Medical School; 36, Berkeley square, W. *Hon. Sec.* 1859-63.

1862 HEWITT, TOM SMITH, M.D., Ivy Cottage, Winkfield, Windsor, Berks.

1860 HICKS, JOHN BRAXTON, M.D., F.R.S., Assistant Physician-Accoucheur to Guy's Hospital; St. Thomas's street, Southwark, S.E. *Council*, 1861-62. *Hon. Sec.* 1863.

Elected

1860 HIGGS, THOMAS FREDERIC, L.R.C.P. Edin.; Wolverhampton street, Dudley.

1859 HINGESTON, JAMES ANSLEY, 22, Clifton terrace, Brighton.

1859 HIRD, FRANCIS, F.R.C.S., formerly Surgeon to the Royal Infirmary for Children, Surgeon to Charing Cross Hospital; 17, Clifford street, Bond street, W. *Council*, 1861-62.

1859 HODGES, RICHARD, M.D., Rochford, Essex.

1859 HODGSON, GEORGE FREDERICK, 52, Montpellier road, Brighton.

1859 HOLMAN, ANDREW, 10, John street, America square, E.C.

1859 HOLMAN, CONSTANTINE, M.D., Reigate, Surrey.

1860 HOLMAN, HENRY MARTIN, M.D., Hurstpierpoint, Sussex.

1861 HORTON, GEORGE EDWARD, Dudley, Worcestershire.

1861 HOUNSELL, HENRY STRANGEWAYS, M.D., Oakfield, Torquay, Devon.

1862 HUBERT, WILLIAM ARTHUR, Markgate street, Beds.

1859 HUSSEY, EDWARD LAW, F.R.C.S., Surgeon to the Radcliffe Infirmary; 104, St. Aldate's, Oxford.

1859 HUTCHINSON, JONATHAN, Assistant-Surgeon to the London Hospital; 4, Finsbury circus, E.C.

1861 HUTTON, CHARLES, M.D., Physician to the General Lying-in Hospital; 26, Lowndes street, Belgrave square, S.W.

1859 ILOTT, JAMES WILLIAM, Bromley, Kent.

1859 IMAGE, WILLIAM EDMUND, F.R.C.S., Senior Surgeon to the Suffolk General Hospital; Bury St. Edmunds, Suffolk.

1859 IRWIN, WILLIAM CROSSLEY, M.D., Belvoir street, Leicester.

1859 JACKSON, HENRY, M.D., Newcastle, New South Wales, Australia.

1861 JACKSON, THOMAS HAYES, M.D., 18, Market place, Darlington, Durham.

1859 JAMES, HENRY, F.R.C.S., Surgeon and Accoucheur to the City of London Lying-in Hospital; Heathfield, Weybridge, Surrey. *Council*, 1862-63.

1862 JAY, FREDERICK FITZHERBERT, L.R.C.P., Pulham, near Harleston, Norfolk.

1859 JENNINGS, JOSEPH C. S., Abbey House, Malmesbury, Wilts.

Elected

1860 JEPSON, HENRY, F.R.C.S., Surgeon to the Kingston Dispensary; Hampton, Middlesex, S.W.

1862 JOHNSON, EDWARD, M.D., 19, Cavendish place, Cavendish square, W.

1861 JONES, EDWARD, M.D., The Park, Sydenham, Kent.

1859 JONES, GEORGE, 12, New Hall street, Birmingham.

1859 JONES, JOHN WILLIAM, 8, Brynteg terrace, Upper Bangor, Caernarvonshire.

1859 JULER, HENRY CUNDELL, M.D., 17, Lower Seymour street, Portman square, W.

1861 JUNKER, F. E., M.D., 56, Gower street, W.C.

1859 KEALY, JOHN ROBERT, M.D., Ashley House, Gosport, Hants. *Hon. Loc. Sec.*

1859 KEELE, GEORGE THOMAS, 1, Bruce villas, St. Paul's road, Highbury, N.

1859 KENDALL, THOMAS MARSTERS, F.R.C.S., Surgeon to the West Norfolk and Lynn Hospital, King's Lynn, Norfolk.

1861 KERBY, WILLIAM HOLMAN, Northiam, Sussex.

1859 KIALLMARK, HENRY WALTER, 46, Princes square, Westbourne grove, W.

1860 KINGSFORD, EDWARD, F.R.C.S., Surgeon to the Sunbury Dispensary; Sunbury, Middlesex, S.W.

1862 KIRKPATRICK, JOHN RUTHERFORD, M.B., T.C.D., Lying-in Hospital, Rutland square, Dublin.

1860 KISCH, JOSEPH, 2, Circus place, Finsbury circus, E.C.

1862 LAMB, JOHN STEWART, M.D., 4, Windsor terrace, Maida hill, W.

1859 LANGMORE, J. CHARLES, M.B., F.R.C.S., 20, Oxford terrace, Hyde park, W. *Council*, 1861-63.

1862 LANPHIER, RICHARD, M.B. Dub., Alford, Lincolnshire.

1859 LEE, NEWTON B. C., 11, Talbot terrace, Talbot road, Bayswater, W.

1859 LEECH, EDWARD, Pallant, Chichester, Sussex.

1860 LEISHMAN, WILLIAM, M.D., 80, Bath street, Glasgow.

1859 LOCOCK, SIR CHAS., Bart., M.D., First Physician-Accoucheur to H.M. the Queen, Consulting Physician to the General Lying-in Hospital; 26, Hertford street, Mayfair, W. *Honorary President.*

Elected

1861 LOVE, GILBERT, Wimbledon, Surrey, S.W.

1862 LOWE, GEORGE, Burton-on-Trent, Staffordshire.

1860 LOWE, JOHN, M.D., Surgeon to the West Norfolk and Lynn Hospital; King street, King's Lynn, Norfolk.

1862 MACKENZIE, GEORGE WISE, Thetford, Norfolk.

1859 MACKINDER, DRAPER, M.D., Consulting Surgeon to the Gainsborough Dispensary; Gainsborough, Lincolnshire.

1859 MACKINLAY, JOHN, M.D., Isleworth, Middlesex.

1862 MACKINLAY, WALTER BOYD, M.D., 2, New Smith Hill street, Paisley.

1859 MACLAREN, ALEXANDER C., 29, Harley street, W.

1859 MACRAE, JOHN, 4, High street, Lewes, Sussex.

1861 McVEAGH, DENIS, L.K. and Q.C.P. Ireland; Hales street, Coventry, Warwickshire.

1859 MADGE, HENRY, M.D., 32, Fitzroy square, W. *Council*, 1863.

1862 MANLEY, JOHN, West Bromwich, Staffordshire.

1860 MARLEY, HENRY FREDERICK, Padstow, Cornwall.

1859 MARLEY, RICHARD, Bromyard, Herefordshire.

1862 MARRIOTT, ROBERT BUCHANAN, Swaffham, Norfolk.

1860 MARSHALL, JAS., M.D., 5, Belvidere road, Upper Norwood, S.

1862 MARSHALL, JOHN, 27A, Aldenham street, St. Pancras, N.W.

1859 MARSHALL, JOHN BRAKE, 21, Princes street, Hanover square, W.

1859 MARSHALL, PETER, 42, Bedford square, W.C.

1860 MARTIN, HENRY VICTOR, F.R.C.S., Staines, Middlesex.

1859 MARTYN, WILLIAM, F.R.C.S., 6, Trevor terrace, Rutland gate, Brompton, S.W.

1861 MATTHEWS, JOHN, M.D., 4, Mylne street, Myddelton square, E.C.

1859 MEADOWS, ALFRED, M.D., Assistant-Physician for Diseases of Women and Children to King's College Hospital, Physician-Accoucheur to the St. George's and St. James's Dispensary; 9, Cavendish place, Cavendish square, W. *Council*, 1862-63.

1859 MERRIMAN, SAMUEL WILLIAM JOHN, M.D., Consulting-Physician-Accoucheur to the Westminster General Dispensary, and Physician-Accoucheur to the Western General Dispensary; 3, Charles street, Westbourne terrace, W. *Council*, 1859-60.

Elected

1859 METEYARD, CHARLES JOSEPH, M.R.C.P., Clunbury, Shrewsbury.

1861 MIDDLETON, WILLIAM, F.R.C.S., 25, Lansdowne place, Leamington, Warwickshire.

1859 MILES, CHARLES, 13, Conduit street west, Westbourne terrace, W.

1859 MILLARD, WILLIAM JOSEPH, Portland house, Whitchurch, Herefordshire.

1859 MITCHELL, JOSEPH THOMAS, F.R.C.S., 8, Percy place, Clapham road, S. *Council*, 1863.

1859 MOORHEAD, JOHN, M.D., Surgeon to the Weymouth Infirmary and Dispensary, Weymouth, Dorset.

1859 MOYLE, JOHN, Chacewater, Truro, Cornwall.

1859 MOYLES, THOS., M.D., 109, Broad street, Birmingham.

1859 MURPHY, EDWARD WILLIAM, M.D., Professor of Midwifery in University College, and Obstetric Physician, University College Hospital, Physician-Accoucheur to the Northern Dispensary; 41, Cumberland street, Bryanston square, W. *Vice-Pres.* 1859-60.

1859 MURRAY, GUSTAVUS CHARLES P., M.D., Medical Officer to the British Lying-in Hospital, Physician for Diseases of Women and Children to the St. George's and St. James's Dispensary; 17, Green street, Grosvenor square, W.

1859 MUSGRAVE, JOHNSON THOMAS, Pembroke place, Finchley road, N.W. *Council*, 1859-60.

1859 NAPPER, ALBERT, Broad Oak, Cranley, Guildford, Surrey.

1859 NASON, RICHARD BIRD, Nuneaton, Warwickshire.

1859 NEAL, JAMES, 85, New Hall street, Birmingham.

1861 NELSON, DUCKWORTH, F.R.C.S., Marlborough road, St. John's Wood, N.W.

1859 NEWMAN, WILLIAM, M.D., Stamford, Lincolnshire.

1859 NEWNHAM, WILLIAM, Richmond villa, Tunbridge Wells, Kent.

1859 NEWTON, EDWARD, F.R.C.S., 30, Fitzroy square, W.

1859 NICHOLSON, WILLIAM HUNTER, 9, Phœnix street, Clarendon square, N.W.

1861 NICHOLS, GEORGE W., Almond Tree House, Rotherhithe, S.E.

Elected

1861 Noverre, Arthur, 25, South street, Park lane, W.

1859 Nunn, Thomas William, Assistant-surgeon to the Middlesex Hospital; 8, Stratford place, Oxford street, W.

1860 Oakshott, John, Highgate, N.

1859 O'Flaherty, Thomas Austin, M.D., 2, Baker street, Portman square, W.

1859 Oldham, James, 53, Norfolk street, Brighton.

1859 Oldham, Henry, M.D., F.R.C.P., Obstetric Physician and Lecturer on Midwifery and Diseases of Women and Children at Guy's Hospital; 26, Finsbury square, E.C. *Vice-Pres.* 1859. *Council,* 1860. *Treas.* 1861-62. *Pres.* 1863.

1859 Orford, William Cockerell, 211, High street, Deritend, Birmingham.

1859 Owen, Edward Robert, F.R.C.S., Surgeon to the Oxford Lying-in Institution; Beaumont street, Oxford.

1861 Owen, William B., 61, Cleveland square, Hyde park, W.

1859 Palfrey, James, M.D., Assistant-Physician to the Metropolitan Free Hospital, and Physician to the Surrey Dispensary; 12, Wellington street, Southwark, S.E.

1861 Palmer, Silas, M.D., London road, Newbury, Berks.

1862 Parker, Theophilus Rt. Bush, Abbotsbury, Dorset.

1860 Payne, Charles Henry, M.D., Wimbledon, Surrey, S.W.

1860 Pearse, George, L.R.C.P. Edin., 10, Regent street, Westminster, S.W.

1861 Pearse, Frederick, L.R.C.P. Edin., 49, Crockherbtown, Cardiff, Glamorganshire.

1859 Peirce, R. King, 16, Norland place, Notting hill, W.

1859 Pinchard, Benjamin, M.D., Cottenham, Cambridgeshire.

1860* Plowman, Wm. T., M.D., St. Austell, Cornwall.

1859 Pollard, William, Jun., Surgeon to the Torbay Infirmary and Dispensary, Torquay, Devon.

1860 Pollock, Timothy, M.D., 26, Hatton garden, E.C.

1860 Porter, Charles, 54, Digbeth, Birmingham.

1859 Potter, Jephson, M.D., 109, Upper Parliament street, Liverpool.

1859 Pound, George, Odiham, Hants.

1859 Powell, Robert George, Buntingford, Herts.

Elected

1859 PRANCE, ROBERT ROOKE, M.D., Heath street, Hampstead, N.W.

1859 PRIESTLEY, W. O., M.D., Physician-Accoucheur to, and Lecturer on Midwifery at the Middlesex Hospital, and Physician-Accoucheur to the St. Marylebone Infirmary; 17, Hertford street, Mayfair, W. *Council*, 1859-60-61.

1862 PRINCE, FREDERICK, Sawston, Cambridgeshire.

1859 PRITCHARD, EDWARD WILLIAM, M.D., 11, Berkeley terrace, Glasgow. *Hon. Loc. Sec.*

1860 PROUDLOVE, THOMAS JAMES, M.R.C.P., Tattenham, Chester.

1859 PYLE, JOHN, F.R.C.S., 56, Oxford terrace, Hyde park, W.

1859 RADFORD, THOMAS, M.D., Consulting-Physician, St. Mary's Hospital, Manchester; Moor field, Higher Broughton, Manchester. *Vice-Pres.* 1859.

1859 RAMSAY, JOHN ALLEN, L.R.C.P. Ed., Great Shelford, Cambridge.

1860 RAMSBOTHAM, JOHN HODGSON, M.D., 16, Park place, Leeds.

1859 RANDALL, JOHN, M.D. Lond., Medical Officer, St. Marylebone Infirmary; 14, Portman street, Portman square, W.

1860 RANSOM, ROBERT, F.R.C.S., 5, Jesus lane, Cambridge.

1861 RASCH, ADOLPHUS A. F., M.D., Hon. Phys. to the Eastern Dispensary of the German Hospital; 7, South street, Finsbury square, E.C.

1859 RAY, EDWARD, F.R.C.S., Dulwich, Surrey, S.

1860* RAYNER, JOHN, 19, Kingsland crescent, Kingsland road, N.E.

1860 RAYNER, THOMAS, M.D., Great Malvern, Worcestershire.

1859 RAYNES, HENRY, Gringley-on-the-hill, Bawtry, Yorkshire.

1859 REE, HENRY PAWLE, L.R.C.P. Ed., Walham green, Fulham, S.W.

1859 REECE, GEORGE, 45, Sussex gardens, Hyde park, W.

1859 REMINGTON, THOMAS, Medical Officer to the Clapham General Dispensary; 1, Grove place, North Brixton, S.

1860 RENTON, JOHN, Shotley bridge, Gateshead, Durham.

1860 RHODES, JAMES, Glossop, Derbyshire.

1859 RICE, JAMES, M.D., Surgeon to the Western Dispensary, Broadway, Westminster; 19, Langham street, Langham place, W.

Elected

1860 Richard, Edward Williams, Prospect House, Finchingfield, Essex.

1862 Richards, David, 8, St. George's place, Brighton, Sussex.

1860 Richards, John Smith Crosland, 36, Bedford square, W.C.

1859 Richards, Samuel, M.D., 36, Bedford square, W.C.

1862 Richards, Smith, 36, Bedford square.

1859 Richardson, Richard, L.R.C.P. Edinb., Rhayader, Radnorshire.

1859 Richardson, William Thomas, Ivy House, Highgate, N.

1860 Ritchie, George, M.D., Billinghay, Sleaford, Lincolnshire.

1859 Roberts, David Lloyd, M.D., Surgeon to St. Mary's Hospital, Manchester; 23, St. John's street, Deansgate, Manchester. *Hon. Loc. Sec.*

1860 Roberts, Robert Price, Rhyl. Flintshire.

1860 Robertson, Charles, L.R.C.P. Ed., 7, Queen street, Scarborough, Yorkshire. *Hon. Loc. Sec.*

1860 Robins, George, L.R.C.P. Ed., 45, Charlotte street, Fitzroy square, W.

1859 Robinson, Thomas, M.D., 64, Lamb's Conduit street, W.C.

1860 Roe, William Hamilton, M.B., M.R.C.P., Assistant Physician to the Westminster Maternity Charity; 57, Park street, Grosvenor square, W.

1859 Rogers, William Richard, M.D., Physician to the Samaritan Free Hospital; 56, Berners street, Oxford street, W.

1859 Roots, William Sudlow, F.R.C.S., F.L.S., Surgeon to the Royal Establishment at Hampton Court, Kingston-on-Thames, S.W.

1860 Roper, Alfred George, High street, Croydon, Surrey.

1859 Rose, Henry Cooper, M.D., High street, Hampstead, N.W.

1859 Ross, Daniel, Surgeon to the Metropolitan Police; 10, Commercial place, Commercial road east, E.

1859 Ross, George, M.D., Surgeon to the Western City Dispensary; 11, Hart street, Bloomsbury, W.C.

1859 Routh, Charles Henry Felix, M.D., Physician to the Samaritan Free Hospital for Women and Children; 52, Montagu square, W. *Council*, 1859-60-61.

Elected

1860 Russell, George, Bawtry, Yorkshire.

1861 Russell, William Alexander, L.R.C.P. Edin.; St. Peter street, St. Albans, Herts.

1860 Sanders, Godfrey, F.R.C.S., 8, Brewer street, Maidstone, Kent.

1862 Sanger, Thomas Frederick, Alfreston, Sussex.

1862 Sankey, William, Extra L.R.C.P., 6, Upper Portland place, Wandsworth, S.W.

1862 Sarell, Richard, M.D., Constantinople.

1860 Saunders, Charles, Foulsham, Norfolk.

1859 Scott, John, F.R.C.S., Surgeon to the Hospital for Women, Soho square; 65, Harley street, Cavendish square, W.

1860 Sedgwick, Leonard William, M.D., 11, Hinde street, Manchester square, W.

1862 Sharman, Malim, 18, New Hall street, Birmingham.

1859 Sharpin, Henry Wilson, Surgeon to the Bedford General Infirmary, Bedford.

1860 Shaw, George, Portland House, Battersea, S.W.

1859 Shaw, James, L.R.C.P. Edin., 52, York street, Cheetham, Manchester.

1859 Shearman, Edward James, M.D., Rotherham, Yorkshire.

1859 Sheehy, William Henry, L.R.C.P. Edin., 4, Claremont square, Pentonville, N.

1862 Shillingford, Isaac Shortland, 1, Hill street, Peckham, S.E.

1859 Shipton, William Parker, Surgeon to the Buxton Bath Charity; Buxton, Derbyshire.

1860 Shirley, Henry James, Hartley row, Hampshire.

1861 Shortt, John, M.D., Assistant-Surgeon H.M.I. Army, Chingleput, Madras District.

1862 Simpson, Henry, M.B. Lond., Lymm, Warrington, Cheshire.

1861 Sisson, Andrew, Reigate, Surrey.

1859 Skegg, Robert, 2, St. Martin's place, Trafalgar sq., W.C.

1860 Skinner, Thomas, M.D., 1, St. James's road, Liverpool. *Hon. Loc. Sec.*

1859 Sleeman, Philip Rowling, F.R.C.S., 16, Buckingham place, Clifton.

1861 Sloman, Samuel George, Farnham, Surrey.

Elected

1861 SLYMAN, WILLIAM DANIEL, 9, Wellington road, Kentish town, N.W.

1860 SMART, THOMAS TOVEY, L.R.C.P. Edinb., South villa, Bedminster, Bristol.

1859 SMILES, WILLIAM, M.D., Physician to the Royal General Dispensary, St. Pancras; 43, Bedford square, W.C.

1860 SMITH, CHARLES CASE, F.R.C.S., Consulting Surgeon to the Suffolk General Hospital; Bury St. Edmund's, Suffolk.

1862 SMITH, HENRY, St. Mary's Hospital, Paddington.

1862 SMITH, J. SIDNEY, Tiverton, Devon.

1861 SMITH, JOHN BRUMBY, 17, St. James's terrace, Liverpool.

1860 SMITH, JOHN, Coseley, near Bilston, Staffordshire.

1860 SMITH, JOSEPH EVANS, Ewias Harold, near Hereford.

1859 SMITH, PROTHEROE, M.D., Physician to the Hospital for Women, Soho square; 25, Park street, Grosvenor square, W.

1859 SMITH, SAMUEL, F.R.C.S., Senior Surgeon to the Leeds General Infirmary; Park place, Leeds. *Council*, 1860-62. *Hon. Loc. Sec.*

1859 SMITH, WILLIAM, M.D., Consulting Physician to the Weymouth Infirmary and Dispensary; Weymouth, Dorset.

1859 SMITH, W. TYLER, M.D., F.R.C.P., Physician-Accoucheur and Lecturer on Midwifery and Diseases of Women and Children to St. Mary's Hospital; 21, Upper Grosvenor street, W. *Treasurer* & *Vice-Pres.* 1859-60. *Pres.* 1861-62. *Council*, 1863.

1860 SNELL, EDMUND, 20, Stepney green, E.

1860 SNOW, JOHN ELLIOT, Walton, near Ipswich.

1859 SOMERVILLE, CHARLES, L.R.C.P., Bloxwich, Walsall, Staffordshire.

1859 SPENCER, GEORGE, 1, Horbury terrace, Notting hill, W.

1860 SPENCER, LAWRENCE, M.D., 129, Church street, Preston, Lancashire.

1862 SPRY, GEORGE FREDERICK, M.D., Staff Assistant-Surgeon, Fort Gomer, Alverstoke, Hants.

1859 SQUIRE, WILLIAM, 6, Orchard street, Portman square, W.

1859 STANTON, JOHN, M.D., 9, Montagu square, W.

1860 STEDMAN, ROBERT SAVIGNAC, Sharnbrook, Bedfordshire.

Elected

1860 STEELE, JAMES, M.D., Miles Platting, Manchester.

1860 STEPHENS, JOSEPH, M.D., 4, Bishop's road, Bayswater.

1859 STONE, JOSEPH, M.D., 84, Bloomsbury, Oxford street, Manchester.

1860 STONE, THOMAS, F.R.C.S., Resident Surgeon to Christ's Hospital.

1859 STOWERS, NOWELL, 30, Newington place, Kennington, S.

1859 STUTTER, FREDERICK AUGUSTUS, Farnboro' House, Upper Sydenham, Kent, S.

1860 SUCKLING, CORNELIUS BENSON, M.D., Surgeon-Accoucheur, Queen's Hospital, Birmingham; St. Mary's square, Birmingham.

1860 SUMPTER, WALTER, M.D., Clay-next-the-Sea, Norfolk.

1860 SUTCLIFFE, WILLIAM, Staleybridge, Cheshire.

1862 SUTHERLAND, WILLIAM, M.D., 22, George street, Croydon, Surrey.

1862 SUTTON, FIELD FLOWERS, M.D., Balham hill, Clapham, S.

1859 SUTTON, JOHN MAULE, M.D., Physician to the Queen's Hospital, and Professor of Clinical Medicine at the Queen's College, Birmingham; Bloomfield, Narberth, Pembrokeshire.

1859 SWAYNE, JOSEPH GRIFFITHS, M.D., Physician-Accoucheur to the Bristol General Hospital; Clifton, Bristol. *Council*, 1860-61. *Vice-Pres.* 1862-63. *Hon. Loc. Sec.*

1860 SWEETING, GEORGE BACON, M.R.C.P., Lynn Regis, Norfolk.

1859 SYDENHAM, JOHN PUDSEY WELCHMAN, Islip, Oxon.

1860 SYKES, RICHARD, Drighlington, near Leeds.

1859 SYMONDS, FREDERICK, F.R.C.S., Surgeon to the Radcliffe Infirmary; 32, Beaumont street, Oxford. *Council*, 1862-63. *Hon. Loc. Sec.*

1861 SYNNOT, ROBERT, M.D., 16, Eaton terrace, Eaton square, S.W.

1860 TAILER, GEORGE WASHINGTON, Bucklesham, near Ipswich, Suffolk.

1861 TANNER, JOHN, Jun., L.R.C.P. Edinb.; Guy's Hospital.

1859 TANNER, THOS. HAWKES, M.D., F.L.S., Assistant-Physician for Diseases of Women and Children to King's College Hospital; 9, Henrietta street, Cavendish square, W. *Hon. Sec.* 1859-62. *Vice-Pres.* 1863.

Elected

1859 Tapson, Alfred Joseph, M.B. Lond., 35, Gloucester gardens, Westbourne terrace, W. *Council*, 1862-63.

1862 Tasker, Richard Thomas, Melbourne, near Derby.

1859 Taylor, Charles, M.D., 4, Bethel place, Camberwell, S.

1859 Taylor, David, 2, Kennington row, Kennington park, S.

1859 Taylor, Edward, Clapham common, S.

1862 Taylor, Thomas, F.R.C.S., 19, Bennett's hill, Birmingham.

1862 Taylor, William, Scarborough, Yorkshire.

1862 Teale, Joseph, 31, Albion street, Leeds.

1862 Thane, George Dancer, M.D., 9, Hart street, Bloomsbury.

1860 Thelwall, William, Farndon, Chester.

1860 Thomas, Frederick, M.D., Tower terrace, Upper Norwood.

1859 Thomas, J. Henry, M.D., Physician Accoucheur to the Royal General Dispensary, St. Pancras; 22, Pentonville road, N.

1860 Thomas, Richard, Menai Bridge, Anglesea.

1860 Thorne, George Leworthy, M.D., Holcombe Regis, Devon.

1862 Thornton, William Henry, M.D., Springfield terrace, Dewsbury, Yorkshire.

1860 Tiffen, Robert, Wigton, Cumberland.

1859 Tilt, Edward John, M.D., Consulting Physician to the Farringdon General Dispensary; 60, Grosvenor street, W.

1859 Times, Henry G., 4, Thayer streeet, Manchester square, W.

1860 Tomkinson, Richard, Cheadle, Staffordshire.

1861 Tomlinson, Robert Sherratt, Burton-on-Trent.

1860 Torbock, Thomas Reddish, M.D., 30, Skinnergate, Darlington.

1862 Tracy, Richard T., M.D., Physician to the Lying-in Hospital, Melbourne, Victoria.

1859 Traer, James Reeves, F.R.C.S., 47, Hans place, Sloane street, S.W.

1859 Trouncer, John Henry, M.D., 6, Mount street, Grosvenor square, W.

1860 Tuke, James Kingdon, 1, Devonshire place, Brighton.

1859 Tulloch, James Stewart, M.D., Surgeon to the Westbourne Dispensary; 1, Pembridge place, Bayswater, W.

1861 Turner, Richard, School hill, Lewes, Sussex.

Elected

1861 TWEED, JOHN JAMES, Jun., 14, Upper Brook street, W.

1859 VAUDIN, CHARLES, L.R.C.P. Edinb., Physician to the Jersey General Dispensary; 60, New street, St. Helier's, Jersey.

1860 VARENNE, EZEKIEL G., Kelvedon, Essex.

1860 VINCENT, PATRICK, Wells-next-sea, Norfolk.

1862 VINE, GEORGE JOHN, 3, Henrietta street, Covent garden, W.C.

1860 WADE, HENRY THOMAS, Trinity terrace, Derby.

1859 WAITS, JOSEPH, 9, Upper Worth street, Poplar, E.

1860 WAKEMAN, PETER RYDER, Bryn Rhûs, Crickhowel, Brecknockshire.

1860 WALES, THOMAS GARNEYS, Jun., Downham, Norfolk.

1859 WALLER, JOHN TURPIN, Flegg Burgh, Norfolk.

1859 WALTON, THOS., 21, Charlotte street, Kingston-upon-Hull, Yorkshire.

1859 WANE, DANIEL, M.D., 20, Grafton street, Bond street, W.

1859 WARDEN, CHARLES, M.D., 39, Temple street, Birmingham.

1860 WATERWORTH, THOMAS HENRY, Surgeon to the Surrey Dispensary; 5, Bengal place, New Kent road, S.E.

1860 WALKER, THOMAS HOUGHTON, M.D., Tolleshunt D'Arcy, Kelvedon, Essex.

1860 WALKER, WILLIAM HENRY, L.R.C.P. Edinb.; Aldborough, near Darlington, Yorkshire.

1860 WARD, JOSEPH, Hill House, Epsom, Surrey.

1860 WARD, JOHN, Penistone, Sheffield, Yorkshire.

1862 WATKINS, CHARLES STEWART, 11, Chandos street, Strand, W.C.

1859 WATSON, SAMUEL, F.R.C.S. Ed.; Cottingham, Hull.

1861 WATTS, GEORGE HENRY, Thatcham, near Newbury, Berks.

1859 WEBB, J. CRASKE, M.D., 23, Grosvenor street west, Eaton square, S.W.

1859 WEBB, HENRY SPEAKMAN, Welwyn, Herts.

1859 WEBSTER, GEORGE, Peckham Rye, S.E.

1860 WELCHMAN, CHARLES EDWARD ELLIOT, Bore street, Lichfield, Staffordshire.

1859 WELLS, T. SPENCER, F.R.C.S., Surgeon to the Samaritan Free Hospital for Women and Children; 3, Upper Grosvenor street, W. *Council*, 1859.

Elected

1859 West, Henry Reginald, M.D., Harpenden, St. Albans, Herts.

1859 West, Robert Uvedale, M.D., Alford, Lincolnshire. *Council*, 1859. *Vice-Pres.* 1860-61-62.

1859 Westmacott, John Guise, M.D., Medical Officer to the Paddington Provident Dispensary; 10, St. Mary's terrace, Paddington, W.

1860 Wheeler, Daniel, Chelmsford, Essex.

1862 Wheelhouse, Claudius Galen, Surgeon to the Leeds Dispensary, and Lecturer on Anatomy, Leeds School of Medicine; 16, East Parade, Leeds.

1860 White, Frederick George, L.R.C.P. Edinb., Erchfont, near Devizes, Wilts.

1860 White, William, Rajshahy, Bengal; East India United Service Club, 14, St. James's square, S.W.

1859 Whitehead, James, M.D., Physician to the Manchester Clinical Hospital; 87, Mosley street, Manchester. *Council*, 1859-60-61.

1859 Wilkin, Henry, 39, Connaught terrace, Hyde park, W.

1861 Williams, David John, M.D., Queenscliff, Geelong, Victoria, Australia. *Hon. Loc. Sec.*

1860 Williams, John, L.R.C.P. Edinb., Llanerchymedd, Anglesea.

1861 Williams, John, Trosnant Lodge, Pontypool, Monmouth.

1860 Williams, Peter Maurice G., Treyarchid, near Trevine, Haverfordwest.

1860 Williams, Robert Hankinson, L.R.C.P. Edinb., Great Eccleston, near Garstang, Lancashire.

1860 Wills, John, M.D., St. Helier's, Jersey.

1861 Wilmshurst, George, Great Hampton street, Birmingham.

1859 Wilson, James George, M.D., Physician-Accoucheur to the Glasgow Lying-in Hospital and Dispensary; Clarence place, Samhiehall street, Glasgow. *Council*, 1863.

1859 Wilson, Jonathan, F.R.C.S., 92, Bloomsbury, Oxford road, Manchester.

1860 Wilson, Robert James, L.R.C.P. Edinb., St. Leonards-on-Sea, Sussex. *Hon. Loc. Sec.*

Elected

1860 WINTERBOTHAM, JOHN, Castleton, near Sheffield, Derbyshire.

1860 WISEMAN, WILLIAM WOOD, Springstone House, Ossett, near Wakefield, Yorkshire.

1859 WITTEN, EDWARD W., 6, Gibson square, Islington, N.

1860 WOOD, WILLIAM JAMES, Brightwaltham, Wantage, Berks.

1859 WORSHIP, J. LUCAS, Riverhead, Sevenoaks, Kent.

1860 WRIGHT, GEORGE, Middleham, W. Bedale, Yorkshire.

1861 YOUNG, WILLIAM BUTLER, 5, Castle street, Reading, Berks.

CONTENTS.

LIST OF PLATES.

WOODCUTS.

ADVERTISEMENT.

The Society is not as a body responsible for the facts and opinions which are advanced in the following papers and communications read, or for those contained in the abstracts of the discussions which have occurred, at the Meetings during the Session.

OBSTETRICAL SOCIETY

OF

LONDON.

SESSION 1862.

ANNUAL GENERAL MEETING, JANUARY 1ST, 1862.

DR. TYLER SMITH in the chair.

Present—48 Fellows and 11 visitors.

The following gentlemen were duly elected Fellows of the Society:—William Braithwaite, M.D., Clarendon House, Leeds; William Gayton, M.R.C.S., 85, Brick Lane, Spitalfields; Richard Sarell, M.D., Constantinople; William Sankey, L.R.C.P., 6, Upper Portland Place, Wandsworth Road; Thomas Frederick Sanger, M.R.C.S., Alfreston, Sussex; Henry Smith, M.R.C.S., St. Mary's Hospital, Paddington; Joseph Teale, M.R.C.S., 31, Albion Street, Leeds; and Charles S. Watkins, M.R.C.S., 11, Chandos Street, Strand.

This was the third annual meeting of the Society. Before proceeding to the proper business of the evening, the propriety of voting an address of condolence to her Majesty was considered, and unanimously decided in the affirmative.

The PRESIDENT observed that the Obstetrical was not a royal or chartered society, and, therefore, it might not have been proper to call a meeting for the purpose of voting an address to her Majesty. The annual meeting, however, falls at a time when no body of Englishmen can assemble together without deploring the heavy loss which has been sustained by the death of that distinguished and good prince, whom all have revered as the husband of our Queen and the father of our future king. It has been thought, under these circumstances, that it would only be decorous and becoming to add our humble tribute to the stream of affectionate and dutiful sympathy flowing from the heart of the nation to the throne, and which, we may hope, will to some extent mitigate the sorrows of our beloved monarch.

Dr. Oldham spoke as follows:—Mr. President, I acquiesce in the observations you have made on the propriety of our offering an expression of condolence and sympathy with her Majesty under her present circumstances of sorrow and bereavement. I feel that it needs some cogent and imperious circumstance to move a body of scientific men from their usual quiet and unostentatious pursuits. But on the deplorable death of the Prince Consort I think that not only may the profession in the larger royal societies address the Queen, but that smaller bodies—like our own—may becomingly offer their tribute of sympathy and loyal devotion to their beloved Queen under her present overwhelming affliction. Indeed, I cannot hesitate to declare that there is not a member of this Society who is not eager to find some channel through which he may convey, as near to the Queen as he may, the earnest feelings in which he desires to participate in the sorrow which now afflicts and desolates her. It is not for me to delineate the characteristics of the prince we have lost. They are known to all here; but if we wanted any additional reason to justify our address, it would be found in the fact that he was associated with the science of this country, not only as being himself a cultivator of science, but as its illustrious and discriminating patron. I feel, however, that the fewer words I use the better, and shall conclude by simply moving that the following address be forwarded to the Right Hon. Sir George Grey, for presentation to her Majesty:

"*To the Queen's most excellent Majesty.*

"May it please your Majesty,—We, the President and Fellows of the Obstetrical Society of London, desire to express to your Majesty our feelings of profound sorrow at the afflicting calamity which has fallen upon your Majesty in the decease of his Royal Highness the Prince Consort, and to give utterance to our deep sense of the irreparable loss the country has sustained in the death of one whose high position and attainments were so constantly and so devotedly used for the advancement of the national welfare, and especially of the interests of education, science, and art.

"We sincerely beg to offer to your Majesty and every member of the Royal Family our most respectful sympathy and condolence upon the present unhappy occasion; and with feelings of the deepest loyalty and affection we earnestly hope that your Majesty may, under Providence, be blessed with tranquillity and resignation in this weighty affliction."

Dr. Druitt said that he felt it an honour to be invited to second this resolution. It was scarcely necessary to add to the few touching and emphatic sentences in which it had been introduced by the President and Treasurer; yet it was one in which the fulness of every man's heart made it difficult to be silent. There were no members of the community so well able to appreciate that profound shock which fell upon us that sad Sunday morning as the members of the Obstetrical Society. They could testify to the intense, he might say the perilous, grief with which the news of this national calamity was received in many a sick chamber, and by many a worn and anxious invalid. Never before had been in our time so fully realised the truth that this English nation, with its diversities of rank, was, in fact, one large and united family; and that at this crisis especially, when there were threatenings from without, this universal sympathy of the whole English people with the grief of their Queen and her children, would show to the world that our loyalty was the symbol of that strength which belongs exclusively to those at peace among themselves. Representing, as the Obstetrical Society does, that portion of the great profession of medicine which is most intimately concerned with the family life of the nation, it was most proper that we should at this crisis offer to the Queen our respectful condolence under her great and irreparable loss.

The Auditors' Report was next read:

"The Auditors appointed to examine the accounts of the Society beg to report to this meeting that they have examined the same. They find that the expenditure of the Society for the year ending December 28th, 1861, amounted to £312 3*s*. 3*d*.; and that the receipts during the same period amounted to £493 5*s*. 1*d*.; while the balance in the hands of the Treasurer in January, 1861, was £291 5*s*. The present state of the funds of the Society is as follows; the balance in the Treasurer's hands, after paying all expenses for the year 1861, amounts to £472 6*s*. 10*d*.

(Signed) "W. TYLER SMITH.
A. MEADOWS.
THOS. E. EDWARDS.
GRAILY HEWITT.
T. H. TANNER.

"December 28th, 1861."

The result of the ballot for the election of the officers of the Society was then read. The following gentlemen were declared duly elected:

Honorary President.—Sir Charles Locock, Bart., M.D.

President.—Dr. Tyler Smith.

Vice-Presidents.—Dr. Babington, Dr. J. Hall Davis, Dr. Druitt, Mr. R. Dunn, Dr. Swayne (Bristol), Dr. R. Uvedale West (Alford, Lincoln).

Treasurer.—Dr. Oldham.

Hon. Secretaries.—Dr. Graily Hewitt, Dr. Tanner.

Other Members of Council.—Dr. Barnes, Dr. Bloxam, Dr. Chowne, Dr. Chas. Drage (Hatfield), Dr. Gream, Mr. Thomas F. Grimsdale (Liverpool), Mr. Francis S. Haden, Mr. Robert Hardy (Hull), Dr. Harley, Mr. Isaac Harrinson (Reading), Dr. J. B. Hicks, Mr. Hird, Mr. Henry James, Dr. Langmore, Dr. A. Meadows, Mr. Samuel Smith (Leeds), Mr. Frederick Symonds (Oxford), Dr. Alfred J. Tapson.

CASE OF SPINA BIFIDA.

By Graily Hewitt, M.D. Lond., M.R.C.P.

PHYSICIAN TO THE BRITISH LYING-IN HOSPITAL, LECTURER ON MIDWIFERY AND DISEASES OF WOMEN AND CHILDREN AT ST. MARY'S HOSPITAL MEDICAL SCHOOL.

The subject of this case was a child delivered by one of the midwives of the British Lying-in Hospital, on October 30th, 1861. The labour took place at the end of the full term of pregnancy. The mother stated that she had had a fall two months before the labour. The labour itself was easy, but the placenta was adherent, and after waiting some time, the midwife was obliged to seek for assistance, and it was removed two hours and a half after the child had been born. No flooding occurred.

The child was a female, and presented no defect in its development with the exception of that about to be noted. The spine was apparently well formed, and the spinous processes easily recognisable by the finger as far as the junction of the lumbar with the sacral region. Over the middle of the sacrum, however, the bony arch was defective, and here there was situated a tumour, smooth, soft, easily compressible, measuring one and a half inch across, and raised above the surrounding surface three quarters of an inch. The tumour evidently contained fluid, which was oozing *guttatim* from a minute aperture in the skin which covered it. When the child was first thoroughly examined by me, two days after birth, the greater portion of the skin covering the tumour was of a deep-red colour; one portion of the skin was, however, of a yellowish colour, and if not in a sloughy condition, it threatened to become so.

The tumour was felt, under the skin, to be surrounded by a slightly elevated margin of bone; on compression, the fluid in greater part was found to pass inwards.

The general condition of the child was good; the motion of lower extremities good; the body warm; the child sucked strongly and slept well.

Means were forthwith taken to protect the tumour from external rubbing or pressure, by pads applied on each side, and it was resolved to attempt more active treatment when the skin covering the tumour assumed a more healthy aspect.

After going on well for the first six days, however, the child became weaker, as regarded its power of sucking, convulsions set in, and twelve days after birth death took place.

The inflammatory action which was set up in the skin covering the tumour extended to the brain, and probably occasioned the fatal result in the case now related. The case appeared, when it first came under notice, a favorable one for an attempt at cure; and it was hoped that, by careful protection of the skin from rubbing, by the use of collodium, and slight pressure kept up by bandaging, retraction of the sac might in time have been produced.

Was there any connection, as cause and effect, between the presence of adhesion of the placenta and the defect in the osseous development of the fœtus?

ADDRESS OF THE PRESIDENT,

W. Tyler Smith, M.D.

The President commenced his Annual Address by referring in terms of congratulation to the prosperous career of the Society. It had been in existence three years, and during that time two volumes of 'Transactions' had been published, which might challenge comparison with the volumes of the older societies, and a third volume was preparing. All the preliminary expenses incidental to the establishment of the Society had been paid, and the Treasurer had a balance of nearly £500 ready for investment. The total number of Fellows was now 482, of which 82 had joined during the

Plate I.

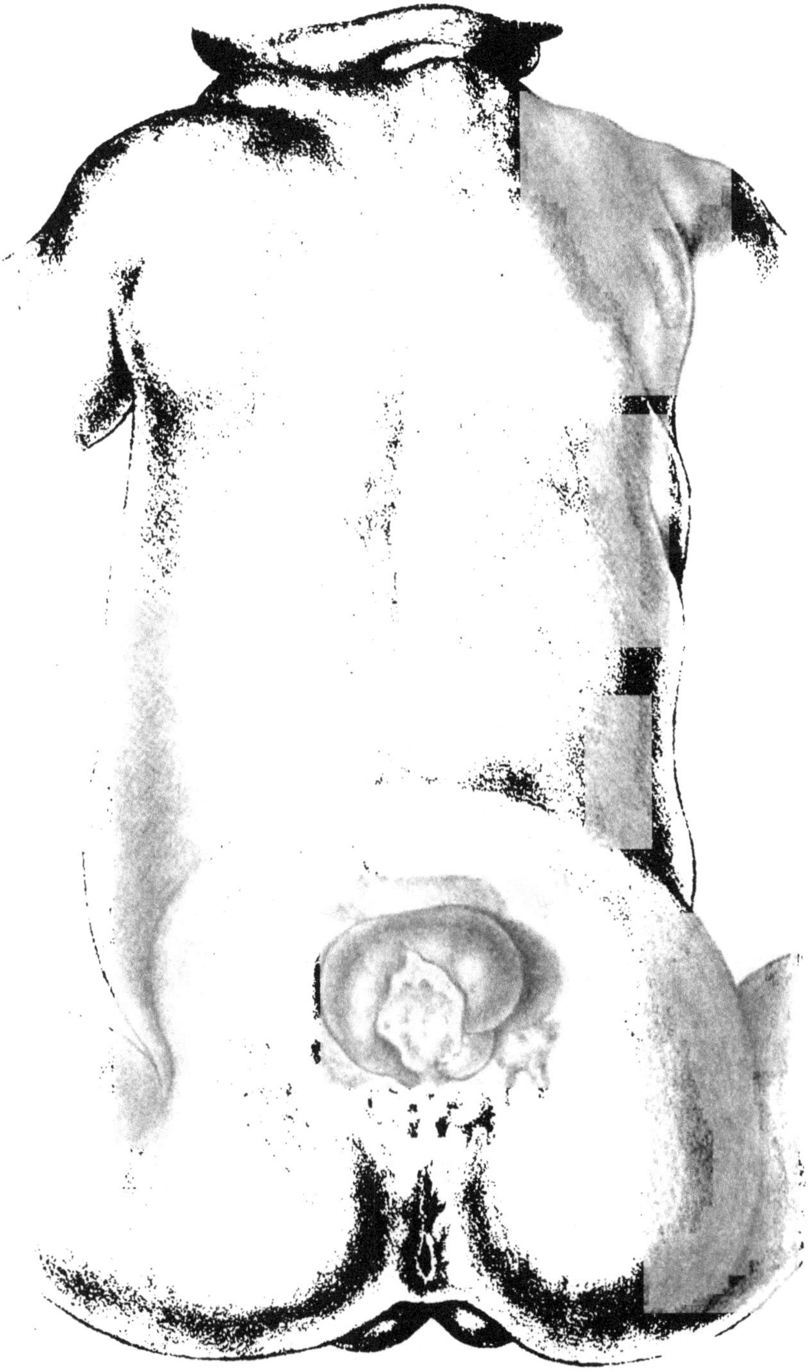

Dr. Westmacott del.t et dir.xit

W. West

The above is reduced from a drawing taken during life. It exhibits

present year. The Society was so cosmopolitan as to include among its Fellows, practitioners in the East and West Indies, Australia, New Zealand, Constantinople, and other places in different parts of the world. During the past year the reputation of the Society had been well maintained by the papers and discussions, and the attendance of Fellows had been uniformly good. The subject of the formation of an Obstetrical Library was next adverted to, as a matter in which little progress has been made, but which required the future exertions of the Fellows and Council. The proceedings in relation to the proposed amalgamation of the medical societies were then passed in review. The points elicited at the meetings of the councils and committees, and at a public meeting of the Royal Medical and Chirurgical Society, seemed to be that our profession greatly needed the existence of some authoritative body, representing the whole profession, which should be the recognised medium of communication between medicine and the state; and that some adequate machinery was required by which reports and decisions should be made upon prominent professional subjects. Without undervaluing the advantages of union, he questioned if any mere organization could give the profession its fair influence in matters of government. The medical profession was steadily increasing its political power and influence by the formation, under various Acts of Parliament, of a considerable body of officials who were in the employ of the State, in connection with Lunacy, Coronerships, Inspectors of Factories, the Poor-law, Registration of Births and Deaths, Sanitary Laws, and other subjects. In the end this must create a political life for the profession, and we could not obtain our legitimate influence, or extend our political arena, until some of our body were found in the Houses of the Legislature. He trusted the time might come when it would be considered as necessary for the legal head of our profession, namely, the President of the Medical Council, to be in Parliament, as the Archbishop of Canterbury or the Lord Chancellor. It was only, he believed, in this way that the profession could achieve its due political recognition. Apart from political life, governments would not refer to any particular body; they would continue, as now, sometimes to consult one college, sometimes another, or, more frequently, some private individual.

Political development was, then, one of the great wants of the medical profession in the present age. With regard to the second point, no doubt any new means for the investigation and discussion of disputed or important points would be useful, but he questioned if the decisions of any body of men would supersede the present machinery, consisting, as it did, of discussion, contemporary literature, the medical press, and the collection of public medical opinion based upon all these. In the meetings of the joint committees of the several societies something like the outline of an amalgamation was proposed and in part adopted. Subsequently, the younger societies were invited to suggest some method by which the objects proposed might be carried out. Various causes operated to prevent the accomplishment of this object. A difficulty arose with the charter of the Royal Medical and Chirurgical. Some of the older fellows of that society strongly opposed any scheme of the kind. In the councils of the younger societies, a loss of independent action was apprehended. Under these circumstances, the proposed amalgamation remained in abeyance. For himself, and he believed he might speak for the Council and Fellows, there was no objection to any union which should preserve the independence and vigour of their own Society. He thought the various societies might unite to form a Supreme Council, just as the colleges and universities united to form the General Council under the Medical Act. To this supreme council might be committed the duties which it was thought might be better performed by a united body than under present arrangements, and the expenses of such a council might be shared in common. This would be a real growth or development of the existing societies, and not a process of mere fusion or remodelling. In any future negotiations he thought the first step should be some understanding between the younger societies. He would now make a few remarks upon the functions performed by medical societies, and by their own Society in particular. Societies, as a means of scientific and practical advancement, had been brought to great perfection in medicine. There was nothing like them, either in the law or the church. Our colleges devoted themselves chiefly to the care of the student from the date of matriculation to the day when he obtained his first professional qualification. After this the medical man was left very much to himself, and the unions of our members in societies were the chief means of public professional intercourse. These bodies also carried on, as it were, and matured, the education of the practitioner, and they also promoted in a very great degree the improvement of medical knowlege. In Obstetrics, the want of such a Society in this metropolis had long been felt. No greater proof of this could be adduced than the remarkable success which had attended its operations. Every evil augury had been falsified, and the best anticipations of its advocates had been more than fulfilled. Our body had not alone the duties pertaining to all other medical societies, but the Obstetrical Society was the only point of union which existed in this country for those engaged in this department of practice. The colleges, which were founded to promote medicine and surgery, naturally preferred these departments to midwifery.

No subject could be more interesting to this Society than any matter relating to the improvement of obstetric education. He was happy to be able to state that during the past year the College of Physicians had completed arrangements for examining and granting a license in medicine and midwifery. The attendance required upon lectures was less than many of them would have thought necessary; but attendance had for the first time been enjoined on clinical diseases of women, which was a step in advance. He ought not to omit to state that in the discussions arising out of this subject their honorary president, Sir Charles Locock, bore a distinguished part. On two occasions he came from the country, at considerable personal inconvenience, to attend the meetings of the College of Physicians, and advocated the interests of midwifery with such zeal and ability as to deserve their warmest gratitude. He begged, in conclusion, to direct their attention to the present social and professional position of obstetrists. There was a tendency to consider us as specialists, against which we should all contend. We were not specialists in the sense in which the ophthalmic or aural surgeon followed a specialty. Midwifery was one of the three great departments into which the wants of society and the lapse of time had divided the profession; and if the charge of specialty was brought against the obstetrist, it might with equal justice be urged against the physician or the surgeon. It should be the aim of the Society to raise the department to which it was devoted, and to obtain the general recognition of its importance. It was often assumed that midwifery was behind medicine and surgery in a scientific and practical point of view, but this was to a great degree untenable. Well-ascertained facts, rules of action, and established principles, were the characteristics which marked the approach of any art to the exactness of science. Viewed impartially, he did not think midwifery could be considered behind either medicine or surgery in these respects. In the many dangerous contingencies met with in the practice of midwifery there were few in which the plan of action was not definitely and clearly laid down. He believed we were advancing in as great a ratio as medicine and surgery. We were fortunate in having to wield some of the greatest resources of medical art. The midwifery forceps was acknowledged to be the most perfect and life-saving application of mechanical genius which had ever been made. No other instrument equalled it in importance and perfection. It also fell to the accoucheur to dispense to mankind the blessings of vaccination, the grandest and most beneficent discovery within the realm of medicine, and perhaps of science. For another world-wide blessing, the use of chloroform, mankind were indebted to an obstetrician. Let us, then, be proud of the privileges we possessed, while we strenuously endeavour to increase and improve them. The mistaken idea has been sometimes broached that the cultivation of midwifery, as one of the great departments of the art of healing, tends to separate it from medicine and surgery. He believed that the more perfect the three great departments became, the more assured would be their union. Who could say that the union between medicine and surgery was not more perfect now than when surgery was in the hands of the barber-chirurgeon? Let us, then, cultivate the department in which we are engaged, not in any spirit of disunion, but with the conviction that the more perfect we become, the more intimate and honorable will be our union with the sister departments. No mere alliance, in which our department is treated as inferior to the others, can ever prove as real or useful as a union cemented by, and depending on, mutual respect, general advancement, and equality.

Mr. SPENCER WELLS proposed a vote of thanks to the President for his address. It was an address so able that it merited more than the usual complimentary vote (which he was sure would be carried by acclamation), and he trusted that at least one of the many valuable suggestions it contained would be acted upon by the gentlemen present, and by every Fellow of the Society. The President had shown very forcibly how necessary it is that our profession should be represented in the Legislature, and he (Mr. Wells) trusted that every Fellow of the Society would do all that lay in his power to attain so desirable an object; and many of them had the power. There were very few medical men who might not exert considerable influence in the selection of candidates for various counties or boroughs, or in influencing the views of candidates. Some, perhaps, might assist in the selection of some eminent medical man, partly retired from very active practice, as a candidate for a seat in the House of Commons. Others, who might be unable to exert such influence as this, might impress upon the mind of some other candidate the necessity for advocating a great constitutional question—one which has already been advocated by an influential section of the press—the creation of life peerages. If life peerages were to become a part of the institutions of the country, we should soon see medical peers sitting in the House of Lords beside the law lords and the bishops. Surely the venerable surgeon (Sir Benjamin Brodie) who was led to this room last night to move the address of condolence to her Majesty from the Medical and Chirurgical Society, would do as full honour to the House of Lords as any lawyer or divine who now has a seat there; and many other medical men might be named who, if they had made the large fortunes gained in the church or at the bar, might accept an hereditary title, and might now do honour to a life peerage. If the profession would really work in earnest for this reform in the general election which is fully expected between February and Easter, we might then see our profession well represented in both Houses of Parliament. At any rate, let the gentlemen present do their best, and show that they appreciate the address for which he now moved that they thank their President, by doing what they could to carry out the objects he had shown to be so desirable.

The motion was seconded by Dr. T. POLLOCK, and carried by acclamation.

FEBRUARY 5TH, 1862.

DR. TYLER SMITH, President, in the chair.

Present—55 Fellows and 6 visitors.

The following gentlemen were duly elected Fellows of the Society:—Thomas Thornely Brooke, M.R.C.S., St. Mary's Hospital, Paddington; John Clarke, M.R.C.S., Lynton, North Devon; John Stewart Lamb, M.D., 4, Windsor Terrace, Maida-hill; Malim Sharman, M.R.C.S., 18, New Hall Street, Birmingham; George John Vine, F.R.C.S., 3, Henrietta Street, Covent Garden, W.C.

REPORT ON MR. SPENCER WELLS' CASE OF EXFOLIATION OF THE FEMALE BLADDER.

By DR. HARLEY.

To decide upon the true nature and source of the above-named specimen has proved a task of more than ordinary difficulty, for while there are several facts in favour of the specimen being, as has been supposed, a slough of the interior of a human bladder, there are, on the other hand, some in favour of the view that the substance in question came from another source, only known to the patient herself.

The following are the facts in favour of the former view:

1st. The patient passed the substance by the urethra six weeks after a severe instrumental labour.

2ndly. From the time of delivery up to the period when the specimen was voided the patient was very ill and bed-ridden.

3rdly. The symptoms she laboured under during the above-named period were those of acute cystitis, associated with nephritis. About three weeks after delivery her medical attendant, Mr. Marshall, brought me the urine for examination. It was then albuminous, contained blood-corpuscles, pus-cells, chylous matter, and renal tube-casts. At the same time the fresh urine was very much loaded with carbonate of ammonia, and was intensely alkaline, even at the moment of being passed. At this period of the case the mere examination of the urine alone would of itself, in absence of any other evidence, have been sufficient to justify the diagnosis of cystic and renal disease.

4thly. Mr. Marshall examined the patient per vaginam on the day preceding the expulsion of the specimen from the bladder, and found nothing in the vagina, although he, at the same time, observed shreds of a sloughy-looking tissue projecting from the orifice of the urethra. There had been a hard swelling felt in the anterior wall of the vagina, which by one practitioner was supposed to be an abscess, and by another a foreign substance in the bladder.

5thly. The patient's health has rapidly improved since the substance came away.

6th and lastly. The woman is married, and there is no apparent cause for her practising deceit.

When we turn to the specimen itself, we find—

1st. An animal membrane of some kind or other—bladder, stomach, or cyst—as large as a child's head.

2ndly. The membrane, which is in the form of a bag, is perfect on all sides except on one, in which there are several irregular rents.

3rdly. The exterior is of a white colour, and even to the naked eye distinctly muscular. On close inspection the muscular fibres are found to be of the involuntary kind, and are distributed in an interlacing manner, as in the urinary bladder.

4thly. The interior is of a dark colour, and everywhere covered with a gritty deposit, on the removal of which a smooth, mucous surface comes into view.

5thly. On analysis, the gritty matter is found to consist of crystalline phosphates and urates.

6thly. While examining the muscular coat of the specimen under the microscope, I found a number of tube-casts and granular cells; but as the specimen had been in water for a couple of days, it is possible that these may have accidentally floated out from the interior of the organ.

7thly. On minute inspection of what appears to be the outer surface of the specimen, there is seen an irregular patch, of about two inches by one in diameter, of a smooth tissue, bearing a strong resemblance to a serous membrane; and if it be really a serous membrane, it is highly probable that it is a portion of the peritoneum.

8thly. The distilled water in which the specimen was steeped during forty-eight hours deposited a quantity of phosphate of lime and of urate of soda and ammonia. The supernatant liquid was of a milky colour, which appearance it even retained after filtration. The fluid, indeed, had very much the appearance of lime-water.

9thly. No ureters, or orifices of ureters, are to be found in the specimen.

10thly. It is impossible to ascertain whether or not the specimen is an entire organ, or only the portion of an organ, in consequence of the torn condition of its lower part.

The above-mentioned data lead me to the conclusion that the specimen is a portion of a urinary bladder, and that at one part it is, probably, of the entire thickness, possessing, as it apparently does, an internal mucous, a middle muscular, and an external serous, coat; the latter only, however, *over a limited portion* half by three quarters of an inch in extent.

The question now is, "Is it a human bladder?" This is a question not so easily answered on anatomical grounds, for in its present state the organ has neither the form nor the size of a human female bladder; and as neither the orifice of the urethra nor the openings of the ureters can be discovered, the specimen may be but a portion of a much larger organ.

Mr. Wells kindly furnished me with a specimen of a human bladder in which was found after death a cast of the interior of the organ, and which he considers to be a parallel case to the one we are now considering. On a careful examination of the specimen, I find that the walls of this bladder are thick and contracted. They are somewhat softened, but the muscular fibres are distinctly visible, and are easily separated from each other. The inner surface of the bladder is lined with a thickened mucous coat. The detached cast of the cavity of the organ has a rough inner surface, and is everywhere covered with gritty deposit, which, as in the doubtful specimen, consists of urates and phosphates. Beyond the latter circumstance, however, I can find no similarity in the two specimens; for the cast is soft, thick, and friable, and contains not a trace of muscular or other organized tissue, being, in fact, nothing else than an exudation, the product of inflammatory action, on one side of which has been deposited a quantity of urinary salts. I have only further to remark that if the bladder, or portion of bladder, sent to me for examination is a true pathological product, it appears to me that we must accept one of the two following theories:

1st. That a woman voided, by the natural passage, nearly her whole bladder.

Or 2ndly. That the entire mucous membrane, with nearly the whole of the muscular coat, has become, by some means or other, dissected from the neighbouring tissues, and exfoliated in the form of a perfect cast.

Mr. Spencer Wells said that he agreed in every particular with the report drawn up by Dr. Harley after minute anatomical investigation. Connecting the result of the examination with Dr. Harley's previous report on the urine, with Mr. Marshall's account of the case, and with his own examination of the patient on the morning the specimen was voided, he could come to no other conclusion than that acute cystitis was followed by sloughing and separation of a very large portion of the bladder.

Dr. Tanner remarked that there was a preparation (Pathological Specimens, No. 1993) in the museum of the Royal College of Surgeons which might help to throw some light upon the nature of the specimen that had just been reported on. The history of the patient from whose bladder the membrane was removed had been communicated to him (Dr. Tanner) by Dr. Knox, and was as follows:—A man, seventy years of age, living in Edinburgh, fell from a scaffold, and in consequence suffered from retention of urine. The catheter was introduced frequently, and a thick, puriform fluid drawn off by it. At the end of the third week, however, nothing would pass through the instrument, while the point of the catheter could be felt to impinge upon a membrane. To relieve the man's sufferings, the late Mr. Liston, assisted by Dr. Knox, cut into the bladder from above the pubes, and thus allowed a large quantity of purulent fluid and a membrane to escape. The patient lived for three months afterwards, discharging his urine partly through the wound and partly through the urethra; at the end of this time he died from exhaustion. On examining the layer of membrane, it is seen to be of saccular form, about six inches in its longer and four inches in its shorter diameter. Its shape indicates that it lined the whole interior of the bladder, and was thrown off from it in one piece. The outer surface is flocculent, and in parts distinctly fibrous; the inner surface is granular and reticulated, like superficially ulcerated mucous membrane. In fact, as the College Catalogue states, it exactly resembles the mucous membrane of a bladder, separated as a slough in one piece.

PROTRACTED RETENTION OF BLIGHTED OVUM.

Dr. Uvedale West exhibited a specimen of blighted ovum, which he said had been expelled two days previously by a woman, æt. 38, who believed that she became pregnant in the early part of February, 1861, her symptoms having been precisely similar to those of her previous pregnancies, which had been four in number, all terminating in normal labours with living children. At the time when she ought to have quickened she began to have frequent hæmorrhages until the full period, in November, when the hæmorrhage became constant. Pains coming on with increase of hæmorrhage, on the 3rd of February the specimen exhibited was, after a few hours, expelled. There was no trace of the embryo to be found in the cavity when opened, it having probably perished at the period of quickening, at which time Dr. West thought the ovum itself ceased to *grow*, although retaining until the full period of nine months an amount of vitality enabling the membranes to blend themselves together into the fleshy, thickened mass exhibited. Independently of the interest attaching to the specimen as an example of protracted retention of blighted ovum, Dr. West thought the case instructive, as being one in which both patient and doctor had been at the same time right and wrong; the former having persisted to the last in the belief that she was not only pregnant, but normally so; the latter having told the patient, when consulted by her after the expiration of her nine months, that he thought she was not only not pregnant normally, but that she had not been pregnant at all; while the ultimate expulsion of the mass exhibited explained everything.

DISCOLORATION OF THE SKIN OF THE FORE-ARMS AND HANDS DURING PREGNANCY.

By J. G. Swayne, M.D.,

PHYSICIAN-ACCOUCHEUR TO THE BRISTOL GENERAL HOSPITAL, AND LECTURER ON MIDWIFERY AT THE BRITISH MEDICAL SCHOOL.

This case is a strongly marked instance of the discoloration of the skin in various parts of the body, which is so often observed during pregnancy. The subject of it was Mrs. A—, æt. 26, a blonde, with rather florid complexion, brown hair, and blue eyes. She had always enjoyed good health. I attended her in her fourth labour on May 12th, 1861, when I was much struck with the peculiar appearance presented by the skin of both forearms and hands. There was a very general discoloration of the skin of the forearms, and this was much more marked on the dorsal than on the palmar aspect. The discoloration attained its greatest intensity at the wrist, where the skin was of a rich, yellowish-brown colour, and as dark as the skin of a mulatto. From that point it gradually faded off up to the elbow, where the skin regained its ordinary hue so imperceptibly that it was impossible to point out the exact place where it ceased. At the wrist, however, the line of demarcation was very distinct, and the colour was deeper and

Discoloration of the Skin of the Fore Arms and Hands during Pregnancy.

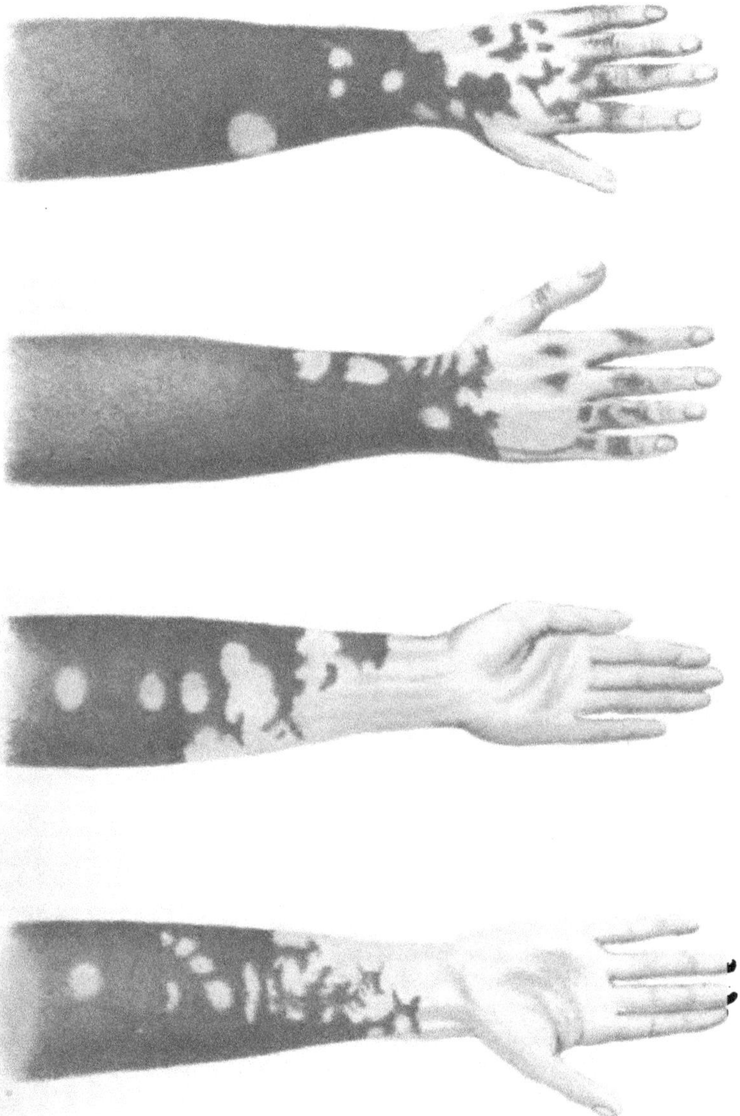

Dorsal Aspect.

Palmar Aspect

extended further on the dorsal than on the palmar surface of each forearm. For instance, on the palmar surface it did not extend quite so far as the wrists, and the hands were quite unaffected; but on the dorsal surface, it extended beyond the wrists, and was noticed partially on the backs of the hands and fingers. Here it assumed the form of isolated patches, with irregular crescentic outlines, and mostly situated on the knuckles. On the forearms these patches coalesced, so as to produce a more uniform dark tint; still, however, with well-defined, irregularly concave edges, and enclosing, here and there, circular patches of white skin. I found, on inquiry, that the skin had been similarly affected in each preceding pregnancy, and that the dark colour first appeared about the end of the third month, and increased, *pari passu*, with the development of the areola until it attained its acme at the time of labour. After delivery it soon began to diminish in intensity, and in about three months had entirely disappeared. This I observed to be the case in the present instance. She informed me, also, that her mother had two children, and that in each of her pregnancies both the arms and neck were spotted in a similar way; and being a very fair woman, the discoloration was still more evident than it was in herself.

DIFFICULT LABOUR FROM LOCKED HEADS.

By Henry Raynes, Esq., Gringley, near Bawtry.

I now beg to lay before the Society a case which occurred in my practice analogous to the one recorded by Dr. Pollock at the meeting of the Society of April 3rd, 1861.

A case of difficult labour from locked heads, literally locked jaws, from mechanical causes, in a twin case, the head of the second child taking precedence of the head of the first, whose body was already in advance. A general outline of the case, as it occurred to me, may be sufficient to direct attention to the possibility of the occurrence of these accidents, which, though rare, yet do occasionally happen.

To be as brief as possible, I may state that the case in question occurred on February 18th, 1838, at Misterton, a remote country village; the patient, the wife of John Gray, of that place, who is now living, and can confirm the leading facts of the case. Labour had considerably advanced before my arrival. The breech presenting, was soon converted into a footling case. Impediment to further progress was now detected, the cause of which was the locking together the heads of the children, which were reversed, and the inferior margins of the lower jaws placed in juxtaposition. I immediately excised the head of the child whose body was just born (being dead) with a penknife, the only instrument at hand. The head of the second child, having taken the lead of the other, preserved its place until labour was so far advanced as to give birth to the second child; the head of the first, from having been truncated, was enabled to retire above the brim and admit of the progress of the second child, which was born by the unaided powers of nature. The child, though born alive, expired soon after its birth. The head of the decapitated child then descended, and was extracted by a little manipulation, the fingers of the operator being placed in the mouth.

This case occurred at a time anterior to the formation of the Obstetrical Society, about twenty-four years ago. I think it, nevertheless, of sufficient interest to induce me to place it before the Society.

I may refer the Society to a similar case published by Mr. Eaton in the 'Medical Gazette,' and recorded by Braithwaite in his 'Retrospect,' vol. xiv. Mr. Eaton's and Dr. Pollock's are the only cases I have seen put upon record.

Doubtless similar cases may occur in the practice of others, but they are of such unfrequent occurrence that they may be ranked amongst those extraordinary cases which happen but once in a man's lifetime.

ON A CASE OF RETAINED MENSES, OF TWO YEARS' DURATION, CAUSED BY ATRESIA VAGINÆ; PUNCTURE OF THE UTERUS BY THE RECTUM; RECOVERY.

By I. Baker Brown, F.R.C.S. (Exam.)

In cases of deficiency or total absence of the vagina in the young female, if not associated with any arrest of development of the uterine organs, it is probable that pain and other symptoms of a desire to menstruate may recur monthly, and yet pass off without any great inconvenience. There is the liability, however, of the accumulation of the menstrual fluid, which goes on augmenting at each period, undergoing inspissation, and ultimately giving rise to painful and continued distension of the uterus, which at last demands surgical interference. Such cases are undoubtedly rare, and where attempts have been made to afford relief by puncture or otherwise in the majority an untoward result has taken place. An exceptional case is related by Dr. Meigs, in his work on 'Woman: her Diseases and Remedies' (Philadelphia, 1859). In this instance there was an absence of the vagina in a girl of sixteen, who had the usual symptoms of menstruation every month, attended with much suffering. The vagina was one inch long, and ended in a *cul de sac.* A hard and solid tumour could be felt jutting upwards in the lower part of the belly like the womb of a woman at quickening. This tumour could be felt also in the rectum; and believing at first that it arose from distension of the womb by the retained menses, an attempt was made to push a small trocar and canula through the rectum quite into the centre of the organ; a few drops of blood only came away. No bad effects ensued, and Dr. Meigs was uncertain as to the true nature of the tumour; at any rate the girl continued in good health, but subject to periodical pains as before, although the uterus did not further increase in size.

On reading Dr. Meigs' description of his case I cannot help thinking that the tumour was a distended uterus and that had he used a larger trocar and canula, the result might have been more positive.

In the 'North American Medico-Chirurgical Review' for July, 1861, is an instance of "occlusion of the uterus," quoted from the 'St. Louis Medical and Surgical Journal' of the previous January, wherein the patient had suffered for two months considerable anguish, without menstruation, though with no other signs of pregnancy. By the finger in the rectum a tumour could be felt; a vaginal examination revealed a shortened vagina. Next day, detecting fluctuation in the tumour, Dr. M. M. Pallen, of St. Louis, introduced a curved trocar into the rectum, and plunged it through the supposed os uteri, and a quart or more of menstrual fluid gushed out, relieving the patient. It is not stated whether this was followed by any bad consequence; if it had been, I have no doubt it would have been mentioned.

A third instance is published in the 'Medical Times' of August 17th, 1861, of a girl, æt. 18, with congenital deficiency of the vagina, admitted into Guy's Hospital under the care of Dr. Hicks. Puncture of the rectum was effectual, and the patient recovered excellently.

Cases of retention of the menses with congenital absence of the vagina must be extremely rare, as so few indeed are placed upon record. The general opinion prevails that a fatal result almost invariably ensues in such cases when the uterus is punctured through the rectum. Whether this is correct or not, the results of experience can alone decide. Dupuytren has opened the closed womb through the vagina in several cases, and the inflammatory symptoms were so severe after the operation that he finally decided upon entirely giving it up, "and rather to allow the patient to die more quietly and slowly than to speedily hasten her death by the operation, which," he states, "always results from inflammation of the womb, and which is the more violent in proportion to its distension." Since his time the distended womb has been punctured on many occasions through the vagina without the terrible effects witnessed by him.

In 1860 I published a case in the 'Lancet' (vol. i, 1860, p. 465) of retained menses in a girl æt. 16, the result of imperforate os uteri. She had never menstruated, but every month she suffered great pain in the belly and back, lasting for a period varying from a few hours to a few days. The vagina ended in a *cul de sac,* but the lips of the os uteri could be obscurely made out, covered, as it were, by the lining membrane of the vagina. An enlarged fluctuating uterus could be felt through the rectum. I punctured the membrane through the vagina, and nearly a pint of treacly fluid flowed out. An untoward result occurred on the third day, from local peritonitis.

Dr. Simpson, of Edinburgh, has operated for retained menses in a case of occlusion of the vagina, the result of adhesion and contraction from sloughing, following a previous difficult labour. A large quantity of fluid was evacuated, and a small amount of irritative fever followed this simple operation of puncture ('Obstetrical Memoirs,' vol. i, p. 292).

Several cases have been collected by Dr. Ramsbotham in which this same fever ended fatally ('Medical Gazette,' October 16th, p. 327).

In none of these, however, had the operation been required by the rectum; in the following case the operation was followed by pain off and on for a few days, the result more of slow contraction of the uterus than of any other cause. And to some extent pain was due to the efforts at natural menstruation, which ended in the appearance of healthy catamenia on the evening of the fourth day of the operation and during the fifth day. Pain also preceded the second menstruation for some days. There was no irritative fever throughout, and the general result I look upon as extremely satisfactory.

CASE (reported from the Case-book).—M. D—, æt. 15, single, admitted into the London Surgical Home, November 13th, 1861, from Yorkshire.

History.—Has always enjoyed good health until about two years ago, when she began to suffer much pain at every monthly period, unaccompanied by any show of menses. She was treated medically for it, but was not examined till a year ago, when Dr. Wright, of Malton, examined her, and described the nature of her complaint, but did nothing for her. She has been under the care of Mr. Teale, of Leeds, who tried to make a vagina, but failed in consequence of the excessively small amount of tissue to work upon. Ever since she has been suffering constant pain from the distended uterus, which has increased much in size.

On admission.—She is a fine, stout, well-developed girl, but with an expression of great suffering in her face; the uterus can be felt externally as large as a four months' gravid organ, and on introducing the finger into the rectum it can be felt bulging and prominent, and something like an os can be distinguished. There are no signs of a vagina, but all the other external parts are perfect.

November 21st.—In the presence of M. Nelaton, from Paris, Dr. Esteva, his assistant, Dr. Gueneau de Mussey, and several other medical gentlemen, Mr. Brown tapped the uterus through the rectum with a curved trocar and canula, which he introduced as nearly as possible where he thought he could feel the os. About an ounce of treacle-like fluid came away immediately; the canula was left in.

10 p. m.—There has been a good deal of pain, for which one grain of opium was ordered. A quantity of the thick menstrual fluid has come away.

22nd.—Has passed a pretty good night until 2 a.m., from which time she became restless. Pulse 100; tongue rather red and dry; very thirsty; there is a peculiar leaden appearance about the countenance; has been no discharge during the night.

23rd, 8 a.m.—Has slept very well all night; possesses a cheerful countenance; pulse 90; tongue clean and moist; there is very little discharge, and no pain.

2 p.m.—Has a good deal of pain in the uterus, for which she was ordered to inhale turpentine and to use fomentations;

these very quickly relieved her; pulse 80; tongue clean; there has been a considerable quantity of the menstrual discharge. This is about the period the catamenia should naturally appear.

24th, a.m.—Pulse 86; tongue clean; has had very little discharge during the night. In the afternoon it assumed a purulent character.

8 p.m.—Has had uterine pain, followed by the appearance of some bright, healthy menstrual fluid.

25th, a.m.—Has had more pain during the night, much relieved by turpentine fomentations and inhalations, and followed by a copious discharge of fresh, healthy menstrual fluid; appetite very good.

26th.—No more discharge. Complains a little of the canula hurting her. The bowels seem inclined to act.

27th.—Is very comfortable; suffers no pain; there is no discharge; passed a little fæces and flatus in the night, at noon, and again in the evening.

December 1st.—Bowels are opened every day, the canula being allowed to remain in. She has no pain, but complains of the canula feeling uncomfortable.

4th, 2 p.m.—Being a fortnight after the operation, Mr. Brown removed the canula; apparently about one inch of it had been in the uterus. The rectum was so full of fæces that no good examination could be made. The uterus could not be felt externally. Patient eats and sleeps well; ordered a dose of castor oil, Mr. Brown particularly wishing that no injections should be used, lest any of the fluid should pass into the uterus.

7th.—Is sitting up; feels very well, appetite good, and sleeps well.

19th.—Has had slight pain in the night, which passed off.

21st, 22nd, 23rd, 24th.—Has had a good deal of uterine pain, but no appearance of any menstrual discharge in her motions, which are carefully examined; the pain generally came on about 5 p.m., and lasted till 10 p.m.; it was much alleviated by turpentine fomentations.

25th.—Mr. Brown examined the rectum with the speculum, but could observe nothing beyond a slight depression, through which, however, he could not introduce any probe or instrument into the uterus. He determined to wait and see, in the event of the uterus becoming enlarged and distended, whether there would be an outlet formed for the menses.

From December 25th to January 2nd she suffered a good deal of pain every day, lasting for some hours, generally in the middle of the day, and unrelieved by any treatment.

January 2nd, a.m.—There appeared a thick muco-gelatinous discharge from the rectum, coloured with blood, no doubt the menstrual fluid; since this appeared she has had no more pain.

3rd.—Very comfortable; there is still a little discharge.

4th.—There is neither pain nor discharge.

10th.—She left Home quite well and in a wonderfully improved state of health.

Dr. Routh, after thanking Mr. Brown for his contribution, remarked that the case was satisfactory as one of recovery after liberating a menstrual accumulation per rectum. It was important, because usually, when an opening for the same purpose was made per vaginam, death was the result. How far, therefore, did recovery depend upon the rectal opening? It was well known we occasionally met with large ovarian cysts within the pelvis, which gave rise to so much distress and pain that the liberation of the contained fluid became imperative. Now, he believed five such cases had occurred in the Samaritan Hospital, all of which, except one, had died after the operation. The continual drain kept up of purulent matter, which usually became very offensive, exhausted the patient in the end, although the immediate effect was relief. Did this depend on the passage of air within the cavity? It was known as a practical point, already insisted upon by Dr. Oldham, for reducing retroverted wombs, that if the vagina was opened and pulled backwards a rush of air took place, and the vagina was pulled out, and so the reduction effected. Did not something like this occur in those cases where the opening was made by the vagina, which was prevented by the sphincter ani from taking place when the opening was made per rectum? *A priori*, we should expect the reverse, from the probable passage of flatus through the opening made per rectum into the cyst or uterus. It was known how intensely putrid were the contents of abscesses near the rectum, from the passage of fæcal matters or flatus within them; yet recovery was not uncommon when the opening was made per rectum. Did anything depend on the vaginal opening, when made, remaining unclosed? Altogether he thought it an important surgical point to determine, which he hoped on some future day to take up and embody in a paper for the Society.

Mr. Spencer Wells agreed with Dr. Routh as to the necessity for inquiry into the relative safety of tapping by the vagina or by the rectum in cases where ovarian cysts were adherent within the pelvis. He had tapped by the vagina in three patients in the Samaritan Hospital. In the first case the operation was performed more than two years ago; and although the woman could not be said to be entirely cured, as some discharge still went on, yet she was in so good a state of health as to be able to walk two or three miles. In a second case the woman died a few months after the tapping, exhausted by continuous discharge. In the third instance the patient gained great temporary relief, but the sac was filling again. In cases where he had tapped by the rectum he had not seen the same suppurative inflammation of the lining membrane of the cyst as after tapping by the vagina, but he had seen troublesome dysenteric tenesmus from the constant discharge of ovarian fluid into the rectum. He could not believe that it was better to have the fetid gases formed in the intestines entering an ovarian cyst than the pure atmospheric air, and he had seen cases where ovarian cysts had opened spontaneously into the rectum, or into some other part of the intestinal canal, prove rapidly fatal after putrefactive fermentation of the ovarian fluid. It was a very important practical question, which required further observation.

Dr. Tyler Smith hoped the further history of the case would be noted.

Mr. Brown replied by stating that this case would still be under the watchful eye of Dr. Wright, of Malton, who was a most careful observer of disease, and deeply interested in this particular case, so that Mr. Brown would be able to report hereafter to the Society the condition of the patient.

ON THE UTERINE DOUCHE AS A THERAPEUTIC AGENT; WITH EXHIBITION OF A NEW INSTRUMENT.

By Graily Hewitt, M.D., M.R.C.P.,

PHYSICIAN TO THE BRITISH LYING-IN HOSPITAL; LECTURER ON MIDWIFERY AND DISEASES OF WOMEN AND CHILDREN IN ST. MARY'S HOSPITAL MEDICAL SCHOOL.

The employment of the uterine douche in the treatment

of certain diseases of the uterus is no novelty. The beneficial action of cold water applied by means of the douche to the portion of the uterus accessible to its action from the vagina, in the treatment of chronic leucorrhœa and allied affections, has been recognised by many authorities. But although the principle in question is recognised, it can scarcely be said that the use of the uterine douche is by any means widely practised; in point of fact, it is very rarely employed by the profession at large. One reason why the douche is so little employed is the want of a ready and efficacious mode of administering it. The various forms of injection apparatus procurable are all more or less open to one of these objections—the quantity of fluid capable of being used is too limited, or manual effort is required, or possession of ingenuity on the part of the patient is essential. In order to administer the douche effectively an instrument is required at once portable, necessitating no mechanical or other effort on the part of the patient, and admitting of the use of a large quantity of water. The fatigue attending the use of ordinary forms of injection apparatus interferes most seriously with their useful employment. The high opinion which the author entertained of the therapeutic power of the uterine douche had induced him to devise an instrument which should fulfil the necessary indications.

The apparatus now exhibited to the Society (ingeniously constructed under the author's directions by Mr. Thos. H. Savory, of the firm of Savory and Moore, of New Bond Street) is extremely portable; the whole is contained in a box seven inches across and four inches deep. It consists of an india-rubber vessel, folding up like a "gibus" opera hat and from the bottom of which a long, flexible tube conveys the fluid. When opened out, the rigidity of the reservoir is maintained by a brass rod screwed in its centre. The reservoir holds nearly a gallon of water, the whole of which can be used at one operation. The action of the douche, which is not that of the syphon, is dependent entirely on gravitation; all that is necessary to set it in action is that the reservoir be placed on some object a foot or two higher than the seat or couch on which the patient is reclining. On turning the stopcock the water flows out continuously, fast or slow, as may be desired, through the vaginal tube, until the reservoir is empty. The instrument possesses all the requisite qualities—it is portable, self-acting, and not liable to get out of order.[1]

In cases belonging to any of the following categories irrigation of the os and cervix uteri, which can be most perfectly and easily carried out with the aid of this instrument, will be found of very great service:—cases of profuse menstruation, dependent on the presence of a lax condition of the vessels of the uterus, giving rise in many cases to prolapsus uteri; chronic leucorrhœa, proceeding from the same cause; enlargement of the uterus, proceeding from defective involution after pregnancy or after abortion; cases of engorgement of the lips of the os uteri, associated with hypertrophied condition of the mucous membrane, and excessive secretion of the mucous follicles of the cervix; in all cases, indeed, in which there is undue fulness of the uterine vessels or defective tonicity of the muscular fibre generally.

Mr. Baker Brown observed, that the principle of Dr. Hewitt's apparatus had long been known, and an instrument is sold by Bucklee, of New Bond Street, which, acting on the principle of a syphon, answered admirably. Mr. Brown had used it for the past twenty-five years.

Dr. Graily Hewitt stated that he was quite aware of the merits of the instrument mentioned by Mr. Brown, to which, however, this was far superior. The motive power—gravitation—was the same in the two instruments, and so far the principle was alike; but in the adaptation of that principle there was an important difference.

Dr. Tyler Smith thought the instrument exhibited would prove most useful and convenient for the intended purpose. He had been disappointed with the instrument alluded to by Mr. Brown; it was not easy to use, and was in a variety of ways in-

[1] The apparatus has been still further simplified since the above was written. The reservoir is now a simple bag, folding up when empty.—G. H.

convenient. Dr. Graily Hewitt's instrument, it was evident, was not open to these objections. The caution was necessary that abortion might be produced by the use of the douche in the early months of pregnancy; the patient being not always aware of her pregnant condition, this circumstance should be borne in mind.

ON THE THROMBOSIS AND EMBOLIA OF LYING-IN WOMEN.

By Robert Barnes, M.D. Lond., F.R.C.P.,

PHYSICIAN TO THE ROYAL MATERNITY CHARITY, ASSISTANT-OBSTETRIC PHYSICIAN TO THE LONDON HOSPITAL; LECTURER ON MIDWIFERY AT ST. THOMAS'S HOSPITAL.

The condition of the blood in pregnant and lying-in women, if thoroughly understood, would furnish the key to much of the pathology of child-bed diseases. That fevers, phlegmasia dolens, and eclampsia, are connected with certain departures from the normal conditions of the circulating fluids, will not now, I believe, be contested. But there is one puerperal affection in which the changes wrought in the blood are invested with a peculiarly striking interest. At a period more or less closely approaching delivery, a woman may be seized with fainting, intense pain in one or more limbs, followed by swelling, arrest of pulsation, loss of heat, gangrene, and perhaps death. What are the antecedent conditions that can lead to this sudden catastrophe? A complete answer to this question would, there cannot be a doubt, indicate the means whereby this catastrophe might, in some cases at least, be averted. In all the cases in which the series of events above enumerated have been observed, and which were subjected to post-mortem examination, clots have been found in the main arteries of the limbs affected.

In another class of cases we witness sudden faintness, irregular action of the heart, distressed breathing, quickly increasing collapse, and rapid death. In these cases it is found that the pulmonic circulation is almost exclusively concerned, and clot-obstructions are discovered in the right heart and pulmonary arteries.

What are the causes which can give rise to coagulation of the blood in the living body? Here is a case in which the physician might, perhaps, be entitled to call upon the chemist for assistance. That organic chemistry has of late years made enough of progress to raise the hope of more effective aid to medicine than has hitherto been acquired, may be freely admitted; but in regard to the particular problem now submitted, we must, I fear, be content for a while to rely mainly upon medical observations. In our search for a solution we must steadily accumulate all apposite observations, in order to multiply the elements of comparison. The cases actually on record are not numerous; but it can hardly be doubted that if cases of sudden death in child-bed had been more closely investigated by dissection, the list might have been greatly extended. It is also certain that if attention be steadily directed, under the light of the few recorded cases, to clinical obstetrics, future experience will be less barren than the past.

The following case is of value as a contribution to the slender mass of facts bearing upon the subject.

Case.—*Swelling of right leg after labour; gangrene; death.*

Mrs. C—, the wife of a surgeon, was thirty-one years of age when she was delivered, on the 23rd Febuary, 1854, of her fourth child. She was attended by Dr. Abraham, who described the labour as easy; the placenta came away entire, and the uterus contracted well. She appeared to be going on favorably, suffering, however, much more from after-pains than on previous occasions, until the 2nd March. The lochial discharge and the secretion of milk continued as usual. She took little nourishment. On March 2nd she was much irritated and excited by the nurse, who did not manage the child properly. She got up in the bed (perhaps was chilled), and was violently agitated. I was sent for late at night, and found her restless, agitated, hysterical, complaining of spasmodic pains in the abdomen. She could bear pressure; it even seemed to relieve her. Pulse 120. She took ten minims of compound spirits of ammonia, twenty minims of sedative liquor of opium, and twenty minims of ether. She complained that this caused a burning pain in the stomach. On the morning of the 3rd Mrs. C— seemed calmer; the pulse was more subdued, having fallen to 100; the pain was relieved; the tongue was red at the tip and round the margin, the papillæ in the centre raised, covered with white fur, and moist. She had taken a saline aperient, which acted fairly. On the morning of the 4th she still appeared to be improving; the pulse ranged from 90 to 110 and back again during the day; the pains in the abdomen were less, but still reappeared spasmodically. On the 5th I was sent for hastily at 9 a.m.; the pains had increased; there was great tenderness all over the abdomen, especially in the region of the uterus; considerable tympanitis; pulse 120, feeble; skin moist, warm; tongue as reported on the 3rd; countenance anxious; she felt as if a tight cord were drawn round the abdomen; dyspnœa. At 1 p.m. Dr. Oldham shared with me the anxieties of the case. He agreed that the uterus was enlarged, and that there was probably phlebitic mischief. The patient could still move and extend her legs freely; there was no tenderness in the legs, or in the groins in the neighbourhood of the large vessels; the uterus was inclined towards the left side; there was marked depression. She took a gentle saline aperient, which acted, and Liquor Cinchonæ, with Liquor Opii Sedativus, every four hours. Nourishment and wine were freely administered.

6th, 9 a.m.—The pain in the abdomen was better. She bore pressure well everywhere, except over the uterus; great tympanitis; some dyspnœa; does not seem to have lost ground.

7th.—Still tympanitis and dyspnœa; free from pain on pressure over abdomen, but there is soreness over the uterus, which, however, seems diminished in bulk; some discharge per vaginam to-day; tenderness in right groin, pain as if after cramp in the right calf; can, however, move the leg freely, and there is no swelling. The tympanitis was relieved by an asafœtida enema, which brought away some fæces as well as wind. No pulsation in right posterior tibial artery. At night she had taken some nourishment.

On the 8th, at 9 a.m., there was pain in the region of the uterus, in the calf and ankle of the right leg; there was slight tumefaction in the groin, but no pain. At 10 a.m. Mrs. C— suddenly fainted. She was restored by stimulants. At noon she was seized with the most excruciating pain in the ankle and calf. I think I never beheld suffering so intense. In her agony she implored her husband to cut off her leg, or to let her die. The pulse was 160. The skin was moist and relaxed; tympanitis; Liquor Opii taken in free doses seemed to exercise no effect. Towards night the intensity of the pain subsided; there was some fulness and pain in the groin; considerable swelling of the ankle, calf, and thigh; still she could bend the knee; on the inner side of the ankle the swelling shows a red blush. At midnight the pulse was 160; there was great prostration, but the intellect was clear. She had taken, with beef tea, wine and Liquor Cinchonæ up to this time. An asafœtida enema again relieved the tympanitis and dyspnœa. The urine, which all through had been passed freely, although high coloured and depositing lithates, was still secreted. On the 9th, at 4 a.m., it was found that the leg, between the calf and ankle, was in a state of gangrene. At 9 a.m. the gangrene had plainly extended; she was now sinking, but in perfect possession of her intellect. She died at 11.

No post-mortem examination was made, but the history of this painfully interesting case can leave little doubt as to the cause of the fatal issue. A coagulum had obstructed the right external iliac or the femoral artery. Mortification had ensued as effectually and as rapidly as if the artery had been ligatured.

To avoid, at least, those fallacies which are apt to arise

from speculations upon isolated cases, I propose to range together such cognate cases as the scanty leisure at my disposal has enabled me to gather. The history of blood-coagulation in the living body is not all of such recent date as has been sometimes imagined. Drs. Richardson[1] and Cohn[2] justly remark that similar facts and arguments to those which have of late years engaged the attention of the profession were known and discussed by Vesalius, Lancisi, Morgagni, Kerkringius, Pasta, Gould, Burserius, Templeman, Quaye, Brown, Cullen, Chisholm, Huxham, and others. But, not to disparage ancestral labours, it must be admitted that contemporary authors have, by more accurate observation, given greater precision to our knowledge of the subject. Amongst the writings that more especially deserve study are those of Baron,[3] Paget,[4] Kirkes,[5] Virchow[6] (1846), Simpson,[7] Richardson, and, lastly, Cohn (1860). The greater part of these writings bear chiefly upon obstructions of the pulmonic circulation and occlusion of the cerebral arteries.

The memoir of Simpson is chiefly valuable as containing the best collection of cases of obstruction in the arteries of the limbs in connection with the puerperal state.

As a means of arriving at definite conclusions, I have abstracted a series of cases in a tabular form.

1 'The Cause of the Coagulations of the Blood,' 1858.
2 'Klinik der Embolischen Gefässkrankheiten,' 1860.
3 'Archives Générales de Méd.,' 1838.
4 'Medico-Chir. Trans.,' 1844.
5 'Med.-Chir. Trans.,' 1852.
6 See also 'Cellular Pathology,' 1859.
7 Collected works, 1856.

TABLE I.—*Cases of Systemic Arterial Thrombosis or Embolia.*

No.	Reference.	History.	Post-mortem appearances and remarks.
1	Dr. Simpson (obstetric works, 1856)	A lady, one year before pregnancy, had rheumatic endocarditis. At eighth month of pregnancy hæmorrhage (plac. prev.). Delivered by forceps. Second week after labour no pulse in right arm, which had been cold, stiff, benumbed; in a few days return of pulsation; then legs affected; at last erratic phlebitis; death five weeks after labour from phlegmasia dolens of left arm and left side of face.	Vena innominata of left side, with its affluent trunks quite obliterated by coagulable lymph. Humeral artery at bend of arm closed by a coagulum. Valves of left side of heart covered with small, wart-like excrescences.
2	Dr. Simpson (obstetric works, 1856)	Patient prematurely delivered of first child; did well for three weeks; fever, diarrhœa, lochia slightly hæmorrhagic. Soon after pains like neuralgia in right leg, then in left, fixed and "occasionally very violent." In seven weeks sudden pain in left groin; a loud systolic bruit in heart. Pulse in right arm suddenly arrested; next day no pulsation in left femoral; then pulse stopped in right femoral; gangrene of left toes; death.	Aortic aperture blocked up by valvular excrescences, friable, granular; on margin of mitral valve small, red excrescences; aorta at bifurcation obstructed by a large, irregular mass, like vegetations in heart; coagula extended down common iliacs. The coats of the vessels were thickened. Right humeral artery obstructed.

TABLE I (*continued*).

No.	Reference.	History.	Post-mortem appearances and remarks.
3	Dr. Macfarlane (Simpson's obstetric works, 1856)	Lady delivered naturally of fifth child. Ten days afterwards acute pain and numbness in right arm, which continued till death at end of three weeks. From first no pulsation below middle of brachial artery; seventeen days from labour, pain in right thigh; gangrene extending to knee; death.	Aortic valves covered with vegetations; aorta dilated and studded with atheroma; middle of brachial, and commencement of lower third of femoral arteries closed by fibrous clots. Cardiac end of clots contained *a small, hard body*, exactly like the aortic excrescences.
4	Dr. Lever (Simpson's works, 1856)	Acute rheumatism during pregnancy; after labour no pulsation in left arm, and subsequently none in left leg; distressing pain in both extremities; hand and foot livid, symptoms of gangrene in both; death in a few days.	Mushroom-like vegetations on valves of heart; in arteries of both affected extremities obstructing vegetations; in veins of both were phlebolithes.
5	Dr. Burrows (Simpson's works)	A lady, six weeks after labour, had rheumatic-like pains in limbs and pain in one calf; remission of symptoms; after exertion sudden hemiplegia of right side. Loud, rasping, systolic murmur over valves; death.	Vegetations on mitral and aortic valves; left corpus striatum a diffluent pulp; artery supplying it obliterated with mass of fibrin. Arteries of limbs not examined.
6	Dr. Risdon Bennett ('Prov. Med. and Sur. Journ.,' 1854)	Patient, æt. 33, had difficult labour; had, before labour, dyspnœa, œdema, occasional palpitations, never rheumatism; seven weeks after labour, pain across chest, and down left arm; a week later apparent syncope, with frothy, bloody expectoration; tumultuous, feeble, irregular action of heart; puffiness of ankles, tenderness of legs, left leg as if	Vegetations under mitral valve; at apex of left ventricle a partially adherent polypus; another in right ventricle. Aorta at bifurcation obstructed by firm clot. Iliac and femoral arteries blocked up. Femoral veins at groins contained a short, recent clot. In kidneys fibrinous or purulent deposits.

		attacked by phlegmasia dolens, then right leg taken; toes of both feet became shrivelled, parchment-like; no pulsation in femoral arteries; gangrene.	
7	Dr. Macfarlane (Simpson's works)	A lady, æt. 38, seven or eight years before, had rheumatism. Three or four years later endocarditis was observed. First labour severe; forceps; six hours before labour violent pain in right arm; no pulse below subclavian; pain violent and incessant for six weeks; collateral circulation partially effected; died of dropsy three months after labour.	Subclavian artery only examined; between clavicle and axilla plugged up by firm, fibrinous clot, consisting of several layers.
8	Dr. James Duncan (Simpson's works)	A primipara; had a protracted labour; two weeks afterwards admitted at Edinburgh Infirmary with pain and acute gangrene of both legs; death in three or four days.	No disease of heart. An inch and a half above bifurcation of aorta, a fibrinous clot completely occluded artery. It was prolonged along common iliacs and left internal iliac. Mass firmly adhered to walls of aorta, which were thickened. Inferior extremities of both plugs in external iliacs did not terminate abruptly, but were continued as a lymphy layer over arterial wall for an inch. Below, the arteries were healthy. Veins healthy.
9	Dr. Cowan (Simpson's works)	A patient, æt. 36, delivered of fourth child; did well for three days; had rigor in night; anxiety, pallor; excruciating pain in left leg and foot, which were cold; pulse small, rapid; lochia arrested; in evening mitigation of pain; foot was gangrenous.	No post-mortem.
10	Dr. Cowan (Simpson's works)	A primipara; had gangrene of a leg ten days after labour. The leg was amputated; not a drop of blood flowed; death next day.	No post-mortem. Amputated limb—some soft clots in artery. (Thrombus probably in iliac; that it was above site of amputation is proved by absence of bleeding.—R. B.)

TABLE I (*continued*).

No.	Reference.	History.	Post-mortem appearances and remarks.
11	Mr. Bottomley ('Laucet,' 1845)	Patient delivered 8th February, 1845; did well for ten days, when pleurisy appeared; this subsided; then pain ("excruciating") in heel, great toe, and ankle; then loss of temperature; gangrene; line of demarcation two inches above ankle. On 3rd May amputation above knee. Both femoral artery and vein were plugged with transparent semi-cartilaginous substance.	Patient survived.
12	Dr. Oke (Simpson's works)	A patient, æt. 24, during tenth week of pregnancy had hæmorrhage and abortion; next day severe headache, giddiness, dimness of sight, vomiting; fingers of left hand felt as though scorched, very painful; next day intense pain and numbness in left arm, which at length became cold and insensible; no pulsation; no disturbance of heart or respiration; had gangrene of skin of thumb and fingers of left hand.	Recovered, but pulsation did not return in the arm.
13	Dr. Barnes	A pluripara, æt. 31, had an ordinary labour; suffered much from after pains. Seven days after labour, after violent mental agitation, had febrile symptoms, and in three days more dyspnœa and swelling of right leg, quickly attended by excruciating pain, which, on subsiding, was followed by gangrene and death on the fourteenth day after delivery.	No post-mortem.

14	J. Baart de la Faille ('Niderl. Tijdschr.,' 1859)	A healthy woman, æt. 36, was delivered 18th August, 1858, of her ninth child. The puerperal week passed favorably; milk copious. On 24th the left leg was very painful; white œdematous swelling of calf, without increase of heat or fever. On 3rd September a third attack of violent quotidian. On the 6th the right leg was seized. On 9th fever, pains in umbilical region, diarrhœa; no distension of abdomen. V.S. ad ℥viij. On 17th diarrhœa ceased; fever still. On 6th October died.	A few pseudo-polypi in the left heart. Liver enlarged, hyperæmic; kidneys, cortical structure hyperæmic. Uterine venous plexuses and pampiniform plexus contained thin, coagulated blood. Common iliac, hypogastric, crural veins filled with black, coagulated blood. Inferior cava in same state. The veins showed no change; no suppuration.
15	Cohn	Patient, æt. 30, had suffered from rheumatism at fifteen; palpitation ever since. Five weeks after labour, whilst walking, suddenly seized with cold of left leg from foot to knee, acute pain in sole; compelled to stop, taken to hospital; in a few hours blue spots observed on leg, which was very cold; motion and feeling quite lost. Gangrenous vesications of leg ensued. Pains in foot often disappeared in day, and returned at night; pulse felt in popliteal space. Right leg natural, but with very weak pulsation. Urine had now become albuminous. Gradual collapse set in. She became somnolent, and sank at end of ten weeks (?) from delivery.	Lungs—numerous infarctions, general œdema, secondary arterial thrombi. Heart enlarged in transverse diameter; at left ostium venosum firm deposits contracting aperture; old, firm clots in vestibule; in left auricle recent clot, containing fatty detritus. In spleen hæmorrhagic infarctus; liver thick, very œdematous; kidneys, hæmorrhagic infarction. Abdominal aorta—a brown-red, fast-adhering clot, quite filling calibre; on right a clot extended into common iliac, on left to Poupart's ligament, there being no clot in femoral or tibial arteries. Veins of both legs contained thin fluid blood.
		(Dr. Cohn concludes that the essential primary embolus came suddenly from the heart and lodged in the external iliac of the left side whilst the patient was walking, being previously in apparent fair health, excepting the endocarditic sequelæ. The original embolus extended by subsequent accretions to aorta. The right leg was not affected, because obstruction had not reached aorta and right iliac till shortly before death.)	

The cases, it will be observed, present several features of similitude, as well as of apparent variation. Cases 1, 4, 5, 7, and 14, are distinguished by a prior complication with rheumatism, a disease which in non-puerperal cases has been frequently found associated with embolia.

The earliest period of attack after labour was observed in Case 12, in which the symptoms were noticed on the second day. The latest period was seven weeks. In eight cases the indications of gangrene arose in less than fourteen days. In twelve fatal cases death ensued in from eleven days to three months. In two instances recovery took place.

It is clear, from the history of these two cases, and from what is known of the history of aneurism and other forms of arterial obliteration, partial or complete, that a collateral circulation may, under favorable circumstances, be established; or that if gangrene be not averted, the necrosed portion may be thrown off, life being preserved by the sacrifice of a part of the body.

Indeed, it has been observed that the arteries are not always completely obstructed by the clot or embolus. A space sufficient to permit the passage of a limited stream of blood may remain open. In this circumstance and the simultaneous extension of the collateral streams is a ground for the hope of recovery.

It must also be borne in mind that death may take place in the primary stage under the commotion attending the coagulation of the blood in the left heart, or so early in the second stage after the transport or formation of coagula in the arteries as to anticipate the development of mortification. Thus, a limb may be only a little swollen, and the persistence or arrest of pulsation in the related arteries may not have been determined. Such a case may pass for one of ordinary puerperal fever with "pyæmia," whilst more perfect observation would have shown it to be one of thrombosis and embolia.

In two cases amputation was resorted to, in one instance (Mr. Bottomley's) successfully, a line of demarcation having been established. In one case, complicated with rheumatism, the symptoms were manifested six hours before labour.

In those cases which are related most circumstantially there appear to be certain premonitory symptoms, whether of the formation of coagula in the heart or of their transport into the arteries. Dyspnœa, syncope, and irregular action of the heart, are mentioned. But in some cases these symptoms have either not occurred or have escaped attention. The earliest condition recorded is pain in the limbs that have been subsequently more overtly attacked. It is especially worthy of recollection for diagnostic purposes that this pain has generally been of the most excruciating kind.

In nine cases special words are used to denote intensity of pain. The same symptom has been observed in non-puerperal cases; and Gaspard and Cruveilhier record that violent pain constantly attended the injections of foreign substances into the arteries, whilst injections into the veins were painless. The pain generally has remitted, and the signs of mortification have appeared. Pulsation has ceased in the arterial trunks leading to the affected limbs; loss of heat and some degree of swelling have followed, then loss of sensation, then gangrene. In cases complicated with rheumatism signs of cardiac disease have been diagnosed.

In all the cases in the preceding table one or more of the limbs were affected.

In three cases the right arm and both legs were involved. In one case the right arm and right leg were affected. In one case the left arm and both legs were affected. In one case the left arm and left leg; in one case the right leg; and in two cases the left leg was the seat of obstruction.

But there can be no doubt that the embolus may be carried to the brain, either in the form of a single clot or of minute particles which may penetrate the finest cerebral arteries or capillaries. Such cases, not, indeed, of a puerperal character, are related by Mr. Paget and others.

Cohn and others give examples, either drawn from human pathology or from experiments upon animals, of embolia of other organs, as of the liver, kidneys, spleen, substance of the heart, and the eye.

The cases may be divided, as to their post-mortem appearances, into two classes:

1. In those in which rheumatism was an antecedent condition there have been found the effects of endocarditis; the valves of the left side of the heart have presented wart-like excrescences. In these cases it has been presumed that the accidents of local arterial obstruction were not always, or, at least, not exclusively, due to the sudden formation of fresh coagula in the heart, but chiefly to the detachment and washing away into the arterial system of portions of the valvular vegetations. Indeed, in some cases portions of matter exactly resembling vegetations attached to the cardiac valves have been found in the arteries at the points of obstruction.

2. In cases not complicated with rheumatism or previous disease of the heart there is evidence to show that blood has suddenly clotted in the cavities of the heart, that the commencement of the mischief was in the heart, and that the local obstructions were the result of the detachment and washing away into the arteries of portions of the heart-clot. It has also been conjectured—and, indeed, before the date of Virchow's researches, this was the favorite idea—that clots or thrombi formed in the arteries at the seat of obstruction, as the consequence of inflammation of these vessels. This question I will not discuss, but refer those who may desire information concerning it to the works of Virchow and Cohn. I will simply observe that the history of the cases seems to support the opinion that the formation of clots is generally of cardiac origin. In those cases where symptoms of cardiac distress have preceded the signs of local obstruction this inference seems clear. In those where pain in a limb or other local distress has been the first thing observed the conclusion that the coagulation did not commence in the heart would be far from certain. At the same time analogy points out that the formation of obstructing coagula in the large arteries is

not impossible. I do not know that there is any evidence to show that the phenomena of senile gangrene, or of gangrene from frost-bite, are produced otherwise than by causes operating *in loco*. So there may be local causes to produce coagulation of blood in the arteries in lying-in women.

It would be unwise to attempt to study the subject of thrombosis or embolia of the systemic arterial system apart from that of the similar affections of the pulmonic circulating system.

In some cases the two systems are simultaneously affected. In contrasting or comparing the phenomena that characterise the disorder as occurring in the pulmonic and the general vascular systems, one circumstance is particularly striking. The left or systemic heart is well known to be especially prone to disease, whilst the right or pulmonic heart is more rarely affected.

Now, in the case of the general system the disease takes its origin in the heart; in the case of the pulmonic system the disease takes its origin mostly in the peripheral veins or larger trunks, whence clots, being carried to the right ventricle, are next transmitted to the pulmonary arterial branches. In certain conditions, as pneumonia, however, there is reason to believe that primary coagulation takes place in the pulmonary arteries.

If we adopt the language of Virchow, we should say that in the system of which the left heart is the centre we have primary central thrombosis and secondary peripheral embolia, and in the system of which the right heart is the centre there is generally primary peripheral thrombosis, secondary cardiac implication, and tertiary embolia of the pulmonary arteries.

Pulmonary embolia is better known and is probably more frequent than systemic embolia.

I have arranged some cases occurring in puerperal women in a tabular form.

TABLE II.—*Cases of Pulmonary Thrombosis or Embolia.*

No.	Reference.	History.	Post-mortem appearances and remarks.
1	Cruveilhier ('Anat. Pathol.')	A woman recently delivered, seized 12th July, 1830, with uterine phlebitis, recovered and suckled; on 3rd August oppression, cough, anxiety, extreme frequency of pulse; died on 9th, twenty-eight days after delivery.	Uterine, ovarian, hypogastric veins like hard cords; they were filled with compact, adherent clots. External iliac veins and left crural veins contained clots less compact and adherent, and evidently recent. At base of left lung several portions of lobular pneumonia; œdema of both lungs behind. Some hard concretions filled divisions of pulmonary artery. The lesser branches were filled with red and scarcely adherent clots. In centre of principal clot was a collection of pus.
2	Cruveilhier ('Anat. Pathol.')	A woman after labour presented typhoid symptoms during latter days of life, dying two weeks after labour.	Iliac vein and divisions filled with adherent sanguineous concretions of different dates; they were pale and contained pus; red and less coherent in smaller vessels; diffuse and lobular pneumonia of right side. Lung, divided, presented sections of vessels full of fibrinous concretions. The right pulmonary artery was obstructed. The concretions in the smaller pulmonary vessels only existed in neighbourhood of lobular pneumonia.
3	Professor Levy, of Copenhagen	A primipara; had an easy labour; next day pain over uterus, relieved by leeches; returned on fourth	Right auricle, ventricle, pulmonary artery, even to small divisions, filled with blood-clots, some fresh;

	('Deutsche Clinik,' 1855)	day with fever and tympanitis; sixth evening, violent dyspnœa, with painful constriction of epigastrium, dry cough, quick pulse, moist rhonchus; bled; improved; on twelfth day, after supper, acute pain in epigastrium, oppression, breathing anxious, laborious; death in a few minutes.	nothing in left heart. Veins of uterus contained concrete pus.
4	Dr. Hoogeeveg ('Preuss. Vereinzeitung,' 1852, and Simpson's works)	A young woman, primipara; three days after labour had phlebitis of left leg, which got better. During convalescence she suddenly *screamed, fell, and died.*	Left crural vein and branches obstructed with coagula. Pulmonary artery filled with similar coagula. These traced into smaller ramifications of pulmonary artery.
5	Dr. Hecker ('Deutsche Clinik')	A primipara, æt. 31; on third day after natural labour seized with phlebitis of left crural vein and œdema of leg; got better; on twenty-ninth day suddenly sank; intellect clear, great anxiety, pallor, gasping, quick respiration, depressed pulse, cold extremities; died in forty-five minutes.	Left crural vein closed by fibrinous clots, extending along iliac to vena cava; hypogastric vein also plugged. Two primary branches of pulmonary arteries filled with fibrinous coagula, reaching to final ramifications. No disease in heart.
6	Dr. Hecker ('Deutsche Clinik')	A woman, æt. 30; had an easy labour, but severe hæmorrhage from adherent placenta; thirty-six hours after had rigor, followed by fever. Uterus tender, pulse 120; anxiety, headache; fever, pulse rose to 140. On sixth day improvement, but still quick pulse. On the eighth she got up, fell immediately, and rose with difficulty; collapse, death in a few hours.	Small portions of placenta adherent; uterine lymphatics filled with pus, veins with fibrinous coagula. Left hypogastric vein obstructed with clots. Heart normal; trunk of pulmonary artery plugged by thrombus, extending into branches, and traced far into ramifications.
7	Mr. Havers ('Med. Times and Gaz.,' 1852)	A woman, æt. 34, delivered of second child; easy labour; did well till twelfth day; while dressing fell on her bed, frothed at mouth, slight convulsion, spoke feebly, lay back and died.	Muscular structure of heart pale, thin. Pulmonary arteries contained clots. Clots were traced to ramifications of pulmonary arteries.
8	Mr. J. H. Hewer (Simpson's works)	Patient delivered of third child; did well for eight days, then complained of slight pain in hip; on lying down she turned suddenly pale, and said "Oh nurse, I am dying!" Pulseless, breathing with difficulty, sensible; death in thirty-five minutes.	Pulmonary arteries filled with hard, cylindrical coagula (attested by Mr. Paget).

TABLE II (*continued*).

No.	Reference.	History.	Post-mortem appearances and remarks.
9	Dr. Meigs ('Phil. Med. Exam.,' 1849, and Simpson's works)	A lady, delivered of fifth child, had some hæmorrhage; next day, sitting up, became suddenly ill; pulse soon 164, breathing violent, irregular; lived forty-eight hours, suffering "inexpressible respiratory distress."	Right auricle and ventricle closed with clot quite free from red globules. Pulmonary artery obstructed with clot, extending into principal branches.
10	Cohn ('Klinik der Embolischen Gefässkrankheiten,' Berlin, 1860)	Patient, æt. 31, delivered of twins (the second child by forceps) on 13th March, 1858; considerable flooding. On 15th shivering, pains in left inguinal region, diarrhœa; general tenderness and swelling of the abdomen followed, with enlargement of uterus; pulse 116; purulent vaginal discharge, collapse; death on 24th.	Serous exudations under arachnoid. In periphery of lungs small pyæmic foci; parenchyma œdematous, full of blood. In pulmonary artery, near hilus of the lung and immediately before division into branches of second order, complete obstruction by a pale-red, firm clot. Ventricular blood loosely coagulated. In spleen, a peripheral focus of mortification (Brandheerd). Uterus recently glued to abdominal wall and left ovary.
11	Cohn (opus citatum)	Patient, æt. 27, delivered of third child after ordinary labour on 31st March, 1859. Lochia ceased second day, but she got up cheerful on ninth day. Rigor, heat and sweat, seized her, then prostration, diarrhœa; no uterine pain, no dyspnœa. Rigors recurred daily; attacks of dyspnœa then appeared. After ten days stabbing pains in right chest; pleurisy; pneumonia of right lung; œdema of both feet; gradual collapse; rigors till last day; death on thirty-first day after delivery.	Lower lobe of right lung compressed by purulent pleuritic effusion; upper lobes of both sides œdematous; pulmonary artery of right, middle, and lower lobes shows numerous obstructed places; the thrombi are mostly purulent, white; the vessel thickened; parenchyma in neighbourhood in state of suppuration, with many foci in stage of hæmorrhagic infarction. Heart—blood scanty, firmly coagulated. Uterus contracted to normal size; veins of placental spot closed with firm, not suppurating, thrombi; parenchyma sound. Veins of pampiniform plexus dilated, containing fluid blood. Thrombosis of vena

			cava from crural vein to hepatic vein and left renal vein of old date.
12	Cohn (opus citatum)	Patient, æt. 42, had floodings three weeks before normal term of gestation from placenta prævia; delivered by forceps; an extremely fetid fluid followed removal of placenta; fever followed; slight icterus; uterus tender; neither cough nor pain in chest, but shortness of breath; repeated rigors, diarrhœa, delirium, death (time after delivery not specified).	Lungs externally very anæmic, in lower lobes œdematous, the branches of the pulmonary artery leading to lower lobes filled with old, firm clots. Heart healthy.
13	G. M. Humphry ('On the Coagulation of the Blood in the VenousSystem during Life,' 1859)	Patient, æt. 35, had a quick, easy labour (the third); did well till fourteenth day, when, after nursing her child, she walked into an adjoining room, and suddenly fell back upon the sofa, as if faint, and died.	The pulmonary arteries on both sides, where they enter the lungs, were plugged with dark clots of moderately firm consistence; these did not appear to have been formed long before death; they extended into the second divisions of the arteries, and were only slightly adherent to the walls. Vessels quite healthy. Lungs, heart, &c., presented nothing remarkable.
14	Dr. Edward Smith	A lady in latter months of pregnancy suddenly uttered a shriek, flung her arms about, and cried, "Oh my head! I cannot breathe! I am going mad!" She died in five minutes.	Blood black and fluid universally, except in the pulmonary veins, where the whole tube was filled by a cylinder of coagulum, having a central clot of blood, enclosed by two layers of condensed fibrin, the outer of which was colourless, and the whole so firm it could be pressed with impunity. The heart was flaccid, and rather enlarged on the right side; the tissue on this side was in the first stage of fatty degeneration; the left side was empty, the right contained fluid black blood; the aorta was preternaturally small; the veins were universally distended.

The following case, although not made clear by dissection, I concluded to be one of pulmonary embolia.

On the 6th May, 1861, I saw, in consultation, a lady who had been delivered of her fourth child, after an easy labour, on the 20th April. Two days after her labour her three children were all ill with scarlatina; one, the most severely affected, lay on a couch near the mother. They were speedily removed by direction of her medical attendant, but next day the patient had shivering; fever followed, but no rash; she had pains in her limbs, but no distinct swelling of the joints or œdema of the extremities. On the tenth day the heart was affected. When I saw her, on the sixteenth day, she was very prostrate; pulse 120, jerking; breathing very hurried and short; she complained of no pain beyond the distress of breathing; she lay inclined to the left side, the head only moderately raised; the countenance was sallow, expression anxious; had suckled till yesterday; the bowels had been purged a week ago, and disposition to loose stools had recurred two or three times since. There was a distinct systolic murmur. The apices of the lungs were free. She died a day or two after my visit. There was a history of primary blood dyscrasia; of secondary endocarditis; of tertiary pulmonic distress, ending in rapid death.

On the following day I saw, in consultation with Mr. Orton, of Stepney, a case similar in almost every circumstance excepting in the suspicion of scarlatinal infection.

The comparison of the foregoing histories will bring out many interesting points in the pathology of the affection.

1. It is especially noted in six cases that there were clots in the peripheral veins, as the crural, iliac, hypogastric, or uterine; and also that signs of phlebitis or of uterine inflammation preceded, often by long intervals, the symptoms of pulmonary distress.

2. The first or peripheral symptoms arose in from twenty-four hours to three days after labour; the secondary or pulmonic symptoms occurred at various periods, from

four days to more than twenty after labour; death occurred in from four to twenty-eight days after labour.

3. In eight cases the death was more or less sudden; in these cases there was great precordial distress, syncope, and dyspnœa.

4. In the cases suddenly fatal it was generally found that not only were the main branches of the pulmonary artery filled with coagula, as well as the smaller ramifications obstructed, but that clots existed in the right heart.

5. In the cases where death was more gradual the symptoms of pneumonia had time to develop themselves.

6. In the gradually fatal cases it was found that the smaller ramifications of the pulmonary artery were obstructed.

It seems reasonable to conclude that the sequence of events in pulmonic embolia is as follows:

1. There is a dyscrasia of the blood immediately proceeding from the puerperal process, which is favorable to the production of clots in the uterine veins and veins of the lower extremities. Imperfect contraction of the uterus, the formation of putrilage in the uterine cavity from the admission of air, which acts upon the blood and serum squeezed out of the vessels and the remains of adherent placenta or of decidua, are often the immediate antecedent conditions of peripheral thrombosis. This process is also favoured by the retardation of the circulation in the veins of the uterus and lower extremities, resulting from pressure. We are, indeed, familiar with tortuosity and thrombosis of the crural veins in pregnant women.

2. The next step is that of embolia. Portions of the peripheral thrombi, attended, no doubt, in many cases by septic matter derived from the uterus, are carried to the right heart. If the solid matters be large enough, or the septic or ichorous matters be irritating enough, to cause a violent perturbation of the heart's action, and to act chemically upon the blood-mass, rapid coagulation of blood in the right cavities may ensue, followed by a similar process in the larger pulmonary arteries. In such cases sudden death occurs.

3. But in those cases in which either minute portions of thrombi are taken up from the peripheral veins or where the septic or ichorous matter is less virulent no clot may form in the right heart, but minute emboli may be carried into the finer divisions of the pulmonary artery, causing lobular pneumonia, ending in slower death, or possibly in recovery.

Pure thrombosis of the venous system, that is, uncomplicated with blood-dyscrasia or fever, is not often fatal. It can only become dangerous when, from some accident, portions of peripheral clots are carried to the heart.

It would, however, be unsafe in the actual state of our clinical experience in this subject, to adopt without reserve, as explaining all cases, the doctrine of Virchow, that arterial-clot obstructions are the result of emboli brought from a distance by the circulating current. As far as careful dissection can show, there seems good reason to conclude that obstruction of the pulmonary arteries may arise from primary, sudden, or gradual formation of clots in those vessels themselves.

4. It has been noticed that in many of these cases some mental emotion or sudden exertion has immediately preceded (and has seemed to be the exciting cause of) the cardiac and pulmonic distress. It seems to me that this association may be explained by the temporary retardation of the blood-current which is occasioned, and which offers a momentary facility for the chemical action of the septic or ichorous matter upon the blood. Possibly, also, sudden exertion may favour the detachment of portions of thrombi from the systemic veins.

But whatever be the explanation adopted, it is difficult to avoid the conclusion that in some of the cases known the fatal catastrophe might not have occurred had the patient been kept in a condition of mental and bodily repose.

It would be an unjustifiable trespass upon the time of the Society were I to enter upon speculations concerning the causes of the coagulation of the blood in the order of cases which form the subject of this paper. The question is one still keenly debated by physiological experimentalists and pathologists. I refer to the works of Virchow, Richardson, and Cohn, for information respecting this matter.

The important question of treatment is obviously closely dependent upon that of etiology. Upon this question want of leisure compels me to touch very lightly. Although there are cases to prove that neither the pulmonic nor the systemic forms of thrombosis and embolia are necessarily fatal, yet it must be acknowledged that our main attention should be directed to prophylactic measures. These should begin with the utmost care for securing a healthy condition of the blood during pregnancy. Exercise in the open air, and thorough cleanliness of the whole skin—too much neglected—good diet, and occasional doses of aperient medicine, are the chief measures. During labour care should be taken to ensure the due and regular contraction of the womb, avoiding as much as possible what is called "kneading," which is another name for bruising, the uterus, and the violent and irregular contraction apt to be produced by ergot. I have certainly seen uterine inflammation caused by the action of ergot.

During the puerperal state the point of first importance is to encourage lactation. There is no agent of equal efficacy in maintaining healthy contraction of the uterus, of promoting its regular involution, and thus of averting many puerperal disorders. The next points are to enforce the recumbent position, to remove all causes of mental or bodily disturbance; not to starve the patient, and thus to give activity to the absorption of foul matters, but to supply the circulating fluid with generous materials.

When prophylaxis is at an end, when we have to deal with the present disease, we must continue the same general treatment, adding bark, stimuli, and the mineral acids. Regarding the alkaline character of the blood in most puerperal diseases, and especially the happy results I have long been accustomed to witness from the administration of nitro-hydrochloric acid in typhoid fever and in puerperal fevers, I insist warmly upon this remedy.

If we adopt Dr. Richardson's theory, that ammonia is the agent which keeps the blood in the living body in a fluid state, we should naturally be led to administer ammonia freely, with the view of dissolving the clots in the heart and the obstructing clots in the arteries. But, without entering upon the general argument, I must state that I do not anticipate any advantage from ammonia given for any length of time. Blood contaminated by the puerperal process, and especially when affected, as it commonly is in these cases, is already prone enough to acquire the alkaline condition which attends the action of septic matter. I may also add that direct clinical observation leads me to reject the use of ammonia in these and in analogous puerperal maladies. Ammonia in the blood may be taken as a constant exponent of exhaustion and of the action of poisonous and depressing agents. It seems contrary to all sound therapeutical reasoning to administer more when there is already too much. Besides, I am not aware that we have any satisfactory evidence to show that we possess in ammonia, or in any other substance, the means of exerting a solvent action upon clotted fibrine in the living body.

The successful issue of Mr. Bottomley's case may suggest the expediency of amputation in certain cases of embolia of the extremities. The course, however, of that case appears to have been exceptional. The strictly puerperal affection is primarily and essentially of cardiac origin; the entire mass of circulating blood is empoisoned or degraded; clots are obstructing the main arteries leading to the limbs, at a point, perhaps, much above the seat of gangrene; in most cases no line of demarcation forms. The uselessness of amputating under these conditions has been long recognised. These conditions differ widely from those of senile or inflammatory gangrene, where the obstructions are capillary and strictly local. The case of Dr. Cowan (No. 10, Table I) is an apt clinical illustration. Not a drop of blood followed amputation. The patient died next day. There was, in all probability, obstruction of the external or common iliac artery, quite beyond reach of relief by the knife. In

Mr. Bottomley's case the general or constitutional symptoms remitted; the patient having survived the first impetus of the disorder, the affection became entirely localized in the leg; a line of demarcation formed, and although there was obstruction of the arterial trunk high up, a sufficient amount of collateral circulation had become established to nourish the stump. So gradual was all this that the amputation was not performed until some months had elapsed.

In post-rheumatic cases, however, the gangrene may be the result of pure embolia, uncomplicated with dangerous blood dyscrasia. Here it is possible that amputation may occasionally be resorted to.

To compass a complete view of the wide subject of thrombosis and embolia, it would be necessary to include the study of those not infrequent cases in which the blood coagulates in the veins of the leg after pregnancy, without giving rise to all that train of symptoms which constitute phlegmasia dolens. These cases are rarely very serious, although important in illustration of the graver varieties of blood-coagulation during life. At some future time I hope to lay before the Society a collection of observations upon this subject. It has been well discussed by Dr. G. M. Humphry, of Cambridge.

It is also of the utmost importance that this subject should not be studied from an exclusively obstetric point of view, but that we should draw illustrations from the domain of general pathology.

MARCH 5TH, 1862.

Dr. TYLER SMITH, President, in the Chair.

Present—33 Fellows and 4 visitors.

The following gentlemen were duly elected Fellows of the Society:—John Moulden Burton, Esq., F.R.C.S., Lee Park, Lee, Kent; Peter Ambrose Cotterell, Esq., M.D., West Bromwich, Staffordshire; William Curry, Esq., M.R.C.S., East Rainton, Fence Houses, Durham; James Ellison, Esq., M.D., 14, High Street, Windsor; Decimus Nelson Frampton, Esq., L.R.C.P., 28, Lower Belgrave Street; Edward Johnson, Esq., M.D., 19, Cavendish Place; John Manly, Esq., L.S.A., West Bromwich, Staffordshire.

NOTE ON THE BRONCHO-PNEUMONIA OF LYING-IN WOMEN.

By ROBERT BARNES, M.D. Lond., F.R.C.P.,

PHYSICIAN TO THE ROYAL MATERNITY CHARITY; ASSISTANT-OBSTETRIC PHYSICIAN TO THE LONDON HOSPITAL; LECTURER ON MIDWIFERY AT ST. THOMAS'S HOSPITAL.

ON account of the close relationship of the subject with that of puerperal thrombosis and embolia, I beg permission to append a note on what I have been accustomed to call puerperal broncho-pneumonia. Reserving for a future opportunity the clinical illustrations of the subject, I am anxious now to submit, as shortly as possible, the general results of my observations.

I have long been familiar with the fact that lying-in women are liable to a peculiar form of broncho-pneumonia. It is generally considered that the pulmonary symptoms which arise during childbed are the consequence of the violent straining attending the expulsive stage of labour, and of "taking cold" during the exposure sometimes incident to that event. To me this explanation is far from sufficient. As in typhoid fever, so in puerperal fever, the lungs are apt to be involved. In either case the cause is similar. I may here observe that a marked characteristic of typhoid fever is extreme alkalinity of the blood. The urine I have frequently found highly ammoniacal on voiding. A similar condition commonly marks the blood in puerperal fever. On one occasion I observed that the bladder, being partially paralysed, and the urine consequently retained in the intervals of being drawn by the catheter three times a day, the urine decomposed so rapidly in the bladder as to evolve large quantities of ammoniacal gas, which escaped in a stream with a gurgling sound when the catheter was introduced. These circumstances, with others which need not be enumerated, indicate a dyscrasia of the blood which must produce certain irritating effects throughout the body. The diarrhœa of puerperal fever and the diarrhœa which frequently appears in childbed apart from overt fever is the simple effect of the irritation of the intestinal mucous membrane by the septic or other offending matter circulating with the blood. Peritonitis, cellulitis of the limbs, synovitis—all arise in the same way.

Accompanying this diarrhœa, or apart from it, we may have broncho-pneumonia. This, in like manner, is simply the effect of the irritation of the bronchial mucous membrane or parenchyma of the lungs by the same offending matter. In some of these cases the breath of the patient has possessed an odour distinctly resembling that of the lochial discharges. Broncho-pneumonia may, in short, be regarded as a symptom, or a part, of puerperal fever. But in many cases the fever is masked, or so slight that it escapes observation, and the attention is fixed upon the pulmonary symptoms alone.

In these cases there is generally a considerable degree of prostration. The whole or the greater part of the mucous tract of the lungs is involved. The expectoration amounts to bronchorrhœa. Large and fine crepitation are heard in almost every part of the chest. The sputa are sometimes tinged with blood. Depletion is not borne. The most successful treatment consists in the administration of cinchona, senega, or serpentaria, in the form of decoction or infusion, with ammonia, and at a later stage with nitro-hydrochloric acid, blisters to the chest, good nourishment, in the form of strong beef tea, eggs and milk, and a moderate allowance of wine or brandy.

The form of broncho-pneumonia I have thus sketched is not to be confounded with that which is the result of capillary embolia of the pulmonary arteries, although there is this affinity between them, that both are set up by offending matter brought to the lung-tissues by the circulating blood.

The importance of recognising this form of broncho-pneumonia will be admitted when its bearings upon child-bed mortality are considered. In some statistical statements I have noticed that certain kinds of death are excluded, on the presumption that labour had nothing to do with the fatal result. Bronchitis and pneumonia are thus treated, although to the informed critic the deaths from these causes may be as plainly traceable to the puerperal process as are the deaths from peritonitis.

It is by the complication of this form of pneumonic irritation that I account for the fatal acceleration of phthisis after labour.

Mr. Ballard said that, although Dr. Barnes did not dwell upon the cause of the formation of the thromboses, he thought, as a practical point, it was one that might be advantageously discussed. He believed all authorities admitted that absorption of pus or putrilage from the unhealed internal surface of the uterus was a principal cause of puerperal disorder, by producing coagulation and infection of the blood in the surrounding veins. It was also generally known that irritation of the mammæ produced uterine contractions. Now, he was under a strong conviction that the mammary irritation which resulted from the efforts to obtain milk from the breasts during the first two or three days after delivery produced that disturbance of the uterus which gave rise to the absorption of pus, and thus to the formation of blood-clots in the neighbouring veins. According to his own experience, no milk was secreted until a period of forty-eight hours after delivery; and in all cases where no means had been employed to obtain it before then, and even after the development of the secretion, excessive irritation of the breasts had been avoided, there had been a complete immunity from puerperal disorders of even the mildest kind; and in all instances of puerperal disorder which had come under his notice one or both of these precautions had been omitted. He knew that it was the general teaching that the child should be put to the breast immediately after delivery, and as this rather encourages than forbids an assiduous application of it afterwards, he was of opinion that a modification of that practice, and a more general recognition of the dependence of puerperal disorder on mammary irritation, would tend much to the prevention of these disorders.

Dr. TANNER observed that Mr. Ballard's views were so startling that he thought it would be better for this gentleman to embody them in a paper for the Society, so that they might be fully and fairly discussed.

Dr. BARNES said that what he meant by the term "causes of the coagulation of the blood in the living vessels" was the immediate causes; and he alluded to the several theories of Richardson, who held that the fluidity of the blood was preserved by ammonia, and of others. The question of thrombosis and embolia was a large one; it belonged to general pathology even more than to obstetrics. He could not, therefore, conveniently do more than give a clinical illustration of the subject in its bearing upon puerperal pathology. That the etiology of thrombosis and of other forms of puerperal disease was one deserving of special study, all would admit; it might also be admitted that one source of puerperal mischief arose from the infection of the blood by the foul matters retained or formed in the uterus after labour; but he was not prepared to hear the doctrine just advanced, that this infection was promoted by applying the child to the breast. The constant aim of the obstetric practitioner was to aid the expulsion of offensive matters by stimulating the uterus to contract. Not only in the puerperal state, but at other times, excitation of the breasts was one of the most efficient means of producing this effect. By it hæmorrhage was restrained; clots, which if retained might putrefy, were expelled; and thus the patient was secured against the very dangers which placing the child to the breast early was accused of promoting. Surely if this theory were true, puerperal diseases would be more frequent. In the Maternity Charity last year upwards of 4000 women were delivered; not one died of puerperal fever; yet he had no doubt that the practice of applying the child to the breast very soon after labour was very generally pursued.

ON OVARIOTOMY, THE MODE OF ITS PERFORMANCE, AND THE RESULTS OBTAINED AT THE LONDON SURGICAL HOME.

By I. Baker Brown, F.R.C.S.,
SENIOR SURGEON TO THE LONDON SURGICAL HOME.

The operation of ovariotomy is now daily becoming a recognised proceeding in surgical practice, the numerous prejudices which prevailed for a long time against its adoption are gradually giving way to practical results, and the collected experience of men like Atlee of Philadelphia, Clay of Manchester, Bird, Lane, Walne, Tanner, Hutchinson, Wells, Tyler Smith, Dunlop, Hamilton, Kiwisch, Langenbeck, M'Dowall, Peaslee, Southam, Paget, and others, most clearly demonstrate that the operation is not only perfectly justifiable and proper in suitable and properly selected cases, but that its mortality is very much less than that accruing from many other capital operations in surgery, among which may be mentioned ligature of the larger arteries, amputation of the hip, or primary amputation of the thigh, the removal of large urinary calculi, herniotomy, and especially the use of the trephine in cases of injury to the cranium. In many of the cases just mentioned operative measures are resorted to as holding out the best chance for prolonging and of saving life; in some, aneurisms for example, it is quite possible that the patients might survive some days or even weeks without any active measures being resorted to. So is it in ovarian dropsy. Patients may go on with life and misery for a time, until their uneasiness and suffering compel them to seek for relief at a dangerous crisis of their disease; whereas, if attempts were made at a much earlier period to cure radically by opening the abdominal cavity, the chances are very much indeed in favour of the best results. Nothing more convincingly proves the correctness of these observations than the fact—and one, too, of a most curious and striking nature—that men who formerly most strenuously opposed and condemned the operation as something barbarous and not to be tolerated, have suddenly become the warmest converts to it. This encourages me to hope and anticipate that those also who still oppose the operation will become convinced of its necessity and high importance, by the efforts of those who perform it, and who faithfully and unreservedly place before the profession their entire experience.

To quote from a surgical writer of experience—"It is not necessary in order to justify an operation, even of a dangerous character, that the patient be in *immediate* peril of death. It is sufficient that the death from the disease which it is proposed to remove should ultimately be certain, though it may be delayed by months or years of previous suffering. From this point of view ovariotomy appears to be a perfectly proper and justifiable operation, and it presents the advantage of the cure, if practised, being complete and permanent. In it there is no mean; the death is speedy, or the cure complete."—*Erichsen, 'Science and Art of Surgery,'* 3rd edition.

I think it is proper here to allude to the important and highly valuable statistics of the results of ovariotomy collected by Dr. Clay, of Birmingham, in his translation of Kiwisch's 'Lectures on the Diseases of the Ovaries;' they are assuredly the most complete that have as yet been tabulated, and the profession cannot be too grateful to him for the trouble he has taken in so accurately and reliably preparing them.

Statistics of Ovariotomy.—Of 537 operations that were performed, 395 were perfect or complete, 24 were cases of but partial excision only, and 118 were incomplete attempts. Of the incomplete cases, 41 deaths ensued and 77 recoveries; of these, of partial excision, 10 recovered and 14 died; whilst of the cases of complete ovariotomy, 212 recovered and 183 died!!! The result in the complete cases, Dr. Clay thinks, strongly illustrates the advisability of the performance of the operation. He also alludes to the fact that in many of the successful cases remedies were used previous to the performance of the operation, and different operative proceedings adopted, with the hope of curing the disease or in arresting its progress, but without success, and in many cases death was imminent. "These cases of recovery may therefore be regarded," he observes, "as triumphs of surgical skill, by means of which so many lives were secured, in several instances for years, which would otherwise have been lost to society." Now, highly favorable as these results must be considered, there is good reason for supposing that they will become still more so when the statistics are collected of the operations that have been performed subsequently to February, 1860, the period to which Dr. Clay's cases extend. Speaking generally, it would seem as if the recoveries are now two to one, or that the deaths are about 33 per cent.

Conditions rendering the operation justifiable.—In determining upon the performance of ovariotomy the surgeon must be satisfied by careful and repeated examination that the tumour is ovarian, and, if possible, that it is not cancerous. The latter is at times not only extremely difficult, but impracticable; the diagnosis will be assisted, however, by the history and aspect of the patient, and the rapidity or slowness of the growth of the tumour, together with the presence or absence of cancer in other parts of the body or in the patient's family.

Heretofore the existence of adhesions was considered as a reason for abandoning the operation of extirpation. At the present time surgeons rarely find an obstacle to the completion of the operation in the adhesions about the ovarian sac, but either break through them with the écraseur or the hand, or divide them by a knife or scissors after tying them, if found vascular. Yet it must be admitted that they may be so strong, so extensive, and so placed, that it is advisable not to run the risk of attempting the removal of the whole tumour, and some other mode of treatment might be resorted to with advantage, as I have elsewhere described in my work on the 'Surgical Diseases of Women.' If it is necessary to secure any of these adhesions by ligatures, I would suggest that they should be silver wire instead of thread or twine, and the ligatures allowed to remain within the abdominal cavity, simply cutting them off short and close. This, I think, is a very material improvement in the operation.

Mode of performing Ovariotomy.—Different methods have been selected by various operators for performing this operation, both in regard to the position of the patient and the manner of making the incisions. My own plan, which has been fully described in my work already alluded to, is as follows:

The patient being placed conveniently on her back, and brought under the influence of chloroform, an exploratory incision, from two to three inches in length, should first be made in the linea alba. Having divided the peritoneum and reached the cyst, two or more fingers should be passed over its surface, to ascertain if adhesions exist. If these are slight and recent, they should, if possible, be broken down by the fingers; or if they are larger and stronger, they may be divided by the écraseur; or if vascular, after being ligatured by silver wire, may be cut through by the knife or scissors. However, cases now and then occur in which adhesions are so firm and vascular, and so extended or so peculiarly situated, that it is not prudent to endeavour to detach the cyst, and then we must desist from the operation of extirpation, and substitute for it one of those other plans of treatment considered in my work—such, for example, as the excision of a portion of the cyst, if, that is to say, it is not deemed more expedient to desist from any further surgical proceeding.

The presence of adhesions and the necessity of dividing them involve an enlargement of the primary incision, a measure otherwise, indeed, necessary to the further carrying out of the operation. An incision of four inches may suffice, but a longer one is often necessary, and on the matter of the length of incision the operator must be guided mainly by his own judgment of what is necessary to enable him to detach and remove the mass with the greater facility.

The next step is to tap the cyst or cysts with a proper trocar and canula, and in the evacuation of the fluid to take care that none of it escapes into the cavity of the abdomen. Then, if there is only one cyst, and that not thick nor vascular, a portion of it only may be excised. If the cyst, however, should be found to be thick or vascular or multilocular, it will be the safest proceeding to have recourse to complete extirpation, in the following manner:—The pedicle of the tumour is to be taken in the left hand and gently drawn outwards from the pelvic cavity, an assistant carefully keeping back by warm flannels the bowels and omentum. A clamp—the best, I believe, being the carpenter's calipers—is now applied around the pedicle. This should be passed as near to the tumour as possible, so that, by the entire length of the pedicle being preserved, the fastened end may be kept external to the abdominal cavity. This done, the tumour should be removed by dividing the pedicle half an inch from the clamp, which should be given to an assistant and held at the inferior end of the opening. The operator then closes the wound, and this, I need hardly say, should be done, as in all operations exposing the peritoneum, as soon as possible, by introducing silver sutures about an inch from the incised edges, and about half an inch apart, through the parietes of the abdomen. This step is best done by passing a tenaculum needle through both sides of the wound and then threading the eye with the wire, and on withdrawing the needle bringing it through and twisting it. In this mode of closing the wound no secondary sutures are required.

The advantages of the clamp are that it can be removed in from one to three days, the wound heals more quickly, and the patient may get convalescent in two or three weeks, whereas when ligatures are applied they take, at the very least, nine or ten days, and now and then as many weeks to come away; and, indeed, an operator has published his cases as successful, the subjects of them having returned to the country many weeks after with the ligatures hanging from the opening; whilst they remain, the patient cannot be considered completely cured.

I used formerly to think that when the pedicle was very short it was better to apply the ligature than the clamp. But now I always use the clamp, taking care, when the pedicle is very short and the drawing gives pain to the patient, to remove the clamp in a few hours.

I have not enjoined the use of any particular length of incision, for this matter must, I am of opinion, be regulated by the special circumstances of each case, the rule on the surgeon's part being to extract the cyst with the least danger to the patient, and through the smallest practicable incision without incurring a risk of failure in the operation. A small incision, of an exploratory nature, should be the first; if the operation be proceeded with, it must be enlarged sufficiently to admit the extraction of the apparent cyst, and further increase will be very easy if its peculiarly compound nature, its position, or relations, or other circumstances, demand it.

It is desirable, when the diseased ovarian mass of one side is removed, and before the abdominal incision is closed, to look at the condition of the other ovary, which not uncommonly is also diseased, and when such is the case may be at once removed. An instance of this sort is described by Dr. Peaslee, in the 'American Journal of Medical Sciences' for April, 1851, in which a cyst, the size of a pullet's egg, was discovered on the right ovary, and the whole organ was diseased. The second tumour was removed. Two somewhat similar occurred to myself, wherein I removed both ovarian tumours; one of them is included in the series which accompanies this paper.

There is one plan lately introduced for placing the patient undergoing the operation, which I cannot but think that extended experience will induce the originator either to change or to modify, namely, placing the patient in an arm-chair during the performance of it. The objections to this are clearly so obvious that it is unnecessary that I should dwell upon them.

In the operation great care should be used not to employ a sponge within the cavity of the abdomen; in fact, it is even better to leave that which cannot be removed with the hand or a piece of flannel than to irritate the peritoneum with a sponge.

Preparations for the Operation.—Previous to performing ovariotomy there are certain preliminary or preparatory measures which deserve to be mentioned, from their importance as bearing on the subsequent results. These are the use of warm baths, repeated on several occasions, to cleanse and soften the skin, and thereby ensure free perspiration after the operation. To these may be conjoined suitable remedial measures of a tonic character, such as steel and arnica. A healthy condition of the skin and of the blood is highly necessary towards recovery afterwards. The bowels should be opened on the morning of the operation. A flannel waistcoat and a pair of flannel drawers should be got ready to wear; the former should be put on before the operation. A hot-water bottle should be prepared for the feet. There should be a thermometer in the room, and the temperature should not be kept lower than 66° nor higher than 70°. A kettle should be kept boiling on the fire, so as to ensure a degree of moisture in the air, so especially requisite when the wind is in the east or the weather hot and dry. The meteorological conditions of the atmosphere should be observed and attended to before the operation, for a low and heavy atmosphere, with an absence or deficiency of ozone, and that condition generally which we describe as depressing, is exceedingly dangerous. Not only does this observation apply to ovariotomy, but to all other serious operations. If a greater regard were paid to atmospheric changes, we might expect much less of gangrene, pyæmia, low fever, and other unfavorable conditions which often arise after operations.

If the operation takes place on the bed which the patient is to occupy afterwards, the lower part should be covered by a mackintosh sheet and an old blanket. There should be a hassock or stool for the feet to rest upon. Warm stockings should encase the feet and legs, and the hands and arms enveloped in a flannel gown. No food should be taken for some hours before the administration of the chloroform, and a supply of ice should be procured for the patient to suck for two or three hours before the operation, to avoid sickness afterwards—this is of some consequence. There should be plenty of hot water in the room, in which in cold weather both the operator and his assistants should immerse their hands before touching the patient; and there should be from three to six basins of warm water ready for immersing sponges or warming the flannels, &c. The duties of each assistant should be clearly assigned and understood before entering the room. Long needles, like those used in operating for ruptured perinæum, should be at hand, with metallic sutures. Several smaller ligatures for blood-vessels should also be ready, and a many-tailed flannel bandage, to go round the abdomen after the operation is completed; also a supply of lint, towels, and a few adhesive straps.

One or two scalpels, a director, a pair of scissors, a pair of vulsellum forceps, a pair of good common forceps, tenaculum, trocar, and canula of large size, together with the needles and ligature, and not less than two clamps, should be ready on a tray; and lastly, as much will depend upon the after treatment, the operator, or some competent surgeon or an experienced nurse, should remain with the patient all night. Indeed, the patient should not be left for more than two hours at a time for the first three or four days.

After Treatment.—After recovery from the effects of the chloroform it will not be necessary to administer opium unless much pain is present, and then either one or two grains are to be given by the mouth. If there is any tendency to sickness, it should be given by the rectum. If the pain should still continue, even after taking the opium, and the patient be troubled with flatus, fomentations must be applied over the abdomen by means of flannels steeped in hot water and freely sprinkled with turpentine. At the same time a cloth with turpentine sprinkled upon it is placed on the bed-clothes, near the mouth, so that its vapour may be freely inhaled. For the first twenty-four or forty-eight hours nothing is given in the way of food, excepting barley-water, iced drinks, &c., until the patient begins to crave for something more substantial, when it is gradually allowed. On the third day, in many of the cases, the patients have taken a mutton chop and a glass of beer.

Analysis of the Cases.—Since the opening of the London Surgical Home up to the present time, March, 1862, ovariotomy has been performed nineteen times by myself. Of that number thirteen have recovered and six have died. The details and special particulars of the whole of these are given in the accompanying tables, which shall now be analysed.

Age.—The ages of the patients varied from 18 to 56; of the successful cases there were one of 18, two of 19, one of 20, one of 21, one of 23, one of 25, one of 27, one of 31, one of 46, two of 48, and one of 56. Of the unsuccessful there were one of 21, one of 30, one of 35, one of 46, one of 50, and one of 55. So that of the successful cases eight were under the age of 30 and five above, whilst of the unsuccessful, one was 21 and five were 30 and upwards. This result agrees somewhat with Dr. Clay's statistics; but it may be stated, without reserve, *cæteris paribus*, that a better chance of success is held out to the female who undergoes the operation before she is 30; this, however, will be influenced by the duration of the disease, the condition of the patient's health, and the nature and extent of the disease, especially as regards the adhesions.

Duration of the Disease.—The duration of the disease in the successful cases was from 4 months to 6 years; six within 1 year, four of 2 years, one of 22 years, one of 4 years, and one of 6, making ten within the 2 years; nine were single and four were married, and of the latter two only had had children. Five only had undergone tapping from one to three times. In the unsuccessful cases the duration of the disease was from 2 to 10 years; four were married women, three of whom had borne families of from three to six children, and one was confined a year before the operation, although the disease was present for two years. Four of the fatal cases were tapped from one to six times.

State of the Health.—The general health was represented as very good in five of the successful cases. In six it was but middling or indifferent, in one it was much shattered, and in another actually bad. One of these had a sharp attack of peritonitis eight months before the operation, and another had a most miserable and unhealthy looking person. With these drawbacks recoveries ensued. In the unsuccessful cases four had bad or indifferent health, yet two were most anxious to undergo the operation; one was in pretty good health, and another had good health up to six weeks before the operation.

The Operation and character of the Tumour.—With respect to the operation and the character of the tumour which it revealed, the incisions varied from three to seven inches in length; in two only did it extend from the umbilicus to the pubes; in one of these the operation was fatal. In eleven it did not exceed five inches.

The tumours were polycystic or multilocular in eleven and unilocular or monocystic in two of the successful cases. In one of the former the opposite ovary was converted into a small fibrous tumour. In the unsuccessful cases the tumour was polycystic in four and monocystic in one, and more or less solid in the sixth, containing hair, steatoma, bone, and many perfect teeth. The sizes of all these varied, but they were mostly medium and large.

Adhesions.—Adhesions were present in all, excepting four of the successful and one of the unsuccessful cases. In the other successful cases they were comparatively slight and easily broken down, although very numerous and extending in various directions in four; they were very firm and strong in two; in one of these they bound the tumour to the uterus and bladder by a band eight inches wide. In five of the six unsuccessful cases they were extensive; for example, in two they were numerous, in all directions, some of them requiring to be cut; in one of these the whole of the omentum was adherent to the uterus; in a third case they were especially strong and thick, requiring a ligature to one attached to the liver. The very extensive adhesions in the fatal cases had much to do with the result.

Anæsthesia.—It may be here remarked that chloroform was given in all the cases; in two it was discontinued because of the great falling of the pulse in one and the alarming congestion of the face and neck in the other; the patients were partially conscious, but suffered no pain; in two instances it was used during the first part of the operation, and ether for the remainder.

Pedicle.—The pedicle was retained outside of the abdomen in all but two of the cases; the callipers were used to retain it in situation externally, in place of the ligature.

Causes of Death.—It now remains to make a few observations on the causes of death in the unsuccessful cases. Out of the nineteen cases in which ovariotomy was performed there were thirteen recoveries, as has been already stated, and six deaths. On looking carefully into the latter it will be observed that in four the fatal result ensued from causes that cannot be fairly attributed to the operation itself. In the eighth and fourteenth cases the fatal result was mainly the result of the operation. In the eighth case an emaciated patient, aged forty-six, had been tapped six times, the adhesions were most considerable, and bled freely on breaking them down, which was the chief cause of the obstinate vomiting and low peritonitis, which ended fatally in two days. Case 14 presented such extensive and firm adhesions that a recovery was not anticipated at the time of the operation; the tumour extended itself into the pelvis, and was glued to the uterus; death was clearly the result of shock in forty hours.

In the other cases, namely, Nos. 2, 3, 18, and 19, other causes influenced the result. In the second case the patient's general health was for some time previous much broken.

She was very urgent to have the tumour removed, and in doing it it was discovered to be congenital, being chiefly solid, containing loose hair, ten pints of steatomatous fluid, bone, teeth, &c. Death occurred in thirty hours; and besides evidence of recent peritonitis, there were the remains of much old disease, the liver being firmly bound to the diaphragm by old adhesions. In No. 3 the patient had been a hard drinker and had softening of the liver; she had been tapped five times, and was very urgent in her demands for the operation. The abdomen contained forty-five pints of ascitic fluid, independently of the contents of the cyst. Death ensued in six days from incessant vomiting of green bile, the result of the diseased state of liver. Cases 18 and 19 almost speak for themselves, for diarrhœa carried off both, the first in eighteen days and the second in eight days after the operation. In Case 18 a large pelvic abscess, which had burst, existed near the rectum, and scirrhous ulceration of the duodenum was observed. In Case 19 the patient went on wonderfully well until the diarrhœa set in, the shock of which, acting upon such a diseased heart as was discovered after death, readily brought about a fatal result by choleraic collapse.

Conclusion.—In this communication I have given the particulars of all these nineteen cases, without any reserve. The details are extracted from the note-books of the Home; the operations were all witnessed by various professional gentlemen from various countries, from different parts of Great Britain and the metropolis, many of whom, at the same time, watched the progress of those that recovered from day to day and week to week; and in now bringing them before the Obstetrical Society of London I do so in the hope that ovarian disease will continue to obtain that attention from practitioners which the last three or four years has given satisfactory evidence of.

No. of case.	Date of operation.	Name and age of patient.	Duration and progress of disease and condition of patient before the operation.	Anæsthetic used, mode of administration, and the preparation.	Length of the incision.	Adhesions.
1	October 20th, 1858	L. P. æt. 20	Married; no children. Two years ago, soon after marriage, noticed an enlargement of abdomen. In March, 1858, had an attack of peritonitis, from the effects of which she was much weakened. Under use of steel and quinine, she in great measure recovered her health before the operation	Chloroform	From umbilicus to pubes	Not very numerous, principally on right side, low down
2	February 10th, 1859	Miss N. æt. 29	Single. In her eleventh year she suffered from pains in the abdomen, recurring periodically, and in 1849 a swelling could be felt in right hypogastric region. Had never menstruated. General health much broken, but was urgent for the operation	Chloroform	Six inches	Not many, but some connected with the omentum, which were torn through
3	February 24th, 1859	Mrs. D. æt. 35	Admitted February, 1859. Married, four children. Four years ago a tumour appeared on the right side of the abdomen, which, in spite of all treatment, increased in size. In August, 1858, was tapped, and four times after, before her admission. Had been a hard drinker, but was urgent for the operation	Chloroform	Seven inches	Few, but strong, and thick, one especially passing up to the edge of the liver, which was ligatured

Nature of the tumour.	Proceedings of and accidents during the operation.	Pedicle within or without abdomen.	Result.
Composed of many cysts containing highly albuminous fluid	The primary incision being made, the tumour was seized by the vulsellum and the trocar introduced, a large quantity of very albuminous fluid escaping. The pedicle, which was long and thin, was enclosed in the calipers, and the wound closed by iron-wire sutures	Outside	She made a rapid and good recovery. On October 27th the calipers were removed, and in a month after the operation she left, quite well. When seen in 1862 she was in perfect health. Whenever the menstrual epoch comes on, the skin over where the pedicle was secured breaks out, and there is a vicarious discharge during the whole period; but as soon as that is over the wound heals up.
Connected with right ovary. A large quantity of solid matter, containing much loose hair, mixed with thick, steatomatous matter. In the centre of the cyst was a large mass of bone, containing many perfect teeth	After the primary incision the tumour was punctured, and ten pints of thick, steatomatous fluid came away, mixed with a thick, pasty, and fatty substance, which obstructed the canula. When the tumour was drawn out it dragged the uterus with it. The calipers were applied, and the tumour separated, when the uterus fell back into its normal position	Outside	The morning after the operation her pulse was 100, and she had occasional pains in the abdomen, which was very tympanitic. At 6 p.m. she became collapsed, and at 10.20 p.m., thirty hours after the operation, she died. At the autopsy the omentum was discoloured, injected, and thickened; the parietal peritoneum inflamed, with scarlet patches around the incision; small intestines on left side slightly glued together. The liver bound to diaphragm by old adhesions; kidneys healthy; heart small, and on the right side very thin, barely an eighth of an inch; lungs healthy; os uteri admitted a sound for about an inch; neck of uterus situated an inch from the body, the two being connected merely by an impervious bone or membrane; mammæ well developed.
Multilocular, of right ovary	After making the preliminary incision forty-five pints of ascitic fluid escaped, independently of the fluid contained in the tumour itself. The pedicle was enclosed in the calipers, and the wound closed with iron-wire sutures	Outside	On February 26th there was some sickness. On 27th the vomiting was incessant; she continued to get worse, and died on March 2nd, six days after the operation. *Autopsy.*—Wound firmly healed; the intestines glued together by lymph; the peritoneum much inflamed; the liver was very pale, and broke down on the slightest touch; kidneys were enlarged and congested; menstruation was taking place.

No. of case.	Date of operation.	Name and age of patient.	Duration and progress of disease and condition of patient before the operation.	Anæsthetic used, mode of administration, and the preparation.	Length of the incision.	Adhesions.
4	December 5th, 1859	E. M. æt. 59	Single. Admitted November 1st, 1859. Increased slightly in size for some time, but did not notice it much till six weeks ago; since then has got rapidly larger. Tapped November 3rd, and five pints of thick, dark fluid drawn off. Cyst soon refilled. General health pretty good	Chloroform	Four inches	Slight, and easily broken down
5	March 22nd, 1860	J. B. æt. 19	Single. Admitted February, 1860. In June, 1859, first noticed a swelling on right side. Had then an attack of peritonitis. She after rapidly increased in size. General health not good, emaciated. Improved under the preliminary treatment	Chloroform	Five inches	Very slight
6	November 1st, 1860	Mrs. B. æt. 31	Married. Admitted October 15th, 1860. One child. Four years ago discovered a swelling on right side of abdomen, which has since gradually increased, but rapidly of late. Never tapped. General health good	Chloroform	Four inches	Very strong to right of uterus. One broad band, eight inches wide, dipped into pelvis, attached to bladder
7	December 27th, 1860	N. L. æt. 48	Single. Admitted October 10th, 1860. Ten months ago had dyspnœa and cough, and felt a lump on right side of belly, which then increased. Complexion sallow, and aspect of malignant disease. Under treatment this changed, and her health improved	Chloroform	Four inches	None

Nature of the tumour.	Proceedings of and accidents during the operation.	Pedicle within or without abdomen.	Result.
Multilocular, of right ovary	The primary incision being made, the tumour was punctured in several places and extracted. The pedicle was broad and short. The edges of wound brought together by iron-wire sutures	Outside	Two hours after the operation peritonitis came on, which yielded to moderate bleeding and opium and calomel. On 8th calipers were removed. On 12th edges of wound looked sloughy; sutures removed. On 16th great pain in pelvis, and restlessness. On 17th a sudden discharge of a pint of pus per vaginam. After that she rapidly recovered.
Multilocular, of right ovary	The primary incision being made, the tumour was punctured and withdrawn. The calipers were first applied, and the tumour separated; then a double whipcord ligature was passed round the pedicle, and fastened tightly. The calipers were now removed, and the pedicle returned to abdomen. Wound closed with iron sutures	Inside	After the operation opium was given as required. She went on without any unfavorable symptoms. On 28th bowels moved; sutures taken out on 31st, and the ligature on pedicle came away. April 5th, a small abscess formed on the track of one of the sutures, which caused a little trouble, but she left May 17th, perfectly cured.
Multilocular, of right ovary	After primary incision, tumour tapped, and fourteen pints of thick fluid drawn off. Part of broad band of adhesions divided by écraseur; other part enclosed in calipers, and divided by knife. The Fallopian tube accidentally torn near the uterus, and as it bled freely, was tied with silver sutures and left in. The pedicle was tied by twine in three parts, and left in. The part of adhesions enclosed by calipers kept outside. Wound closed by iron sutures	Inside	She had no unfavorable symptoms. On the 4th the calipers were removed. On 11th the ligatures on the pedicle came away, and on December 10th she left, quite well.
Multilocular	After primary incision was made, the tumour was tapped, and eight pints green fluid drawn off. Pedicle was very short, and was enclosed in calipers. Wound closed with iron sutures	Outside	Patient had no unfavorable symptoms. On 30th calipers were removed. Left in five weeks from date of operation, quite well.

No. of case.	Date of operation.	Name and age of patient.	Duration and progress of disease and condition of patient before the operation.	Anæsthetic used, mode of administration, and the preparation.	Length of the incision.	Adhesions.
8	December 27th, 1860	M. M. æt. 46	Single. Admitted 27th. Two years ago got thin and weak, and felt pain in right side, with small swelling, which rapidly got larger. First tapped a year ago, and four times since, the last time six weeks ago, and thirty-eight pints drawn off. December 11th, her sixth tapping, and forty-four pints drawn off. Albuminous. General health not good, emaciated. Submitted to usual treatment	Chloroform	Six inches	Numerous in all directions
9	March 2nd, 1861	Miss W. æt. 48	Single. Admitted February 1st. A year ago suffered from spasms in belly, when she first noticed a swelling at lower part, which has since much increased. Catamenia regular up to September last, but not since. General health not good. Ascites besides multilocular tumour	Chloroform at first, then stopped, from its lowering the pulse	First two inches, then enlarged to six inches	None of any consequence
10	September 19th, 1861	L. H. æt. 21	Single. Two years ago first noticed a swelling in abdomen, which has gradually enlarged. Tapped a year ago, and again in March last, and four gallons drawn off a second time. General health good	Chloroform	Three to four inches	None of any consequence
11	October 24th, 1861	F. W. æt. 19	Single. Two years ago noticed a lump on the right side, which has gradually increased. General health very good. Never been tapped	Chloroform	Three to four inches	None

Nature of the tumour.	Proceedings of and accidents during the operation.	Pedicle within or without abdomen.	Result.
Large cyst, with fluid and numerous solid masses, resembling honeycomb or colloid cancer, formed of numerous cysts, one inside of the other; right ovary	In consequence of adhesions, the primary incision cut right into the tumour, and twenty-two pints of albuminous fluid escaped. Bleeding considerable from broken-down adhesions, surface so large that nothing could be done to stop it. Pedicle enclosed in calipers, and the tumour separated. Wound closed with iron sutures	Outside	After the operation she was very sick for many hours, nothing stopping the vomiting. Symptoms of low peritonitis came on, and on the 29th she suddenly sank. *Autopsy.*—Traces of peritonitis all over abdomen, with very much fresh lymph; traces of pus in kidneys; several clots of blood among bowels; right lung very much engorged; liver enlarged and fatty; spleen enlarged.
Polycystic, of right ovary, and hard fibrous tumour of the left ovary	The primary incision let out some ascitic fluid and some hydatidiform cysts. With the hand a large cyst could be felt, containing fluid and two large masses of cyst. The large cyst was tapped, and the tumour then brought out. The calipers were applied, and the tumour separated. The pedicle of the tumour attached to the other ovary was tied in two portions with twine, cut off, and allowed to remain in	Outside	She was rather faint after the operation, and some brandy was given; but she subsequently progressed favorably. On 4th calipers were removed. On 10th the ligature came away, and in about a month after the operation she left quite well, and when seen some months after was fatter and in perfect health.
Principally one large cyst, with some smaller	After incision was made, cyst was tapped, and seventeen pints of fluid drawn off. The pedicle was not large, and was enclosed in the calipers. Wound secured by silver sutures	Outside	Some peritonitis after operation. Calipers removed on the 22nd. Left quite well, on October 31st.
Multilocular	After incision was made, cyst was tapped, and fourteen pints of fluid drawn off. Pedicle secured by calipers. Wound closed by silver sutures	Outside	Sickness and symptoms of peritonitis on the second day, much relieved by turpentine fomentations and inhalations. Calipers removed on evening of 27th. Left one month after operation, quite well. When seen, some months after, was quite well and strong.

No. of case.	Date of operation.	Name and age of patient.	Duration and progress of disease and condition of patient before the operation.	Anæsthetic used, mode of administration, and the preparation.	Length of the incision.	Adhesions.
12	October 31st, 1861	C. S. æt. 46	Married. Six years ago first noticed a swelling on the belly, which has steadily increased; attributes it to a fall on a chair. Tapped once before and once after admission. Twenty-five pints of fluid, dark brown, drawn off. Miserable looking, but improved after second tapping	Chloroform	Four inches	Numerous; one firm band near the liver was tied
13	October 31st, 1861	M. S. æt. 23	Single. Two years ago first noticed a largeness in her body. General health good. Never was tapped	Chloroform	Three inches	None
14	October 31st, 1861	M. A. M. æt. 50	Married; no children. Admitted October 14th. An invalid for three years before. She discovered some months ago a swelling in belly, the size of an adult's head. General health not good. Very urgent for the operation	Chloroform	Umbilicus to pubes, subsequently enlarged	Very numerous, deep in pelvis, to whole of anterior wall of uterus; also one to liver, ligatured
15	November 14th, 1861	S. D. æt. 27	Single. Admitted October 15th. Fifteen months ago received a bruise on the right side from a box. In November, 1860, she noticed that she was stouter than usual. In June, 1861, was tapped. Also on 24th October, and twenty-three pints drawn off. Much emaciated; general health bad; urgent for operation	Chloroform at the first, and then ether for the rest	Six inches	Numerous in all directions. One very broad, going to the liver

Nature of the tumour.	Proceedings of and accidents during the operation.	Pedicle within or without abdomen.	Result.
Tumour composed of two principal cysts, but with a number of smaller ones	The primary incision went through the walls of the abdomen, which were very thin, and at the same time opened into cysts, and eleven pints of fluid escaped. Pedicle enclosed in calipers, and wound closed by silver wires	Outside	Suffered much pain from flatus for two days after operation; much relieved by turpentine fomentations and inhalations. Calipers removed on the 4th November. Left the Home 4th December; she had perfectly recovered from the operation, but did not gain strength fast, and was found to be constantly irritating the clitoris.
One large cyst, the walls of which studded with thousands of smaller; right ovary	After primary incision, cyst was tapped, and twenty-three pints of clear fluid drawn off. Pedicle enclosed in calipers. Wound secured by fine silver sutures	Outside	She had only one grain of opium after the operation. On November 22nd the wound was quite healed, and on December 4th she left the Home, quite well and strong.
When cut into resembled honeycomb; multilocular	After primary incision but five pints of albuminous fluid drawn off; different cysts. Tumour modelled to the pelvis, difficult to extract from adhesions. Those attached to uterus divided into four parts, separately ligatured. The pedicle thick, and enclosed in calipers. Several large vessels were tied, and wound closed by eleven silver sutures	Outside	Had three grains of opium, but never rallied, and sank forty hours after the operation. Autopsy showed partial peritonitis; the pedicle covered with clots, and some blood in peritoneum. Nothing found sufficient to account for death. Evidently must have arisen from shock.
Multilocular, of right ovary; twenty-two pints drawn off	The primary incision cut into the tumour, owing to the adhesions. One broad band was ligatured and divided. Pedicle was thick, and fastened by the calipers; very little bleeding from the adhesions. Wound closed by silver sutures	Outside	She had no pain after the operation, nor a single grain of opium. On the 17th the calipers were removed. On the 24th the sutures were taken out; and on December 17th she left, perfectly well in every respect.

No. of case.	Date of operation.	Name and age of patient.	Duration and progress of disease and condition of patient before the operation.	Anæsthetic used, mode of administration, and the preparation.	Length of the incision.	Adhesions.
16	November 21st, 1861	K. S. æt. 18	Single. Admitted October 28th. Three or four months ago first noticed a swelling in the right side, which has increased very rapidly. General health not good. Not menstruated for eight months. Improved under treatment	Chloroform	Five inches	Numerous and firm in all directions
17	January 2nd, 1862	E. H. æt. 56	Married; six children. Admitted November 7th. Two and a half years ago noticed a swelling on the right side, which has gradually increased. Tapped once eight months ago. Health much shattered. Tapped twice in the Home. Health much improved; urgent for the operation	Chloroform	Five inches	Some in front readily broken down
18	January 9th, 1862	Mrs. D. æt. 30	Married; three children. Admitted December 7th. Last child born twelve months ago; but two years ago had noticed enlargement of the belly, and three months before being pregnant. The labour was natural, but succeeded by a severe attack of peritonitis. Health good until lately; suffering from pain after food, flatulence and want of sleep. After admission, much pain at nights. December 11th, tapped, and thirty pints drawn off; after this her health improved	Chloroform at first, and then ether	Six incisions	Numerous in all directions. Some had to be cut, and did so like cartilage; whole of omentum adherent to tumour
19	January 9th, 1862	Mrs. D. R. æt. 55	Married; no children. Admitted January 6th. Good health until two years ago, when she noticed an enlargement of the abdomen, which has since much increased in size. In October, 1860, first tapped, and seventeen pints fluid drawn off. Tapped twice since, with increase of the fluid. General health good; was urgent for the operation	Chloroform at first, but stopped, from alarming congestion of the face. Partly conscious during the operation	Three inches	None

Nature of the tumour.	Proceedings of and accidents during the operation.	Pedicle within or without abdomen.	Result.
Multilocular, of left ovary	Operation difficult, owing to the strong adhesions. In separating the pedicle a part of the corner of the uterus was sliced off and bled freely, but was fastened by six silver sutures, cut short, and left in. Pedicle enclosed in the calipers. Wound closed by silver sutures	Outside	She made a very good recovery. On the 24th the calipers were removed. On 27th she menstruated the first time for nine months; and on December 28rd she left, perfectly well. She has menstruated since she left the Home.
Multilocular, small cysts, inside larger; were suppurating	Primary incision had to be extended, owing to the large amount of solid matter. Pedicle long and thin, and enclosed in the calipers. Wound closed by fourteen silver sutures, the walls of abdomen being very thin	Outside	She recovered very nicely; the calipers were removed the morning after the operation. On the 12th the wound was quite healed, and she left the Home, well, in less than a month after the operation.
One large parent cyst, enclosing masses of smaller ones in stages of suppuration	Primary incision of four inches, had to be extended to six, from the strong adhesions. Tumour tapped in several places; only eight and a half pints fluid drawn off. Omentum was tied and divided, and the cut surface drawn up in apposition with the abdominal parietes in the hope of producing adhesions, the ligature being fastened to a piece of wood outside of the abdomen. Pedicle enclosed in the calipers. Wounds closed by silver sutures	Outside	During first forty-eight hours signs of low peritonitis; pulse 120; constant vomiting, and for many hours was fed by bowel entirely. She recovered from this, but diarrhœa set in on 17th December, and could not be checked; she lived till 27th, when she sank, a discharge of pus occurring from the rectum few hours before death. *Autopsy.*—Wound perfectly healed; omentum adherent to parietes; a large pelvic abscess was in connection with the rectum, and a scirrhous mass attached to the duodenum, and ulcerated through its coats. Intestines glued together by lymph.
One large cyst, containing smaller ones and a mass as large as a goose's egg full of cysts; right ovary	Nothing peculiar; ten pints of fluid were drawn off. The pedicle enclosed in calipers, and the wound closed by silver sutures	Outside	Went on wonderfully up to the evening of the 14th, when diarrhœa came on, continuing till the morning of the 16th, when the pulse became intermittent and the extremities cold; she sank on 17th, at 10 a.m., in spite of enormous quantities of stimulants. *Autopsy.*—Lymph present in intestines, but not enough to account for death; the left kidney fatty; heart distended and flabby, the walls, especially of the auricles, very thin, about that of a wafer. Contents of thorax all adherent, and the pericardium adherent to the heart.

Mr. Spencer Wells said that the recommendation of the author of the paper to tie adhesions with silver wire, to divide the adhesions, and then cut off the wire short, leaving a portion of dead tissue strangulated by the wire within the peritoneal cavity, was advice which he should not be disposed to follow. The material of which the ligature was composed could be of little importance. Either wire or twine would equally cause gangrene of the strangulated part, and there would be great danger that the whole system might be poisoned by absorption of the fetid matter of the decomposing slough. He felt convinced that if this practice were followed the mortality after ovariotomy would increase. He preferred a ligature of wire-rope, tightened by a screw, to the caliper-clamp; and he thought (after trying both seton-wire and harelip-pins for the closure of the wound) that harelip-pins were generally to be preferred. The lateral pressure made by the cotton twisted round the pins fixed the two wounded surfaces more closely and securely than the wire. He differed entirely from the author in his preference to flannel over sponge in cases where it was necessary to cleanse the peritoneal cavity from blood or ovarian fluid. A soft, clean sponge did the work more effectually, and there was not the danger, as there was with flannel, of leaving portions of fine wool, or *fluff*, adhering to the peritoneum. He also thought that the author's advice would lead to a want of care in thoroughly cleansing the peritoneal cavity from ovarian fluid. In a recent case he had been led by some such advice, and by what he had heard of the practice of other surgeons, to leave some ovarian fluid in the cavity, thinking that as the intestines were exposed it might be more dangerous to sponge away the fluid than to leave it; but the result had very much disappointed him. There was little else unfavorable about the case, yet the patient died, thirty hours after operation, of acute peritonitis, and the whole membrane was covered by a layer of the albuminous portion of the fluid. The peritoneum seemed to have acted as a dialyser, allowing the water to pass through, and leaving a coating of albumen on its surface. He (Mr. Wells) could hardly suppose that either inhalation of the vapour of turpentine after the operation, or the exhibition of arnica before it, could have any great influence upon the result. He had never used either, and his results were not less satisfactory than those of the author. It was singular that he had had exactly the same number of cases in the Samaritan Hospital as Mr. Brown had had in his Home—namely, 19. Mr. Brown's returns showed 13 recoveries and 6 deaths. His (Mr. Wells'), 11 recoveries and 8 deaths. His cases in private practice had been 15, of whom 8 recovered and 7 died. The total gave 34 cases, with 19 recoveries and 15 deaths. He trusted that Mr. Brown would also give the Society the result of his *whole* experience of ovariotomy. He (Mr. Wells) had not been able to do more than compare their first 20 cases; and it was singular that with these 20 the number of recoveries and deaths was directly reversed, for Mr. Brown had had 13 deaths and 7 recoveries; while he (Mr. Wells) had had 13 recoveries and 7 deaths. He was also of opinion that in some of the fatal cases brought before the Society this evening, the operation ought not to have been performed. The patients died of serious organic disease of the heart, or of some other important organic cancer of the intestine, for example; or the uterus was so closely surrounded by adhering pelvic portions of the ovarian tumour that separation could not be effected. Such conditions could generally be detected during life, and ought, with rare exceptions, to lead the surgeon to refuse to operate. It often became our duty to operate in very unfavorable cases, and many of his own fatal cases had occurred under conditions so unfavorable that a good result could not fairly be expected; but the operation was decidedly contra-indicated in any case of serious organic disease of heart or lungs, or of malignant disease in any important organ.

Dr. TANNER made some observations on the importance of not resorting to ovariotomy in cases where the operation was almost certain to prove fatal. There were many women afflicted with ovarian tumours, where extirpation was quite impracticable. This was proved by some cases that had been under his care, and where he had resisted the patient's desire for an operation. In two recent instances in which the disease proved fatal, it was found impossible after death to remove the tumours withont tearing the viscera. The existence of very firm adhesions had been diagnosed during life; and though it was distressing to witness the gradual sinking of these poor women, yet it would have been very improper to have added to their sufferings by any operative procedures.

Dr. HALL DAVIS observed, that the success recorded in the paper, of thirteen recoveries out of nineten ovariotomy operations, was highly gratifying. Of those cases, he (Dr. Davis) had had the opportunity of watching the course of twelve, of which number eight recovered. It was his opinion that such success as that presented by the nineteen cases now reported by Mr. Brown, and the equal success of Dr. Tyler Smith, Mr. Spencer Wells, Dr. Clay, and of other recent operators, of 67 per cent. of recoveries, as compared with the unfavorable results of former years, was an advance in surgery of which we might well be proud. We are now, therefore, no longer justified in opposing the wishes of our suffering patients, anxious for the operation, as affording them a chance of escape from a miserable death,—at least in any case which furnishes a hope of a favorable issue. For many years he had taught, in his lectures, that ovariotomy was not justifiable; but the mortality which then attended it, of at least two in every three operations, as fully authorised his so doing as the present improved method of operation, with its happy results, has justified a change of opinion. He still did not think we should take upon ourselves the responsibility of actually recommending the operation, but after fairly laying before our patient the proportion of recoveries from it, we should then, in a case which offers no obvious objection to the operation, leave the important decision to the patient herself.

Dr. ROUTH said he had seen a large number of cases of ovarian disease; he spoke, therefore, from experience. First, he believed we could never be certain beforehand on some of the most important points of diagnosis in ovarian disease. Extensive adhesions had been often diagnosed before operation, which were afterwards found to be limited or absent. In other cases their absence was predicted, while the operation revealed that they were very firm and numerous. The presence of coexisting ascites greatly increased the difficulty, so as to make a preliminary tapping necessary before ovarian disease could be made out at all. Secondly, he had known some of the most eminent men in the diagnosis of ovarian disease mistake a large cyst of the kidney, extra-uterine pregnancy, and fibroid disease of the uterus, for ovarian dropsy. Thirdly, Mr. Wells objected to the expediency of operating in cases of cancer of the intestines, which he stated was always to be made out before operation. In one of Mr. Brown's cases there was cancer of the duodenum with a large ovarian cyst in front of it. How could such a disease be made out? It was simply impossible. In honesty he (Dr. Routh) was bound to add that post-mortems often revealed the coexistence of other disease which not only could not have been made out before operation, but which could not even have been suspected. Fourthly, his impression was that the non-existence of adhesions, and a perfectly healthy peritoneum, were not necessarily favorable to recovery. He had seen such cases followed by severe peritonitis; while others, in which the peritoneum was almost entirely disorganized by extensive adhesions, which needed very great force to tear them asunder, recovered without one bad symptom. Lastly, he thought that the practice of sponging out the contents of a cyst, if accidentally effused during the operation, was better than leaving the fluid in the cavity of the peritoneum.

Dr. GRAILY HEWITT thought the facts contained in Mr. Brown's paper interesting, as showing the improvements which had occurred of late in the results obtained in the operation of ovariotomy. If he recollected aright, Mr. Brown's former experience, as summed up in Mr. Clay's work on 'Ovariotomy Statistics,' exhibited cures only to the extent of 31 or 32 per cent., whereas in the series of cases now brought forward the mortality was 31·5 per cent., and the cures 68·5 per cent. It was very satisfactory to find that the attention paid to the subject had produced improvement such as that now referred to—an improvement which had more or less attended the operation in other hands also. He thought it would be interesting to the Society if Mr. Brown would state to what he considered the very marked difference in the results of his recent and former experience was due. Further, would Mr. Brown inform the Society whether the results related included all his ovariotomy operations, both those carried out and those only attempted, as was done in Mr. Clay's statistical account? With reference to the existence of adhesions, and their influence on the mortality of the operation, his own observations induced him to think that the point was comparatively unimportant. Any danger attending the use of sponges in the operation was, he believed, connected with want of attention to cleanliness, and consequent introduction of noxious matter into the system.

Dr. TYLER SMITH observed that the remarks of the author upon the semi-recumbent position of the patient during the operation evidently applied to himself. He could only state that he believed this position to be superior to the horizontal, inasmuch as it facilitated the removal of fluid from the abdominal cavity, was convenient to the operator, and it certainly did not produce syncope. In some patients the horizontal position was impossible, as they could not lie down without danger of suffocation. He was glad Mr. Brown had modified his plan of giving opiates as the rule after operations, as he thought it could be shown in some cases to lead to bad results. His own plan had been not to place ligatures upon adhesions when bleeding took place immediately after their division, but to wait till towards the end of the operation, by which time all bleeding from adhesion had generally ceased. He used warm flannels to prevent the protrusion of the intestines, but thought soft and perfectly clean sponges preferable to flannel in removing fluid and coagula. The sponges should be large, so as to render it impossible for them to be left in the abdomen. He thought neither good nor harm could result from the use of arnica and turpentine in the way recommended by the author. It appeared to him that we were quite able to estimate beforehand the chances of recovery in particular cases; but in the interests of humanity, and when death was inevitable without operation, he thought we were bound in some cases to operate, even though the chances of recovery were slight. The general recognition of the value of the operation would diminish such cases, and also those which were now met with of a hopeless character, by leading to its timely performance. He could not but remark that the present discussion had been chiefly occupied with the minor but still important points relating to the details of this great operation. The subject had now been several times before the Fellows, and, as far as the Obstetrical Society of London was concerned, no voice had been raised against the principle of the operation. It must be held to have been accepted as a recognised operation of the highest value. His own cases had been ten in number, of which seven had been entirely successful.

Mr. BAKER BROWN, in reply to the observations of Mr. Spencer Wells, stated that he had used the silver wires as ligatures with the best results. In one instance, in the presence of M. Nélaton, of Paris, and others, he had used four silver sutures to a wound in the uterus, and the patient made an excellent recovery. The theoretical opinions of Mr. Wells were completely upset by practical facts, as proved both by Mr. Brown and by Dr. Tyler Smith. Mr. Brown repeated, that his experience of the injurious effects of sponges on the peritoneum was founded on actual facts, first suggested by observing that Mr. White Cooper avoided the use of sponges in operations of the eye, and by also hearing the practical experience of Mr. Webber on the same subject. Mr. Wells' observations about leaving any of the ovarian fluid within the peritoneal cavity were repeatedly controverted by the non-injurious results of spontaneous rupture of ovarian cysts. Mr. Brown had recommended the use of the inhalation of turpentine, after the operation, in cases of pain, upon the well-known principle of its vapour being an excellent anæsthetic; and he felt sure that if any gentleman would administer it to patients suffering pain he would be speedily convinced of the advantages arising from its use. Mr. Brown had no intention in this paper of comparing the results of his operations with those of Mr. Spencer Wells; but as that gentleman had alluded to the number of his own cases, he had not the slightest objection to state that the results of his whole practice, in private and in St. Mary's Hospital, had been nineteen cases, with six recoveries; and in the London Surgical Home, nineteen cases, with thirteen recoveries: total, thirty-eight cases, and nineteen recoveries. Mr. Brown was surprised at the opinion expressed by Mr. Wells as to the facility of detecting other organic diseases during life in patients suffering from ovarian disease, because he knew that Mr. Wells had operated on a patient, with a fatal result, which he and others of great experience had condemned as totally unfit for operation. The Society had also heard from Dr. Tanner of another case of like nature; and Mr. Brown believed that in two other cases Mr. Wells had operated, in his hospital, where the adhesions were so great as to forbid the completion of the operation. Mr. Brown believed that the greater beneficial results obtained in the London Surgical Home over his former practice were due to the skilled nursing and perfect organization of that establishment affording such facilities in the after-treatment. He had mentioned the minute details of the preparatory and after-treatment because a large experience in operative surgery had convinced him that success arose from a strict attention to these points, rather than from the brilliancy of the operation itself.

APRIL 2ND, 1862.

DR. TYLER SMITH, President, in the Chair

Present—46 Fellows and 5 visitors.

The following gentlemen were duly elected Fellows of the Society:—John Brickwell, M.R.C.S., Sawbridgeworth, Herts; Joseph Thomas Holt Dunn, L.R.C.P., 7, Carlton Place, Westbourne Park; John Marshall, M.R.C.S., 27A, Aldenham Street, St. Pancras; Henry Simpson, M.B., Lymm, Warrington, Cheshire; Sidney Smith, M.R.C.S., Tiverton, Devon; Richard Thomas Tasker, M.R.C.S., Melbourne, near Derby.

The PRESIDENT congratulated the Society on the appearance of the volume of 'Transactions' for the past year (vol. iii). A copy was handed round for inspection.

DESCRIPTION OF A SPECIMEN OF AN OVUM IN OVO.

By ROBERT BARNES, M.D., F.R.C.P.,

PHYSICIAN TO THE ROYAL MATERNITY CHARITY, ASSISTANT-OBSTETRIC PHYSICIAN TO THE LONDON HOSPITAL; LECTURER ON MIDWIFERY AT ST. THOMAS'S HOSPITAL.

THE egg now submitted to the Society I will describe in the words of Mr. Hora, R.I.N., who sent me the specimen, premising that my friend is fairly accomplished as a naturalist and a very accurate observer. "A farmer here (Newcastle-Emlyn, South Wales) has a pullet which commenced laying some six weeks since, and has laid pretty regularly an egg a day since. Now and then, at various intervals, she lays these double eggs; up to the present time she has laid nine, all alike in every respect, even to the colour of the shells. The inner shell is always of a red tint like the Cochin fowl's and the partridge's; the outer shell always a dull chalky white, without any gloss or polish upon it. The pullet is evidently a half-bred between a Cochin and a Dorking. But is it not curious that the eggs should always bear the distinguishing marks so plainly, the Cochin egg being always inside the Dorking egg? The two yolks in one shell is common enough, but I never before met with a case like this of two perfect eggs, one contained within the other."

The inner egg is of the size of an ordinary pullet's egg. It is a perfect egg, having a hard shell of a reddish tint, containing a full-sized yolk in albumen. It lies in the larger egg, the two shells not being adherent, surrounded by the albumen of the larger egg, the yolk of which lies somewhat compressed in the big end of the shell.

The length of the outer egg is three inches, breadth two and a quarter inches. Total weight, four and three quarter ounces.

The average length of a fowl's egg is two and a quarter inches, and the breadth 1·7 inches.

That two yolks or ovarian ova may descend along the oviduct together, getting a common investment of albumen, and then of shell, is an intelligible circumstance. But it is not so easy to understand how an egg after obtaining its albumen and shell, the latter of which is added near the cloaca, can become associated with another ovum and be invested in the albumen and shell of its fellow. Does the first ovum after receiving its own albumen and shell get carried back up the oviduct to meet the second ovum, and descend along with it through those tracts which supply successively the albumen and shell? Or does the first egg after completion lie in the lower part of the oviduct waiting the arrival of the second egg, and get immersed in its fluid albumen before the deposit of shell has commenced?

A. *Inner egg of a reddish colour; the "cochin egg."*

B. *Albumen of outer egg, surrounding yolk of its own egg, and the cochin egg.*

C. *Yolk of outer or Dorking egg lying in larger end.*

Shell of outer egg of dull chalky white.

The preservation of the distinctive characters of the Cochin and Dorking egg in this ovum in ovo suggests an interesting speculation concerning the transmissibility of parental peculiarities. There are two double shells of a similar kind in the Museum of the College of Surgeons. But these specimens do not appear to exhibit the remarkable variety in the character of the two shells presented in the specimen submitted to the Society.

A CASE OF OVARIOTOMY, AND A REPLY TO A STATEMENT RESPECTING IT MADE BY MR. BAKER BROWN AT THE LAST MEETING OF THE SOCIETY.

By T. Spencer Wells, Esq., F.R.C.S.

Mr. B. Brown inquired of the President by whose authority his name had been mentioned in the title of this paper?

The President replied, that the usual regulations respecting the admission of papers had been complied with as regarded the paper in question.

Mr. B. Brown then protested against the title of the paper, wherein his name was used, as he considered, in an unjustifiable manner, and protested against its being read.

The President stated that the Council had determined that the paper should be read.

The paper was then read, the following being an abstract of the same:

Mr. Brown having said at the last meeting, "He knew that Mr. Wells had operated on a patient, with a fatal result, which he and others of great experience had condemned as totally unfit for operation," Mr. Wells now narrated the case at length to the Society:—The patient was single, thirty years of age, the subject of a multilocular cystic tumour of the left ovary, of about two years' growth, which was removed by Mr. Wells on the 13th of January last. There were some adhesions, both to the parietes and to the colon; but they were easily separated. From an unusual tendency to protrusion of the intestine, Mr. Wells did not sponge out all the ovarian fluid which had escaped into the peritoneal cavity; and he partly attributed to this fact the diffuse peritonitis which proved fatal twenty-nine hours after the operation. In order to prove that Mr. Brown had *not* "condemned" this case as "totally unfit for operation," Mr. Wells produced a letter from the uncle of the patient,—a Fellow of the Royal College of Surgeons,—which this gentleman authorised Mr. Wells to bring before the Society, in which he stated that Mr. Brown had written to him saying that his niece's was "a fair case for operation." The uncle also enclosed for the information of the Society a letter from Mr. Brown to the father of the patient, in which Mr. Brown said that the tumour "could be removed by a dangerous operation. No one, however, can recommend it to be removed; yet if Miss — determines she will elect to have the trial made, being fully aware of the danger, then I will undertake the operation, with the sanction of her uncle, feeling that there is a fair prospect of success—*i. e.*, as much reason to hope as to fear." These letters, and the history of the case, were read without any comment from Mr. Wells.

Dr. Barnes observed that each gentleman having had the opportunity of submitting his own account of the case to the Society, there could be no cause for discussing the matter any further in that place. In affording this opportunity, the Society had done all that it could fairly be called upon to do. Any further discussion should be carried on elsewhere. He deprecated the idea of making the Society the arena of a personal contest of this kind.

Mr. Brown then again protested, and declined making any observations.

COMPLETE OCCLUSION OF THE OS UTERI, WITH RETENTION OF THE MENSES AFTER DIFFICULT LABOUR.

By John Hall Davis, M.D.,

PHYSICIAN TO THE ROYAL MATERNITY CHARITY, TO THE SAINT PANCRAS INFIRMARY, AND TO THE ST. GEORGE'S AND ST. JAMES'S DISPENSARY.

Mrs. —, æt. 33, of healthy conformation and medium stature, married in December, 1858, was taken in labour of her *first* child, July 15th, 1860, at 8 in the evening.

At 6 the following morning (July 16th), Mr. Hayman, of Axminster, Devon, was summoned. The liquor amnii had escaped just before his arrival. The labour advanced very slowly for two days. By the husband's request three medical gentlemen were then called in; ergot and antimony were given, but scarcely any dilatation of the os uteri took place till the third day (July 18th). The labour then advanced, and the head was well within reach at 2 o'clock.

At 4 o'clock Mr. Hayman used the long forceps in the presence of these gentlemen, and with great difficulty a female child of ten and a half pounds weight, and stillborn, was thus delivered. A slight rent of the perinæum took place at the birth. No shivering nor fever followed the delivery, and the patient left her bed at the end of a fortnight, but was unable to sit comfortably till Mr. Hayman united the sides of the rent by a small plastic operation. The menstrual period had not returned when she was placed under my care, fifteen months after delivery. A thick, yellowish discharge flowed from the vagina for three months after her confinement, and the patient had at times suffered since from pains in the abdomen; always felt uncomfortable, dull, and heavy; soon fatigued. She could not lie on her back, and driving over uneven ground was painful to her.

On August 7th Mr. Hayman brought the patient to London for my advice. I found the os uteri completely obliterated; the cervix of the uterus did not dip into the vagina in the least, and was softer than the unimpregnated uterus, under ordinary circumstances, is found to be; it was perfectly smooth, without the least indication in any direction of where the orifice of the uterus had once been. I could at this time detect no enlargement of the uterus above the pubes; no fluctuation in the uterus per vaginam; that passage presented no cicatrices, and was of ample capacity.

As I was leaving London for a few weeks, saw no great urgency in the case, and deemed that August was not the most favorable month, in a sanitary view, for an operation which might be postponed, I requested to see the patient again in October.

October 28th.—The patient returned to me at this date. The uterus could now be felt above the pubes, enlarged to the size of a four months' gravidity. A soft, somewhat elastic prominence of the uterus was perceived at the top of the vagina with distinct fluctuation. The patient's discomfort had increased, and she now fancied herself pregnant; but I informed her that she was not so, and of the nature of her case, which I looked upon as one of retained catamenia.

November 2nd.—The bowels having been regulated, I re-examined, and having fixed upon the point of greatest prominence, I punctured the uterus in the axis of the organ with a canulated stilet, to the depth of a quarter of an inch. I then withdrew the stilet and advanced the canula into the uterus, when a portion of the retained catamenial fluid came away. It was of the consistence of treacle, but not offensive. As the discharge did not flow freely I very slightly enlarged the aperture to each side with the hysterotome, when the collected menses readily escaped to the extent of six ounces, and more followed during the next two days. The aperture was subsequently maintained by leaving in a No. 12 gum-elastic catheter for two hours daily.

15th.—All had gone on well till to-day, when, after walking up and down stairs, contrary to advice, and insufficiently clad, yesterday and the previous day, she now complained of violent pain in the pelvic region; she had also shivering; pulse 100; dry skin. A return to bed, turpentine stupes, an enema, and a Dover's powder, were followed by great relief.

16th.—Much better; some pain remaining was followed by turpentine stupes and an anodyne enema.

17th.—The menses reappeared without pain.

19th.—To save the patient inconvenience, and thinking it might be dispensed with, the catheter was now discontinued.

26th.—Re-examining to-day, I found the orifice so contracted as not to admit a small probe; I therefore enlarged it so as to readmit No. 12 catheter, as before.

December 1st and 2nd.—The patient took a drive in a close carriage, but not sufficiently clothed for the season; shivering followed, and pain in the umbilical and pelvic regions. Turpentine stupes, a morphia draught, with an opiate enema, gave relief as before. Catheterism was again discontinued.

3rd.—Pain severe in the night in the pelvic region; skin hot and dry; pulse 120. Turpentine epithems, a hot hip-bath, followed by free perspiration and relief; but a relapse of pain soon ensued.

For the next seven days the patient passed through a period of much danger, during which I watched her day and night; the symptoms were those of pyæmia. Pulse 110 to 140; shiverings, heats, profuse sweats, vomiting, diarrhœa, tympanitic abdomen, insomnia, imperfect vision, and delirium. These were met by appropriate remedies, and the strength was well sustained by tonics, stimulants, and nourishment given very frequently. On two nights I found the patient in a cold sweat, her pulse intermittent. The brandy was here given still more freely, and food too, which the patient took with the greatest craving. During this time there was no marked tenderness, even on considerable pressure of the abdomen, yet the patient would at times complain of pain in the region of the uterus, which was felt enlarged above the pubes. There was no redness nor swelling over any of the joints, or any part of the surface. Urine high-coloured, scanty, never albuminous; dirty, viscid sputa.

16th.—More sleep and less craving for food in the night. Examination per vaginam to-day discovers one effect of the patient's illness in the enlarged and fixed condition of the uterus. Catheterism of the os uteri was not yet returned to for fear of rekindling inflammatory action. A few days later I was gratified by a return for a few hours of menstruation.

January 7th.—Improvement has continued steady. The uterus was again examined to-day, and found to be reduced to the size it presented previous to the above attack. The os uteri was now sufficiently open to admit a small uterine sound. Three days later the patient was permitted to walk about her adjoining rooms. About this time brandy and wine were replaced by stout.

24th.—The catamenia reappeared freely, and lasted the patient's normal period—between two and three days.

30th.—The weather being warm and the patient much stronger, I sanctioned her return to Axminster. The patient reached home with scarcely any fatigue; has since, without any drawbacks, gone on favorably, and says she is quite well.

Two perfectly satisfactory menstrual periods have occurred since, commencing respectively February 10th and March 7th, so that I apprehend there is no fear now of a recurrence of the closure of the os uteri in this patient.[1]

I have brought this case before the Society as illustrating a cause of retained catamenia, of which we have very few recorded instances, and therefore one most probably rarely met with. I find no case of the kind in any of the Transactions of our societies; nor in any of our systematic works or monographs do I find such a cause referred to, excepting in the 'Obstetrics' of Dr. Tyler Smith.

I do not refer to congenital, but acquired or secondary occlusions of the os uteri as a cause of amenorrhœa, the vagina not being also involved.

[1] The above patient was in London in June; I found her in good health, and able to visit the International Exhibition several times. The periods, I have heard snce, continue regular.

Examples of such obliteration acting as an obstacle in labour are now pretty numerously recorded, and in them it has been generally traced, I will not say always, to the influence of a previous labour and resulting inflammatory action. In those instances it is obvious the *complete* obliteration could not have taken place till after conception. M. Cazeaux mentions one case of its occurrence in labour in which, six weeks before, the os uteri had been found as yet open. Smellie, Hamilton, Gooch, Naegelé, Dubois, Ashwell, Lever, Waller, Mayne, Lauverjat, Gautier, Trask, and others, give instances of this condition in labour.

In July, 1858, Mr. William Jeffreys and Mr. John Hainworth, of Camden Town, submitted a case of this kind for my advice. The uterus presented per vaginam a smooth, globular prominence. There was no trace of orifice, or of indication of its former site. It was the patient's first labour. She had had inflammation of the neck of the uterus in the fifth month of pregnancy. I determined to follow Naegelé's practice, advocated also by M. Cazeaux and the late Dr. Rigby, at least should it prove sufficient, viz., to make the necessary uterine orifice by pressing strongly during uterine action upon the centre of the globular swelling. I thus with my index finger made an aperture with a jagged edge. The liquor amnii came away at the same time, and the child, head presenting, was born soon after, having been dead apparently some days.

In some recorded cases incisions have become necessary, and when these have been omitted or too long delayed a fatal issue has been the consequence.

In the case of retained menstruation, which I have brought before the Society, it appears to me that the occlusion was the result of inflammatory action occasioned by the long-continued pressure of the head against the os uteri after the discharge of the protecting bag of waters. My friend gives it as his opinion that the rupture of the perineum was unavoidably produced by the forceps' delivery, and states that after a first trial of them he was in favour of craniotomy, but was overruled in consultation. Mr. Hayman, however, skilfully remedied the slight injury thus occasioned, and had the satisfaction of feeling that every possible effort was made to save the child. I cannot conclude without thanking Mr. Hayman for the case and its early history. My thanks are also due to Dr. Arthur Farre for his valuable advice in consultations upon the case after the attack of pyæmia had declared itself. That attack appeared to have been the conjoint result of the necessary interference and the premature exertion of the patient, with exposure to cold afterwards.

I should state that Dr. West saw the patient once with us to quiet her fears about a "phantom tumour" which had appeared at the end of the pyæmic fever. This abdominal enlargement, a liniment of cajeput oil dispersed in a few days.

ON THE NATURE, TREATMENT, ETC., OF PUERPERAL PERITONITIS.

By Joseph Thomas Mitchell, F.R.C.S.E.

The favorable notice accorded to my former paper has led me again to appear before the Obstetrical Society of London. And now I am anxious to bring forward the result of my experience in the treatment of puerperal peritonitis in a general and parochial practice during a period of nearly forty years, among 4349 recorded cases of labour among which I have been called on to treat twenty-seven cases of well-marked urgent puerperal peritonitis, of which only four cases have terminated fatally. But in stating this result, I would also remark that I never had to encounter epidemic puerperal fever, and that I never attended a case that I could trace to contagious origin, and that every case to which I have alluded was attended at the patient's own residence, and not either in an infirmary or hospital.

When I was the pupil of the late Dr. Haighighton and

Dr. Blundell, at Guy's Hospital School, in 1819 and 1820, I was taught by their lectures that the greatest fatality always attended this dreadful disease, and I left the theatre earnestly desiring that I never should have to treat it, as I then fully believed that all remedial means would avail but little to avert a fatal issue: a sentiment much in accordance with that lately expressed by our esteemed President.

In the winter of 1825, when I had been some years in practice, and had never seen a case of puerperal peritonitis, I was present at what was then called the "celebrated lecture of Dr. Armstrong on puerperal fever," delivered at the Maze Pond School of Medicine, when he boldly asserted that in a very large practice of midwifery, in which he had been engaged in Sunderland for many years, he had never lost a case which he had been able to see within two hours after the shivering fit, which invariably ushers in the unmistakeable symptoms of this appalling disease, unless it had originated in extensive mechanical lesion, produced in labour, or otherwise.

The treatment he adopted was bleeding to syncope, followed by the administration of large doses of opium, by which, all peristaltic action of the bowels would be suspended, and the excessive alarm and consequent irritability of the whole nervous system subdued, at the same time enjoining implicit rest to the patient in the recumbent position, and applying extensive counter-irritation over the whole abdominal surface. The lecture took place at four in the afternoon, and an immense crowd of practitioners from all parts of London, as many as could gain admission to the theatre, was present to hear it. I left the lecture, which occupied two hours in being delivered, with feelings very different from those with which I had gone away from the theatre at Guy's after having heard Dr. Blundell's lecture on the same subject a few years before. On my arrival at home, strange to say, I found an urgent message awaiting me, that my immediate attendance was required on a poor woman who had been delivered two days previously, and who was suffering excruciating pain, and had sent for me several times within the past hour. I went to her immediately, when, to my dismay, I found myself confronted for the first time with the direful enemy which I had so much feared. I immediately put in practice Dr. Armstrong's remedies, and the result was that I had the gratification of seeing my patient snatched from what appeared to be impending death. After the pleasing termination of this case my inordinate fears in having to contend with this disease subsided, and from that time to this I have always adopted the same practice, and with almost the same invariable success.

What is puerperal peritonitis? It is a disease marked by the following symptoms, occurring under the following circumstances. A woman in apparently normal condition of health or otherwise, who may or may not have received some shock or accident, is taken in labour, the process of which is either natural, easy and quick, or lingering and preternatural; it may have required manual or instrumental aid, or it may have been accomplished without either. After delivery, all the attendant circumstances may give hope of a speedy recovery to health and strength, or it may be otherwise; generally, on the second or third day after delivery, she begins to feel pain in the abdomen, slight, perhaps, at first; but from time to time it becomes augmented, as it were, by slight colic or spasmodic action of the intestines, which may be taken for ordinary afterpains; this condition lasts, perhaps, for an hour or two, or even for a day, when suddenly she is seized with a violent spasm in the belly, which is quickly succeeded by a fit of shivering, more or less severe; this ushers in symptoms alarming to the patient and all around her, who become impressed with the belief that death is fast approaching; her countenance has become pale, shrunken, and deeply anxious in its aspect; her extremities cold; her pulse almost uncountable, and scarcely discerned, from quickness and feebleness; by this time the most excruciating, permanent pain is felt over the whole internal abdominal surface, which is greatly augmented by the slightest pressure made externally, and this all present without retention of urine or other accountable cause; indeed, she is in a condition not unlike that which speedily follows the taking of corrosive mineral poison, except that there need be no vomiting, and from which, if she be not speedily relieved, will be followed by swelling and tenderness of the abdomen, produced by the rapid outpouring of serum, coagulable lymph, and pus, which, in some instances, is even attended by sloughing of small patches in the membrane, as has been seen in post-mortem examinations.

The question then is, have we any means to prevent such results? My answer is, we have none except what are most active in their operation, and that require to be applied with the earliest and greatest promptitude. Under these impressions, in order that I might be ready promptly to apply my remedies when such emergencies may occur, my rule has always been to instruct the parish midwives, and others in attendance on lying-in women, immediately to send for me whenever any symptoms might appear, such as I have described as characteristic of the approach of this disease. This rule has often given me unnecessary trouble, when no real cause for alarm has existed, but it has enabled me, promptly, to apply my remedies where it has.

Then, what have been these remedies? Bleeding to a greater or less extent, generally adopted but once, yet in some instances, twice, and in some few cases even thrice, followed by the administration of full, almost poisonous, doses of opium, and then extensively irritating the whole abdominal surface by fomentations of hot water and turpentine, or by the application of large sinapisms; at the same time enjoining the strictest quiet, and confining the patient in the horizontal position on her back, even when called on to pass her urine, taking care to prevent all action of the bowels, during even four or five days, if necessary, and then to relieve them only by an injection of gruel and turpentine, and not by any purgative given by the mouth. Indeed, I urgently warn every practitioner against administering any purgative by the mouth during the continuation of any symptoms of this affection.

Perhaps many will exclaim—" What! bleed a woman in

whom life appears almost already extinguished, as is evidenced by the depressed condition of the nervous system, and by all the other attendant symptoms! And how can you bleed a woman almost pulseless, with cold extremities, and apparently sinking? A vein may be opened, but no blood can flow." Under such circumstances the operation may appear to be difficult; but by preliminary preparation the difficulty will be removed. Let the hands and the feet of the patient be placed in water, as hot as can be borne, for a short time; then tie up the arm, when the veins at the bend will be found to be distended, and easy to be opened. At first the blood will flow slowly, but very soon, as the operation proceeds, and the engorged congested vessels of the inflamed membrane become relieved, the blood will flow freely; the heart, which, under the direction of the alarmed nervous system, had almost ceased to push the blood forwards to the diseased surface, where a destructive process had begun, recovers its action, contracts more firmly and normally, and the blood becomes freely and equally circulated throughout the whole system, and the circulation being restored, the blood is made to flow "plæno-vivo," until, as the overloaded vessels of the affected part become more relieved, the excruciating pains in the abdomen are lessened, perhaps entirely removed, never to return; when, by producing almost narcotism and active counter-irritation, the violent action commenced in the peritoneum, and which must, if left unchecked, become speedily disorganizing, is directed to the vessels of the skin, and nature, relieved from her alarm, gradually recovers her normal action.

I am aware that, in advocating this plan of treatment, I am placing myself at issue with the generally received opinions of the present day. I expect to be told that disease is always of asthenic origin, and that an asthenic condition is the cause of its perpetuation, and that the cure is only to be hoped for in the adoption of repleting and stimulating, rather than depleting, means; but my answer is in the result of the practice.

Of the four fatal cases among the twenty-seven cases

treated, the first that died was one to which a physician-accoucheur, then of repute, was called in during the progress of labour, in consequence of a large thrombus having formed high up in the vagina, by the giving way of a large varicose vein in labour, when the tumour prevented the descent of the child's head. In that case I wished to divide the tumour by a longitudinal incision, made parallel to the axis of the passage, thereby to allow the blood to escape, and then to let the head pass over it by the natural expulsive efforts of the uterus, as there was ample space in the bony canal to allow of transit through it; but to this the friends of the patient objected, and then I sent for this gentleman, who also objected to my suggestion, and he immediately applied the forceps to the head, and delivered hastily, by dragging it violently over the tumour, which, of course, burst under the pressure, and by which the vagina was much lacerated, even to the vulva. Peritonitis followed, and death.

In the second case death was accelerated, if not caused, by the injudicious administration of a full dose of castor-oil, given, also contrary to my approbation, by another eminent physician-accoucheur, who was called in on the second day of treatment, and on the fifth from the delivery, when all the acute symptoms had been subdued and the case was progressing favorably; the action of the purgative revived the mischief, and she died on the ninth day.

The third was a woman in most impoverished circumstances, who was suffering under great deprivations, who was seized with labour at the seventh month of gestation; she was evidently suffering from peritonitis when labour began, and was convulsed in labour; she died on the fifth day.

The last was a similar case of six months' gestation, where there was a placenta presentation, requiring turning, which, from the urgency of the hæmorrhage, was effected hastily, and was followed by peritonitis, and she died. This woman was not bled.

Now, how do free, sudden abstraction of blood, the administration of opium in large doses, and the application of extensive counter-irritants on the skin, affect such deranged phenomena as are present at the onset of puerperal peritonitis, such as I have described, indicating such universal depression of the nervous system and almost paralysed condition of the circulating? By the mere sudden, temporary, but universal, relaxation produced on the ordinarily normally distended condition of the blood-vessels generally, acting mechanically and specially in relieving the congested or distended condition of the particular vessels of the part affected, the condition varying in degree, according to the nature of the structure affected, found in every part suffering under inflammation before disorganization has actually commenced, and becomes more or less destructive in its consequences; according, also, to the peculiarities of the structure. It is rapidly so when it occurs in the serous membranes lining the great cavities of the body. And this relief given to the congested vessels by the bleeding is perpetuated by the sedative effects of the opium, assisted by the deriving influence of the artificial erysipelas set up on the whole abdominal skin by the application of the hot-water and turpentine fomentations.

But with the treatment which I have commended I do not deem it necessary to starve the patient, whose powers I sustain with light, nutritious food, as beef tea, milk, and farinaceous food, and, perhaps, even with wine, in moderate quantities. Yet in no instance did I ever give wine or other stimulant until many hours after all the acute symptoms, of which, I esteem the acute pain as the chief, had subsided.

Those who universally condemn depletion by bleeding, do it under the conviction, that, as the system is thereby deprived of so much of its necessary pabulum of life, it ought never to be wasted; but retained, to sustain it, under the destructive tendency of disease; and, also, because they deny that, by bleeding, the active disease is ever suspended. From these opinions I differ. Moreover, nature, in her own operations shows us to what extent loss of blood may be borne, not only with impunity, but with advantage, as in extensive epistaxis when apoplexy is threatened; in hæmatemesis where gastritis exists, or in hæmacatharsis during an attack of enteritis, as well as by the rapid recoveries often made by women, after deliveries, in which they had suffered immense losses of blood.

The twenty-three cases of recovery, here alluded to, out of twenty-seven cases treated, are proofs of the safety of the practice of bleeding when adopted to a moderate extent, not one of which suffered afterwards, as from an anæmic state, or had her recovery retarded thereby. A near relative was one of the subjects of this treatment. She was bled twice within twelve hours; first to sixteen ounces, and secondly to six ounces; she recovered well, and within sixteen years of the occurrence was afterwards delivered of eight living, healthy children, and she is now a healthy woman of fifty-nine years of age.

Dr. Tilbury Fox regretted that he had not been present to hear the commencement of the paper, as he understood that reference had been made to his paper on 'Puerperal Fever.' The plan of treatment which Mr. Mitchell's paper inculcated might, no doubt, be serviceable in sporadic cases, but was totally inapplicable to the epidemic form of disease. In the present instance the death-rate of the author, four in twenty-seven cases, which was very little below the average mortality of epidemic puerperal fever, as derived from large statistics, did not certainly warrant the practice of bloodletting and the like. Hæmorrhage and venesection were identical in their action, and yet the former was no preventive, but a large number of women attacked by fever were the subjects of post-partum hæmorrhage. From a very careful study of the records of the General Lying-in Hospital, he had come to the conclusion that bleeding did harm. It could not certainly lessen materies morbi. Then there were certain local-tissue actions which were necessary to the cure of many cases of puerperal fever. These were eliminative, and might be called pyæmic. It was necessary to save up the power of the system for these operations. Bleeding appeared in the epidemic form to check these; nay, moreover, it appeared in every way to prolong convalescence. Further than this even, in many instances after bleeding, the pulse has positively risen in frequency, and the patient has quickly died, evidently in consequence of the loss of blood. Hæmorrhage favoured absorption, opium checked it. Hence the combination should be resorted to as a rule, in order to keep in check the taking into the system of the putrid matter, especially from the uterine cavity. The most suitable case for bleeding would be sporadic, where the disease was localized, so to speak, the aim being to moderate excessive local action. No general rule could be laid down. The treatment must be eclectic. On account of not having heard the early part of the paper, he was a little uncertain whether he had noticed its most important point.

Dr. J. BRAXTON HICKS thought that it was very difficult to be certain that peritonitis was really present in cases where the pain in the lower abdomen and pelvic region was even very severe. The majority of these cases proved to be cellulitis, not involving the peritoneum, but probably produced by inflammation of the lymphatics, which passed so freely within the folds of the broad ligament. The treatment adopted in the Guy's Lying-in Charity was not so heroic as that of the author, but Dr. Hicks thought the death-rate would not by any means prove to be greater.

Dr. ROUTH said he should be sorry to learn that the profession had been influenced by Mr. Mitchell's paper to treat *all* cases of puerperal peritonitis by bloodletting. Casual cases met with in private practice were very different from those occurring in lying-in hospitals. There were, moreover, several varieties of the disease—the dynamic and adynamic, the contagious and non-contagious, &c. In his early career Dr. Routh had seen a fearful epidemic in Vienna, where sometimes six hundred died a year. That fever was found to be non-contagious, and caused by direct inoculation of dead matter carried from the dead-house beneath the nails of the medical attendants. All kinds of treatment had occasionally succeeded—generally, however, failed. In some examples, in which a particular kind of *facies* made its appearance, it could be surely foretold that death would occur, in spite of any treatment. In others, in which this *facies* was not observed, instances of recovery could be found under all kinds of treatment. Again, the fatal cases gave indications of *blood* poison. Almost the first symptom observed, even before the mother became seriously ill at all, was the death of the infant taking place suddenly with narcotic symptoms, poisoned by the breast-milk. In others the false membranes effused in the abdominal cavity with serum was so rapid that they seemed rather to be the result of decomposition of the blood than inflammation. The acid state of the serum was to be noted in other examples. Bleeding in such cases, he believed, was contra-indicated by all known physiological rules. So also in puerperal peritonitis, which prevailed at the same time as erysipelas. He believed every epidemic, as well as every case, was to be studied by itself, and treated upon broad, general principles, and not necessarily by bloodletting as a panacea. Some of Mr. Mitchell's cases might probably be only of the nature of those examples observed in hospitals for women, which generally yielded to local depletion, with turpentine stupes, and without venesection.

Mr. CLEVELAND thought the paper would have been more valuable if the cases had been more minutely detailed. In all diseases of such importance as the one under consideration the cases should be reported at sufficient length to furnish, as far as possible, the means of forming an independent diagnosis. Had not an error of diagnosis been made in reference to some of the cases that had been adduced? He (Mr. Cleveland) had met with only two cases of puerperal fever. The first he had treated with calomel and opium and stimulants. In the second he had resorted to venesection, as well as leeching. In both cases the result was unfavorable. In one an inspection revealed pus in the uterine veins. In both there was a dark, sloughy state of the placental surface of the uterus, as well as intense peritonitis. With regard to treatment, he would, in the event of meeting with another case, give quinine in large doses, combined with opium. His experience of the marked benefit resulting from the use of the former remedy in some low forms of inflammation, but more especially in erysipelas, would induce him to pursue this plan of treatment.

MAY 7TH, 1862.

DR. TYLER SMITH, President, in the Chair.

Present—34 Fellows and 3 visitors.

The titles were read of upwards of 200 works on obstetric medicine, presented to the Society by Sir Charles Locock, Bart., M.D., &c., the Honorary President.

The following gentleman was duly elected a Fellow of the Society:—Robert Henry Spencer Carpenter, L.S.A., Carr Villa, Durham.

NOTE ON THE STATE OF THE INTERNAL SURFACE OF THE UTERUS AFTER DELIVERY.

By J. MATTHEWS DUNCAN, M.D.,

HONORARY FELLOW OF THE OBSTETRICAL SOCIETY OF LONDON, ETC.

No greater step has in modern times been made in the department of obstetrical physiology than the establishment of the true anatomy of the decidua vera and decidua reflexa, and the light shed by these discoveries on various natural and morbid functions and processes has led to a great extension of obstetrical knowledge. The unsatisfactory nature of the old, erroneous theories of John Hunter regarding the decidual membranes is quite equalled by the unsatisfactory and unscientific doctrines generally taught regarding the same parts after labour or miscarriage. Although it appears to me that the unreasonableness of these doctrines and their inconsistence with facts have been well demonstrated, and that satisfactory though incomplete descriptions of the true anatomy of the mucous membrane of the uterus after delivery have been substituted for the old errors; yet it is evident, from an extensive acquaintance with obstetrical literature, that the old errors still flourish in the schools. Many authors, indeed, seem quite insensible of the immense importance of the subject. Others, among whom I may cite the justly eminent and highly enlightened Baron Dubois, of Paris, still appear to cling to the old doctrine, connected with the name of Cruveilhier, that after delivery the muscular tissue of the body of the uterus is everywhere laid bare. In describing the internal plane of muscular fibres of the uterus after delivery, Dubois makes the following remarks:*—"Nous avons cherché à distinguer sur la coupe même de l'organe, de trois à sept jours après l'accouchement, les traces de la muqueuse en voie de régénération, nous n'avons jamais pu les distinguer. . . . La couche musculaire existe immédiatement au-dessous de la masse sanieuse d'un gris brunâtre, qui après la coction, remplit constamment l'organe chez les nouvelles accouchées." But while this great accoucheur adheres to these views, his compatriot, M. Robin, has contributed to this department of science microscopic researches of great value, tending to the establishment of rational views which I long ago espoused. My object in presenting this note to the Obstetrical Society of London is to call the attention of that body to the present state of the subject, with a view to its further elucidation by the members, and to the extension through the profession of the true doctrines. It is needless to remark how extensive the bearings of this subject are; their importance is at once attested by the recollection that puerperal fever is one of the diseases for whose comprehension the knowledge of this subject is essential.

The very few remarks I wish to make may be conveniently arranged according to the topics; first, regarding

[1] 'Traité complet de l'art des accouchements,' par MM. Dubois et Pajot, tome i, livr. 2me, p. 430.

the internal surface of the body of the uterus, exclusive of the placental site; second, the placental site; and third, the reproduction of uterine mucous membrane after delivery or during pregnancy. The condition of the internal surface of the cervical portion of the uterus may be left entirely out of this note, for no great difference of opinion has ever existed regarding it.

1. THE INTERNAL SURFACE OF THE BODY OF THE UTERUS, EXCLUSIVE OF THE PLACENTAL SITE.

I have elsewhere[1] taken pains to show that the modern errors regarding the condition of this part, as taught by Cruveilhier and others, are departures from the older and truer teaching of the great William Hunter. I have shown that the anatomy of the decidua truly given and carefully described by William Hunter was supplanted by a jumble of errors introduced into science by his brother John. In like manner, William Hunter's views as to the condition of the mucous membranes of the uterus after delivery have been lost sight of, and it only remains for us now to restore them to their proper place. On this subject he says, in his 'Anatomical Description of the Human Gravid Uterus,' "This membrane (the decidua) is an efflorescence of the internal coat of the uterus itself, and is, therefore, shed as often as a woman bears a child or suffers a miscarriage. It is of considerable thickness, and *one stratum of it is always left upon the uterus after delivery*, most of which dissolves and comes away with the lochia."

My own observations support the conclusion of William Hunter, and appear to me further to justify the statement that at no time during pregnancy or after it is the decidua thrown off in mass or the muscular tissue denuded. In the course of pregnancy, as the superficial layers of the decidua gradually become obsolete and caducous, new growth of mucous membrane takes place beneath the old; and at whatever time miscarriage may take place, the separated decidua leaves always a layer covering the internal surface of the uterus.

[1] 'Edinburgh Medical Journal,' February, 1858.

The observations of the late Dr. Chisholm,[1] of Virchow,[1] of Priestley, and of M. Robin, confute the unphilosophical views of Cruveilhier and his followers, and support those just referred to as having been long ago published by William Hunter, but subsequently forgotten.

A thesis of M. Colin is mentioned by Priestley,[2] and cited by Robin,[3] as enunciating views identical with those supported in this note, but I have not been fortunate enough to see it.

2. The placental site.

It is natural to suppose that this part of the interior of the uterus will, more than any other, be completely denuded of mucous structures; for here we have, not merely the supposed throwing off of old decidual membrane, but the separation of the highly vascular placenta, suddenly and in the midst of its functions, leaving a bleeding surface behind. I have been represented as holding that the persistence of a layer of mucous membrane at this part was less probable than its persistence over the rest of the uterine surface.[4] Now, in my original paper on this subject, published in October, 1853, I assert that after delivery the persistent layer of mucous membrane "is found, as in early pregnancy, to be thicker at the site of the insertion of the placenta than elsewhere."[5] It was, indeed, the examination of this part, and especially the observation of sinuses still opening upon its surface after the thick mucous membrane was easily and plainly seen, that first strongly attracted my attention to the subject; for this observation made it plain that the old theory of Cruveilhier and, I may now add, the young theory of Heschl, were fundamentally erroneous, their view being that a new mucous membrane was developed over the denuded uterine surfaces, and, therefore, covering

1 'Edinburgh Medical Journal,' December, 1857.

2 'Lectures on the Development of the Gravid Uterus,' p. 98.

3 'Mémoires de l'Académie Impériale de Médecine,' 1861, p. 150.

4 Churchill, 'Theory and Practice of Midwifery.' Edition 1860, p. 230.

5 'British and Foreign Medico-Chirurgical Review,' October, 1853, p. 509.

up the sinuses, the demonstration of whose open condition made the view untenable.

Since my first investigations I have had opportunities of carefully examining the uterine surface at the placental site after natural labour and in a suicide near the full time, in whom I artificially separated the organ with a view to this question. In some of these studies I had the valued assistance of the late Mr. Barlow, of this town, who, by microscopic examinations, made out the existence of structures such as have more recently been fully described by Priestley,[1] and especially by Robin. This last observer has now arrived at the same conclusions as I had previously announced. In his elaborate paper, published in the 'Memoirs of the Imperial Academy of Medicine,'[2] he says that of the utero-placental area of the mucous membrane of the uterus there is only a small, superficial portion caducous, the greater part remaining permanently adherent to the uterus, and that this persisting portion has a thickness increasing in proportion to the contraction of the muscular layer of the organ.

3. THE REPRODUCTION OF UTERINE MUCOUS MEMBRANE AFTER DELIVERY OR DURING PREGNANCY.

M. Robin and Dr. Priestley believe that, in the course of pregnancy, after its fourth month has passed, the whole mucous membrane of the uterus, or the whole decidua, with the exception of the serotina, is thrown off from the subjacent muscular layer, being displaced by a new mucous lamina which at that time springs up beneath the old decidua. Up till 1858 Robin believed that a somewhat similar series of changes occurred after delivery at the site of the serotina or old site of the placenta, but now[3] he holds that the layer of serotina persisting after delivery is, in no sense, caducous, and continues attached to the muscular uterine wall.

The part of M. Robin's views last described, as only

[1] 'Lectures on the Development of the Gravid Uterus,' p. 97.

[2] 'Mémoires de l'Académie Impériale de Médecine,' 1861, p. 137.

[3] Loc. cit., p. 137.

recently adopted by him, coincides with what I have ever maintained. From all the other opinions of Robin and Priestley on this point I dissent. Their published observations do not seem to me to afford any good grounds for their statements. Every one admits that a great amount of effete decidual structures is observed outside the chorion in advanced pregnancy, and it is only natural to suppose that, as superficial layers are shed or exfoliated, new structures are springing up to replace them. In this way it may be quite true that the old decidua is removed and a new mucous membrane appears. But in this sense the same may be asserted of the muscular layer of the uterus after delivery; the old has disappeared by absorption, and new muscular structures have replaced it; yet, after all, it is the same muscular layer. This is not the meaning of M. Robin and Dr. Priestley. They adhere to the old and, I believe, erroneous notion that the whole uterine mucous membrane of early pregnancy is deciduous or caducous, and is replaced by an entirely new membrane, the peculiar difference of their opinion from the older notions being this, namely, that while, according to the latter, it was at delivery that the decidua was torn off or thrown off, leaving the muscular structure denuded, according to the former it is about the middle of pregnancy that the decidua is separated and a new mucous membrane begins to be regenerated. This implies that at some time the muscular layer is laid bare, and produces on its surface a mucous tissue heterologous to it. On theoretical grounds this view appears to be untenable, and my observations in cases of miscarriage lend no support to it.

Dr. PRIESTLEY said that he would not long occupy the time of the Society, but as Dr. Matthews Duncan had made frequent reference to his published observations, he craved permission to say a few words. The chief questions at issue were, 1st, What is the condition of the interior of the uterus after delivery? and 2nd, By what process does the interior of the uterus regain the condition of the unimpregnated organ? In reference to the first point, Dr. Priestley had no hesitation in expressing his conviction that the sagacious opinion of William Hunter, so ably discussed and confirmed by the researches of Dr. Duncan, was the correct one. The plane of muscular fibres lying next the cavity of the uterus was not denuded in the way described by M. Cruveilhier, and the interior of the uterus was only so far analogous to a stump after amputation that large divided vessels were found open at the placental spot. In reference to the second point, he differed from Dr. Duncan so far that he believed the chief portion of the laminæ lying next the uterine cavity after delivery not to be composed of regularly formed epithelial particles, such as form mucous membranes generally, but to consist of irregular cells, fibro-cellular structures, and fat-granules, identical with those found in the decidua in the latter periods of pregnancy. Shreds of these laminæ floated out when the preparation was placed in water, and they were gradually shed off as lochia during the patient's convalescence. Beneath these, however, the microscopic observer found small and regular epithelial particles, not mature at the time of delivery, but embryonic in character, and probably the progeny of the original mucous membrane. The epithelial cells forming the mucous membrane of the uterus at the time of conception were, no doubt, transformed into the fibro-cellular structures of the decidua, and hence the reproduction from the basement membrane, during the latter half of pregnancy, of those cell-particles which were intended to replace the original mucous membrane.

A CASE OF UNSUSPECTED PREGNANCY AND LABOUR.

By Thomas Hawkes Tanner, M.D.,

ASSISTANT-PHYSICIAN FOR THE DISEASES OF WOMEN AND CHILDREN TO KING'S COLLEGE HOSPITAL, ETC.

I was sent for on Thursday morning, 17th April, 1862, at nine o'clock, to see Mrs. G., forty-two years of age, who had been suffering great pain in the abdomen since eleven o'clock on the preceding night. This lady had previously sought my advice on some half dozen occasions. She last consulted me at the beginning of March for an attack of indigestion, on which occasion no mention was made of any enlargement of the abdomen, nor was there any swelling perceptible through her dress. She has been married rather more than three years (since February, 1859), and stated that she had never been pregnant. The catamenia were last on some time in June, 1861; but as they had been very scanty for five or six months before, this circumstance did not particularly attract her attention. In fact she attributed the cessation to the change of life.

On my arrival at the patient's house I found her in bed, complaining of great abdominal pain, which had kept her awake the whole night. Her husband and mother-in-law were present, as well as a married sister who had borne children. I was told that Mrs. G. had not been well for a fortnight, her breath having been short on making any exertion, and her legs having become swollen. On Wednesday night, at eleven o'clock, she suddenly began to suffer from pain in the stomach, for the relief of which her friends applied a mustard poultice. At 2 o'clock a.m. the sufferings were so great, that a neighbouring medical man was sent for. This gentleman was unable to attend, but sent his assistant, who stated that the illness was due to "flatulence and inflammation of the bowels." He gave a bottle of medicine, the second dose of which, however, caused sickness, and failed to afford any relief.

On examining the abdomen I discovered an oval tumour distinctly, occupying the right side, and extending from the pelvis to some two inches above the umbilicus. It seemed to be about the size of the adult head; but although the abdominal parietes were thin, the tumour was by no means distinct to the sight, though it was readily made out on palpation. On making a vaginal examination I found the os uteri dilated to the size of a crown piece, and the head of a fœtus entering the brim of the pelvis, with the vertex presenting. The membranes were ruptured; but the patient was not conscious of any discharge of water having taken place, and there was no appearance of moisture on the bed upon which she had been lying all night. On inspecting the breasts a narrow brown areola was seen; but it certainly did not exceed half an inch in width. When Mrs. G. was asked if she had felt any movements in her abdomen, she allowed that she had occasionally experienced curious sensations for some weeks past, but these were attributed to flatulence. During the whole period of pregnancy there had been neither sickness nor any feeling of nausea. The moderate increase in size which was perceptible had been attributed to the natural deposition of fat, for all the members of her family are disposed to be stout.

As the pains were not violent, and the head did not advance, I left the case at nine o'clock, after explaining its nature; but this explanation was received with incredulity, neither the patient nor her husband having the slightest suspicion that pregnancy existed. The sister, however, took steps for obtaining the loan of some baby-linen, &c.

At half-past one in the afternoon, when I returned, the pains of labour were strong and of frequent occurrence. The head was low down and the parts fully dilated. After waiting an hour the violence of the pains and their slight effect upon the fœtal head led me to fear that rupture of the uterus might take place, unless relief could be quickly afforded; and therefore I applied the short forceps, and easily effected delivery. The child, a female, was born with animation suspended; but, by a persevering use of artificial respiration, it was resuscitated at the end of half an hour. Although small it seemed to be a mature infant; and it is now (6th May) strong and healthy.

The medico-legal bearings of the foregoing curious case are so apparent, that they need but little comment. The history, however, seems to establish the fact that a woman may conceive, may go to the full term of gestation, and may be in labour for ten hours, without having any suspicion that she is pregnant. It ought perhaps to be mentioned that from all I have seen and heard of Mrs. G. no doubt whatever is entertained but that her statements may be taken as strictly true. Independently of this circumstance it so happens that both parents, though they despaired of ever having a child, were most anxious for one; and the birth of the little girl is, therefore, regarded as the happiest event which could befall them.

BRIEF REMARKS ON ANÆSTHESIA IN MIDWIFERY.

By Thomas Skinner, M.D., &c.

The object of the author was to show the safety with which chloroform could be employed to relieve the pains of parturition, and to exhibit a simple apparatus by which anæsthetic agents might be economically administered.

Dr. Priestley considered Dr. Skinner's apparatus ingenious; and as it allowed air to pass freely through its texture, it was not open to the same objections as a mask or other instrument. It seemed to him somewhat fragile, and might be easily broken when clutched by partially insensible patients. The bottle arrangement he believed would prove useful, and might effect an important economy in chloroform.

Dr. Graily Hewitt thought it important that the duration of the labour in cases where chloroform was given should be stated. He had found that chloroform sometimes exercised a most decided effect in putting a stop to the progress of labour, and that in cases where anæsthesia was for other reasons most indicated.

A PRACTICAL INQUIRY INTO THE PROPERTIES OF NITRATE OF SILVER, WITH AN ACCOUNT OF A NEW INSTRUMENT FOR ITS USE IN UTERINE DISEASE.

By Robert Ellis,

OBSTETRIC SURGEON TO THE CHELSEA AND BELGRAVE DISPENSARY.

The nitrate of silver is a substance so familiar to the surgeon that the author feels as if an apology were needed for an inquiry into its properties before the members of this Society. It is, however, because the subject is so commonplace, and the substance so much in our hands, that such an inquiry becomes important, and especially if there exist erroneous views as to its therapeutic influence and physiological properties,—and such is really the case. By some obstetrists this substance, in its fused state as the lunar caustic, of which alone the writer proposes to treat in this paper, is reckoned an active escharotic; by others as not entitled to any such consideration. Since these opinions necessarily influence and determine the practice of those who hold them, it becomes very desirable, if possible, to decide the true position of this most valuable agent.

Many years ago Mr. Higginbottom, in his excellent treatise on the properties of this substance, denied the escharotic power of the nitrate of silver, and attributed simply stimulant and astringent characters to this salt. Others have since then repeated this opinion, and in a recent communication to a medical journal the following expressions are employed in reference to this subject:

"My experience," says this writer, "teaches me that nitrate of silver is no more a caustic than tincture of cantharides, as Mr. Higginbottom has long ago asserted. The distinction that Dr. Meigs draws between the antiphlogistic touches and the escharotic action of nitrate of silver does not bear examination. Use it as you may, the nitrate of silver does not cauterize. Leave it in the neck of the womb, it will cause more pain, loss of blood, and subsequent discharge, but no destruction of tissue, unless coagulated mucus mixed up with epithelial scales and insoluble chlorides of silver can be called such. Even when applied to a fungous ulcer, the slight loss of substance is rather due to the friction of a hard body on a pulpy surface than to the chemical combination of the neutral salt and the diseased tissues. A densely hypertrophied neck of the womb might be whitened with the solid nitrate of silver every fourth day until doomsday without much reducing its bulk. Indeed, I have seen such a plan of treatment injudiciously continued for a year or longer in a case of hysteralgia, the neck of the womb being healthy and of an average size, and the effects were rather astringent than caustic, condensing the tissues, narrowing the cervical canal, and rendering its dilatation necessary and difficult. Thus, while nitrate of silver may be repeatedly applied without inducing a loss of substance, the slightest application of the potassa fusa to the neck of the womb produces an evident loss of substance; and therefore the two agents, however applied, produce totally different effects in similar cases."

In opposition to this statement the opinion of Dr. Meigs and of Recamier, of Dr. Tyler Smith, and of others, is that the nitrate of silver is strictly an escharotic substance, producing loss of tissue and a slough. By some obstetrists it is regarded as an active escharotic, but by others as a substance the caustic properties of which greatly depend on the manner in which it is employed. The large and constant employment of this substance in the treatment of uterine disease seems to justify some attempt at gaining the truth in regard to its real properties, and the remarks now about to be made are intended by the writer for this end.

An escharotic is defined by pharmacologists as a substance capable of destroying both the structure and life of a part, and consequently giving rise to the formation of a slough or eschar. The precise views of Liebig on the influence of poisons on the living tissues express the true action of an escharotic in a more complete manner. And in reference to the particular substance under consideration, he remarks —"When nitrate of silver is applied to skin or muscular fibre, it combines with them instantaneously. The compounds thus formed are so stable that they cannot be decomposed by other powerful chemical agents. Parts of the body united to salts of silver no longer belong to the living organism, for their vital functions have been arrested by combination with the oxide of silver; and if they are capable of being reproduced, the neighbouring living structures throw them off in the form of an eschar." The opinion that nitrate of silver is an escharotic is here clearly entertained, and is based upon the consideration of its chemical behaviour when in contact with organic substances.

Without an unnecessary refinement, it may, perhaps, be taken for granted that the action of an escharotic substance, —confining our attention only to chemical escharotics, is that it disorganizes living tissue, and by giving a fixed chemical character to it prohibits the continuance of the functions of life in the part which has undergone this change. That there should be a difference in the chemical activity of different escharotics may well be understood. And those are most powerful, for the purpose of the surgeon, which have their chemical affinity for combination with organic substances most intensely active. But beyond this no proper distinction can be maintained between what are called the stronger and such as are esteemed the weaker of these agents. Their common character is that they destroy life and structure, and the product of their destruction, being no longer capable of metamorphosis in the living body, is cast off in the form of the eschar.

Nitrate of silver is characterised by these properties, and it is of much practical importance that this should be clearly understood, and the mistake of comparing it to such an agent as the tincture of cantharides fully exposed. This salt forms definite chemical combination with the albumen and fibrin of the structures to which it is applied, and in so doing renders them incapable of further change—in fact, kills them. The writer has a special object in insisting on this definition of the action of this substance, which will immediately be made evident. It is, however, objected to this view that the action of this salt is well known in practice to be extremely superficial when applied to the skin, and scarcely deserving of the name of an escharotic. Dr. Pereira classifies it as among the substances which do not effect the complete destruction of parts, which the escharotics do. This error has arisen from a want of consideration of the proper action of this caustic. When applied to the skin it undoubtedly acts quite superficially, if *the epidermis be intact;* but if that be removed, and nitrate of silver be applied to the surface of a blister, or to that of an ulcer, its action is no longer superficial. Being permitted by the increase and irregularity of surface to penetrate deeper into the tissues, it is capable of destroying their vitality and producing a slough.

This substance may therefore be defined as a true escharotic, of a low power of penetration. Its action is limited by two circumstances—first, by the remarkably dense and impermeable character of its compound with the albumen and fibrin of the structures, by reason of which its penetration is to a great extent impeded; and second, by the abundance of chloride of sodium to be found in the tissues to which it is applied, and with which it forms an insoluble compound of chloride of silver. An interesting and simple experiment may be made, which in a remarkable manner illustrates the first of these statements. If a strong solution of nitrate of silver be poured into a glass vessel, and a few drops of fluid albumen (as from an egg) be dropped into it, the albumen becomes immediately converted into a dense, white, semi-solid substance, a true compound of organic matter with silver. On making a section of this it will be seen that the action of the salt is chiefly confined to the surface, while the central part remains unaffected. In this manner we have a distinct evidence of the great impermeability of the albumen-silver compound, and can well understand the low penetration of the nitrate of silver into the living structures. With the abundant presence of the chloride of sodium in the body we are all familiar. In the perspiration it is brought to the surface of the skin, and thus limits the action of the nitrate applied there. And in the mucus secreted by the mouth or in the genito-urinary passages sufficient is contained, also, to impede the caustic effect of this salt.

But considered in its relation to our uses as obstetrists, it must not be forgotten that the substance is applied to a region of the body, the canal of the cervix uteri, which of all others exposes the largest amount of surface, by reason of the rugose character of the membrane and the large size of the villi which stud its surface. Numerous orifices of excretory glands likewise present additional facilities for the deep penetration of any caustic substance. The application of the lunar caustic to such a structure cannot fail to be attended with the large decomposition of living tissue, since it is penetrated by it on every side, and the result is the production of a true slough or eschar. Provided the stick be held in contact with this surface for a minute or two, the delicate structure of the villi, and that of a superficial portion of the mucous membrane underlying the fine epithelium of this part, cannot fail to be destroyed. In practice, as is well known, this is really the case, and a true slough is thrown off. That this eschar is something more than coagulated mucus the writer has satisfied himself by an examination of it under the microscope. The effect of the nitrate of silver on tissues is such as to confuse their structure when microscopically examined, but it is not difficult to get a certain amount of proof in support of this statement if care be used.

In order, as far as possible, to end all question on the action of the nitrate of silver on organized structures, the writer has carefully investigated the subject, by observing the behaviour of the web of the frog under the microscope, when treated with minute portions of this escharotic. Some very interesting phenomena presented themselves in the course of this inquiry. Immediately after placing a minute crystal of the caustic on the surface of the web there was a sudden cessation of all circulation in the capillaries, not merely beneath the caustic, but in a large area around. This was apparently not so much due to the mechanical obstruction to the passage of the blood-globules in the part touched as to a kind of nervous shock communicated to the blood-vessels. Then there was a gradually lessening freedom of circulation in the larger blood-vessels beyond; to this succeeded a great dilatation of those vessels, and of the capillaries, as much as to double their former size. The crystal of nitrate of silver was the focus of this mischief, which radiated from it on every side. The eschar was remarkably distinct, in the form of a minute circular spot just under the caustic. The tissue here, seen under a 1-8th object-glass, was contracted, and evidently dead and destroyed. It consisted of a blackish mass of capillaries, choked with burst globules, and of basement membrane and epithelial scales, all as if fused together by the caustic. Its limits were most precisely defined and sharp cut, even under the eye of the microscope. Its margin was marked by a livid-red line, consisting of gorged capillaries, and in part of blood-globules forced out into the surrounding interspaces. For some little distance around there was no movement of globules in the capillaries, and, in fact, a condition of congestion and inflammation was already begun. The death of tissue was thus manifested to the eye, for it was obviously impossible that circulation of blood could ever be re-established in a part so entirely altered and confused in its structure as that underlying the caustic.

The subsequent events were also interesting. In twenty hours lymph was effused all round the eschar, and at its edges a process of separation of the dead from the living was commenced by the softening of the marginal tissues. A new direction to the circulation was given, and the eschar became surrounded by a vivid zone of blood-vessels, in which great activity of flow was evident. The eschar, as a dot of dead structure, lay in a little hollow formed by the living, raised margin around it. A crowd of colourless corpuscles lining the walls of these marginal blood-vessels seemed to be occupied in the work of separation going forward. In from seventy to eighty hours the little eschar separated and dropped out, leaving a small, round hole in the web, as clean as if punched out. At the end of a week the edges of the perforation were smoothed down, and in a little time became covered with epithelium and pigment-cells. Whether the hole is ultimately sealed up or not the writer was unable to ascertain. In the animals under observation it remained unclosed for several weeks.

In contrast with the action of this substance, a crystal of cantharidine was placed on the web. It produced distinct vesication, with effusion of serosity under the epithelium, but there was no eschar or separation of tissue whatever. An intense degree of inflammation, with effusion of lymph, were the sole results.

These experiments, which were very often repeated by the writer, seem to exhibit to the eye what chemistry already teaches us as to the true action of nitrate of silver, and they represent it as combining with and killing the animal structure, the dead portion being then cast off by the living around it. Many other irritants and escharotic substances were used, with differing results. Among other interesting observations it was constantly remarked that the more powerful the escharotic the less the degree of pain given to the animal. Thus, for example, the actual cautery, in the shape of a white-hot wire, was scarcely perceived by the animal when the web was touched by it, while severe struggles followed the application of a small fragment of nitrate of silver, thus giving force to the principle already laid down by the author—that in the human subject the weakest escharotics are far more painful than the more powerful.

The writer has thus attempted to illustrate thetrue chemical and physiological behaviour of this important and valuable substance. To the obstetric surgeon it is indeed invaluable. It is essentially characterised by its strict limits of action, a point well made out under the microscope; by its active and yet most manageable properties as a caustic substance; by its powerfully astringent and stimulant qualities, and by the healthy and kindly healing surface which results from its escharotic use. These are properties possessed by few, if any other, of our escharotic substances, and they render this one in a special manner applicable for the treatment of most of the ulcerative diseases of the os uteri. To produce its full effect as an escharotic it is necessary to use it most firmly, and with a certain degree of friction and rotation. By this means it penetrates below the surface, and an eschar of sufficient depth can be readily obtained. But nitrate of silver, in its ordinary form of lunar caustic, is wholly unfit for this kind of service, in consequence of its great brittleness; and the constantly recurring annoyance which has arisen to obstetrists out of this defect has led of late to several attempts at its removal.

Commercially, the nitrate of silver is sold in large, tabular crystals. These contain a certain amount of water of crystallisation, with a very little free nitric acid. When heated to a certain point, the crystals fuse and the nitrate may be run into moulds; in this manner the ordinary lunar caustic is made. The mould, which is usually made of brass, and electro-plated inside, has a number of cylindrical grooves in it, and thus many sticks are cast in one operation. In order to ensure perfectly white caustic, it is necessary to melt it with care in a silver ladle. It is probably because the fused material is very quickly cooled that it is so extremely brittle, as it is generally found in commerce; and a good way of procuring caustic much less friable than common is to allow the mould very slowly to become cooled.

Many attempts have been made to remedy this defect, with more or less success. Within the last year or two great efforts have been made by the operative chemists to give to their caustic the character of toughness while preserving its purity. The admixture of a certain proportion of chloride of silver,—which may be fused into a substance called by the old chemists horn silver,—with the nitrate, to a great degree diminishes the brittleness of the latter. But this kind of caustic has the disadvantage of being much less active as an escharotic, and also, owing to the photographic properties of the chloride of silver, it becomes quite black by exposure to the light. Its use was consequently soon discontinued. Another method of communicating a certain degree of toughness to the caustic consists in the addition of a small quantity of the nitrate of lead to the fused mass. The effect of this is certainly sufficiently good to justify the addition, and a tolerably firm pencil is secured thereby. But in this, as in all other instances, the caustic is weakened in exact proportion to the amount of foreign matter introduced. The admixture of a small per-centage of the nitrate of potash (the toughness of which in a fused state is well exemplified in the common sal-prunel ball) is likewise of service in destroying the brittleness of the caustic cylinder, and the varieties of tough caustic now sold by different London chemists will be found to contain one or other of the ingredients named, in addition to the nitrate of silver. The very slow cooling of the fused mass may also be taken advantage of in preparing these specimens of a not-friable caustic. Some of the best makers of this variety of caustic have sent specimens to the author for practical use, and some are now shown to the Society.

The writer has been pressed by the makers of tough caustic to give an opinion as to its value in practice, and he would observe with regret that, without any exception, this caustic fails to answer the expectations that might be formed of it. After the first or second use it is no longer tough, but nearly as friable as common caustic, and the writer has more than once broken off a considerable piece of it high up in the cervical canal. It would appear as if the moisture of the surface to which it is used penetrated its substance and robbed it of the strong cohesive property which it possesses when newly fused. It will be observed that the makers enclose this caustic in sealed glass tubes, evidently because of the injurious action of damp upon its tenacity.

If it be desirable to produce a very firm and tenacious caustic cylinder, the writer has long since suggested the best way of doing this, which is by mixing up with the fused material a small quantity of long asbestos fibres. These will hold the crystalline particles together, and the preparation is not influenced by damp. The tenacity given to common mortar by the mixture of hair with it gives a practical example of the value of this suggestion.

But the whole difficulty has, in the writer's opinion, been long since removed by the simple and useful instrument now shown to this Society. A modification of this instrument has been in constant use by the writer for more than ten years, and was exhibited by him with the perforated caustic more than eight years ago at a meeting of the Western Medical Society. More recently this invention has been taken up by the French surgeons, whether with or without the knowledge of its original source the writer is unable to say. But the author desires to put on record this claim to the originality of his instrument, a condensed account of it being contained in the proceedings of the society just named.

The simple idea of the instrument is the solid and unyielding support given to the brittle caustic by passing a metallic pin through the centre of the cylinder. To effect this the caustic must be cast hollow, and after some little

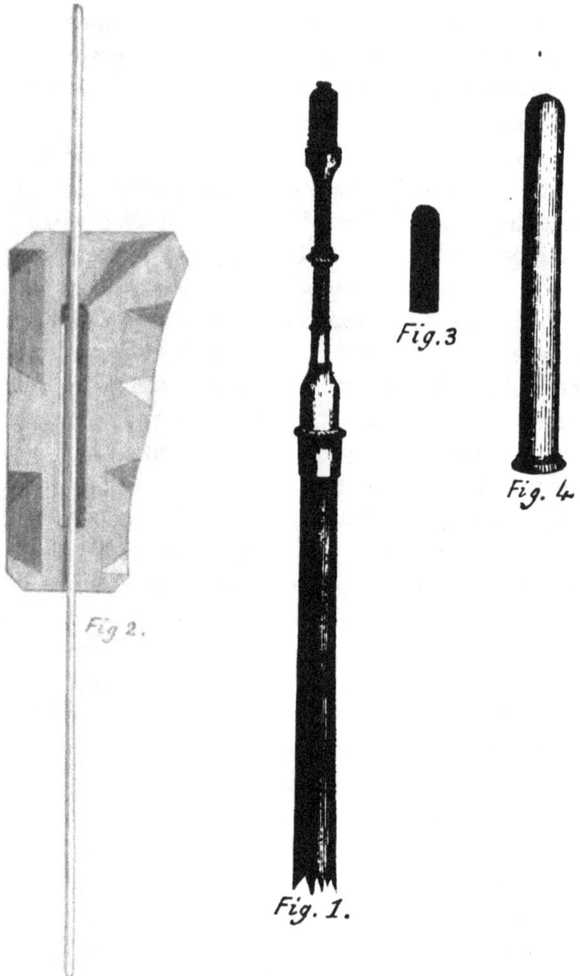

Fig. 1 represents the caustic-holder mounted on the quill, and fitted with perforated caustic.

" 2 shows the mould for the caustic, in section, with the steel wire which forms the core.

" 3, a piece of perforated caustic.

" 4, the cover, with the aperture at its end.

trouble the writer succeeded in making a simple mould by which it can be accomplished. The moulds employed are of two forms, that for casting cylinders and the original one for casting bullets of caustic. In each case the central perforation is produced, as shown in the cut, by passing a polished steel pin through a hole in the upper and lower halves of the mould, and the fused caustic is then poured into the mould. On solidifying, the pin is easily withdrawn, and a hollow bullet or stick of caustic is produced. In practice it is found best to lubricate the mould and the steel wire with a little oil occasionally. The caustic is thus readily detached from both. Specimens of hollow sticks and bullets of this substance are now on the table, together with the moulds used in their fabrication.

The caustic-holder differs in many respects from the ordinary form, but is really quite as simple, and by no means liable to injury or derangement. It consists of a small socket of silver, bisected and carried on the halves of a slender metallic support, grooved internally, and externally cut to a spiral thread, on which a nut works to and fro. The cylinder of caustic drops about one eighth of an inch into this socket, and a platinum pin, exactly like a common pin, is passed through it and between the halves of the stem. The little nut is now worked upwards, and the pin being secured by its pressure, a perfectly firm and unbreakable cylinder of caustic is held by the instrument.

There are two parts of this caustic-holder to which, in addition, the author invites the notice of this meeting—the stalk and the cover. The former is made of a large porcupine quill, the polish, elasticity, lightness, and strength of which make it an invaluable handle for a surgical tool, and especially for one frequently immersed in water. The cover is *perforated* at its end, and by this simple contrivance the caustic is always kept dry and hard, instead of in the half deliquescent and filthy condition in which it is found in the holders with covers hermetically closed at the end. The small perforation at the end admits the air to the caustic, and causes the evaporation of any fluid which may hang about it. The comfort and handiness of this instrument is promoted to no slight extent by these two features in its construction, and the writer can strongly commend them to the notice of other obstetric practitioners.

For many years the author has used no other caustic holder or caustic than that here described; and having had during that time a very large experience of the value of this simple invention, he would now beg to offer it for the use of others similarly engaged. The instrument and the perforated caustic may be procured at several of the best instrument makers,[1] and the writer can assure any who make trial of it that in a very short time it will save its cost in the extraordinary economy with which it can be used, the caustic being available to the last fragment. In conclusion, the writer would observe that it has been objected to him by some surgeons that it is rather a benefit than otherwise to leave a piece of caustic behind in the cervical canal. The severe pain, the great amount of hæmorrhage and discharge, and the extensive excoriation of the external parts, which follow this surgical blunder in treating diseases of the cervix uteri are, in the writer's opinion, a sufficient condemnation of the accident. The deliberate practice of breaking it off intentionally is certainly not warranted by its results nor necessary to the cure of disease.

[1] Mr. Coxeter, who was employed by the writer in the first instance to make this instrument, has succeeded extremely well in its production, and also in that of the perforated caustic.

June 4th, 1862.

Dr. TYLER SMITH, President, in the Chair.

Present—33 Fellows and 5 visitors.

The following gentlemen were duly elected Fellows of the Society:—John Ellam, Esq., L.R.C.P. Lond., Nottingham; Thomas Prytherch, Esq., L.R.C.P. Edin.

CASE OF A LARGE FIBROUS TUMOUR IMPEDING DELIVERY.

By Henry M. Madge, M.D.

Nearly all the cases of the above description that I have been able to find in the writings of our leading authors have been fatal to both mother and child, the primary causes of death in both instances being the same, namely, protracted labour and the manipulations rendered necessary to effect delivery. This great fatality has given rise to various suggestions in the way of treatment. Among other plans the induction of premature labour and the Cæsarean section have been recommended. When the state of the patient is actually known, I think we should be disposed to adopt the induction of premature labour as the very best and safest proceeding; but in primiparous patients, who are frequently disposed rather to keep in the dark than to enlighten the medical attendant, and, where there are no very striking circumstances to excite suspicion, the case is almost certain to go on to the full period; we must then have recourse to other measures, and, as far as I have investigated the subject, where the tumour is large, requiring much force to push it upwards, the Cæsarean section appears to me to offer the best chance for the patient's safety. It has been found that, whether the patient is left to the fearful odds of struggling through labour with a large tumour in the pelvis, whether removal by excision or enucleation of the tumour is attempted, or whether the tumour opened, or unopened, is pushed above the brim of the pelvis, the result is nearly always the same—death in a few days from peritonitis, shock, and exhaustion. The following history forms another addition to the list of these unfortunate cases.

Mrs. H—, æt. 27, primipara, well grown, in robust health, and who had gone her full time, was taken with slight labour pains on the morning of May 21st. On making an examination in the after part of the day I found the pelvis occupied by a large, round tumour, which at first appeared to me to be the child's head. It seemed, however, to be lifting up, as it were, and pushing forwards the posterior wall of the vagina. It was low down, and came lower, but receding again, with every pain. It appeared to fill up every niche in the pelvis, so that the finger could not be passed around it. The os uteri could not be felt. Next day the tumour was occupying precisely the same position. The pains were still slight and not frequent, and, as the patient was in her usual health and spirits, it was considered advisable to wait. In the evening, with considerable difficulty, by hooking my finger high up behind the symphisis pubis, I was enabled to reach the os uteri; it was directed forwards, dilated to about the size of a crown-piece, and, as well as I could make out, some part of the breech presented. On the following day Dr. West, Mr. Spencer Wells, and Mr. Newton, met me in consultation. Pains getting more frequent. As some parts of the tumour felt soft and yielding, a trocar was introduced, and a small portion of fluid drawn off. Vain attempts had been made previously to push the tumour above the brim of the pelvis. Chloroform having been administered, and the catheter used, the opening in the tumour was enlarged. Mr. Spencer Wells was then enabled to push the tumour upwards, and, with the aid of a blunt hook, the child was brought down by the buttock. When born it had some faint signs of life, but could not be made to breathe. In the early part of the following day the patient seemed to be doing well; as the day advanced, by fits and starts she became very excited, and could not be persuaded to lie still. Peritonitis set in in the afternoon, and she died on the third day after confinement.

Autopsy, eighteen hours after death.—The peritoneum was universally inflamed, and here and there were large, dark-red patches. There was but little effused lymph; some of the small intestines, a good deal distended with gases, were slightly glued together, and lying underneath the viscera there was about a pint of bloody serum. The tumour was lying above and in a line with the uterus, nearly reaching by its upper border the epigastrium. It was attached to the posterior aspect of the fundus uteri by a large pedicle, and had thus been allowed to drop into the pelvis at or before the commencement of labour. I removed the uterus and tumour together (the preparation, with a drawing, was exhibited to the meeting). The whole weighed upwards of four pounds; the tumour forming, perhaps, about a third of the weight. Involution of the uterus had not proceeded to any extent. The length from the fundus to the os uteri was eight inches, and width at widest part of body seven and a half inches; average thickness of walls, an inch. *Internal surface* covered with a soft, pulpy substance, easily scraped away from the uterine wall to the naked eye leaving the interlacing muscular structure quite bare. A friend of mine, more successful than myself, found in it the elements of a mucous membrane. He thus describes his microscopical examination:—"The piece taken from the uterine surface appeared to me to be basement membrane, covered with an unusually large quantity of tesselated epithelium-particles, chiefly detached." The placental surface had a torn, clotty, sanguineous appearance, caused by the breaking up of the decidua and consequent exposure of the uterine sinuses at this part. The shreds of decidual membrane were very evident, thus corroborating views of mine described elsewhere.[1] (The point just noticed I had also an opportunity of observing a short time ago, through the kindness of Dr. Rogers, of Dean Street, in an examination, very soon after death, of a woman who died in labour from ruptured uterus.) *External surface of uterus* studded with small, fibrous tumours, about the size of walnuts. Diameter of the large tumour, six and a half inches; it consists of fibro-cellular tissue, of a dusky-white colour, with irregular channels, containing straw-coloured fluid, the whole enclosed in a capsule consisting of uterine substance and fibres; the fibres of the capsule are so intimately blended and interlaced with the white, tendinous fibres of the interior, that enucleation would have been very difficult, if not impossible. On cutting partly through the pedicle, which was about an inch in diameter and the same in length, very large vessels were found, showing that the danger of hæmorrhage would have been added to the other dangers attending an operation for the removal of the tumour by excision. The small tumours were six in number, and of the same anatomical characters as the larger one. There did not appear to be any old adhesions or disease about the broad ligaments, Fallopian tubes, or ovaries. There was, as might be expected, more congestion and signs of inflammation about the neighbourhood of the opening in the tumour than elsewhere; still the opening could not be considered the sole cause or starting-point of the peritonitis. The dark-red patches and apparently bruised condition of the peritoneum in several parts showed, as the histories of other cases have shown, that peritonitis must follow, whether the tumour under similar circumstances is returned to the abdominal cavity opened or not

[1] 'On the Anatomical Relations between the Mother and Fœtus.' A pamphlet, 1859, Renshaw, Strand.

DESCRIPTION OF PLATE IV.

The drawing is an anterior view of the uterus and its appendages, with the tumour attached.

a. The tumour attached by its pedicle to the posterior aspect of the fundus uteri.

b, *b*, *b*. The uterus, and portions of the broad ligaments, Fallopian tubes, ovarian and round ligaments.

c, *c*, *c*. Three of the smaller tumours described in the paper.

d. The os uteri.

e. The vagina laid open.

W Searson lith. Dr Woodmacott dir.

W West imp.

opened. With the exception of what has been stated the abdominal and pelvic viscera were in a good state of health. *Head and chest* not examined.

Remarks.—The history of this case presents one or two singular and instructive features. First, it is a little remarkable (though common in parallel cases) that the patient should have had all these tumours growing from her womb without having had the slightest suspicion of their existence; they did not interfere with her health or her movements. Up to a very few weeks before her confinement she was in the habit of taking active walking and even dancing exercise. Second, the embarrassment to the practitioner caused by having what seems (at least through the vagina walls) to be the child's head low down in the pelvis, without being able to find the os uteri, may be lessened by his bearing in mind the possibility of cases like the one I have related.

Dr. Tyler Smith observed, that when fibrous tumours of the uterus existed below the pelvic brim, the best method of treatment was to induce premature labour. He had once been called to a case similar to the present, in which, with a large fibrous tumour in the hollow of the sacrum, there were placenta prævia and arm presentation. Turning was performed with great difficulty, and the child slowly extracted. The woman ultimately did well, and the tumour disappeared.

TWIN (?) ABORTION.

Mr. J. C. Langmore showed a twin abortion. One fœtus, apparently of between three and four months, which was flattened, and had been dead some time, was expelled at the fourth catamenial period, after very slight pain, the placenta being retained and the hæmorrhage inconsiderable. After waiting three hours he consulted Dr. Priestley, who removed the placenta; and on again introducing the finger into the uterus to remove the clots, brought away a second and perfect ovum of about four weeks: it was adherent near the fundus; its membranes were healthy, and the embryo as seen through the amnion was fresh and vascular. The whole circumstance seemed to raise a strong presumption in favour of superfœtation having occurred.

A discussion then took place respecting the question as to the existence of superfœtation in this case, Dr. Priestley believing it to be an instance of the kind, but an opposite opinion being expressed by Dr. Routh. Dr. Braxton Hicks also remarked on the presence of certain appearances militating against this view of the case.

Dr. MADGE said, that besides the anatomical and physiological arguments which might be employed against the possibility of a superfœtation, it should be borne in mind that among a large portion of the community, more especially among the unthinking working-classes, pregnant women, during nearly the whole period of pregnancy, were exposed to the risk of superfœtation; so that if the possibility of superfœtation were to be accepted as a sound doctrine, we ought occasionally to meet with a series of fœtuses, in various stages of development, belonging to the same patient. It is rarely, however, that even twin fœtuses are met with, varying so much in size and development as to make the medical attendant think of superfœtation. When such an occurrence happens, Dr. Madge would subscribe to the opinion that it would be capable of receiving the usual explanation, namely—"That morbid changes, difficult perhaps to trace, have been so situated in connection with the respective embryos or their appendages as to cause the healthy and stronger embryo to go on growing at the expense of the other!" With regard to the stress laid by Dr. Priestley on the perfect condition of the membranes of the small ovum in Mr. Langmore's case, Dr. Madge thought that it did not prove much, because the ovum, with the membranes entire, may be detained in the uterus for a considerable time without undergoing important changes; and in the case under discussion it was probable that the presence in the uterus of the somewhat developed fœtus was the chief cause of the detention in the same cavity of its blighted neighbour.

It was finally determined that a committee, consisting of Dr. HARLEY and Dr. TANNER, should be appointed to report on the specimen at the next meeting.

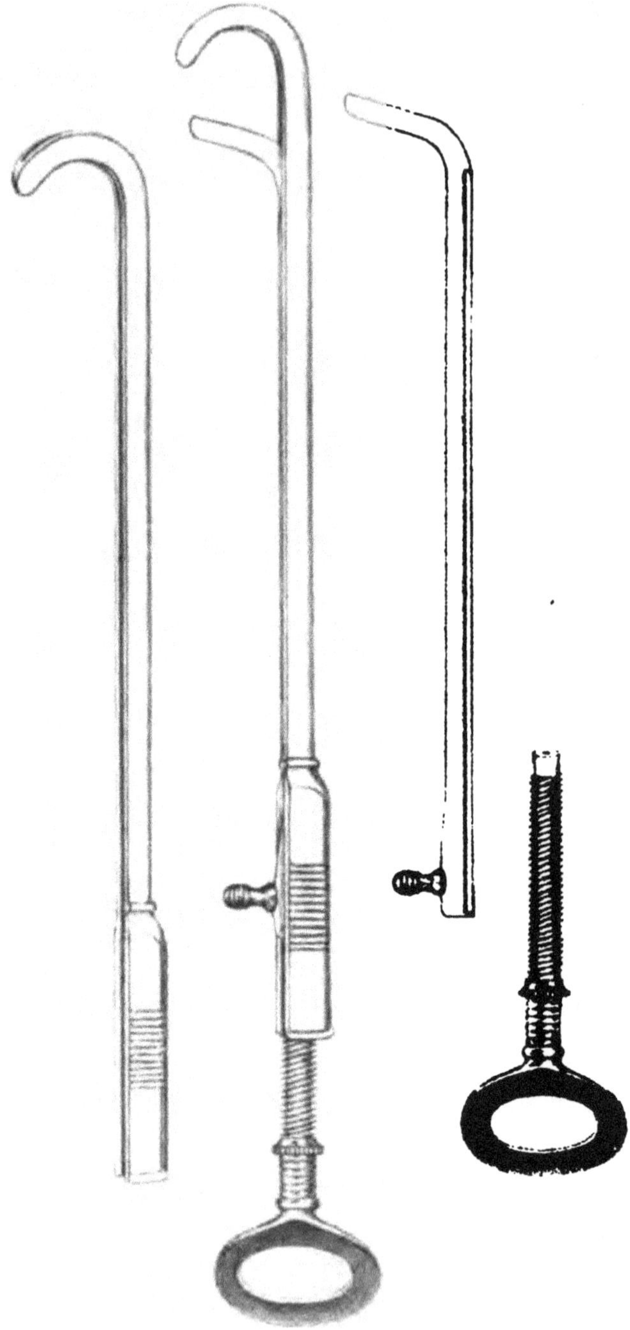

Dr Westmacott del.t

W. West imp.

THE POLYPTRITE: A NEW INSTRUMENT FOR CRUSHING THE NECKS OF UTERINE POLYPI.

By J. H. Aveling, M.D.

This instrument consists of a long hook, a slide, and a screw. In using it the hook alone is first passed over the neck of the polypus; the slide is then pushed up as far as it can be made to go by the hand; and then, by means of the screw, the operation is completed by forcing the blunt blade of the slide into the concavity of the hook, and through the neck of the polypus. Dr. Aveling stated that he and others who had used the polyptrite had found its application easy, rapid, and safe, and in no instance had he heard of the slightest hæmorrhage having followed its employment. He had used it in a case of intra-uterine polypus with perfect success, having previously dilated the os with sponge-tents. The present instrument, manufactured by Messrs. Weiss, he considered a great improvement on two other instruments of a similar kind, and for a like purpose, which he had invented in 1849 and 1857.

Mr. Spencer Wells asked what advantage the polyptrite had over the polyptome.

Dr. Aveling said that his instrument could be as easily applied as the polyptome, and that, from the character of the wound inflicted by it, there was less chance of hæmorrhage; it being a recognised fact that crushed wounds are not as liable to bleed as cut ones.

ON A NEW DESCRIPTION OF NIPPLE SHIELD, AND THE TREATMENT OF SORE NIPPLES.

By H. Cooper Rose, M.D., M.R.C.S., L.S.A., &c., &c., Hampstead.

Having been repeatedly annoyed by the suffering of patients (chiefly primiparæ) from sore and tender nipples, so frequently the forerunner of mammary abscess, I have been induced to try all the mechanical appliances that are to be found in the extensive repertory of nursery require-

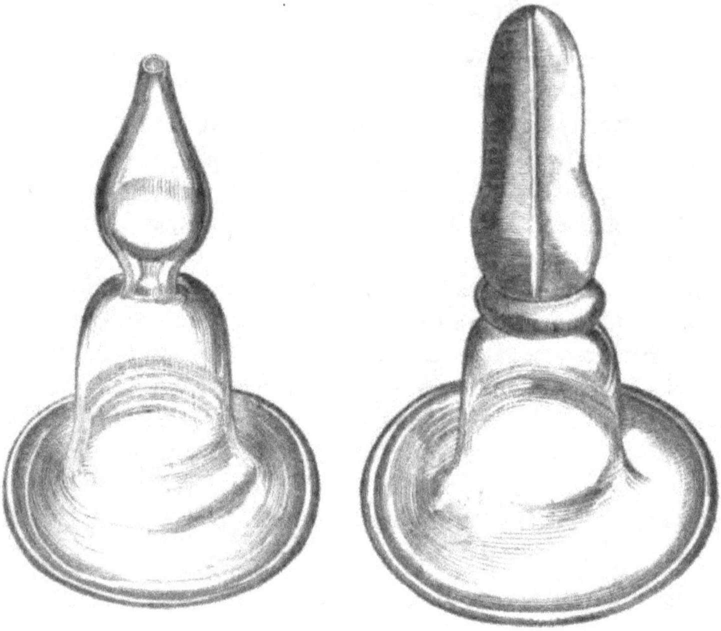

ments, with a view to shield the nipple from the irritation produced by the secretions and friction of the infant's mouth. Their name is legion.

The success attending the use of those generally to be found is so very uncertain, and too frequently entirely unattainable, that I have been endeavouring to fill the void by suggesting some improvements in their construction.

In the first place I modelled a shield in gutta percha, based upon the following principles:

1*st*. That the cylindrical portion should be long enough to ensure a space or vacuum between the end of the nipple of the mother when fully drawn out, and the end of the shield (the prime error generally being that this portion is made too short; the nipple is consequently drawn up to the top, entirely filling it, and the lactiferous ducts are, therefore, blocked against the hard substance of the instrument).

2ndly. That the diameter should be sufficiently large to render strangulation of the nipple impossible.

3rdly. That the shield should be smooth and unyielding, so as to avoid friction; *transparent*, so that the flow of milk may be observed, and the position of the nipple ascertained.

And *4thly.* That the substance used for the mouth-piece should, as nearly as possible, resemble the parent's nipple; so arranged that it cannot collapse and allow the child to suck in air.

All these indications are entirely fulfilled by the accompanying glass appliance which I have had made by Messrs. Gilbertson of Ludgate Hill. A calf's teat, a piece of wash leather, or an india-rubber nipple, is simply tied over the cone-shaped appendix or mouth-piece, which the infant readily takes, and when not in use it should be kept immersed in clean cold water.

I have not yet met with a *single case* where it has failed to answer the purpose for which it was designed, and I believe their general adoption would prevent many cases of bad breasts.

My plan is to recommend the use of the shield for the first week or two, or longer if there be a tendency to tender nipples; and at the same time I employ the application of a saturated alcoholic solution of gum benzoin and glycerine in equal proportions to the nipples after every time the child is nursed.

This application succeeds better than any other I have tried, in all stages, and in every variety, of chapped and tender nipples.

A glass shield is no novelty, but I have never met with one constructed upon the above principles. The advantage of the mouth-piece is twofold: its cavity increases the vacuum produced by the suction of the infant, and the artificial nipple, of whatever composed, is prevented from collapsing; thereby rendering it impossible for the child to suck in the air, which is often followed by considerable distress.

This is apparently a trifling matter, but every successful attempt to alleviate the sufferings which are too commonly met with amongst nursing mothers will be duly appreciated.

CASE OF DOUBLE UTERUS, WITH SIMULTANEOUS GESTATION.

By Henry Grace, M.R.C.S., L.M., &c.

(Communicated by Dr. Graily Hewitt.)

On March 28th I was summoned by my father, Mr. H. M. Grace, of Downend, to hold a consultation on Mrs. Beunett, a married woman about twenty-six years of age, who had been in labour about fifteen hours.

It was her fourth pregnancy. Twice the child was born prematurely; the third child did not live; and with this, the fourth, she considered herself not to have gone her full time.

When her labour first commenced she sent for a midwife, who found herself unable to manage the case; and my father being therefore summoned, I was called in on his discovering the following most unusual complication.

The midwife's account was to the effect that during her charge of the case the escape of the liquor amnii occurred at an early period; that the pains gradually increased till about two hours prior to our arrival; and that since then they had been gradually subsiding in force and frequency.

On my arrival I found the patient lying on the bed, her countenance anxious, with a pulse feeble and accelerated; but the pains were very slight, and not of a bearing down character.

On examination per vaginam a hand presented; and upon my introducing my left hand into the vagina and tracing the arm upwards, the os was found about half dilated, the edges, thick and unyielding, being near the symphysis pubis, and lying directly posterior to the above. Another os was discovered in a similar state of dilatation, with the head of a second child presenting itself in the normal position. The septum between the first and second os was about half an inch in thickness; and having passed my second finger through the anterior os, and my first through the posterior, the septum was found to pass up as far as could be reached, and to be of a like thickness. We then determined to dilate the anterior os (from which the hand and arm were protruding), which we did with some little difficulty; and seizing a leg we turned and delivered, having to use much force, as the pains were inefficient; but the placenta was expelled unwontedly quick, without any unusual hæmorrhage. The child proved to be dead, and appeared to be rather under seven months in development. From external examination of the abdomen I considered that each uterus was separate at its fundus.

We then dilated the second os, which yielded more readily than the first had done, and again turned the child, which this time was born alive, though it did not live many hours. The placenta was again expelled soon after the birth, of its own accord. Both children were females, of the same size, and apparently of a like age.

The poor woman suffered from no flooding or any unfavorable symptom; she is now following her customary avocation. I have examined her since her convalescence, and I found the neck of each uterus to be much in the same position—the anterior os being much more readily reached than the posterior.

She had always menstruated regularly at intervals of rather more than three weeks. I consider the doubly formed uterus to be not unlike fig. 28 in 'Churchill's Theory and Practice of Midwifery,' but I cannot satisfactorily account for the position of each os.

ON A CASE OF PRESENTATION OF THE RIGHT ARM AND SHOULDER. DELIVERY BY THE NATURAL POWERS, OR SPONTANEOUS EVOLUTION.

By Richard Hodges, M.D., F.R.C.S.

On Sunday, the 8th of January of the present year, I was summoned to visit a lady in labour with her fourth child. At eleven o'clock on that day the os uteri was found fully dilated, and the membranes protruding through it distending the vagina; but no presentation could be ascertained. During a pain the liquor amnii escaped, and no more uterine action occurred throughout that day, the following day, Monday, or the next, Tuesday, until towards the evening, when, on account of slight pains, I made an examination, and found a hand high up presenting. The patient was cheerful throughout this interval, sat up the greater part of each day, felt as if nothing was the matter with her, and considered it strange that the process of labour should have been so suspended. The pains, however, did not forget to return; they kept returning and increasing in intensity, and with their return the presenting part was more and more easily recognised. Ascertaining that the right hand, arm, and shoulder presented, and believing it unlikely that delivery would take place without assistance, I cautiously introduced my hand into the uterus with the view of bringing down the feet; but I was unable to do so from the uterus firmly embracing the fœtus, and preventing my hand passing on far enough to seize them. By the continuance of the pains, however, the presentation was forced lower and lower; the arm and shoulder now protruded at the pubis, and the side of the chest pressed out the perineum; the breech, by further efforts at this time descended and turned forwards, and was expelled as in an ordinary breech presentation, the body of the child curving or bending to a sufficient degree to admit of delivery quickly taking place, the arm and shoulder all the while remaining under the arch of the pubis, and not receding. The head was now alone left, and soon excluded, and the whole process was over at two o'clock on the morning of Wednesday, and in less time than on previous occasions when the presentation was natural. The child was above the average size, and, there is reason to believe, had been dead several days.

The case just narrated is interesting, not only on account of showing the fact that nature is, for the most part, adequate to the end in view—that she is the best and safest physician; but also in exemplifying a mode in which expulsion under such circumstances takes place, and regarding which a diversity of opinion has prevailed: one supposing that the lower extremities descended during a pain, and made room for the upper, which ascended as the others came down, till, the body turning round on its axis, the breech was expelled, as in an original presentation of that part; while another believing it impossible for the upper extremities to mount up into the contracting uterus, and that, consequently, no part which once protruded ever receded.

FOUR ADDITIONAL CASES OF OVARIOTOMY.

By W. Tyler Smith, M.D., F.R.C.P.

The present cases are in continuation of those presented to the Society in February and July, 1861, and numbered from 1 to 8.

Case 9.—*Polycystic disease of both ovaries; operation; death.*

The subject of this case was fifty-nine years of age, unmarried, and had suffered from ovarian tumour for thirty-eight years—a longer period, it is believed, than has been recorded of any similar case. She was of immense size. The operation was by the long incision, the bulk of the tumour being solid. Professor Simpson was present, and assisted at the operation. Numerous adhesions rendered the removal of the tumours very difficult. The pelvic adhesions were especially firm. In breaking them down, the rectum was slightly wounded. The patient died from shock six hours after the operation.

Case 10.—*Polycystic disease of both ovaries; operation; death.*

Mrs. M— had been suffering from ovarian tumour for two years. She had been once tapped, but ineffectually. The tumour was large, and chiefly solid. There was dropsical swelling of the feet, legs, and abdominal walls; a quick pulse, and great emaciation. The tumours were removed by a moderate-sized incision, but the adhesions were extensive and firm. As in the former case, the pelvic adhesions were the most formidable. The peritoneum was found to be extensively diseased, being covered in patches with masses of scirrhous hardness nearly an inch thick. The pedicles were secured by ligatures, which were left hanging from the lower part of the wound. This patient lingered for three days, and then died of exhaustion.

Case 11.—*Polycystic disease of the left ovary; operation; recovery.*

This patient (Mrs. H—) had suffered for upwards of two years. In the first instance tapping was attempted, but nothing escaped through the trocar, save a little blood. The tumour was large, and almost entirely solid. There were adhesions to the small intestines, the omentum, and the abdominal walls. The pedicle was of large size, and the clamp was used to secure it. Great irritation and some hæmorrhage were caused by the sloughing of the large pedicle; but with these exceptions her recovery was uninterrupted, and she is now convalescent.

CASE 12.—*Polycystic disease of the left ovary; operation; recovery.*

Mrs. H—, æt. 58, was first tapped and pressure applied. Two cysts were emptied, but a considerable quantity of solid matter still remained. After the tumours had refilled, the operation was decided on, and performed in the presence of Professor Nélaton. The tumour was removed by a small incision. It was adherent to the omentum and the abdominal walls. The pedicle was slight, and after being tied with a silk ligature the pedicle and the ligature were cut off as short as possible, and dropped into the abdomen. The wound was then closed entirely. It healed by the first intention. There was not a bad symptom, and in ten days she was convalescent. This is the second successful case in which the author has returned the pedicle and ligature into the abdomen.

Thus, up to the date of the paper, the author has performed ovariotomy in twelve cases. Of these, three have died, and nine have perfectly recovered. One of them has since become pregnant.

Mr. SPENCER WELLS said that he had been especially interested during the reading of the paper by the account of the two cases in which the pelvic adhesions had been so extensive, and by the mode in which the author had secured the pedicle in two other cases. He (Mr. Wells) felt that those who were learning how to lessen the mortality after ovariotomy had no more difficult problem to solve than the best way to deal with the pedicle. The fact that the author had in two successful cases tied the pedicle and returned it, with the ligature cut off short, into the peritoneal cavity, leaving the ligature and the portion of pedicle which it strangulated within that cavity, and closing the wound entirely, was very surprising; but it taught a very important lesson; and if it did not lead him (Mr. Wells) to follow the example so set without modification, it would certainly encourage him, in any suitable case, to tie the vessels only (not the entire pedicle) with wire, to cut off the ligatures short, return the pedicle, and close the wound. With regard to pelvic adhesions, he would remark that he looked upon them as one of the most serious indications against ovariotomy. He had several times refused to operate where dislocation of the uterus and the presence of fixed portions of an ovarian tumour between the uterus and rectum or the uterus and bladder had been detected; and in cases in which the patients had died of the natural progress of the disease the justice of the decision had been proved. In one case, the rectum, uterus, cyst, and bladder were found so fused together that it was almost impossible to separate them after death. Occasionally, it was extremely difficult to say whether portions of ovarian tumours in the pelvis were adhering there, or were simply pressed downwards and non-adherent. He had two cases of this kind now in the Samaritan Hospital, and he intended to tap the abdominal cysts to see if (when those were empty) the pelvic portion could be pushed upwards. In this manner he had cleared up the diagnosis in other cases. It was only by carefully observing various cases that we could arrive at the knowledge of the conditions which render ovariotomy advisable or otherwise; but we are now beginning to learn this, and to be able to say to a patient or her friends either that the case is one where recovery may be hoped for very confidently, or one where the prospect of success or failure was about equal, or one where the conditions are so unfavorable that no reasonable hope of success could be entertained. Among these conditions he was disposed to class pelvic adhesions. At least this was the result of his own experience, and the two fatal cases narrated this evening supported that view. The profession in general, and those who were endeavouring to diminish the mortality after ovariotomy in particular, were much indebted to the author for this addition to their knowledge.

THE VESSELS CONCERNED IN THE PRODUCTION OF PHLEGMASIA DOLENS.

By Wm. Tilbury Fox, M.D. Lond., Univ. Med. Scholar.

Some time since the Obstetrical Society accepted some general remarks from me upon the subject of phlegmasia dolens, more especially in reference to the circumstances attending its production; my aim being to show that, in the majority of cases, the obstructive disease was not an inflammatory condition, but a thrombosis in the lymphatic vessels produced by the sudden absorption of extraneous matter through sudden loss. I now desire to raise a discussion touching the aspect of the disease, in so far as the various vascular channels are concerned; and do not hesitate to confess that this wish on my part is intensified, especially on account of the doctrines promulgated so recently in the Lettsomian Lectures of Dr. Mackenzie, which the profession appears to receive with an almost entire concurrence.

In the 'Gazette Médicale,' 1845, Bouchut states "that phlegmasia dolens was due, not to a primary inflammation of the veins, but to a coagulation of the blood in them, resulting from some peculiar change in the quality of the constituent elements of the blood, which rendered it specially liable to become coagulated." Dr. Simpson, in the 'Med. Times and Gazette,' 1859, sums up thus:—"But in the great majority of cases it seems to me that we must look for the primary cause of the disease in some morbid condition of the circulating fluid, leading, first of all, perhaps, to some peculiar change in the lining membrane of the veins, and through this, secondarily, to coagulation of blood, occlusion of vessels, and obstruction to the circulation in the limb." Dr. Watson writes:—"The painful disorder called phlegmasia dolens is caused by a stoppage in the femoral veins."

The following propositions of Dr. Mackenzie best express modern belief:

"1. Crural phlebitis in a pure uncomplicated form cannot give rise to all the local and general phenomena of the disease, and therefore cannot be its proximate cause.

"2. Phlebitis itself is for the most part not a primary but a secondary affection, and in the great majority of cases is a consequence of the circulation of impure or morbid blood in the veins.

"3. The proximate cause of the disease is therefore pre-eminently a morbific condition of the blood, which I have experimentally shown to be capable of producing not only the lesions of the veins met with in the disease, but all its phenomena."

Dr. Mackenzie remarks, in searching for a cause, "It must be remembered that an inflamed and obstructed condition of the iliac veins constitutes one of the most important and, indeed, pathognomonic features of the complaint; and therefore in seeking for a theory we must exclude any which does not equally account for this as well as for its other pathological conditions."

I propose to run counter to the opinions of these high authorities, to show that they are founded in error, and that the occurrence of phlebitis should be put out of view in our estimate of phlegmasia dolens, which latter may, no doubt, be brought about, among other modes, by a vitiated state of blood, but certainly not by such causes as of necessity tend to produce phlebitis. Though the veins have nothing to do essentially with phlegmasia dolens, it is convenient to notice their influence, when obstructed, upon contiguous parts.

It has been clearly established by research that the local application of irritants to veins produces, either through irritation of the lining membrane or direct action upon the blood, coagulation, which may or may not be followed by actual phlebitis, almost invariably not. The experiments of Pirigott, performed in 1839, and Reumert in 1840, in the case of dogs, which have been confirmed, especially by Dr. Mackenzie and Mr. Henry Lee, showed very clearly that the action of chemical and mechanical irritants was limited, and the extension of inflammation uncommon. Modern pathology, however, has relinquished in great measure the belief in phlebitis, and given to the obstructive lesion the name thrombosis.

It would be superfluous to recount the experiments and clinical data which prove that a blocking up of the fem vein results in an *œdematous* state of limb, and is incapable of giving rise to phlegmasia dolens. No doubt in its character as a coincidence it influences to some extent the latter, and reference will be made to this presently. We pass then to the consideration of obstructed veins, produced not by local means, but through the action of a vitiated blood-current, when the phenomena of phlegmasia dolens are looked upon as evidence of the existence of a "blood disease," and which is also merely a modification of the relinquished hypothesis, so far as the pathology is concerned.

Now, *à priori*, it appears of little moment, touching the effect, whether the obstructive lesion is caused by local agencies, or through the medium of the general circulation, since the obstruction is certainly as complete frequently in the one case as the other; and if there be a real difference under the two conditions, of course the changes over and beyond œdema, which characterise the lesion as phlegmasia dolens, must be ascribed to the action of the blood state (which is absent in the locally produced venous disease) upon the general textures of the limb: hence, moreover, *à priori*, it would seem that the actual venous disease must have less to do with phlegmasia dolens than is usually supposed, and that we must look (according to the theory now under notice) for the true explanation of the production of white swelling in a special action carried on between the blood in an abnormal state and the tissues. It has been argued that, in the instance of coagulation resulting from a general vitiation of the blood, the smallest radicles of veins are affected; but exceptions to this are by no means uncommon, and it is equally true of obstruction produced by local measures. Wherein does the *modus operandi* of obstruction in the two cases differ? To those who hold that the proximate cause of phlegmasia dolens is a morbific condition of the blood, giving rise to phlebitis secondarily, we must offer the alternative—either that phlegmasia dolens is a result in and through the production of venous obstruction—but since this *per se*, as a local state, is incapable of producing phlegmasia dolens, we offer a contradiction;—or that the disease is due to the action of the blood state—not upon the vessels, but the general tissues; and in this instance we offer an assumption, inasmuch as no clinical or experimental facts can be adduced in confirmation. Turn we now to the clinical aspect of the case. They who hold the belief in the blood origin of phlegmasia dolens use, as their chief argument, the frequent occurrence of the disease after labour, when blood vitiation is particularly common. (By the term blood vitiation is meant such as tends to give rise to "phlebitis" as a secondary matter.) Now, I appeal to the experience of those most competent to give any opinion, to decide whether "blood disease," which gives rise to coagulation (these being the conditions advanced as necessary by Dr. Mackenzie's propositions), be not very frequent in the after-parturient state, and very, very rarely followed by phlegmasia dolens, but only by œdema. The affirmative will be readily conceded me; cases of the kind might be quoted in any number: but it is unnecessary. Why, then, does phlegmasia dolens ensue in the one case and not in the other? Why is it that the disease does not result from all cases of blood poisoning with obstructed veins, because the conditions which are said to be necessary and sufficient, as the cause, are certainly fulfilled most amply in these instances? A contradiction of the prevailing doctrine lies upon the surface of the clinical history of phlegmasia dolens. How comes it, moreover, that the latter is unproduced in the various blood poisonings which occur, irrespectively of the parturient state where the supposed conditions of evolution (according to the modern theory) are abundantly manifested in a large majority of cases without the accredited result? Directly we step beyond the boundary of obstetrics into the wide domain of general medicine we are compelled to relinquish the doctrine which ascribes anything beyond œdema to an obstructive disease of veins produced in the course of any blood disease; and we perceive at once how necessary it is to mark closely the distinction between œdema and phlegmasia dolens. It is very interesting to note, as Dr. Lee has it, that Mr. Lawrence, who examined the first fatal case which occurred to Dr. Davis, and whose history of morbid appearances threw more light on the nature of the affection than all hypotheses that had previously been advanced—and which were merely speculative, unsupported by facts—declared at the Medical and Chirurgical Society, in 1828, that he was fully convinced, from what had fallen under his observation, that Dr. Davis's views were incorrect, and that phlegmasia dolens did not arise from inflammation of the iliac and femoral veins. (*Vide* 'Medical Gazette,' vol. ii, 1842-3,

p. 855.) The phlebitis, in this instance, resulted during blood-poisoning, but Mr. Lawrence clearly saw the distinction that is to be drawn between œdema and white leg.

The frequent occurrence of phlegmasia dolens after parturition may equally be ascribed to the existence at that time of the causes of thrombosis, extreme hæmorrhage wound, and vitiated fluid. Again, if phlegmasia dolens be a disease of so-called blood origin, why is it limited to the lower limbs almost invariably? *A priori*, this is an argument in favour of its local production. It occurs in connection with certain local determining causes—for example, in the lower limb in connection with organic changes in the uterus, in the upper limb with disease of the breast or adjoining parts; and leaving out of consideration the cases of direct pressure, there exists always the probability, to say the least, that the obstructive disease in the vessels, be they and it what they may, can travel from some seat near whereat organic change is going on, and in which the absorbents are actively at work, so as to affect the main current of the limb. Example, from the uterus to the iliac, from the mamma to the subclavian vascular channels. The local circumstances, the activity and hypertrophy of the absorptive vessels (as in the parturient state), their thin coats, the presence of wounds, the occurrences of hæmorrhage, acute diarrhœa, and the like, which demand compensation; the presence of vitiated fluid, the character of the local lesions (*i. e.* the ulcerative kind), are so commonly linked with the onset of the disease, that the mind grasps the conclusion that these are more than any other connected with the production of phlegmasia dolens, though the latter may be helped out by the disposition of the general blood state. It must not be forgotten that in the lower limbs the effect of gravitation, the long-continued pressure of the gravid womb, and the like, materially tend to stagnate the free circulation, and hence coagulation is here less guarded against. It is not at all uncommon to see in persons out of health, after standing for a long time, thrombosis in the popliteal vessels. I have observed several well-marked cases of the kind, and in one or two instances extravasation of blood into the hamstring muscles has followed.

Again, the character of the swelling is not that of venous stasis produced by blood diseases, the enlargement being unequal, and commencing above and extending downwards.

Again, *there need be no venous disease at all in phlegmasia dolens*, and this is an insurmountable argument as tending against the existing theory. I shall quote two cases presently substantiating this point, but it is to be noticed that the swelling in these instances appears not to be so great—due, no doubt, to the absence of superadded œdema.

Again, blood vitiation capable *per se* of giving rise to "phlebitis" is accompanied by general symptoms, and in phlegmasia dolens these may be positively *nil;* and this leads me to observe—

Sixthly. That the death-rate of uncomplicated phlegmasia dolens completely sets aside the theory of its production by a vitiated state of the general blood-current as its proximate cause; death occurring in conjunction with venous obstruction, complicating blood poisoning, is by no means uncommon. Whence, thence, this contradiction, since, according to the prevailing opinion, white leg is the most perfect and complete condition of these two concurrences, and should possess a high death-rate.

Seventhly. Phlegmasia dolens occurring in phthisis, cancer, dysentery, from pressure of all kinds, suppressed menstruation, after abortions and the like, remains unaccounted for by the phlebitic theory.

Eighthly. The experimental evidence of artificially produced phlegmasia dolens through venous obstruction is open to very grave objection. Dr. Mackenzie, in his 'Lettsomian Lectures,' p. 222, details an experiment of the injection of lactic acid into the general blood-current, after first ligaturing the femorals, so as to prevent localized action. "In twenty-four hours the affected extremity was greatly swollen throughout, its temperature was raised, it was painful on pressure, and the dog moved it with difficulty. In forty-eight hours its general condition was the same, the swelling was still considerable, the limb was tender on pressure, and the dog still moved it with difficulty." Can it be doubted that these are among the most characteristic symptoms of phlegmasia dolens? asks Dr. Mackenzie. With all due respect, I am credulous with regard to the nature of the result. It does not appear that the disease was aught else but œdema, and there are no symptoms or appearances whatever mentioned as characteristic of phlegmasia dolens. Again, the post-mortem showed, in addition to the extensive lesion of the veins, "that the subcutaneous and intermuscular cellular tissue was morbidly vascular and infiltrated, and that the muscles themselves were in places swollen and congested." Why, assuredly these are the very conditions linked with disease, not of the veins, but of the lymphatics; the cellular tissue is never seriously affected without involving lymphatic disease; and supposing phlegmasia dolens to have existed, of which no evidence is forthcoming, it was not shown to be independent of lymphatic disease.

Nature of the so-called phlebitis.—The term "phlebitis" has been freely used, and a few remarks are necessary in connection therewith. I by no means deny its occasional existence, but in the instances in which I have examined inflamed veins, so-called, the evidence has been deficient; the lining membrane of veins is, perhaps, the one least disposed to take on inflammatory action, and coagulation can in nowise be regarded as proof thereof. Virchow's views find almost universal acceptance in the use of the term thrombosis, as applied to the coagulations in the venous tract; though its mode of production is still a question *sub judice*, it is a matter of surprise that in the recent Lettsomian lectures no reference has been made to this aspect of the pathology, which has been widely debated among the profession, since it is the weak point of Dr. Mackenzie's theory, which assumes the existence of a cause, such as tends to produce what is altogether absent in the vast majority of, if not all, cases of phlegmasia dolens. I hope I deal fairly in this matter, since there is no mention made of any such condition as thrombosis; but if the latter state is implied by the term phlebitis, my objection holds equally good in regarding it as a cause of white leg, since phlebitis cannot produce the latter, and may be altogether absent.

It remains, then, to show what vessels are concerned in the production of phlegmasia dolens. Let it be admitted that œdema is not white leg, and we must remove venous obstruction and its proper elements from the list of the components of phlegmasia dolens. Moreover, let it be granted that the latter may exist as a purely local disease, without any general symptoms, and all such associations as puerperal fever, blood poisonings and the like, must be renounced as necessary parts. It is of first consequence to distinguish between the essentials and the mere coincidences of the disease. For example, in instances of phlegmasia dolens occurring during the existence of puerperal fever, take away from the general total all the proper puerperal fever symptoms, and the phlegmasia dolens remains in its entirety; take away the hot, tense, elastic, white swelling, and the puerperal fever remains in all its integrity. The two cannot be associated as necessary parts, the one of the other. I hold this position most tenaciously, for even the greatest authorities have failed to mark the distinction, and thereby countenanced error.

The pathology of phlegmasia dolens is sadly behindhand, perhaps on account of its rare fatality. From the time of Mauriceau, who described first the malady, nearly a century and a half elapsed before a post-mortem examination was recorded; and it certainly is an opprobrium to obstetricians that the opportunities that have occurred have elicited so little interest in the determination of the question of causation as revealed by post-mortem lesions.

Modern opinions run in the wrong tract; and if we go back to the writings of Hull, Trye, and White, we shall find that these were not far from finding the correct theory. Hull looked upon the disease as an inflammatory exudative condition of the whole structures of the limb, certainly not a very satisfactory explanation. Trye regarded the disease as an inflammation of the lymphatic glands, an error that common observation might have taught him. White evidently drew his conclusions from certain experiments of Sir A. Cooper ('Med. Records and Researches,' art. vii, p. 86, 1798), who ligatured the thoracic duct, and found that the receptaculum chyli burst in consequence of the peristaltic action of the vessels acting in opposition to the obstruction.

"Is it not, therefore, probable," says Mr. White, "that this disorder is owing to the child's head pressing the lymphatic vessel or vessels which arise from one of the lower extremities against the brim of the pelvis during a labour pain, so as to stop the progress of the lymph? The number of valves will effectually prevent it from regurgitating; and if the head continues any time precisely in that situation, while the lymph is driven on through the valves, by the peristaltic action of the coats of its vessels, by the great exertion of the muscles and the strong vibration of the inguinal artery which are greatly increased by the labour-pains, the lymphatic vessel, though its coats should be allowed to be stronger than those of the blood-vessels, must at last burst and shed its contents." "When the orifice made in the lymphatic is healed, and the diameter of the tube is contracted, or, perhaps, totally closed by the cicatrix, the lymph is retained in the lymphatic vessels and glands of the limb and labium pudendi, and distends them to such a degree and so suddenly as to occasion great pain and swelling, which always begin in that part next to which the obstruction is formed," &c.

White correctly looked upon the disease as local, but incorrectly as connected necessarily with parturition, with rupture of the lymphatics, with obstruction of the latter commencing at Poupart's ligament, inasmuch as this travels up from the pelvis to the main lymphatic vessels of the limb. It is curious, too, that White did not see a fatal objection to his theory in the fact that, if rupture took place originally from obstruction, the same thing would occur again when the cicatrix had produced further obstruction.

White was compelled, moreover, to assume, as a predisponent, the existence of thin coats in the lymphatic vessels of those affected by phlegmasia dolens; lastly, post-mortem evidence is entirely wanting to support White's hypothesis. But although he miscarried as regards the *cause*, he was correct in estimating the *nature* of the disease as "an obstruction, detention, and accumulation of lymph in the limb." Mr. White had by far the most correct appreciation of the disease of any writer, either prior or subsequent to his time, and his remarks show him to be a most able and sound surgeon; and there is no doubt that, had he possessed the opportunity of testing his views by actual post-mortem observation, he would probably have still further advanced towards the truth. He is the only one, at any rate, of early writers who had prominently in view the all-important distinction between œdema and white leg, and was particularly emphatic in pointing out the neglect in the writings especially of Hull, Trye, Puzos, and Levret (*vide* 'Inquiry,' part ii, p. 37 *et seq.*).

It is but fair to notice the objections that have been urged against the doctrine, that lymphatic obstruction alone produces phlegmasia dolens, by Dr. Hull.

First, the absence of swelling, &c., of the lymphatic vessels and glands. Now, the seat of obstruction is usually high up in the pelvis, out of reach, having travelled there from the uterine lymphatics; the spot, perhaps, where they are most manifestly affected is the broad ligament of the uterus; then the obstruction is thrombosis, and not accompanied by inflammatory swelling, as the rule. Moreover, it is not usual to feel diseased lymphatics. The glands, yes; but not the actual vessels. No doubt they may enlarge, as shown by Mr. Trye (p. 42 of his essay) in the records of a case of tumour pressing upon and making them become varicose; there is always hypertrophy of the pelvic lymphatics in the pregnant; again, the lymphatics, even when inflamed, are generally obscured by the brawny swelling, which is not the case with obstructed veins in an œdematous swelling.

Dr. Hull (p. 127 of his work) remarks, "If it were necessary, I could adduce other cases to prove that the tumefaction of the limb, produced in consequence of inflammation of the lymphatic vessels, is neither so painful at first, nor so tense and tender, nor so free from discoloration, nor so difficult of removal, as the swelling incident to the lower extremities of lying-in women."

Now, in these cases the obstruction is seldom that of many trunks, and it is seldom complete, as in the case of pressure upon, or thrombosis of, a large pelvic trunk; then, again, inflammation of the lymphatics takes place in consequence of the action of a septic poison (ex., erysipelas), and hence there are certain tissue actions—abscess and the like—accompanied by hyperæmia, and which take rise in consequence of the circulation of a general blood poison, which may give rise to lymphatic obstruction as one of its effects; but then the character of the phlegmasia dolens is considerably modified by these tissue actions. In true phlegmasia dolens the tissues are quite passive; there is no vascular action beyond the healthy limit. It is quite true that lymphangitis is by no means followed by phlegmasia dolens; but then this is no proof that simple obstruction of the *main* trunk may not be the cause.

Dr. Hull further observes, with regard to the time of the occurrence of the disease, that "if it consisted of an inflammation of the lymphatic system, instead of seldom happening within the first week, it should almost invariably take place within this period, because the lymphatics may be supposed at this time to have suffered more, either from injury during labour or from the absorption of acrimonious lochial discharge." This statement is valueless, because we know that lymphangitis depends upon septic disease, which may occur at very varying post-mortem periods. Moreover, the coagulation in the vessels may take some time to travel up from the uterine to the iliac channels, so as to affect the main current of the limb.

Again—"the manner in which intumescence makes its appearance in phlegmasia dolcus is generally the reverse of what happens in swellings that are produced by inflammation of the lymphatics." (Hull, p. 128.) In the former case from above downwards, in the latter from below upwards. The explanation of the two cases is clear; in the one case a poison is introduced usually at the extremity of the limb—ex., in whitlow, erysipelas—and the swelling occurs necessarily from below upwards; in the other case the obstruction is seated high up, the lymph is sent forwards by the contractile action of its vessels, and collects especially above where the swelling first takes rise. We see here an important difference in the action of obstructed veins and obstructed lymphatics.

Again—"the appearance of the complaint in the other lower extremity, sooner or later, appears to me," says Dr. Hull, "to present another material objection." However, he does no more than mention this, which merely depends upon any cause acting alike upon both sides, or the obstructive disease travelling up from one so as to affect the common trunk leading to both limbs.

Again—"the nature of the effused fluid of phlegmasia dolens differs from that of lymphatic inflammation." Had Dr. Hull knowledge of present pathology, he would, no doubt, have grasped what Mr. White's remarks implied, viz., the distinction between lymphatic obstruction conjoined to a healthy blood state, and the same condition plus the circulation of septic poison in the system and the consequent so-called "effusions."

Lastly. It has so happened that in cases in which the thoracic duct has been tied the derivative evidence has been negative, since the receptaculum chyli has invariably burst.

I believe, then, that the non-œdematous, tense, white, elastic swelling is due to obstructed lymphatic circulation, and that White was perfectly correct in his estimate of the *nature* of the disease, but not of its *cause*. Further, that lymphatic disease *per se* will and has produced phlegmasia dolens beyond a doubt, and that venous disease, as a primary state or one secondary to a blood irritation, is beside the question, can be established by facts indisputable.

I argued out before this Society, some time ago, the relation between the connective tissues and lymphatic distribution, and the probability the lymphatics are the agents specially concerned in regulating the nutritive condition of the former; that the connective tissue is the great tract which, running throughout the body, is the seat of most inflammatory changes, and wherein are found the reparative and eliminative actions and agents. Ex.—Formation of abscess. And inasmuch as the demand for these is necessarily variable, nature does not leave herself unprepared for emergencies; that the lymphatics are the agents which carry off waste, and such reparative material as is not required, from the spot where it was given by the blood (or, as Virchow affirms, *produced* by the tissues themselves) for the emergency, whatever it was. According to this view, to which modern pathology is rapidly tending, indurations, circumbscribing poisons—ex., chancre, suppuration, and its climax, pyæmia, and the like—must be regarded as salutary.

In the natural condition of nutrition a large quantity of lymph travels from the cellular tissue towards the thoracic duct. Mr. Patch, of Exeter, in vol. v of 'Medical Essays,' p. 399, relates the case of a boy, eleven years old, who had an almost imperceptible orifice near the left groin, which discharged in three days from two quarts to five pints of lymph. In Henson's 'Exp. Inq.,' part ii, p. 198, is another case referred to by Mr. White. Hence, where the lymphatics are obstructed, the effect is felt in the part from whence the vessels spring, and phlegmasia dolens results. Now, in cases in which tissue actions are being carried on in the limb, and a large amount of fibrinous material is present, if the lymphatics become obstructed the same result may ensue; but if these tissue actions are well marked, that is, if such a state as suppuration occur, the phlegmasia dolens is thereby materially modified; and it is unfair to deny in such instances that lymphatic obstruction can give rise to white leg, since the latter is completely marked by superadded changes. Take, for example, the case of introduction of poison into the cellular tissue, which was the example adduced, in the discussion that followed the reading of my first paper, by Dr. Druitt, in refutation of the proposition advanced by myself. "It was impossible," said Dr. Druitt, "to regard phlegmasia dolens otherwise than as one member of that class of pathological exudations which includes also diffuse inflammation of the areolar tissue, erysipelas, carbuncle, and snake-bite, which last the author had alluded to, though he did not seem to appreciate the fact that it afforded a complete solution of the phenomena of the disease under consideration." And "a poison introduced into the cellular tissue, whether locally or through the medium of the circulation at large, was all that was required to explain the phenomena. I repeat again, with all due humility, that the introduction of a poison into the cellular tissue may or may not obstruct the lymphatics in either case; the areolar tissue receives an increased supply of fibrinous material for repair of the damage done through the eliminating process of circumscription by lymph and subsequent absorption, or by the formation of abscess. If the lymphatics be free, no phlegmasia dolens ensues, the limb is quasi-œdematous, brawny, and the lymphatics remove in part the fibrinous material; if the lymphatics, on the other hand, be obstructed, so as to *affect materially the main current of the limb*, then phlegmasia dolens ensues; and if inflammation, abscess, and the like occur, they are merely matters of special elimination *engrafted upon and modifying* the phlegmasia dolens, for the purpose of removing a blood poison, which produces two distinct things, phlegmasia dolens and inflammatory actions, which may exist the one without the other in perfect integrity. In proof of what I say, let me refer to two cases of snake-bite, the one recorded in the 'Obstetrical Transactions,' vol. ii, in which phlegmasia dolens arose in consequence of sudden coagulation of lymph, and was unaccompanied by general symptoms; the other detailed in the 'Lancet' for August 8th, 1857, briefly as follows.

G. S—, æt. 16, bitten in his right thumb. "His thumb,

hand, and arm, as far as the elbow, were found considerably swollen. This swelling was of rather a peculiar character, being shiny, tense, and elastic, not pitting on pressure." The deep-red line of absorbents could be traced to the axilla, and from thence to the thorax. No suppuration occurred. Discharged twelfth day. The veins became implicated towards the end of the case. It is needless to refer to cases in which extensive abscess occurs.

There are various other proofs that obstruction of the main lymphatic current is all that is necessary to the production of phlegmasia dolens.

In cases of cancer of the large glandular collections, whenever the disease is so far advanced as to merely cause slight obstruction, the swelling around is doughy; and if there be pressure upon the veins, œdematous; if perfect obliteration exist, then phlegmasia dolens results. This is exemplified by the cases of cancer of the mamma recorded by Dr. Mackfarlane. I am enabled to give the further details of the case of cancer of the iliac glands to which reference was made in a former paper, in 1860. There existed a larger tumour in the right groin, with a white, tense, elastic, swollen condition of thigh. In October, 1861, this tumour had considerably lessened, and the phlegmasia dolens also. On the opposite side, however, the same changes had taken place as on the right side, and the glands of the left axilla were hard, enlarged, and accompanied by a similar condition of swelling to that of the thigh. The disease was confined entirely to the lymphatic glands, and travelling from the inguinal to the intra-pelvic glands; and when I last examined the case there was a non-œdematous, tense, white, swollen condition of the sacral and lumbar regions. The patient died in the country, of which I was unaware, and so lost a post-mortem. But the disease was unmistakeably scirrhus of the lymphatic glands. I never saw any case which so strongly impressed upon my mind the conviction that phlegmasia dolens is really produced by lymphatic obstruction.

A case of the same kind is recorded by Dr. Ferriar, in

the 'Medical Museum,' vol. i, p. 335, where, post mortem, were found, "scirrhus-glands greatly enlarged, and surrounding the crural vein," &c.

Another argument is to be found in the fact that in œdema the lymphatics are free; this, however, is *negative* merely in its application.

Again, the changes in anæmia lymphatica, when it exists in an extreme degree, must interfere with the lymph-current; and the condition of the surface in severe cases is white and pungent. Perhaps further observation is required before any conclusions can be drawn from this case; at any rate, the *probability* must be admitted that future experience will find in this disease a very powerful argument in favour of White's theory of the production of phlegmasia dolens.

Lastly, there is the evidence of direct observation to show that phlegmasia dolens is the result of lymphatic obstruction.

Dr. Rigby's case, recorded in the 'Medical Gazette,' 1835, is as follows, in reference to the post-mortem:—Left thigh one third greater than right; slight peritonitis; on raising the peritoneum from iliac fossa, the cellular membrane which envelopes the round ligament where this passes under the epigastric vessels after quitting the peritoneal cavity was found infiltrated and condensed with lymph and pus; the whole of this cellular membrane (which, it will be borne in mind, is the fascia propria of Sir A. Cooper, and which fills the femoral ring, and, moreover, forms the medium of transmission for the lymphatics of the thigh) was in the same condition, densely matted by lymph, and containing pus in the interstices." No disease whatever of the veins existed; the whole of the neighbouring glands were diseased. Dr. Rigby still thought the case lacked perfection in the absence of venous disease. The swelling in this case was not so great as usual, hence we see the influence of venous disease here exemplified—it adds to the general enlargement of the limb.

Case 2, 'Obstetrical Transactions,' vol. ii, is briefly as follows:—Cancer of sacro-iliac synchondrosis, involving lymphatics, and evidenced by the presence of a tumour to the left of the mesial line, followed by phlegmasia dolens, subsidence of tumour, disappearance of the white leg; no signs of venous disease, though carefully searched for during life and after death. This case shakes the foundation of the doctrine that ascribes white leg to a blood vitiation.

Mr. White mentions in his 'Inquiry,' part ii, the case of a gentleman who fractured his pelvis, and in whom subsequently phlegmasia dolens ensued, evidently in consequence of the pressure exercised upon the main lymphatic trunks during the progress of reparation, though Mr. White believed the main lymphatics were ruptured by the fractured bones.

Nature of the lymphatic obstruction, and causes.

1. Extrinsic pressure upon the vessels.
2. Thrombosis, due to sudden absorption of acrimonious fluid.
3. True inflammation (tolerably rare).

By far the greatest number of instances occur under the second head; the discussion of this point was the aim of my former communication.

The relation between venous obstruction and phlegmasia dolens can now be appreciated. Venous obstruction results in œdema and nothing else, and adds to the general enlargement of the limb.

Most of the causes which produce lymphatic obstruction also give rise to venous obstruction, hence their frequent association.

It has further appeared to me that, in the cases in which venous obstruction is not superadded, that the decline of the swelling has been unaccompanied by pitting on pressure, except in so slight a manner as is accountable by the want of elasticity in consequence of the preceding distension.

Summary.

1. Phlegmasia dolens is a local disease.

2. No general symptoms need be present (implies absence of blood poison).

3. Phlebitis, however produced, cannot give rise to *phlegmasia dolens*, but *œdema* only.

4. Phlegmasia dolens may occur in, but forms no necessary part of, blood poisoning (such as tends to phlebitis), but is modified thereby frequently; and any tissue conditions over and above the presence of fibrinous serosity, and the consequent hypertrophous state of areolar tissue, are in nowise essential components of phlegmasia dolens, but common alike to very many different "blood diseases."

5. Obstruction of the main lymphatic channels alone is capable of giving rise to white leg, and acts by preventing the removal of lymph from the affected limb.

6. The obstruction may be the result of—

A. Extrinsic pressure. Ex.—Tumours of all kinds.
B. Thrombosis, due to sudden (compensatory) absorption of vitiated fluid after sudden loss of any kind.
C. Inflammatory changes in the vessels themselves.

7. The effect of the action of venous obstruction upon the phlegmasia dolens is an intensification of the general swelling and the presence of œdema during the subsidence of the enlargement of the limb.

Finally, in connection with this disease, I would call attention to a source of blood poisoning which was noticed in a former paper of mine, and which appears to me to deserve very careful attention. In cases of diffuse inflammation, erysipelas, pyæmia, and the like, in which large tracts of cellular tissue are undergoing rapid change, it has been noticed in fatal cases that, as Mr. Busk has observed, "the lungs are highly congested, and on close inspection the small pulmonary vessels found to contain pus." The most prevalent opinion is that the corpuscles are ill-developed, pale blood-corpuscles. However, the point I wish to note is this, that the lymphatics take up all the waste, the superabundant fibrin, &c., from the diseased cellular tissue, and pour their contents, together with an increased number of corpuscular elements formed in their glandular part, into the venous system, at the junction of the subclavian and jugular veins, and that this may be a means, when very extensively carried out—that is, when the cellular tissue is largely involved—of producing coagulations at the right side of the heart, and pulmonary obstructions, especially in cases of already existing pulmonary retardation, weak heart, or blood vitiation. It is a pathological condition, the existence of which is fully borne out by reference to cases of ulcerative disease, extensive burns—indeed, all cases in which the cellular tissue is much involved.

Dr. Tyler Smith thought the Society very much indebted to Dr. Fox for the able way in which upon several occasions he had brought forward this important subject. His own view was that all the symptoms of phlegmasia dolens might be produced either by obstruction of the veins, arteries, or lymphatics; but that pathology and clinical observation combined to show that obstruction of the veins was the lesion most frequently found in these cases. The author of the paper had rendered a service by directing special attention to the lymphatics in this disease—a point which had been somewhat lost sight of in the present day.

Dr. Fox, in reply, asked the President to explain how phlegmasia dolens resulted in cases where no trace whatever of venous disease existed post mortem; and how it was, supposing blood vitiation and venous obstruction to be the cause, that sometimes œdema, and sometimes phlegmasia dolens resulted; why the swelling commenced sometimes above and sometimes below; why phlegmasia dolens, which was a greater degree of disease than œdema, resulting from blood vitiation (according to prevailing theories), possessed so low a mortality. It was evident in blood disease, as appears from recent pathological inquiry (especially brought out in the late discussion on puerperal fever at the Parisian Academy), that the lymphatics are as frequently affected as the veins, as in the broad ligament of the uterus. A distinction must be drawn between thrombosis and inflammation of the lymphatics, which was usually due to septic poison, obstruction being uncommon, and certain tissue actions, set going in answer to the blood state, modifying the whole character of any swelling. He (Dr. Fox) did not throw cold water upon pathological facts, for the paper was based upon such; but thought that experimental evidence, such as that brought forward by Dr. Mackenzie, should not set aside clinical facts.

JULY 2ND, 1862.

DR. TYLER SMITH, President, in the Chair.

Present—30 Fellows and 12 visitors.

The following gentlemen were duly elected Fellows of the Society:—Richard Lanphier, Esq., M.B., Alford, Lincolnshire; William Taylor, Esq., M.R.C.S.E., Scarborough.

A REPORT ON A TWIN (?) ABORTION EXHIBITED TO THE SOCIETY BY DR. LANGMORE ON JUNE 4th, 1862.

By GEORGE HARLEY, M.D., and T. H. TANNER, M.D.

IN accordance with the wish of the Society expressed at the last meeting, we beg to say that the preparation of a twin (?) abortion exhibited by Dr. Langmore has been carefully examined, and that we have been led to entertain certain views as to its nature. Before stating our conclusions, however, it will be convenient to give a brief history of the case. This, as furnished to us by Drs. Langmore and Priestley, seems to be as follows:

Mrs. B—, æt. 38, has had nine children, the youngest being three years old. Has never had twins. The catamenia were on for the last time in January, 1862, and they ceased on the 20th. On the 22nd May, when she was probably about four months advanced in pregnancy, she noticed a slight vaginal discharge; a fortnight previously having had shivering and a continued feeling of coldness in the abdomen. In the evening pains came on, and a fœtus, apparently of about four months' gestation, was expelled. It was flattened, and more or less atrophied; and on examination immediately afterwards, it was apparent that it had been *dead some time*. Serious hæmorrhage set in, and therefore Dr. Langmore, who, up to this time had been in charge of the case, summoned Dr. Priestley for consultation. This gentleman, on his arrival, removed the placenta, which corresponded in size with the fœtus expelled. As the flooding was not checked by this proceeding, Dr. Priestley again introduced his finger into the uterus; when, by depressing the organ with the hand applied over the pubes, he reached a smooth, soft body, which was adherent to the upper part of the cavity, but was removed without much difficulty. On withdrawing this body it was found to consist of a second bag of membranes. The chorion and amnion were unruptured, healthy, and transparent; and through them an embryo of about five or six weeks could be plainly seen, floating in clear liquor amnii. The embryo appeared fresh and perfect, not at all atrophied, and minute vessels could be distinguished ramifying on its dorsal surface. There was a little fresh blood-clot, adherent here and there to the villi of the chorion; and as this was not removed before putting the preparation into spirit, it became hardened and incorporated with the villi. There were, however, none of the appearances of ordinary apoplectic ovum. The decidua of this second ovum came away separately, and was healthy; there were no indurations in its substance, but here and there it was infiltrated with fresh blood.

When the preparation came into our hands it had been in spirit for thirteen days. The first fœtus was of about the fourth month of utero-gestation. It was a male, the penis and scrotum being distinct; it measured five and a half inches in length from the occiput to the heel. The eyelids were separable. Mouth, lips, and tongue, perfectly distinct. The ears were tolerably advanced in formation, the meatus being distinct. The nails were already defined.

The placenta was pale and exsanguine in some portions, in others dark and filled with clotted blood. The membranes and cord were distinct. The cause of death appeared to have been strangulation from twisting of the cord.

In the second preparation we found the membranes unruptured, but opaque; and through them an ovum could be indistinctly seen floating in liquor amnii. A portion of the chorion villi was imbedded in blood-clot, but this could be separated, where it was attempted, in one small portion only. The whole seemed healthy, allowing for the changes produced by the spirit. The sac of the membranes measured two and one-eighth inches. On opening the bag a small embryo, in a good state of preservation, was discovered. It measured five-eighths of an inch in length and five-sixteenths in breadth. The head, with the eye, was perfectly distinct. So, also, were the branchial clefts. The legs and arms already projected from the trunk. The interior of the sac was at one spot unusually vascular.

After examining this preparation we have come to the conclusion that it is, in all probability, an example of superfœtation. That superfœtation is possible during the first few days after conception is generally allowed, and, indeed, cannot be disputed. In no other way can be explained the cases, related on good authority, where negro women have brought forth twin children, one being a negro, the other a mulatto, after successive impregnations by black and white men. So, again, a mare, covered first by a stallion and afterwards by an ass, has produced at one parturition a horse and a mule.

The question, then, arises, is there any physical obstacle to the occurrence of superfœtation at a later period? There seems to be none until about the end of the third month. As is well known, the *decidua vera* is only the hypertrophied mucous membrane of the uterus. It is not, as it was once thought to be, a complete bag, occluding the os uteri and the orifices of the Fallopian tubes. The new structure is the thin *decidua reflexa*, which springs from the mucous membrane and envelopes the ovum; but it does not come into contact with the decidua vera, and so close up the uterus, until about the third month of gestation. Dr. Matthews Duncan has described a preparation which well illustrates some points in regard to the decidua. This gentleman says ('Monthly Journal of Medical Science,' vol. xvi, p. 326, Edinburgh, 1853) :—

"The woman from whom this preparation was taken died from causes quite unconnected with the uterus or its functions. Judging from the development of the fœtus, she had arrived, at least, at the eighth week of pregnancy. The mucous membrane lining the uterus, or the decidua vera, is seen to be of great thickness; that lining the cervix is unchanged. The openings of the cervix uteri and of the Fallopian tube of the left side are easily seen; that of the right tube has been destroyed in dissection. The decidua reflexa completely covers the ovum, being a thin layer, without glands, springing from the decidua vera. The cavity of the uterus is still not closed, there being ample space all around the ovum between the two parts of the decidua, from the os uteri to the tubes."

Then, as regards the supposed mucous plug which fills the cervix during pregnancy, there seems to be no difference between it and that found in the unimpregnated uterus. Moreover, in cases where the catamenia continue regular for three or four periods after impregnation, the supposed plug in no way impedes the flow, nor does the flow seem to endanger the ovum.

Dr. Tyler Smith has related ('Lancet,' April 12th, 1856) a case very similar to the one under consideration. A young married lady, pregnant for the first time, miscarried at the end of the fifth month, and some hours afterwards a small clot was discharged, enclosing a perfectly fresh and healthy ovum of about one month. There were no signs of a double uterus in this case. The patient had menstruated regularly during the time she had been pregnant, and was unwell three weeks before she aborted.

In conclusion, we are led to assume that the case under consideration is one of superfœtation, for this reason :—If the second, healthy, six weeks' ovum were the product of the same conception as the first, four months' fœtus, which had been *dead some time* when expelled, then we must believe that although the latter perished some days before its expulsion, and manifested symptoms of putrefaction, yet the small, second ovum died when six weeks old, was retained for about ten weeks afterwards, and, nevertheless, when removed, was perfectly healthy, and did not present any trace of decomposition. We cannot subscribe to this improbable view. As, theoretically, we see no physical obstacle to the occurrence of superfœtation during the first three months of pregnancy, so we think the specimen now reported upon proves, so far as anything of the sort can prove, that superfœtation is a positive fact.

ENORMOUS DEVELOPMENT OF HYDATIDS IN OMENTUM, ETC., SIMULATING AN OVARIAN TUMOUR.

By William Newman, M.D., Stamford.

(Communicated by Professor Harley.)

Mrs. M—, æt. 43, married twenty years; has had three children; first born five years after marriage; the others each after an interval of two years; has not had any miscarriage. The labours were always easy.

States that she has not had good health for eleven years past; had "spasms" very frequently; more or less of nausea, and sometimes actual vomiting. At times a good deal of pain about the abdomen, never very severe—twisting, uneasy kind of pain. Never had jaundice or any yellowness of skin.

Menstruation quite regular since the birth of her last child.

Five years ago (in 1857) she first consulted Mr. Eaton, of Ancaster. The symptoms were, as a whole, indefinite; there was some enlargement of the abdomen on the left side, and dulness on percussion, radiating from the left iliac fossa, where it was most evident. Ulceration of the os uteri was detected, and much benefit was derived from local cauterization and general treatment. Within a few months after Mr. Eaton first saw her he detected a hard lump on the right side of the abdomen, situate about the outer border of the hypogastric region. This could be felt per vaginam, and could be balanced—one hand on the abdomen, and the fingers of the other introduced per vaginam.

States that the said lump increased for four years, steadily but slowly, until, in October, 1860, she was very ill, with much pain and sickness, and the swelling became much larger between the spinal column and the crest of the ilium on the right side. The skin became red and very tense. Mr. Eaton made an incision and let out, with very great relief, a quantity of matter, one or two hydatid cysts escaping at the same time. The discharge of pus continued until March, 1861 (five or six months); from twelve to twenty-four hydatid-cysts escaping altogether from the artificial opening. The discharge ceased, and the opening healed.

She is now (January, 1862) in fair health; oppressed by size and weight; the abdomen is of very considerable size.

I learn, on inquiry, from Mr. Eaton, that he had no doubt that the swelling and lump in the right iliac fossa was due to some enlargement of the right ovary, and that he believed the subsequent increase in size of the abdomen to be due to the steady increase of this local disease.

He had never thoroughly satisfied himself as to what was the cause of the dulness on percussion and the increase in size in the left iliac fossa, existing when he first saw the patient.

After the apparent increase of the tumour detected in the right side, the right side of the abdomen became the largest, and remained so for a year or more; then the left side of the abdomen was also increased. There was no indication of fresh development of disease in the pelvic viscera of the left side, and percussion and manipulation gave no distinct evidence of the existence of two separate masses.

The percussion signs noted at different times during her

illness were always those of thorough dulness in the right iliac region and the right flank, with good resonance in not at all more than the upper third of the abdomen; while on the left side there was uniform dulness, specially marked up to a line midway between the crest of the ilium and the ribs, and resonance above.

I may add that the case was looked upon by the medical men who saw the patient as one "of multilocular ovarian cyst." No question was entertained on this point.

May 10th, 1862.—Had not been so well for a fortnight or more. Symptoms of acute peritonitis showed themselves about forty-eight hours back, and she sank rapidly, dying at 4 p.m.

11th.—*Post-mortem examination,* 6·30 p.m.—Body much emaciated; no œdema of lower limbs; abdomen very large, thirty-eight inches over umbilicus; most prominent below umbilicus; projecting forwards and downwards, not laterally; presenting nodulated appearances, more especially on right side; more resistent in some parts than others; fluctuation evident in patches, not uniformly present.

On opening the abdomen the large omentum was seen stretched over a mass of glistening cysts on both sides; the transverse colon in usual position above.

The sternum was dissected up, and then came into view—the diaphragm, pushed up nearly to level between third and fourth ribs, by soft, fluctuating tumour, formed by two masses of hydatids, lying imbedded in upper and anterior surface of the right lobe of the liver, in hollowed-out depression, this probably from four to six inches in diameter by one and a half inch or two inches deep. Lined, each of masses, by dense, white, thick membrane, and containing abundant hydatid-vesicles of every size.

So far as could be ascertained, the exclusion of the cysts from the mass of the liver was complete, and the hepatic structure was normal in appearance and free from appearance of morbid growth, excepting quite at the posterior and lower part of the right lobe, where cysts of the same character and appearance were again found to exist. From this second deposit ran an unbroken chain of hydatid-cysts, prolonged in front of the right kidney, across the spinal column, deep down into the pelvic cavity, occupying more especially the left iliac fossa. Springing from this, or continuous with it, was a huge mass of hydatid-cysts, closely embracing the uterus, left ovary, bladder. The right ovary was apparently represented by a firm, solid mass, the size of a small fœtal head, tough in texture, and whitish-red in colour, having no cysts in its interior, though an independent cluster, imbedded in the mesentery, closely surrounded the whole mass.

The great omentum, stretched over the masses just mentioned, presented numerous unconnected cysts in its texture, not very large.

On the left side, lying almost parallel with the crest of the ilium, was a single, enormous cyst, having many smaller ones shooting from it, and deeply attached to the mesentery.

The kidneys were *in situ*, and not implicated in the morbid growths; healthy in structure. Spleen healthy.

The contents of many of the larger cysts (those of a large, superficial one in particular, on the right side) were puriform, broken-down cyst-walls, &c. The contents of the smaller ones were pellucid, clear, and unbroken. In others, again, numerous smaller cysts were contained.

The intestines were pushed up and behind the cysts, in an agglomerated mass, and recent lymph coated them, as well as the surfaces of the omentum and the internal wall of the abdomen; the rupture of some superficial cyst had, in all probability, induced the fatal peritonitis.

Adhesions were abundant between the abdominal wall and the mass of contents; some soft and recent, others, specially about site of abscess, near right ilium, very firm and resistent.

This case seems to have been just one of those where an absolutely correct diagnosis during life was next to impossible. In the conditions of area and character of dulness on percussion—external appearance of the abdomen, its firm, nodulated character, unaltered by supine position—characters of resistance to pressure and localized fluctuation

—there was absolutely no difference between this tumour and the characters which the multilocular ovarian disease would present.

Dr. Simpson, in his published lectures on ovarian dropsy ('Medical Times and Gazette,' December 3rd, 1859), refers to two states which might aid in the diagnosis—the history of the growth of the tumour and its early direction, and the possibility sometimes of pushing the tumour up in the abdominal cavity, so as to prove its non-attachment to anything in the pelvic cavity.

The history in this case tended to prove the tumour "ovarian," and the adhesions were of such an extent as to make the test of raising the whole unavailable, had there not been any direct development of hydatid disease within the alæ of the pelvis.

A CASE IN WHICH AIR WAS EXPELLED FROM THE VAGINA.

By George Harley, M.D.

The chief points in the case are these:—The expulsion of the air is accompanied with a loud noise, and, although odourless, is attended with great personal discomfort. It began about eighteen months ago, at a catamenial period, and has recurred with increasing severity at each period, until now there are several discharges in the course of a few minutes. The patient is married, and the mother of three children. The vagina was carefully examined, in order to find if any communication existed between it and the rectum, but none was found. In order to ascertain, if possible, the source of the air, Dr. Harley took a full-sized male catheter, to which was attached a long india-rubber tube with a stop-cock at the other end. The catheter was introduced into the uterus, the end of the tube with the stop-cock being placed in a tumbler of water. No air escaped when the instrument was in this position; but on placing the open end of the catheter in the vagina an instantaneous discharge of gas took place. Soon afterwards the water was found to be sucked up through the tube into the vagina; and after one or two other experiments it was found that the vagina sucked in and expelled the air by spasmodic action. It was further observed that the abdominal muscles materially assisted in producing this result; and although the patient has not the power of commencing the action, once it has begun and gone on for a few minutes she has the power of continuing it.

The uterus is completely retroverted, and the posterior lip of the os is ulcerated. The lady's health is far from good. She looks careworn and anæmic. She had dysentery while in India.

Treatment.—The uterus was got into its normal position, and a course of strong nervine tonics, together with astringent vaginal injections, completely arrested the spasmodic affection of the vagina in the space of two or three weeks.

Dr. Druitt was glad to find that the phenomena of this case had been described by so acute and exact an observer, otherwise the case might have been narrated as one of physometra. He had once been consulted about the case of a lady who, after her confinement in a hot country, complained of want of sexual feeling, and likewise of discharges of air from the vagina. He had attributed both maladies to relaxation, and prescribed cold alum baths. Air would readily enter a relaxed vagina in large quantities; for example, when a woman was placed upon her hands and knees for the purpose of examination.

Dr. Graily Hewitt had seen a case of the kind mentioned by Dr. Harley. The lady, to whom the passage of flatus from the vagina was very distressing, was the subject of enlargement and hypertrophy of the vaginal part of the cervix uteri. No fistulous opening existed between the rectum and the vagina. In this case Dr. Graily Hewitt considered that the air passed into the vagina by a kind of suction movement. The rigid, flat roof of the vagina, constituted by the indurated cervix, acted as a dilator of the vagina; when during certain movements of the body the uterus was drawn upwards, air entered the vagina.

Dr. Braxton Hicks remarked that the admission of air into the vagina was by no means rare. It might be witnessed not unfrequently in those whose vulvæ were lax and uteri heavy, when they lie down on the examining couch; the weight of the uterus causing it to fall on to the sacrum in the recumbent posture, whereby air was drawn in; while on assuming the erect position it was expelled again by the descent of the uterus.

CLINICAL MEMOIR ON TURNING IN CASES OF DISPROPORTION.

By Alfred H. M'Clintock, M.D., F.R.C.S.I.,
LATE MASTER OF THE DUBLIN LYING-IN HOSPITAL.

The practice of turning in cases of pelvic deformity is, to borrow the language of Dr. Tyler Smith, "one of the agitated questions of the present day, which requires the sober and dispassionate consideration of all who are interested in the establishment and advance of obstetrics."

This, like every other question of a practical bearing, can only be decided by clinical observation. The primary object, then, of this communication is to lay before the Society the results of my own experience of this practice. As to the rationale of the measure and the principles upon which it is based, Dr. Simpson has discussed them so fully as to leave nothing to be said thereupon. At the same time I must observe that Sir Fielding Ould—one of the earliest authors to recommend the practice, and whose treatise was published 120 years ago—had a very good notion of the peculiar advantages belonging to it, for he observes, "It may be objected that the same narrowness of the passage through the pelvis which hindered the natural expulsion with the head foremost may hinder its extraction when brought forth by the feet; this is also allowed; but yet, if we consider the matter properly, it will appear that, by drawing from a small end, which is the feet, in order to bring forth the larger, with the additional assistance of holding the legs in one hand and having the finger of the other in the child's mouth, there is a far greater probability of bringing it forth, than when the large end comes first, and that without any probability of assisting the mother's efforts but by the destruction of the child."

Some writers have been at much pains to make out the

exact limits of pelvic capacity within which the operation should be restricted. I confess I do not see much utility in this, for the very obvious reasons that the size of the child is liable to considerable variation, even at the full time, and also because the exact capacity of the pelvis cannot be determined with precision during life.

Version has been performed by myself, or under my direction, *seventeen* times in the Dublin Lying-in Hospital, on account of disproportion between the child and pelvis.

The following table gives at one view the leading particulars of each of these cases (*vide* opposite page):

The actual number of different patients operated on was only *twelve*, in consequence of three having been twice or thrice under treatment. Of the *seventeen* operations, *one* was followed by the death of the mother. (Case 2 in Table.) But it is hardly fair to attribute this event to the effects of the operation. Her labour was only twelve hours long from first to last, and the version was not attended with any unusual difficulty. She was in a depressed state of mind from domestic causes, and died of puerperal fever—then rather prevalent—on the eighth day after delivery. This child was born alive, but the right parietal bone, which had lain next the sacrum, showed a great depression. This disappeared in the course of a few days, however.

Her first labour was difficult, her second also difficult, and terminated by instruments, the child being lost on both occasions. On her third labour she came for the first time under my care. (Case 1 in Table.) Having waited for four hours after the rupture of the membranes, to see if the pains, which were vigorous, would cause the head to descend into the pelvis, and finding that no impression was made on it, I had her put under chloroform, and Dr. Byrne, one of the assistant-physicians to the hospital, turned the child without much difficulty. Considerable delay took place in the extraction of the head; and though the fœtal heart pulsated at birth, and the child made two or three gasps, still respiration could not be established.

Table of Cases in which Turning was performed for Disproportion.

No.	Age.	Hours in labour.	Child.		Former births.		Got chloroform.	Result to mother.	Observations.
			Alive.	Dead.	Alive.	Dead.			
1	25	15	—	G.	—	B. 2 G.	Yes	Recovered	Same patient: Child's heart beating at birth.
2	27	12	B.	—	—	B. 3 G.	Yes	Died	Same patient: Of puerperal fever.
3	42	22	G.	—	4 G.	4 B.	Yes	Recovered.	
4	32	36	—	B.	G.	2 B. 2 G.	Yes	Recovered	Same patient: Funis presented. Craniotomy; head locked in brim.*
5	34	6	B.	—	G.	3 B. 2 G.	Yes	Recovered	Same patient
6	35	12	G.	—	B. G.	3 B. 2 G.	Yes	Recovered	Same patient: Indentation of parietal bone.
7	30	26	—	B.	—	2 G.	Yes	Recovered	Child's heart beating at birth.
8	34	11	—	B.	G.	3 B.	Yes	Recovered	Child's heart beating at birth.
9	30	16	—	G.	4 G.	B.	Yes	Recovered	Child's heart beating at birth. All her labours difficult.
10	23	23	G.	—	—	2 B.	Yes	Recovered	
11	35	14	—	B.	3 G.	B. 4 G.	No	Recovered	Child's heart beating at birth. Parietal bone fractured.
12	28	38	—	G.	—	G.	Yes	Recovered	Child's heart beating at birth.
13	32	18	—	B.	—	—	Yes	Recovered	Same patient: Craniotomy necessary to complete version.
14	33	33	G.	—	—	B.	Yes	Recovered	Same patient
15	36	16	B.	—	G.	B.	Yes	Recovered	Same patient
16	27	17	G.	—	B.	2 G.	Yes	Recovered	Boy saved by bringing down leg, after fifty-five hours' labour, breech having presented.
17	30	18	B.	—	B. 3 G.	2 B.	Yes	Recovered	All her previous labours difficult; two instrumental.

The gross average mortality of the mothers after the operation of turning is stated by Churchill to be about one in fifteen. Hence its performance in the class of cases now under consideration would not seem to be attended with any increased risk to the parent.

The average length of the labour in the seventeen cases was considerable, viz., *nineteen* hours; the extremes being *six* and *thirty-eight*. In *twelve* instances the membranes had been ruptured for some hours before turning. With one exception (Case 11) chloroform was administered on every occasion. In this solitary instance it was not given, in consequence of the woman's determined opposition. Neither entreaty, threats, nor arguments, could prevail on her to inhale it, so I conceded the point. She told us she could and would bear any amount of pain without flinching, and she proved as good as her word. She was in labour of her ninth child when admitted to the hospital, and though the pelvis did not present any notable indication of deformity, yet the history of her former labours led me to suppose that there must be some defect in it. All her children were delivered artificially, and five of them were dead, three girls only having been born alive. Immense difficulty was experienced in withdrawing the head, and the child was lost, though the fœtal heart pulsated for fifteen minutes after birth. I shall have occasion to allude to this child again.

In *fifteen* instances the extraction of the infant was effected by manual assistance alone, and in *two* cases I was compelled to resort to the perforator and crotchet, having failed, after prolonged efforts, to get the head away by any other means. One of these cases I must here relate, as it has a strong practical bearing upon the operation of turning.

M. M—(Case No. 13 in Table), in labour of her first child, was brought into hospital at 9 a.m., the waters having come away the preceding day. Moderate pains were present; the hand and funis partially protruded through the os, which was soft, and nearly fully dilated; the head could be felt immediately above. There was some pulsation in the cord. She was immediately chloroformed, and the hand was introduced into the uterus, and one leg of the child seized and brought into the vagina, though not without some difficulty; but all the force we could use, pulling at the leg, or pushing up the head, or doing both simultaneously, could not make the child revolve. Having vainly endeavoured for upwards of two hours to draw down the breech into the pelvis, we had to abandon the attempt, and, as all pulsation in the cord had long ceased, I made an opening into the head. This done, a great deal of cerebrum came away, and now I was able, with moderate exertion, to pull down the breech and deliver the child, which proved to be a large male. This case recalls to my mind an observation by Madame La Chapelle. She says that, where the head has been the presenting part, it is very difficult to terminate the delivery by drawing down a single leg, and that this difficulty is produced by the head being pushed into the brim before the breech of the child; the buttocks acting in the same way, she says, as the knot on a cord with which we extract a cork from the interior of a bottle. When both feet, on the contrary, have been seized, there is much less difficulty, she asserts, in pushing up the head, and getting the child to make the turn or revolution.

This woman seemed to have a pelvis, not actually deformed perhaps, but of the deep, masculine kind. It was her first labour, and she was the only primipara among the twelve patients. I should not have felt justified in giving it a place in this collection, did not her two subsequent labours prove that there existed some deficiency in the size of the pelvis. Her second labour (Case No. 14 in Table) lasted nearly thirty-three hours. I waited for some hours after the full dilatation of the os uteri, to see if the head would descend, but it remained quite at the brim. I endeavoured, as carefully as I could, to measure the pelvis with my hand when she was under chloroform, and the result showed the conjugate diameter to be about three and three eighths inches, but this can only be an approximation. The child was a girl, and born in a very weakly state, but was brought round by the persevering employment of restoratives. On the posterior part of the left parietal bone was a marked depression, which, I consider, was caused by the sacrum before the version was undertaken, the head having presented in the first position.

The other patient on whom I had to perform craniotomy (Case No. 4 in Table) first came under my care in her sixth labour, all her previous labours having been difficult, and four of her children dead-born. When admitted, she had been many hours in labour, and the funis was presenting along with the hand and head. Version was effected under chloroform without any great difficulty. The head stuck fast in the brim, and no amount of force could extract it, so that eventually it became necessary to perforate, which I did by fixing the small end of a blunt hook on the lower jaw, and then carrying up the perforator through the mouth and base of the skull. This woman I delivered by turning and saved the children in her two succeeding labours. The latter of them (Case No. 6 in Table) took place in January, 1861. It required very powerful exertion to bring the head of the child through the upper strait of the pelvis, and it presented a considerable depression in the situation of the anterior inferior angle of the left parietal bone,—the one which had lain next the sacral promontory. A very large, sanguineous tumour formed on the left side of the head and around the indentation immediately after birth. This disappeared in some days, but the depression remained, and when I saw the child a month afterwards had undergone little change.

In Case 11, to which I have already adverted, as the only instance where chloroform was not administered, the turning and extraction of the child went on very well till it came to the head, but at this stage immense difficulty was encountered. The pulsations ceased in the funis, and I really thought it would be necessary to employ the perforator and crotchet. At length the head was pulled through the brim, and instantly it cleared the outlet. The fœtal heart was beating, and continued to do so for a quarter of an hour. Respiration could not be established. On the right parietal bone (that next the sacrum) was a marked depression, and, as in the case last mentioned, a tumour speedily formed in this situation. Upon dissection, this tumour was found to be caused by the extravasation of blood between the scalp and pericranium. This parietal bone was fractured; the solution of continuity extending upwards from the inferior or temporal edge, and nearer to the coronal than the lambdoidal suture. There was a slight depression of the posterior portion of the bone. The woman recovered without any untoward symptom.

One other case, No. 17 in Table, requires that I should give a short sketch of its history. It was the woman's seventh labour. Three of her children had been boys and three girls. With each of the former parturition was most difficult. One of them I delivered with the forceps, by the high operation. Great force had to be used, and though the fœtal heart was beating when the instrument was applied, the child was dead-born. Another boy was also dead-born, having been delivered instrumentally by my predecessor, Dr. Shekleton. And the third boy was expelled alive by the natural efforts; but from the time of the breaking of the membranes till the child was born—a period of twelve hours—the pains were incessant, and of the most violent, expulsive kind. On the present occasion the waters were discharged about five o'clock a.m., after which the pains became more frequent and very much stronger than before. The fœtal heart was audible high up and to the right side. For five hours this strong uterine action continued, the head meanwhile remaining stationary at the brim. Seeing no prospect of an advance of the head, and apprehending rupture of the uterus, I put her fully under the influence of chloroform, passed up my left hand, and turned the child. The head was entering the brim in the second, or right occipito-anterior, position. I had brought down only one leg, and had some little trouble getting the child to turn. There was much difficulty extricating the arms, and very great difficulty with the head, which was a good deal compressed laterally, and presented a depression on the right parietal bone, this having borne against the sacrum. The humerus of the sacral arm had sustained a partial or green-stick fracture. This was the only occasion on which I ever broke the humerus when extracting the arms, though I own to having several times broken the clavicle. There was scarcely any cardiac pulsation in this child when born; nevertheless its resuscitation was speedily effected. The woman recovered very well.

I do not conceive it necessary to occupy the time of the Society with any further details of the several cases. Those I have related will serve very well as examples, and in the tabular statement are shown the leading particulars of each. Let me now mention the chief circumstances of interest connected with the infants.

Of the *seventeen* children, *nine* survived birth, that is to say, they lived and breathed. Just permit me here to remark that I have never regarded a child as saved by an obstetric operation, nor have I recorded it as born "alive," unless respiration was fully established. In all other cases the child was reckoned among the "dead-born;" for unless it breathe I consider its life to be but intra-uterine life, and no more. This may be bad physiology (though I doubt it), and contrary to the law of the land; but still it is the principle I acted on in the registering of births. The fœtal heart continued to pulsate for a period varying from fifteen to twenty minutes after delivery in five of the children recorded as "dead-born" in the Table.

Of the *nine* children born alive, *four* were boys and *five* were girls; whilst of those dead-born the numbers were reversed, *five* being boys and *three* girls. The influence of sex upon the result of labour, *quoad* the fœtus, is thus well illustrated. But a more striking exemplification is to be found in the general result of all the births which the twelve women had. The total number of mature children born to them was sixty-four, viz., twenty-seven boys and thirty-seven girls. Of the boys, twenty-one were born dead, which is a proportion of 78 per cent. upon all the male births; whilst of the girls only sixteen were dead-born, being in the proportion of 43 per cent. of all the female births. Who could have supposed that so small a difference between the size of the male and female fœtal head could have produced so great a difference in the results!

In every instance where turning was performed, before determining upon the operation, the child was ascertained by auscultation to be alive.

What now, it may be asked, is the practical value of this measure, and what are the limits of its utility? These are important questions, and in answering them I would particularly wish to guard myself from the imputation of speaking authoritatively or dogmatically. Of course, I have formed some opinion of my own, and have drawn some general conclusions from what I have seen; and I shall honestly state, under a sense of duty, the impressions that have been made on my mind. In so doing, the members present will not, I trust, consider me to be egotistical or presumptuous. In the first place, let me observe that in none of these patients was there any considerable contraction of the pelvis. The evidence, in nearly all of them, tended to prove that the amount of narrowing must have been, comparatively speaking, slight, and altogether confined to the upper strait, as most of these women had given birth by the natural efforts to mature children. Nevertheless, in every instance force had to be employed, subsequently to turning, and in some instances powerful force, in order to bring the head into the pelvic cavity; and on one occasion the perforator and crochet had to be used before this could be effected at all. Of the children, we have already seen that rather less than one in two was lost. Upon the gross average of all cases of turning, the infantile mortality, according to Dr. Churchill's statistics, is a fraction more than one in three. Here is a difference of about 17 per cent. in favour of the latter over the former class of cases.

Looking to the interests of the child, then, I think that the value of this measure has been exaggerated by its advocates, and that it is only where the degree of pelvic contraction, or, more properly, of disproportion, is *very slight*, we can resort to it with any certainty of saving the fœtus. Hence I would not deliberately advise a patient who had a decided contraction of the pelvis to await the natural accession of parturition, and trust to turning, in preference to the induction of premature labour, for the saving of herself and child.

I am very far from wishing to underrate the value of turning as a means of saving fœtal life in the class of cases under consideration. That it really gives an increased chance of safety to the child is a proposition which admits of being proved from the Table I have given. The eleven women (for the primipara need not be included) were delivered of 47 children by *other* modes than turning—some by the natural efforts, some by the forceps, some by craniotomy; of these 47 children, 18 were born alive, that is 38 per cent.: whilst of the children of the same women (including the primipara), delivered by turning, the proportion born alive was almost 53 per cent. If we carry this comparative analysis to the sexes of the children, we find the proportion of boys born alive after turning to be four ninths, or 44 per cent.; whereas of those delivered by other means, only 2 out of 18, or 11 per cent., were alive. With the female children the contrast is not so great. Five eighths, or 62 per cent., were extracted alive by version; and of 29 children delivered by other means, sixteen, or 55 per cent., were living. The results of these comparisons are, no doubt, favorable to turning; but they must be accepted with reserve, the data they are based on being so limited.

Setting aside all theoretical considerations, and looking merely at the results of practice, I cannot help thinking that the limits within which version is strictly applicable are so confined that it can hardly, if at all, supersede the artificial induction of labour, especially with the improvements which Dr. Barnes has pointed out to us for ensuring and accelerating this operation. In nearly all the cases upon which this memoir is based the existence of any defect in the capacity of the pelvis was rather a matter of inference than of demonstration. The character of the woman's previous labours led us to *infer* that there probably existed some deficiency of space, but in only three or four instances was this palpable to the examiner. Yet how great was the force required to bring the head through the brim! A much less degree of force, applied for a longer time, would, no doubt, suffice. But the very nature of this mode of delivery absolutely precludes a delay of more than a very few minutes if the child is to be saved.

There may be room for instituting, in these cases of slight pelvic contraction, a comparison between the relative advantages of turning and of the long forceps, or, rather, of the high operation with the long forceps. This is a controverted point, however, which I shall not now stop to discuss, as my experience in the use of the long forceps, when the head is at or above the brim, is, perhaps, too limited; but I freely confess that in cases of disproportion I would confine the high-forceps operation to those in which turning is impracticable, or would be attended with great risk.

Where the results of a patient's previous labours, or of careful admeasurement of the pelvis, warrant the conclusion that a live birth is not to be expected with a natural, that is, a head presentation, under such circumstances I would resort to turning as early in the labour as the state of the os would admit.

But another and more perplexing class of patients comprehends those where things are so nicely balanced that the slight difference depending on the child being male or female, above or below the standard bulk, may seriously affect the results of parturition. If the case be consigned to nature till the woman's vital forces begin to give way in the prolonged struggle, it may then be too late to attempt turning. In a few instances of this doubtful kind what I did was this—I gave nature a few (three or four) hours' trial after the os was fully opened, to see whether the head was likely to descend or not. In our prognosis of these cases of obstructed labour, rupture of the uterus is a contingency which must never be left out of view,

Looking to the interests of the mother only, I think this operation has stronger claims than when viewed in its relation to fœtal life. By an early resort to turning, the duration of the labour may be materially abridged; and if successful, all danger from rupture of the uterus, or from the alternative measures of craniotomy, and the high-forceps operation, is completely avoided. On the other hand, it must not be forgotten that if the operation fail, and the head become locked in the brim, not only is the child lost, but the woman must undergo a second operation.

This brings me to the last point I have to notice, namely, whether, in cases requiring craniotomy, is version more likely to diminish or increase the difficulties of delivery? This question is not decided by authorities; but, judging from my own experience, I should prefer using the perforator and crotchet when the head is coming *first* than when it comes *last*; therefore, on the ground of convenience alone, I would not substitute the feet for the head. A regard for the patient's safety should prompt the same course, for craniotomy by itself, is surely not so dangerous to the patient as craniotomy superadded to version.

The mechanical advantage of this mode of delivery in cases of disproportion depends altogether, I should say, upon the opportunity thereby afforded of supplementing the contractions of the uterus to an almost unlimited extent. I do not believe that the diameters of the head are more advantageously placed with regard to those of the pelvis, nor can I believe that the head is more compressible when entering the strait with its base than when it does so with its vertex, till this be demonstrated by direct experiment.

Dr. Barnes expressed his thanks to Dr. M'Clintock for having brought this important practical question before the Society, the more especially as his paper was based on so broad a foundation of facts. Dr. Barnes hoped that, as one who had some personal experience of the operation, he might, without impropriety, respond to the invitation of the President. He observed that the revival of the application of turning to certain cases of disproportion constituted one of the greatest merits rendered by Professor Simpson to obstetric practice. He felt he was justified in calling it a revival, for he thought there was abundant evidence that the great accoucheurs who practised one and two hundred years ago were accustomed to trust to this operation much more freely than was now done. To this course Dr. Barnes said they were almost compelled by the want of those instruments with which, in our day, we were enabled to encounter cases of disproportion. Having no forceps, and but inefficient instruments of any kind, they were forced to trust to their unarmed hands. With their hands they extricated themselves and their patients from many difficulties, in which we resorted to the perforator or other instrumental aid. He entertained a strong conviction that we should return to a more sedulous cultivation of the hands as an obstetric instrument, and that material improvement in obstetric practice would result. The extension of the operation of turning as a substitute for more hazardous operations, and as a means of extricating patients from a variety of dangers, was especially to be desired. The particular application of turning to cases of disproportion was one of which he had formed a favorable opinion. At first, after Dr. Simpson's proposition to revive it, he distrusted its utility. He tried it by the favorite test of statistics. But he had since learned that we possessed no such statistics as would serve for the determination of any great question in obstetric practice. He had put the question fairly to the test of experience. He might state the general result of his observations as follows:—Disproportions might be divided into three degrees: First, there were slight disproportions, giving rise to protracted labour, which admitted of being relieved by the long forceps; but the forceps must be not only long, but double-curved, well-made, and capable of being worked by the two hands. There was then a second degree, or class of cases, lying between the class capable of relief by the forceps and the third degree, or class, in which craniotomy was necessary. This second or intermediate degree it was that properly admitted of treatment by turning. Beyond the third degree might be added a fourth, in which the Cæsarean section was the resource. It was thus seen that the operation of turning stood between the patient and craniotomy, promising to avert the necessity, in some cases, of resorting to that repulsive operation. It did not appear that the disproportion in most of Dr. M'Clintock's cases was great. It seemed probable that in some of them the long forceps might have been successful. Where there was only slight pelvic contraction, he (Dr. Barnes) thought it right to try the forceps first, and, failing in this manner, to proceed to turning. It was true that the practice was necessarily experimental. Dr. M'Clintock had fairly said that we could not determine beforehand the size of the child's head. We could not, therefore, tell beforehand what the degree of obstruction would be. But if the child were born dead after turning, we had, at least, the satisfaction of reflecting that the child was not sacrificed, of necessity, by the mode of operating, as was the case in perforation. If it perished, it was because it had to pass through a pelvis whose condition was incompatible with the birth of a living child. He did not assent to the opinion of Dr. M'Clintock, that the head did not come through the pelvic brim more easily when drawn through base first than in the ordinary mode of entry by the crown. He thought the passage much facilitated. It might seem strange, but he had seen reason to believe, that in these cases of disproportion the child had a somewhat better chance of being born alive than after turning under ordinary conditions. The common cause of disproportion was slight projection of the promontory of the sacrum; on either side a marked hollow was preserved, in one or other of which the cord would lie protected. A very valuable application of the practice was found in the completion of delivery after perforation. In cases where much difficulty had been experienced in extracting the head by the crochet and craniotomy-forceps he had, on several occasions, delivered with ease in a few minutes by turning. Much labour to the practitioner, exhaustion and distress to the patient, were thus saved. He would make one more remark; it was that, although great force had occasionally been necessary in extracting, he had never seen the smallest injury result to the mother. The patients had recovered as speedily and as well as after ordinary labours. Dr. Barnes concluded by again expressing his sense of the high value of Dr. M'Clintock's communication.

Dr. Kidd thought that no comparison could be drawn between the statistics of former times and the present, because the influence of chloroform must be taken into account.

Dr. Braxton Hicks considered that the cases brought forward by Dr. M'Clintock could scarcely be fairly quoted as examples of the value of turning over the use of the long forceps, in either delivering the child or in saving its life. Those cases only could be admitted as absolute proof on that point in which the forceps had been applied, and had failed to bring the head through, but where turning had been subsequently resorted to with success. Dr. Hicks instanced a case which occurred to him recently, in which the long forceps failed to bring the head through the brim, but where, by version, the child was delivered after some detention, its heart pulsating for an hour and a half after, inflation of the lungs being continued till it ceased. In this case the forceps failed. Turning gave the child a chance, to say the least, of life, which the only other treatment left—namely, perforation—could not.

Dr. Graily Hewitt had an observation to make with reference to the difficulty the author of the paper had alluded to of effecting the transit of the body of the fœtus, after turning, where only one foot had been brought down. He believed that the difficulty in question was not confined to cases in which the head had originally presented, as the author seemed to infer was supposed to be the case; and that, on the contrary, the same difficulty was found in other cases—in transverse presentations, *e.g.* He had met with a case which bore out this view of the matter. It had been a sort of maxim that the bringing of one foot down was sufficient. He thought that the erroneousness of this teaching should be pointed out, and the necessity of bringing down both feet, in cases of turning, inculcated. In common with other speakers, he begged to express his thanks to the author for the very valuable contribution he had made to obstetric science in the paper now read to the Society.

Dr. M'Clintock, in reply, said that, before answering the questions which had been put to him, and making such explanatory remarks as the discussion called for, he would wish to avail himself of this the first opportunity which had presented itself, of personally thanking the Society for having elected him an honorary Fellow, a distinction of which he felt truly proud.

He concurred to a great extent in the objections urged by Dr. Barnes against conclusions based merely on statistics, as he felt convinced that there was no proposition, however absurd or monstrous, which might not be sustained by statistical calculations. At the same time he could not help thinking that all questions touching the value of any mode of treatment, or of any remedy, must eventually be decided by an impartial appeal to statistical facts.

He entertained the highest opinion of chloroform, given to the induction of complete anæsthesia, in the operation of turning; and in all the cases, one only excepted, contained in his memoir, chloroform had been so exhibited. In fact, he had long entertained the opinion that there was no other class of obstetric cases in which chloroform contributed so directly to the *safety* of the patient. On other occasions it may conduce to the comfort of the patient, or to the convenience of the accoucheur, but it was more than questionable whether it decidedly lessened the danger attendant upon parturition. He had been in the habit of using it in all cases of turning where there was reason to apprehend any resistance from the uterus; but he considered that nothing short of complete anæsthesia would be of use. He had purposely abstained in his memoir from entering into comparison between the respective claims of turning and the high-forceps operation in cases of disproportion. Although by turning, in the cases under consideration, the chance of saving the fœtus was far from certain, still we might reckon with much confidence upon delivering the woman, at all events; and even if the child was lost, we had the gratifying reflection that it was in the attempt to save its life, and from a cause utterly beyond our control. Some of the speakers considered that a decided mechanical advantage was gained by the base of the skull passing foremost through the pelvis, which only strengthened the opinion he entertained of turning being superior to the forceps where disproportion exists; for if, with this advantage, such enormous force was required to draw the head through the brim, it was surely next to impossible that the forceps could accomplish this with the vertex coming foremost. He had been misapprehended about the cases to which he should restrict the forceps. His meaning was that he would confine its use to those cases where the contracted state of the uterus forbade turning altogether, or rendered the attempt highly dangerous.

As his opinion had been asked relative to the value of turning in cases where the funis presented, he would venture to make an observation or two upon this point. In several cases he had resorted to turning on account of the funis presenting; he could not state, from memory, however, the results of these cases; but he was in favour of the practice where the child was still strong, and the circumstances of the labour were such as to render the operation easy of performance. He believed a careful research would show that a much larger proportion of children were saved by turning than by any other mode of treating this complication of labour.

OCTOBER 1ST, 1862.

DR. TYLER SMITH, President, in the chair.

Present—22 Fellows and 3 visitors.

The following gentlemen were duly elected Fellows of the Society:—Field Flowers Sutton, M.D., Balham Hill, Clapham; William Henry Thornton, M.D., Dewsbury, Yorkshire.

NOTES OF A CASE OF SPINA BIFIDA, FOLLOWED BY HYDROCEPHALUS.

By D. RICHARDS., M.R.C.S.E., Brighton,
FORMERLY PHYSICIAN'S ASSISTANT TO UNIVERSITY COLLEGE HOSPITAL, LONDON.

(Communicated by Dr. TANNER.)

ON the 4th of April, 1860, I attended Mrs. F— in her confinement. She was strong and healthy, and the pelvis was well-formed. After the child's head was born nearly twenty minutes elapsed before the shoulders and back came into the world. The birth being complete, I found that the difficulty had arisen from the extraordinary position of the legs, which were doubled up to the shoulders, and forcibly detained there. From this posture they could not be removed.

The child was a female, and alive. On examining it, I found spina bifida in the lower part of the dorsal region,

As seen July 22nd, 1860.

As seen about beginning of October, 1860.

three spinous processes being entirely wanting. The integument was also wanting, so that there existed an *aperture* in place of the *watery tumour* usually seen in such cases, exposing, as it seems, part of the spinal canal, about an inch in depth. There was also angular curvature of the spine at this part. The palate was cleft, and there was talipes varus of both feet.

The head was healthy, and normal in size.

The child was born on the 4th of April, 1860. The aperture in the back immediately began to close by granulation. On the 2nd of May the left leg descended from its position on the shoulder into its proper place. A fortnight after, the right leg partially descended. At this time the cavity in the spine became entirely closed up with granulations, which rose to the level of the surrounding skin, and so remained.

In *wet weather* the granulating surface appeared wet and inclined to throw out a thinnish discharge, but in *fine weather* the surface looked dry and as if covered with skin.

As the cavity closed, *the head* was observed to enlarge. On the 5th of May it measured in circumference $18\frac{1}{4}$ in.; May 19th, $18\frac{3}{4}$ in.; June 2nd, 19 in.; 16th, $19\frac{1}{2}$ in.; 30th, $19\frac{3}{4}$ in.; July 22nd, 23 in. About this size it remained until the 2nd of October, when a *diminution* was observed.

Some degree of anasarca, which had existed of late, now also began to diminish, and by October 7th had altogether subsided.

The *head* had now diminished to about the same size as at birth, and the *aperture in the spine* was completely healed. The child died October 11th, 1860, from exhaustion.

No post-mortem examination could be obtained.

IMPERFORATE RECTUM; ATTEMPT AT RELIEF BY OPERATION; DEATH.

By William Tilbury Fox, M.D. Lond., University Medical Scholar.

On June 5th I was requested to take charge of the following case:

William M—, aged four days, has passed nothing per anum since birth. The child was lying apparently free from actual pain, seldom crying, evidently exhausted; there has been vomiting of very offensive, dirty fluid, and everything taken into the stomach is now rejected; a good deal of flatus; surface coolish; has made water freely. The belly is greatly distended, tympanitic, and somewhat tender; there is a small but normal-looking anus; a probe, however, merely passes about one eighth of an inch from the opening into a little cul-de-sac; there is no fulness to be seen or felt; on pressing the point of the finger firmly and deeply into the pelvis, it passes in the direction of the rectum without meeting with anything like a distended rectum; there is, however, some impulse on crying, but this appears to be communicated from the general mass of tissues rather than a loaded bowel. Two modes of relief were open for adoption, either to go in search of the rectum or to make an artificial anus by opening the colon. I determined (inasmuch as *some* impulse was felt in the situation of the rectum when the child cried, and the natural outlet was present, indicating *the probability* that the gut was not obliterated very high up) to pass a trocar through the resisting structures, in the hope of hitting upon the rectum. I accordingly passed into the anus the canula, pressing it deeply in the direction of the rectum, and then the trocar in the usual manner, so that the point of the latter must have reached, at least, to a spot an inch and a half from the anal orifice. No good resulted; very little bleeding occurred. An hour or two after this I passed a full-sized bougie (urethral) along the tract of the wound. Neither flatus nor fæcal matter passed through the latter. Looking chiefly to the absence of any distinct impulse, I thought it useless to make any further attempt per anum to restore the bowel, but proposed to the friends to open the colon, putting the inconveniences which would probably result in their true light. An objection was raised, and I left (it being late at night), intending to abide by the decision of the parents, if the child were alive in the morning; at 3 a.m., however, death took place, with apparently an entire absence of suffering.

Post-mortem.—General peritonitis, with hæmorrhagic spots here and there; all the bowels were much distended, except the colon, near the sigmoid flexure, which was less inflamed than other parts; the pelvic fascia and peritoneal reflections were normal. The rectum terminated in a cul-de-sac, about an inch and a half from the anus, with which it was connected by cellular tissue. No effusion in pelvis, and there was less peritonitis about the seat of operation than elsewhere, there being very little, if any, change about the rectal portion of the gut; *its commencement* was loaded with feculent matter of good consistence, but its *termination* was empty almost entirely for the space of more than an inch, and this accounted for the absence of impulse during life, no doubt, in a great measure. The trocar had passed into the very central point of the rectal termination; this is well seen in the actual preparation. There appeared to be no sphincter ani.

Remarks.—The above case is important in several points.

1. Most surgeons agree that, where no impulse is to be felt, the operation of searching for the obliterated rectum is useless; however, this case shows that the absence of impulse is no bar to operation, because the lower part of the bowel may be not fully distended, but, indeed, almost empty.

2. The probability is that, where an anus exists, be it ever so rudimentary, the bowel is not far off.

3. If a trocar be used, it should be a full-sized one.

4. Before withdrawing the canula itself the injection of fluid is desirable; had this been done in the present instance, before instead of after the withdrawal of the canula, it is very likely that some fæcal matter might have been dislodged and expelled, which would have guided us to further procedures.

RUPTURED VAGINA DURING LABOUR; CHILD IN ABDOMEN THREE AND A HALF HOURS; PELVIC CELLULITIS; RECOVERY.

By John Henry Bell, M.D., Bradford.

(Communicated by Dr. Tanner.)

Previous history.—Mary S—, æt. 28, says that generally she has enjoyed very good health; when fifteen years of age, she had typhus; when twenty, she had a child; at twenty-four, she got married; since then she has had two children, both born alive after easy labours; was not more than a quarter of an hour right ill when last confined; never required the attendance of a surgeon; was always up and going about the house on the fourth day. Between her confinements was always very healthy. During her last pregnancy she worked at the mill; appetite was very good, and did not notice anything different to what she had experienced in her previous pregnancies.

Labour commenced on Tuesday, August 6th, 1861, at eight o'clock in the evening, when the membranes ruptured without any previous pain; during the night she had slight, lingering pains in the back and loins; these continued regularly during Wednesday morning, getting what she called "middling strong" in the afternoon, but nothing like so strong as what she had experienced in her previous labours before the birth of the child; about five in the afternoon the pains entirely ceased, her legs became quite numb, and powerless, so that she was unable to move about; she continued in this state until twelve o'clock on Wednesday night, when she was seen by my assistant, Mr. Pritchard; the head had then passed the os uteri, and was well in the pelvis, and he thought it would not be long before being over. There appeared to be plenty of room, the external parts were relaxed, and as she had not had any pains for seven hours, he gave her half a drachm of ergot; this producing no effect, in half an hour the dose was repeated; shortly afterwards, without complaining of much pain, she said she felt "*a tear, a burst, and a flow,*" and thought that the child was born; there was a great discharge of blood. On examination, the head was found to have receded considerably, and receded still further before the finger; the hand was carried forward over the side of the head into the abdominal cavity. It was half-past one on Thursday morning, three quarters of an hour after the rupture had taken place, when I first saw the woman; she was then laid in the middle of the bed, on her right side; everything about her was saturated with blood, although there was no bleeding going on just then; she did not complain of any pain; there was no sickness, no collapse, no restlessness, no unusual anxiety of countenance; the pulse was small, quick, and regular, and she said she felt rather faint. As she was not laid in a favorable position, she turned herself in bed without assistance, and did not complain of it giving her any pain. On making an examination per vaginam, the head was felt at the brim of the pelvis; the hand passed readily, without the slightest resistance, over the side of the head into the abdominal cavity; the bladder, containing some urine, could be felt in front, the intestines above, and the contracted uterus behind; the limbs of the child were felt with the right hand when applied to the abdomen externally, although not so distinctly as I had expected; the head, when grasped with the hand, could be moved about freely, and brought down considerably into the pelvis. As there appeared to be abundance of room, and the external parts were very much relaxed, one blade of the forceps was applied to the under side of the head, the left hand on the upper side acting as the opposing blade; by this means the head was brought to the outlet of the pelvis, but my hand lost its power, and I was obliged to desist. I had some difficulty in applying the other blade of the forceps, owing to the head of the child receding considerably and being very movable; after I had got them nicely adjusted, having a very good hold of the head, without giving much pain to the mother, considerable force was applied, at short intervals, for about three quarters of an hour; the head came readily to the outlet of the pelvis, but could not be brought further, and the forceps were then necessarily withdrawn. She was now left for about twenty minutes, to receive the consolations of her spiritual adviser. The pulse and powers were then apparently the same; she was quite calm, able and willing to do anything required of her; I therefore determined to turn. The hand was introduced into the abdominal cavity, almost as high as the stomach; one foot was laid hold of and extricated from the folds of intestine, and the umbilical cord, and gradually drawn downwards; the body of the child was soon born, but considerable force and time were required before the head would come. The operation of turning did not give any pain that was complained of; she was very quiet and patient the whole of the time. The child, of course, was dead. Nothing remarkable in its appearance.

The fingers were now passed along the umbilical cord, and its insertion into the placenta was readily felt; by gentle traction it came easily away, but whether from the uterus or abdominal cavity I could not be sure. I then passed the hand into the vagina, expecting to find that the rupture was of the lower third of the uterus, involving the vagina, but was surprised to find the os uteri very high, near the sacrum, elongated laterally, but *entire,* and in the position of the left antero-lateral reflection of the mucous membrane of the vagina a large rent, through which the hand passed readily into the abdomen; fortunately there was no prolapsion of the bowel. Immediately after delivery she expressed herself as feeling "nicely;" had no pain or even uneasiness, no faintness; pulse small, weak, and 140. The delivery was completed at four o'clock on Thursday morning, the child having been in the abdominal cavity, and subjected to rather rough usage, for three and a half hours.

Thursday forenoon.—Pulse 145; no pain, no tenderness, no sleep; abdomen tympanitic; not much discharge.

Second day.—Pulse 125; no sleep; "feels nicely" has made water; abdomen as large as at the full time of pregnancy, no tenderness, or other unfavorable symptoms.

Third day.—Pulse 120; bowels moved during the night, after taking castor oil; dozed a little occasionally in the afternoon; after a slight sleep she seemed lost for a short time, and complained of great weakness.

Fourth day.—Pulse 120; in other respects much the same; she complained this morning of some tenderness in the left side, but nothing to excite any alarm. From this date she continued improving daily; although the pulse was never below 120, at times she had a little abdominal pain, but never severe; the tympanic state of the abdomen daily subsided; after the first week there was no lochial discharge. I could not but remark that she progressed daily, just the same as a placenta prævia patient from which I was called to attend to her.

August 17th, tenth day.—Was up for a short time.

Thirteenth day.—Was up for four hours, and walked about the room; the feet were rather swollen, more particularly the left foot; she also complained of soreness of the left hip. No pain or swelling of the body.

Twentieth day.—She has not been out of bed for a week; the swelling of the left leg, from slight phlegmasia dolens, has continued up to now, but is almost gone; the soreness of the hip continues, with pain striking downwards into the groin; over the crest of the ilium is a large, diffused swelling cannot lie on the left side. No discharge of colours. Pulse never under 120.

September 7th.—Had some discharge to-day; in other respects much the same.

8th.—Some slight discharge again to-day; the soreness and swelling over the crest of the left ilium continues increasing; there is also some deep-seated fulness in the left groin; this is, no doubt, a large abscess from pelvic cellulitis; but what struck me as the most remarkable about it was that, when pressure was made upon it with the hands alternately, the sound of the matter churning backwards and forwards could be distinctly heard; the sound was more like a splash, as of some thick fluid against the inside of a barrel, than of churning. She would not allow a vaginal examination.

13th.—Pulse 130; tongue clean; appetite bad; the soreness and swelling over the crest of the ilium are much the same; it will now be about a foot in diameter. The night before, when turning in bed, she was surprised at having a very offensive discharge from the vagina, and wondered whatever it could be.

16th.—Pulse 120; no pain; not so much soreness of the hip; complains of nothing but weakness; tongue clean and moist; bowels regular; great and very offensive discharge from vagina on the 14th and 15th. The swelling had partly subsided; firm, continued pressure upon it increased the discharge; air-sound continued the same, but the splash seemed larger.

On September 17th she was admitted into the Bradford Infirmary, and I now lost sight of her for six weeks. She tells me that the discharge from the vagina ceased altogether a few days after her admission. On September 25th she began to be "*unwell,*" and continued so (as usual) for three or four days. On October 3rd the abscess over the crest of the ilium burst externally; there was a great discharge of *very offensive* matter; this continued in great quantities for several days; whenever she moved, it came out very freely. On October 17th all was healed, and she was gaining her strength nicely.

On October 24th she was discharged.

August 5th, 1862.—For many months she has enjoyed her usual good health, and has menstruated regularly until lately; it is now nine weeks since she was "poorly," and it appears likely that she is again pregnant.

On making an examination per vaginam, the position of the rent is felt at once; anteriorly to the os uteri, in the position of the left antero-lateral reflection of the mucous membrane of the vagina is a prominent ridge, about an inch and a quarter in length; between this and the anterior lip of the os uteri is a deep furrow, which, with the ridge in front, feels something like the os uteri; the os uteri is, however, behind this.

A SINGULAR CASE OF UNSUSPECTED PREGNANCY AND AWKWARD DELIVERY.

By John Shortt, M.D.,

ZILLAR SURGEON, CHINGLEPUT, MADRAS.

A. B—, æt. 40, European, married in India in 1844, and has been residing there for the last eleven years; of a tall and rather spare conformation of body; the mother of two girls; the second, now alive, was born in 1846.

Statement.—Has been long out of health; suffered from fits (hysteria) in 1852, and became "crazy," as she terms it. Two years previous to the occurrence about to be related she resided at a hill sanitarium, during which time she suffered, as she believes, from displacement and inflammation of the womb, for which she was subjected to medical treatment. In March, 18—, she accompanied her husband to a favorite station on the eastern coast, and, being still an invalid, immediately placed herself under medical treatment for the same old complaint, viz., inflammation and displacement of the womb. The treatment, according to her account, consisted of drastic purgative pills, composed of aloes, scammony, cambogia,[1] &c., to relieve obstinate cos-

[1] These prescriptions I have seen.

tiveness, from which she suffered. The speculum was had recourse to, and caustic, iodine, &c., were frequently applied to the mouth of the womb. Whilst this treatment was going on a gradual and visible enlargement of the abdomen was taking place, which the medical attendant pronounced to be ovarian dropsy. During a temporary and short visit to the station, in the month of October following, having been previously acquainted with the lady and her husband, I called to see them, when she complained of her state, and, with tears in her eyes, spoke of the dropsy from which she believed herself suffering, and said that "that very morning she had to let her dress out to the extent of four inches." Shortly after this, owing to some misunderstanding, her medical attendant refused to attend her, and all treatment ceased. About the end of the month of November following she found that she was passing small quantities of fluid by the vagina, and supposed it to be caused by a rupture of the ovarian cyst. Believing it a favorable termination of the disease, she did not seek medical advice for a couple of days, when she was seized with violent pains, and the husband called in the nearest surgeon. To this gentleman the case was made out as rupture of the ovarian cyst into the abdominal cavity, both by the patient and her husband. She was ordered an opiate draught, &c., and was directed to be placed in a warm bath, when, to the surprise of the patient, the husband, and the others present, a living child dropped into the bath, and, but for the activity of an assistant, would have met with a watery grave. The child (a boy, arrived at maturity) was well-proportioned, of good average size, but of rather lanky appearance, and slightly deformed in the chest (pigeon-breasted).

There are several points of interest connected with this case. During the whole period of gestation the patient was ignorant that she was with child, although a mother before; she attributed all her feelings to disease; so firm was her belief in this respect that the pleasing fact of all her fancied pain and suffering terminating in the birth of a son was, as she states, "the greatest surprise she ever experienced."

The only way in which the mistake that was made in the diagnosis of this case can have occurred must have been from the medical attendant failing to use his own judgment, and being led away by the patient's statements and feelings, which, no doubt, were morbid. When we take into consideration the long time the patient was an invalid from disease of the womb, the real existence of which was, I believe, certified by several medical men, the patient's age, and the long interval (nearly nine years since the birth of her second daughter) she had ceased to conceive, the mistake in the diagnosis may be accounted for.

The most remarkable point in this case is, that for nearly two thirds of the period of gestation the speculum, caustic, &c., were applied to the mouth of the womb, and the most drastic purgatives administered, without any injurious effects.

The patient arrived on the coast early in the month of March, and in the month of November following brought forth a living child, so that conception must have taken place soon after her arrival on the coast. The caustic and speculum treatment commenced about the same time; nevertheless the course of nature was not interfered with. The change from the hill sanitarium to the coast, together with the previous treatment at that place, no doubt paved the way for what followed.

This patient has since been to and returned from England, and I have lately seen a certificate from an eminent member of the profession (one of the Presidents of the Obstetrical Society), to say that she is suffering from adhesion of the neck of the womb to the rectum, in consequence of which she continues a martyr to obstinate constipation.

Having seen a case of unsuspected pregnancy and labour by Dr. Tanner, read before a meeting of the Obstetrical Society on the 7th of May, 1862, published in the 'Lancet,' I forward this case as a proof that a woman may not only conceive and be in labour, but bring forth a living child, without any suspicion of being pregnant.

ON THE USE OF MEDICATED PESSARIES IN THE TREATMENT OF UTERINE DISEASE.

By Thomas Hawkes Tanner, M.D.,
ASSISTANT-PHYSICIAN FOR THE DISEASES OF WOMEN AND CHILDREN TO KING'S COLLEGE HOSPITAL, ETC.

The great value of a variety of local applications in the treatment of uterine disease seems to be insufficiently appreciated by the profession at large. This is somewhat strange, considering the time which has elapsed since Dr. Simpson specially directed attention to their exceeding utility. Yet it is certain that a large number of practitioners know of no agents which may be directly applied to the uterus and vagina save the various kinds of caustics and injections. The latter are certainly of great benefit in many cases; but it must be allowed that, even when properly used, they are often of only temporary service, since they cannot be kept in contact with the diseased part for more than a few minutes.

The chief reason, I believe, for the non-employment of medicated pessaries has been the difficulty of so making them that they can be efficiently applied by the patient herself. When formed of certain drugs mixed into a mass with lard and wax, they are either so soft that the sufferer cannot introduce them into the vagina; or, on the contrary, they are so hard that they fail to dissolve, and are expelled in just the same condition as that in which they were introduced. Although I have now employed these agents very freely for some years, I have found very few druggists who would take the trouble so to make them that they were of any service. The difficulties just alluded to have, however, been overcome since Mr. White Cooper directed attention ('Lancet,' 28th June, 1862) to the utility of the butter obtained from the *Theobroma cacao nut*, from which chocolate is made, as the basis for ophthalmic ointments. This material possesses many valuable qualities, the chief being these:—It has an agreeable smell, and does not soil the fingers when handled; it does not become rancid; while, more particularly, though very firm, it has the property of becoming fluid at a low temperature. It is sometimes a little too stiff, but this fault is readily obviated by combining with it a little olive oil or glycerine. Pessaries made with cacao butter, though they have the consistence of wax while cold, are dissolved in the course of a few minutes when introduced into the vagina.

If ophthalmic surgeons are much indebted to Mr. White Cooper for directing attention to the uses of this butter, obstetric physicians are under no less an obligation. For although it had been used in America for making ointments for some time before this gentleman wrote of its merits, yet no physicians in this country were acquainted with its value, as far as I can learn from many inquiries.

There are few uterine diseases in which the use of medicated pessaries may not advantageously form a part of the treatment. But they are more especially valuable in acute and chronic inflammation of the cervix uteri; in internal metritis, with exfoliation of the lining membrane of the uterus; in slight prolapsus or procidentia; in cancer; in all varieties of ovaritis; as well as in many affections of the female bladder. By means of them the diseased parts may be kept constantly bathed in such drugs as mercury, iodine, lead, zinc, belladonna, opium, conium, &c. They are not only most efficacious in relieving pain, but they also shield the diseased and irritable surface from contact with the vaginal walls. Owing to this latter property, they are of great utility in healing excoriations about the labia uteri; though, of course, part of the benefit derived from their use in these cases must be attributed to the absorption of the materials composing them. By their employment, moreover, the necessity for frequent examination of the morbid structures is greatly diminished.

The following formulæ are given as examples of the way in which I generally prescribe these remedies. It is only necessary to premise that rather large doses of the different drugs are necessary, inasmuch as absorption through the walls of the vagina is slow and uncertain:

1. *Iodide of Lead and Belladonna Pessaries.*—℞. Plumbi Iodidi, ℈ij; Extracti Belladonnæ, ℈j; Butyri Cacao, ʒiv; Olei Olivæ, ʒj. Misce. Divide into four pessaries, and order one to be introduced into the vagina every night or every other night.

2. *Mercurial Pessaries.*—℞. Unguenti Hydrargyri, ℈iv—ʒij; Butyri Cacao, ʒiv; Olei Olivæ, ʒj. Misce. Where there is tenderness of the cervix uteri, one scruple of extract of belladonna or two scruples of extract of conium should be added to the mass. Divide into four pessaries.

3. *Lead and Opium Pessaries.*—℞. Plumbi Acetatis, ℈j; Extracti Opii, gr. xij; Butyri Cacao, ʒiv; Olei Olivæ, ʒj. Misce. Divide into four pessaries. Order one to be used every other night.

4. *Zinc and Belladonna Pessaries.*—℞. Zinci Oxydi, ʒj; Extracti Belladonnæ, gr. xij—℈j; Butyri Cacao, ʒiv; Olei Olivæ, ʒj. Misce. Divide into four pessaries. One to be used every night.

5. *Iodide of Potassium and Conium Pessaries.*—℞. Potassii Iodidi, ʒj; Extracti Conii, ℈iv; Butyri Cacao, ʒiv; Glycerinii puri, ʒj. Misce. Divide into four pessaries, and direct one to be used every night.

6. *Tannin and Catechu Pessaries.*—℞. Tanninæ, ℈ij; Pulveris Catechu, ʒj; Butyri Cacao, ʒiv; Olei Olivæ, ʒj. Misce. Divide into four pessaries, and order one to be used every other night.

In some diseases of the uterine cavity, attended with copious muco-purulent discharges or with hæmorrhage, the greatest benefit may be obtained from the local use of astringents. Once or twice a week a pessary made of tannin and the cacao butter, about two and a half inches long, and of the size of an ordinary stick of nitrate of silver, may be introduced up the canal of the uterus, and left there. It soon dissolves, and thus coats the whole seat of the discharge with the medicament, the coating remaining attached for many hours. Such a pessary, weighing about thirty-six grains, will usually contain from twelve to twenty grains of tannin. Of course other substances—as alum, sulphate of zinc, dried sulphate of iron, &c.—may be employed in the same manner, if their use be indicated. This plan of treatment has none of the objections which apply to throwing fluids into the cavity of the uterus, a proceeding that is certainly not unattended with danger. There is no necessity, moreover, for dilating the cervix with sponge-tents prior to the introduction of the pessary; inasmuch as, when sanguineous or purulent discharges have long been present, the os and cervical canal will always be found sufficiently patulous to permit of the introduction of these astringent rods.

Dr. TYLER SMITH said that he thought the Society was much indebted to Dr. Tanner for bringing the present communication before them. He had occasionally resorted to the use of various medicated pessaries made with lard and wax; but, probably for the reasons which the author had mentioned, he had not found them of the utility he expected. He believed, however, that these pessaries, made in the elegant form recommended by Dr. Tanner, would probably prove very valuable, and he should therefore give them a full trial.

November 5th, 1862.

Dr. TYLER SMITH, President, in the Chair.

Present—29 Fellows and 3 visitors.

The following gentlemen were elected Fellows of the Society:—Stephen John Burke, M.R.C.S., Sydney, New South Wales; Laurence Trent Cumberbatch, M.R.C.S., 25, Cadogan Place, Belgrave Square; Thomas Fender, L.R.C.S., Alnwick, Northumberland; William Hall, M.R.C.S., North Street, Leeds; Charles Harris, M.D., Northiam, Sussex; T. Smith Hewitt, M.D., Winkfield, Windsor; William Arthur Hubert, M.R.C.S., Markyate Street, Bedfordshire; Frederick Fitzherbert Jay, L.R.C.P., near Acle, Norwich; George Lowe, M.R.C.S., Burton-on-Trent, Staffordshire; George Wise Mackenzie, M.R.C.S., Thetford, Norfolk; Walter Boyd Mackinlay, M.D., 2, New Smith-hills, Paisley; Robert Buchanan Marriott, M.R.C.S., Swaffham, Norfolk; Theophilus Robert Bush Parker, M.R.C.S., Abbotsbury, Dorset; David Richards, M.R.C.S., 8, St. George's Place, Brighton; Smith Richards, M.R.C.S., 36, Bedford Square; William Sutherland, M.D., 22, George Street, Croydon; George Dancer Thane, M.D., 9, Hart Street, Bloomsbury; Richard T. Tracy, M.D., Melbourne, Victoria; Claudius Galen Wheelhouse, M.R.C.S., 16, East Parade, Leeds.

The Honorary Secretaries announced the donation of about 390 valuable works on the medical sciences from Dr. Charles Clay, of Manchester. A special vote of thanks to Dr. Clay was proposed by Mr. Marshall, seconded by Dr. Drage, and carried unanimously.

A CASE OF SUDDEN AND UNCONSCIOUS DELIVERY.

By John Shortt, M.D.
ZILLAH SURGEON, CHINGLEPUT.

Some years ago, as I was crossing the esplanade at Villare, between the hours of 7 and 8 a.m., I perceived three Hindoo women preceding me at about the distance of thirty yards, with large baskets on their heads, filled with *bratties*, or cakes of dried cowdung, which they were conveying into the town for sale from a village some four miles distant. Suddenly I noticed one of the women, as she was walking along, stand still a second and stoop; when, to my surprise, I observed a fully developed male child drop on the ground. One of her companions immediately ran into the town, which was about a hundred yards in front, for a knife to divide the umbilical cord; and by this time a few female passers-by having assembled, a screen was formed around her by their clothes, and when the knife arrived the cord was divided. The after-birth coming away soon after, she was removed to an open shed in the town for the day; and in the course of the evening was taken to her own village, her female friends consoling her with the fact of being able to call her son the "esplanade boy." As she was a woman of caste, they would not permit me to approach her to render any assistance in my power.

The woman to whom this accident happened was in good health, about twenty-eight years of age, and the mother of two living children. Although aware of her state, she did not expect her confinement to take place for some days. Moreover, when she left her hut there was not the slightest indication of approaching labour; while she experienced no pain or other inconvenience, and was not aware of her confinement until she actually felt the child slip between her thighs.

This case is interesting: the absence of pain or other indication of approaching labour renders it very remarkable.

I am convinced that the woman in this case must have had a very capacious pelvis, to account for the sudden birth of the child in the manner described above.

A CASE OF OBSTRUCTED LABOUR FROM THE PRESENCE OF THE HYMEN.

By Silas Palmer, M.D., F.S.A.

Mrs. W—, æt. 31, residing at Speen, sent for me early on the morning of the 8th of August, 1860, stating that she had been in labour all night.

On examining I found the os uteri slightly dilated, the membranes entire, the pains few and far between. But what struck me as singular on making this examination was that a band caught my finger as I introduced it, and which appeared to hang from the right labium. My impression at the moment was that the patient had probably met with an accident, that the parts had been lacerated, and the surfaces had not united. The band, being lax and not likely to interfere with the progress of the labour, attracted little more attention, as I did not attach any importance to its presence. My patient being inclined to sleep, I left her to attend another case. Several hours having passed, I called to see what progress had been made, when I found she had slept for upwards of an hour, that the pains had then returned, and that the nurse had again and again been urged to send for me, as the patient felt certain that there was something which prevented the child's head advancing, and that she should be torn during her pains.

On making the usual examination I found the band which I had noticed in the morning tightly stretched over the presenting part of the child's head, the perinæum distended, and the advance of the head evidently arrested by the band.

I uncovered the parts, to get a better view of them, and then discovered that the source of delay was the *hymen*, evidently of that type figured (I think) by Cloquet, and which I have ventured to call *fenestrated*. The band extended from beneath the meatus urinarius to the fourchette. On the left side, its margin was smooth and rounded, and on the right, it was fringed. *Les rapports sexuels* having more frequently taken place on the left side would, I think, account for the difference in the surfaces. I then rapidly sketched the parts in my note-book (from which the accompanying drawing was copied); then waited to see the effect of a few more pains, and as there appeared no chance of its yielding, I divided the band with a pair of scissors. It bled freely, and almost immediately the child's head passed into the world. The scalp was greatly tumefied; and there was a deep sulcus where the band had pressed, which did not disappear for ten days.

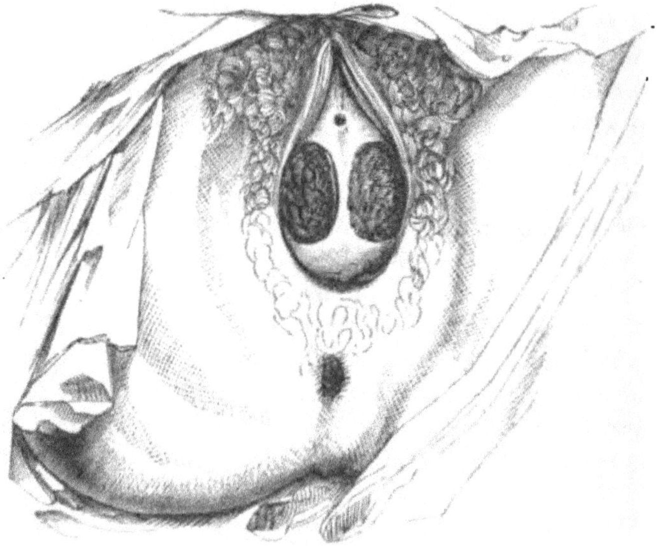

A CASE OF ACEPHALO-CYCLOPEAN MONSTROSITY.

By Robert Hardey.

LATE LECTURER ON OBSTETRICS, HULL AND EAST RIDING SCHOOL OF MEDICINE.

Case.—On August 8th, 1848, I was desired by my esteemed friend and colleague, the late Edward Wallis, Esq., to visit with him a patient of the Hull Lying-in Charity, residing in Salthouse Lane, in this town. His attendance had been recently desired by the attendant midwife, who could neither deliver the woman nor make out the presentation. The labour had already continued about forty-eight hours. Mr. Wallis had himself diagnosed the part presenting as being a greatly swollen mouth, with protruding tongue; but he could neither find nose, eyes, or any other part which he could recognise.

On examination I found his diagnosis strictly correct, the centre of the presentation consisting of the swollen mouth and tongue, and, all around, nothing to be felt but the cheeks of the fœtus, it being apparently minus both eyes and nose. We agreed on immediate delivery, which was accomplished after some difficulty by securing the blunt hook in one of the axillæ. The fœtus was found to exceed the usual size of full-grown fœti; the cuticle was separating from the cutis vera, proving death to have occurred previous to, or at the very outset of, the labour.

EXTERNAL APPEARANCES.

On examining the part which had presented at the os uteri it was found to be the face of an acephalous fœtus, which was in immediate contact with, and forming a rounded and somewhat protuberant termination of, the upper part of the chest, the cheeks and mouth being directed upwards. *The face* was of full size, *mouth* unusually round, and the *protruded tongue* very thick and firm. *The cheeks* large, protuberant, and livid (no doubt from long-continued pressure sustained during the labour). *Chin* scarcely discernible, but situated at the usual distance from the mouth. *Nose* entirely wanting. From the centre of the upper lip there ran posteriorly a sulcus, separating the cheeks, and terminating at the central, pointed margin of *a rounded cavity,* which was one and two thirds of an inch from before backwards, and about one and a quarter inch across. This cavity, surrounded by a ciliary margin and a few cilia, contained *a large globe, possessing two pupils,* one on each side of the mesial line. The eye itself was protruded forward.

Immediately above (or posterior to) the orbit was seen *an appendage,* about one and a half inch long, tongue-shaped, directed towards the left shoulder, and containing either bony or cartilaginous deposit. The sides of the face terminated on the shoulders, and the ears (which were very large) were situate still further backward. Beneath the chin was a column of fat, terminating at each ear and resting on the chest. The lower jaw was perfect and movable; the centre of the oral arch was present, but its two sides wanting.

The upper extremities were perfectly formed, large, and firm. *The lower limbs* were of proper size; the thighs, however, appeared unusually short, from their being placed by the sides of the pelvis, and the right foot was thrown inward (*talipes commune*).

The chest was rather contracted, its centre soft and flat, as if the sternum and costal cartilages were wanting.

The abdomen was unusually broad, measuring round it seventeen inches immediately above the umbilicus. On the right side of the navel were protruding several folds of intestine; these had evidently escaped during the labour, and were easily returned into the abdominal cavity. The abdomen from funis downward formed a large hernial pouch, containing intestines, completely hiding the parts beneath it, and reaching downwards nearly as low as the knees. On

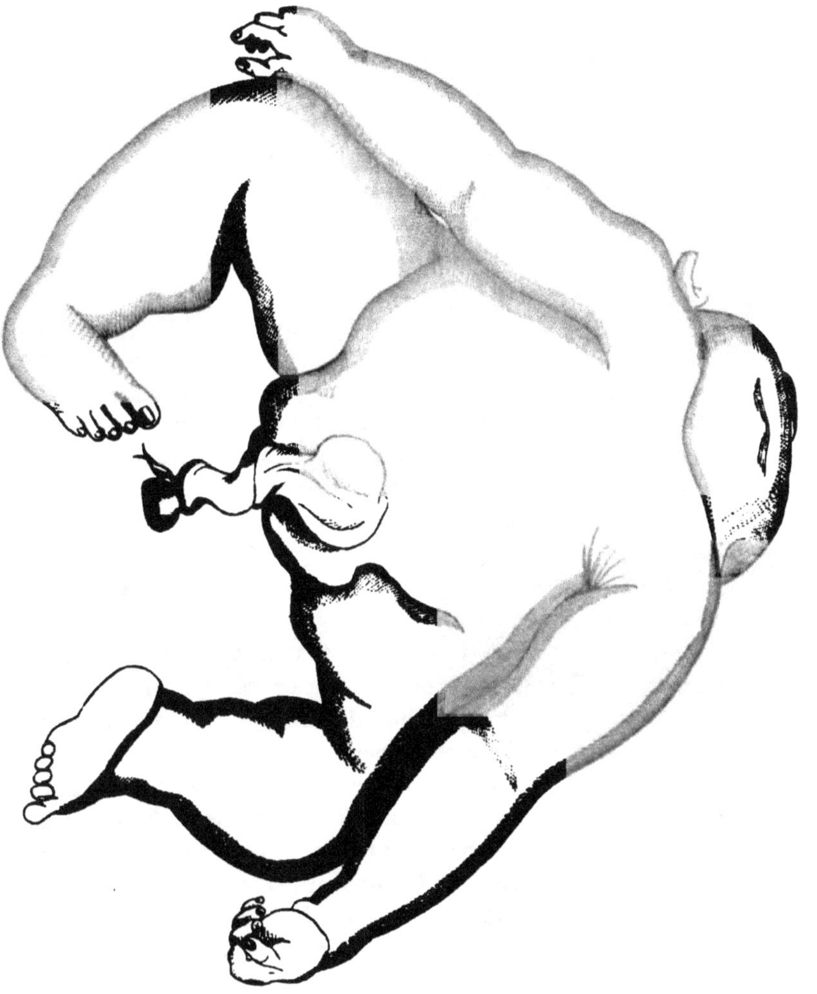

raising this bag upwards the anus was found in its usual situation, but there was a complete absence of external organs of generation. On each side of the mesial line, towards the groins (and about three quarters of an inch apart from each other), was found a small, loose fold of skin, about the size of a split pea, attempts, probably, at the formation of labia pudendi majora. In the mesial line, about one inch in front of the anus, was found a small, well-defined aperture, admitting the point of a probe, and leading to a cavity extending full half an inch towards each groin and backwards towards the rectum.

Viewed from the front, each hip appeared raised upwards to within one and a half inch of the axilla, and the thigh spread itself outwards from that point; hence the immense breadth of the fœtus opposite its pelvis, and the seeming shortness of the thighs. Looking on the fœtus from behind, we were struck with its general resemblance to that of a frog, arising from the spread position of the arms, its widely separated lower limbs, the outward aspect of the knees, with its legs drawn inward toward each other. The back was unusually flat, and there was a central depression, giving the impression that the spinal column was either cleft, or altogether wanting.

Immediately below the tongue-shaped appendage already referred to, was a large oval space, or cavity, three inches across, two and a half inches downwards, and reaching to the loins, covered by a thin membrane, and apparently containing coagulated blood. The lateral spaces between the ears and this cavity were thickly covered with hair, which also formed a fringed border around its periphery. The ears were large, and projected unnaturally outward; and the spinal depression inclined to the left side, giving to the right half of the fœtus much larger proportions than its fellow.

INTERNAL ORGANIZATION.

Having obtained a plaster cast by a clever artist, we proceeded to examine the interior structure of this *lusus naturæ.* We first directed our attention to its large Cyclopean peculiarity. In doing this, we found the globe of the eye one, the cornea two, one on each side the mesial line, and the conjunctiva continuous and one.

Muscles.—A narrow muscular band, corresponding to the inferior oblique muscle, was proceeding backward and upward from the inferior edge of the orbit, in its mesial line, and then passing inward, was inserted at the bifurcation of the inferior rectus, next to be described. The rectus inferior, arising from the floor of the orbit, passed forward, sending a strip to each rectus externus, and terminated by a bifurcation, inserted into the sclerotica on each side, having between these (as before observed) the insertion of the inferior oblique muscle. The external oblique muscles were situated normally, and were unusually large. There were two superior recti muscles. Also supra-orbitar arteries and nerves on each side of the mesial line, apparently lost on the conjunctiva. Likewise two inferior orbitar arteries and nerves, also lost on the conjunctiva. There were two lachrymal glands, in the usual situation. The optic nerve was single.

The tongue-like process behind the orbit, contained a cavity lined by serous membrane, within which was found a little caseous matter, and a minute, sebaceous opening. This sac was covered in front and above by a cartilage, articulated to the central posterior margin of the orbit, and terminated by a bifurcated extremity; between these two forked terminations was found a second cavity, lined, like the larger one, by a serous membrane.

Muscles of the throat.—The anterior belly of the digastricus was much lengthened, the os hyoides being much nearer the sternum than the chin. The left sterno-cleido-mastoideus muscle terminated in a fascial structure beneath the ear; the right one was folded on itself, and terminated on the back of the occiput.

The cranial cavity was situated on the back of the chest, and there was an entire absence of the upper and lateral cranial bones. Dividing the scalp longitudinally, the proper cerebral coverings were found contained therein, divided by the tentorium into two equal parts. There was an entire absence of cerebral substance, but the cerebral cavity contained some small coagula. The base of the cranium assumed the normal aspect.

Front of the chest.—The muscles were all present, and more developed than usual. The breast-bone and ribs, with their cartilages, all in their normal condition.

Abdomen.—All the muscles present, and in their healthy condition. The large abdominal pouch, situated below and associated with the funis, was found to be formed by the aponeuroses of the abdominal muscles.

Abdominal viscera.—The liver, stomach, and intestines situated correctly, and of the ordinary size and appearance. The pancreas was situated low in the lumbar region, and below the left kidney.

Pelvic viscera.—The bladder and urachus were lying in the lumbar region, the former communicating with the orifice in the perinæum. The uterus was situated normally. Ovaries near to the internal abdominal rings. The two kidneys were joined together, occupying the lower and anterior aspect of the spinal column, and having but one artery, passing from the aorta just below the superior mesenteric artery. There were two ureters, which were lost in the walls of the abdominal sac.

Behind or below the external orifice of the bladder or urethra, a rudimentary vagina or *cul-de-sac* was found; the left ovary situated in the left iliac fossa.

The skeleton of this "monster" was examined by Mr. Wallis, whose notes were unfortunately mislaid, and have not been recovered. The peculiarities found referred chiefly to the absence of the nose, the defective hard palate, the single orbit, the acephalous formation, the talipes of the right foot, and the abnormal condition of the spinal column, which was found cleft from the chest downward, and thereby was accounting for the amazing breadth of the lumbar region.

It is worthy of remark, relative to this interesting case,

that the mother had previously borne several children, all healthy and well-formed; that nothing had happened to her during gestation which, according to popular prejudice, might be supposed to have conduced to the malformation of her infant; and that she had not the slightest idea or expectation that it would be otherwise, when born, than healthy and normally constituted.

This circumstance leads me further to observe, that my own obstetric experience, in nearly 6500 cases, attended during the last forty years, is in direct opposition to the prevalent opinion that these monstrosities are traceable, in a large number of cases, to strong impressions made on the mother's mind during early gestation, and producing a full expectation that the child, when born, would be found affected in the particular way expected by the mother.

In the long period just named, I need scarce say I have met with numerous cases of monstrous formation in infants; but I can most distinctly affirm that in not one solitary instance have I found a fœtus malformed or affected by nævus where it was confidently anticipated by the mother; or, on the occurrence of such malformation or nævus being made known to the mother, have I ever received from her such an account of occurrences or mental impressions during the previous gestation, as made it in the slightest degree probable that the monstrous production was resulting from the same.

In a large number of instances I have found the patient's mind firmly impressed with the notion that the infant, when born, would be found misshapen in some particular way, or the subject of nævus in some particular situation, arising out of one or more circumstances which had happened to her during the previous gestation; but in no instance whatever have I found her anticipations verified, the infants being found, on birth, in all respects perfect. I think it, therefore, extremely improbable that the mother's imagination, during early gestation, can so act on the uterine ovum as to be productive of those malformed and imperfect organisms which are so frequently met with in the human species.

CASE OF PUERPERAL CONVULSIONS COMPLICATED WITH MANIA; APPARENT RECOVERY; SUDDEN DECEASE.

By Archibald Hall, M.D. Edin.,

PROFESSOR OF MIDWIFERY, M'GILL UNIVERSITY; PHYSICIAN-ACCOUCHEUR TO THE UNIVERSITY LYING-IN HOSPITAL; CONSULTING-PHYSICIAN TO THE MONTREAL GENERAL HOSPITAL; ASSOCIATE OF THE COLLEGE OF PHYSICIANS OF PHILADELPHIA; HONORARY FELLOW OF THE OBSTETRICAL SOCIETY OF LONDON; ETC., ETC.

About midnight of the 13th or 14th of September I was summoned to meet Dr. Peltier, of this city, in consultation on the case of Mrs. N. D—, then in labour with her first child, the first pains of which had come on about 6 p.m., continuing with apparent regularity until about 11 p.m., when, a convulsive attack occurring, Dr. Peltier, her engaged attendant, was immediately sent for. A second attack of convulsions occurred almost immediately after his arrival in the house, with strong evidence of maniacal delusion during the interval or afterwards; and concluding that the termination of the case might prove unfavorable, I was sent for in the course of half an hour after Dr. Peltier had seen the patient.

On entering the sick room I found the patient sitting up in bed, tossing her arms wildly about, and uttering various exclamations of a desponding, religious character, which increased in vehemence at what we supposed to be the recurrence of every pain. She recognised no one. An examination per vaginam scarcely permitted the entrance into the os uteri of the point of the forefinger, while the uterine orifice itself was detected with difficulty high up, and directly facing the promontory of the sacrum, thus indicating considerable anterior uterine obliquity.

I must now observe that the patient was a young woman of twenty-one years of age, with profuse, light, sandy hair, of a highly nervous and irritable disposition, of a very fair complexion, and apparently tall and stoutly built; fond of reading light literature, highly imaginative, but withal of a strictly religious turn of mind. In this latter respect she had been apparently well brought up.

No cause for the convulsions or the maniacal condition which developed itself between 6 and 11 p.m., and which was increasing in intensity, could be discovered, except the idle tales of officious, kind friends. These persons had narrated to her, during the two months preceding her accouchement, stories about the severity of the sufferings which she would have to undergo, and had advised her on no account to permit a cloth to be applied to her face (reference here evidently made to the use of chloroform), as it would kill her, &c., &c.; until finally her mind became so intensely wrought upon that, when Dr. Peltier entered her room, she regarded him with an expression of intense horror. A convulsive attack almost immediately followed, succeeded by others almost every half hour; while maniacal delusions, chiefly of a religious character, and increasing in intensity, displayed themselves. Such was the condition in which I found Mrs. D— at midnight, and it must be confessed that the case was by no means an enviable one.

At this period a vaginal examination disclosed the uterine orifice as barely permitting the entrance of the point of the forefinger, the exact condition in which it was when Dr. Peltier first saw her; and although we could judge, from an apparent forcing down, that the uterine efforts had not relaxed and were not relaxing, yet their influence seemed rather to have the effect of depressing the vertex, with the uterine segment before it, lower and lower into the cavity of the pelvis, than to have the least agency in dilating the os. After a free withdrawal of blood from the arm, the application of a blister to the nape of the neck, the removal of her hair, the application of ice to the head, and the periodic exhibition of small doses of calomel, I advised the employment of chloroform, as well to combat the attacks of convulsions as to allay the maniacal excitement. As another very severe attack of convulsions supervened within a period of an hour, it was deemed advisable to repeat the abstraction of blood, thus making a total loss of about forty ounces. But I must here observe that the loss of blood was much greater than this, as, in consequence of the continual loosening of the bandages, resulting from the jactitation of her arms, and necessitating the continual readjustment of them, the loss of blood was undoubtedly much greater than that specified. After waiting until between 2 and 3 a.m. of the 14th, as not the least change had taken place in matters since 11 p.m., Dr. Peltier and myself deemed it advisable to request the presence of Dr. Campbell, who came promptly, and advised perseverance and the employment of the chloroform until the uterine orifice was sufficiently dilated to allow of either manual or instrumental interference. The os uteri was yet in the same non-patulous condition, but it was now perceived that the fœtal head had about half descended into the cavity of the pelvis.

About 3 a.m. Dr. Campbell left, and I accompanied him, leaving Dr. Peltier in attendance, to superintend the administration of the chloroform and to report the dilatation of the uterine orifice. At 10 a.m. I received a note from Dr. Peltier, signifying the important fact that the os uteri was considerably dilated, and requesting my presence I was in immediate attendance. On examination I found the os dilated to about the size of an English shilling, but with a rigidity of the lip which defied all attempts at further dilatation, the vertex now almost pressing on the perinæum, and, under such circumstances, utterly negativing manual interference, but entailing on us the necessity of taking advantage of the first opportunity for instrumental assistance.

After waiting for some time I imagined that I could succeed in the application of the short forceps; but on attempting to apply them I found myself foiled, as the orifice would not admit of sufficient dilatation without risk of laceration. But after another half hour had elapsed, during which the pains had been more severe and more efficient, I succeeded in applying them, and in a few minutes delivered our patient of a *dead* child, but evidently only so recently.

Our patient had one, if not two, attacks of convulsions

after the labour had terminated and after the delivery of the placenta, but she continued in a state of maniacal abstraction—the subject invariably that of a desponding, religious character—until Friday, the 19th, when the severity of the symptoms abated. She now chiefly complained of a slight pain over the forehead. There was not the least heat of skin; her pulse was soft and regular, 82; and her intellect evidently regaining its sway. The lochial discharge, which had been suppressed, was resumed, but there was no secretion of milk, probably due to the severity of the depletory measures employed.

All this time the calomel had been perseveringly employed, without the least influence upon her gums, while the other treatment consisted of an anodyne draught of morphia, hyoscyamus, and chloric ether, in full measure at bedtime, and during the day in divided doses, so as to quell the violence of the maniacal symptoms. During the whole period the alvine evacuations were free, and, until now, passed unconsciously; but at the present period she exercised control over them, and signified to her mother and her nurse her necessities in these respects. I forgot to mention that, on one occasion during the progress of her labour her phrenzy proceeded to the extent of throwing herself suddenly and violently out of her bed, striking with her head the side of one of her attendants, knocking her almost over, and herself falling at full length on the floor.

On Saturday morning, September 20th, I visited her, as I supposed, for the last time. She presented every possible appearance of being on the fair road to a complete restoration to health. She was perfectly sensible. The lochial discharge existed. There was not the least feverish condition of the skin. Her pulse was perfectly regular and normal in its peculiarities, yet she still complained of a slight pain over the forehead.

On Sunday evening, the 21st, at 7 p.m., a message was left at my house, while absent on professional duty, to visit Mrs. D——. I instantly went to her house, where I met Dr. Peltier. I found her almost pulseless, and with the same insane delusions as previously described. Her skin was cold and clammy, and her pulse, imperceptibly quick and feeble, with intermissions, announced the speedy approach of dissolution. She replied to no question sensibly. Powerful diffusible stimulants were immediately resorted to. At 4 a.m. of the following Monday morning my colleague was summoned to her bedside. He found her comatose, a condition which had come on within the preceding two hours, and she died in about two hours after his visit; a melancholy termination to a case which, although severe, promised at one time the most favorable results.

During the whole of this illness it is to be remarked that the pupil of the eye, although generally dilated, was perfectly sensitive to the impression of light. It was on no occasion seen in a contracted condition.

It is to be regretted that we were not permitted a post-mortem examination. The cause of death must have been cerebral effusion, either within the ventricles or upon the surface of the brain, or possibly both.

Having thus given a sketch of the main features of this interesting case, I may be permitted to transcribe the concluding portion of a short report of a nearly analogous case in Ramsbotham's 'Midwifery,' American edition, 1855, pp. 508-9. This was a case of mania *without* convulsions, whose termination was much of the same character.

"The pulse varied from 80 to 100, according as she had been calm or excited. It was only necessary to restrain her during one day, and that by two long towels—one placed across the chest and fastened to the bedstead, and the other over her thighs, just above the knee, in the same manner. Both I and her general attendant, who had for nearly twenty years superintended a very large establishment for the reception of lunatics in the neighbourhood of London, gave it as our opinion that her life was in no immediate danger. Things went on in this way for six days from the date of my first visit, when I was summoned hastily, late in the evening, and found that after a tranquil night and day, which gave her friends reasons to believe her much better, she had become comatose. Her pulse was at 160. Her legs and feet were cold, her head hotter than it had previously been, and she was bathed in a profuse perspiration, which had continued for eight or ten hours. The pupils had contracted to a pin's point, and the eyes suffused. Notwithstanding her apparently insensible state, she swallowed fluids by two or three teaspoonfuls at a time. She continued to sink, and died in the course of the night."

A few words in conclusion.

During the early period of her illness she never once asked for her husband, who was out of town at the time, and did not arrive until fully twenty-eight hours after her accouchement. She recognised him, however, but betrayed no peculiar affection for him. It was not until her apparently complete restoration, on Saturday, 20th, that she appeared to entertain any idea whatever that she had been delivered of a child; while during the two days preceding the 20th she chiefly complained of her mouth, imagining that there was something wrong with her gums or her throat, very probably due to the irritation of her mouth, produced by the biting of the sides of her tongue during the convulsive attacks, and which could not be prevented. When spoken to she very frequently replied correctly, although sometimes not until after evasion; but her condition mentally may be correctly described as that of *active melancholia*, if these words can convey my idea.

To conclude. I believe that puerperal convulsions complicated with puerperal mania is an extremely rare affection, and when occurring should be recorded for the benefit of obstetric science. I by no means pretend that the treatment adopted in the case, of which a general outline has been given, was the best that could have been devised. It was such, however, as the predominance of symptoms seemed to require at our hands, and was mainly guided by the existing pathological condition, with the further view of combating other pathological conditions which might subsequently arise. It was upon this latter principle that mercury was administered, a point which will be readily recognised and appreciated.

A discussion followed the reading of this paper, in which Dr. Braxton Hicks, Dr. Tanner, and Dr. Graily Hewitt took part.

Dr. Graily Hewitt exhibited, for Mr. Francis Taylor, of Romsey,

A NIPPLE-SHIELD.

Mr. Taylor had forwarded the instrument in question for inspection by the Fellows of the Society, having seen in the report of a recent meeting of the Society that a nipple-shield had been shown by another gentleman, with which his (Mr. Taylor's) instrument was, he believed, identical. Mr. Taylor's invention was of glass, with a caoutchouc nipple, and had, it was stated, been long sold by Messrs. Barclay and Sons.

FIVE CASES OF VAGINAL CLOSURE.

By J. Braxton Hicks, M.D., F.R.S.,

ASSISTANT-PHYSICIAN-ACCOUCHEUR AT GUY'S HOSPITAL, AND PHYSICIAN TO ROYAL MATERNITY CHARITY.

Two Cases of entire Atresia of Vagina.

Case 1.—*Complete absence (atresia) of vagina, with retained menses; puncture per rectum; recovery.*—E. H—, admitted under my care on April 3rd, 1861, æt. 18, a well-built, healthy looking girl. Two years ago she first felt pain in the abdomen, with bearing down; her breasts also gave her pain, and became somewhat swollen at the time of the pain in abdomen. These symptoms repeated themselves regularly every month, with few exceptions, when they did not return for six or seven weeks. With some of these attacks there was vomiting.

There had at no time been any discharge of menses, nor any vicarious secretion.

The pain lately had been so severe as to require opiates for its relief. She had been under the care of Dr. Sharpe, of Grange Road, Bermondsey, who had detected the abnormal condition, and who had advised her coming to the hospital.

On examination I found the external parts of the sexual organs well developed; the urethra natural, and beneath it the corrugated edge of the hymen. But within the hymen no trace of any canal existed. There was no appearance of any septum, or of the previous existence of any opening. The rectum was normally placed.

On examining per rectum I was able to carry my finger almost to the meatus urinarius, behind the position of the hymen. The recto-urethral membrane was very thin, as proved by the introduction of a catheter at the same time; there was no cord-like feeling, as if any canal had previously existed. About three inches within the rectum I felt a hard tumour, lying above and external to it, in the centre, of about the size of the fist. Pressure above pubes caused this to descend. This I concluded to be the uterus, distended by menstrual fluid.

As the recto-urethral septum was so thin that the chance of a successful result of any attempt to form an artificial vagina was very small, I determined to puncture the uterus through the bowel at the next period, in order that I might find the uterus larger, and therefore more readily tapped. She was sent home till the time arrived. She was readmitted on April 21st, and the bowels having been previously opened by a purgative, on the 22nd I operated. I found the uterus twice the size it was upon the previous examination. The curved trocar and canula (such as are used to puncture the bladder per rectum) were employed, and introduced rather anteriorly, in order to escape the peritoneal pouch behind the uterus. About three or four ounces of dark, thick fluid flowed, and when it ceased the canula was withdrawn. An ounce or two of the same fluid followed next day. The portion through which the canula passed was, from its density and thickness, doubtless the walls of the uterus.

The cessation of pain was immediate, and the patient recovered without a bad symptom. A small dose of opium was given every six hours for a day or two; she was kept in bed for five days, and she left the hospital on the seventh day.

The next menstrual period was marked by severe pain for three days, after which it subsided, but without any menstrual flow. The next two periods occurred only three weeks apart, the pain being but slight, lasting only one day, still without any appearance of menses per rectum.

For two periods after these she had no discharge nor suffering, but as she was pale, it is possible that the secretion was deficient. After this the attacks of pain repeated themselves with vigour, so that about seven months after the first operation it became necessary to repeat it. Her sufferings were intense, so much so that her shrieks were heard across the road.

I examined her rectum, and found the uterus again distended as before.

The operation was repeated at the monthly period, and about the same quantity of menses came away. It was, as before, dark and thick. The canula was left in for six hours, and in order to prevent any air entering by it the aperture was plugged. There were some slight irritative symptoms the next day, after which everything went on favorably. Menses flowed away for some days afterwards, and a slightly blood-coloured discharge for three weeks, when it ceased. On the occurrence of the next period pain again appeared, but after a few days' suffering the uterus overcame the obstacle, and a quantity of menses flowed from the rectum. This was followed by speedy relief from pain.

From that time to this she has been quite free from

pain, and every month a discharge of menstrual fluid takes place by the bowel. She complains of a discharge of yellow fluid in the interval, but over its passage per anum she has perfect control. This is probably uterine leucorrhœa, to be expected after the irritation to which the uterus has been subjected. Her health was perfect.

In this distressing condition we have, at present, but three plans open to us—1st. Leaving the case to nature. 2nd. Forming an artificial vagina. 3rd. Puncturing the uterus per rectum.

In respect of the *first*, the excessive pain recurring every month or oftener, as shown in this and the following case, as well as the danger of rupture of uterus or Fallopian tubes (as shown in the cases collected by Puech[1]) will, I think, be sufficient to determine us to employ some plan for its evacuation. With regard to the *second*, in these cases, where the recto-urethral septum is sufficiently thick, for many reasons it seems desirable to form an artificial vagina. This certainly appears the more scientific plan, but it is a point of much practical importance to ascertain beforehand whether the thickness of the septum be such as to be capable of being split, so as to leave a wall before and behind strong enough to bear the violence to which the vagina is liable; in other words, what is the least thickness for this purpose. I think it will be conceded that, as in this case, where the septum between the catheter in urethra and the finger in rectum feels only of the thickness of the normal vagino-urethral septum, then the operation can scarcely be expected to be practicable. I may instance Mr. Baker Brown's case read before this Society, where the attempt had been made to open up a vagina, but which had to be relinquished in consequence of the thinness of the membrane, and puncture substituted.

When, from these and other reasons, it is deemed advisable to puncture the uterus per rectum, it is a matter of some

Puech, A., "Atresia of Genital Passages in Women," 'Comptes Rend.,' December 9th, 1861, p. 1066. Also 'Year Book,' 1861.

importance to know for what period should the canula remain in the uterus. Upon this it is desirable to gain some clue to a rule. In the case just recited the time given in the second operation (nearly six hours) seemed to produce more satisfactory results than when it was removed directly. Comparing it with the results in the case alluded to and read by Mr. Baker Brown a short time since, in which severe irritative symptoms resulted, the canula being left in for two weeks, perhaps ten or twelve hours would be found to be the best period for it to remain in.

Again, I think if we look to the records of other cases of opening up of the uterus by an artificial vagina, we shall find the principal danger arises upon opening the uterus. As it is very probable that the admission of air has much to do with this, I would recommend in all such cases that the canula be plugged just before the complete evacuation of the uterine contents.

CASE 2.—*Entire atresia of vagina; retention of menses; partial operation; recovery.*

The following case possesses some points of interest, and, as far as it goes, may help and assist our knowledge of this disease and its remedies.

J. M—, æt. 28, married, was admitted into Mary Ward September 14th, 1861. She was a dark, healthy, spare Irishwoman.

She had never menstruated, but for some years had had intense pain every month in the lower abdomen, so much so that she was uncontrollable at the time.

I found the labia majora natural. The urethra was patent enough to admit the forefinger readily. Behind this there were no nymphæ, nor hymen, nor any channel; but the ordinary vulval mucous membrane passed over the part, marked by a raphe in median line. By pressure upon this part the point of the finger passed between the rectum and urethra about an inch. Examination per rectum showed the recto-urethral septum to be thick, perhaps three times more so than in the foregoing case.

A hard, elongated, irregularly shaped tumour was situated above the pubes, rather to the right side, which could be plainly felt in the rectum about three or three and a half inches from anus. It appeared, from its form, to be the enlarged uterus, with the right Fallopian tube distended also. As it tapered downwards, it did not present a very favorable form for tapping through the bowel; and moreover as the patient was already married, and the recto-urethral septum of considerable thickness, I resolved to attempt the formation of an artificial vagina.

It was contemplated to do so in three operations, in order that the constitutional irritation might be lessened as much as possible.

After she was placed under chloroform I divided the raphe superficially from just beneath the meatus urinarius to the perinæum, a line of about two and a half inches long. The cellular tissue between the rectum and urethra was broken down by the sharp ivory handle of the scalpel about an inch on either side of the median line, and to a depth of rather more than an inch. The finger was kept in rectum and a catheter in urethra during this time. Oiled lint was passed into the artificial canal, and she was kept in bed perfectly quiet for five days, the lint being changed daily.

Not a bad symptom followed. Five days after the first operation she was again put under chloroform, and I extended the opening to within half an inch of uterus. I found that immediately behind the urethra there was some yellow tissue, an inch wide and a quarter of an inch in thickness, much more easily broken down than the other portions; this, taking the direction of the tumour, I followed, considering it to be the relics of the vagina. Having filled the canal with oiled lint, she was placed in bed. Very little blood followed this or the other portion of the operation. It was intended to have completed the operation the next time. She went on exceedingly well afterwards. But when the day for the completion of the operation arrived she refused to undergo any further operation, her friends having prejudiced her against chloroform (it had been very difficult to bring her under its power); and without it the chance of success was very slight, as she was very intolerant of pain. However, as she was impracticable, I was obliged to forego the satisfaction I might have felt had the last portion of the operation turned out as successful as the first.

As I have already in the other case remarked, hitherto the principal danger has been in the last portion of the operation, namely, in the opening the uterus. It was my intention to have used a canula, drawn off most of the fluid, plugged the canula, and enlarged the wound so made subsequently.

The three following are cases of severe constriction of the vagina, the result of lingering labours.

In the first and second the dysmenorrhœa had been very severe, in consequence of the small opening only giving way after considerable accumulation of menstrual secretion. In the first, however, impregnation had been entirely prevented; in the second it occurred only after twelve years.

CASE 8.—*Excessive dysmenorrhœa from almost complete occlusion of the vagina; division of cicatrices; recovery.*—L. H—, æt. 25, married, was, three years ago, delivered of a live child, after ninety-six hours of lingering labour, for the last twelve of which the head was allowed to remain in the outlet without any assistance. She was exceedingly ill after this for six months, suffering severe pain in vagina, uterus, and pelvic region, with purulent discharge, having for three months after delivery incontinence of urine. After her recovery sexual connexion was found to be nearly entirely impeded, and gradually menstruation became painful and difficult. For this she was under treatment in two of the London hospitals, in one of which a slight opening was made, with temporary relief to menstruation. The pain and difficulty soon returned, and before admission the menses could not flow till after two or three days' severe pains.

On admission, March 2nd, 1862, into Guy's Hospital, it

was found that the vagina was so completely closed by cicatrices, at about one inch within that canal, that not the smallest opening could be detected. It was therefore decided to wait till menstruation commenced; this took place the day following, when, through a speculum, an aperture the size of a pin was detected to the left side of the vagina, by the small stream of secretion which oozed through it. A small probe was, after some trouble, inserted, and the opening enlarged by slight incisions with a pointed bistoury. Finally, a catheter was introduced and retained six hours, through which the menses flowed, with complete comfort to the patient. When the menses had passed off, about six days after admission, she was placed under chloroform on her back. The speculum was again passed, and the opening easily recognised. The speculum was then removed, and the finger alone trusted to during the remainder of the operation. I used a guarded, sharp-pointed bistoury first of all, to enlarge the aperture of sufficient size for the introduction of the left forefinger. After this was accomplished the firm and tense bands were divided by a blunt-pointed bistoury, till the finger was introduced about an inch, when it came to a firmer band, with a small opening in it. This was enlarged by many small incisions, when the finger entered the cavity formed by the upper third of the vagina. This had been distended by the periodical accumulation of menses, and its walls had become dense. I was anxious not to run risks of constitutional irritation, and therefore postponed further operation for a second occasion. She had no bad symptom after. In five days I again put her under chloroform, and divided the remaining cicatrices so as to admit two fingers. Some of the thick intervening portions were removed, and the vagina, although somewhat rigid, admitted the introduction of two fingers. A very large bougie was placed in the vagina before she was put into bed. During the first three days a dilatable india-rubber bag was introduced, but afterwards the largest bougie was daily used. The vaginal douche was employed frequently, both after the first and second operation.

She had no bad symptom, and left the hospital on the 24th of March.

At the end of two months the vagina remained the same size, and during that time she had become pregnant and aborted. She still continues the use of the bougie.

(Since the reading of this paper I have seen her, and find that the vagina is nearly natural, only a slight band remaining.)

The two cases following are of cicatrized vagina, the effects of former protracted labours, the patients being in actual labour at the time of my seeing them.

CASE 4.—*Almost complete obliteration of the middle third of vagina; conversion of the upper third into a large sac, distended with pus; at the seventh month of pregnancy; enlargement of vagina; delivery: recovery.*—Mrs. W—, Hackney, aged about thirty, well-formed, healthy. Twelve years ago was delivered after a lingering labour by the forceps, which were used on account of convulsions, and not from any obstruction. I was informed there was no difficulty in applying them or in bringing away the child. However, shortly after her recovery, she noticed impediment at coition, which has continued ever since. She had had ever since very much difficulty, and intense pain at the menstrual periods. About six years ago the menses were completely retained, to remedy which a slight opening was formed, with temporary benefit. Latterly the difficulty had returned, the secretion flowing with great pain, which generally has yielded to warm baths and opiates.

I was called in by Mr. Wright, of Clapton Square, on the evening of March 3rd, 1862, to see her, and who had detected the condition of the vagina.

She was in the seventh month of pregnancy, and had been suffering from pains, at intervals, for three or four days, in the uterus and lower abdomen, which was very tender upon pressure. The uterus contracted and relaxed alternately.

I found a closure of the vagina about one third up; it ended gradually in a funnel-shaped point. I was able to pass a uterine sound, and then an elastic catheter, about an inch beyond the termination of the funnel. There was no evidence of any expansion in the narrow channel.

I considered that, as so complete an obstruction would preclude any reasonable hope of the child's head being able to expand it, and as her symptoms were becoming urgent and the tenderness considerable, it would be better to open up the vagina at once. She was already under the influence of chloroform, for such was her intolerance of pain that it was found impossible to touch her without her being thrown into a state of the greatest irritability; few persons could be found more intolerant of pain, and few in which chloroform was longer producing anæsthesia, circumstances which added much to the inherent difficulties of the case.

Having placed her on her back, I introduced a director, along which was passed a bistoury, guarded nearly up to the point, as far as about half an inch. With this slight incisions were made in many directions, gradually, till the tip of the left forefinger was able just to enter. Upon this the bistoury was passed flatwise, and by means of its guidance numerous bands of rigid cicatrices were detected in all directions; these were divided at many points by turning the edge of the bistoury towards them, assisted by the pressure of the finger. By this mode and by dilatation by the finger I was able to advance an inch, when I came upon a firm septum, apparently stopping further advance. However, a small hole was detected in it, into which I passed the bistoury, and enlarged it also by slight incisions in many directions, till the forefinger was admitted through. It then entered a cavity, the lower end only of which it could explore. Upon withdrawing the finger about four or five ounces of pus flowed. I again examined the cavity, dividing more bands, and then found a membranous bag coming down from above, evidently containing fluid. This was found to be subject to the influence of pressure above, and also it became tenser when uterine contractions came on, and relaxed upon their subsidence. This I supposed to be the amnial membranes. After a time I was able to reach the upper part of the cavity, and found the bag protruding through a thickened ring, which proved to be the os uteri dilated to about the size of a crown-piece.

Chloroform was suspended, to see what the uterus would do. After about two and a half hours the patient was again placed under its influence. The membranes were found lower, but the fœtus could not be felt. The membranes were then ruptured, in order to secure the continuation of the pains. A large quantity of liquor amnii flowed, which assisted in relaxing the vagina. In addition to this, I again carefully sought for any remnants of bands, and divided them by drawing the point of the bistoury lightly over them, assisted by stretching them by the finger. By these means two fingers were admitted through the narrow part of vagina without difficulty, so that at last the head of the fœtus was detected as the presenting part. One point was very noticeable, namely, that upon each occurrence of the uterine contractions the narrow part of the vagina became smaller and rigid, relaxing on their subsidence; this it did also each time directly the finger was introduced, but it went off upon keeping the finger quiet.

By this time the vagina was so altered in form from its former abnormal state that, if the well-lubricated finger were carefully and quickly passed in, the whole canal seemed of almost natural shape; for the upper distended part had now contracted, and its narrow part had been so distended that the whole seemed to form a canal of nearly the same calibre throughout. Very little bleeding took place during the operation.

I left, therefore, the labour to come on naturally, considering that the rest would be accomplished by the pressure of the child's head. This it did, and for the remainder of the report of the case I am indebted to Mr. Wright, under whose care I left her. He says, "She continued without uterine pains till midday of the 5th of March, when they reappeared; the vagina was dilated slowly but gradually under the pressure of the head, the right hand coming down with it, and she was delivered at 5 a.m. on the 6th of March. The child was dead, but it was not apparent how long it had been so. For the last two hours she was kept under the influence of chloroform, in consequence of her excitability under pain."

She recovered without any bad symptom. After a few weeks Mr. Wright found the vagina continued open, but not more so than I left it before the head passed through it. He has continued the use of a bougie ever since.

Remarks.—The mode in which the incisions into the cicatrices is made in these cases, as also in the succeeding one, is a point of considerable importance; for, by making them in only two or three directions, it is evident that the chief expansion of the canal must come from the healthy tissue at the bottom of the cuts; there must be, therefore, great danger that it would be rent through upon the descent of the head. This calamity seems to me to be much less likely to take place if the cicatrices are scored in many directions, and not completely through, at least at first. If the finger guides the bistoury, it will readily detect the resisting point, and by first passing the instrument on the flat, turning it, when required, towards the band, a very slight pressure will suffice to destroy its rigidity; the finger feels it yield, and the bistoury can be again laid flat upon it. This can be frequently and easily repeated without any danger wherever any resistance is detected.

The best form of bistoury for this purpose is a straight, blunt-pointed one, with only about one inch of cutting edge.

It will be of considerable assistance if it be so very slightly curved that the cutting edge, just behind the blunt tip, can cut as it is drawn towards the operator. This will facilitate the section of the firmer bands.

But should we only have the curved, sharp-pointed kind at command, then it must be covered to within an inch or so of its point; and instead of being pressed against the bands, its point should be drawn lightly over them towards the operator, guided carefully by the finger, which is also at hand to protect the point in case the patient should move.

The form the vagina had assumed in this case was peculiar; the wall of the upper part, which was largely distended, was very much thickened and firm. The accumulation of secretion of purulent matter had gone on also to dilate the os uteri, and was evidently exciting labour-pains, which subsided for a time upon its evacuation. It also caused much tenderness throughout the lower abdomen, and it seems difficult to conjecture in what manner such a case would have terminated had it been left entirely to nature. Whilst the menses existed the very narrow channel was kept open periodically, but when pregnancy ensued then it ceased to convey away the natural discharges; irritation of the mucous membrane was set up, and an accumulation of puriform matter followed.

CASE 5.—*Middle third of vagina contracted to size of a quill; enlargement of vagina; impaction of fœtal head at brim; perforation; delivery; post partum hæmorrhage; recovery.*—A. M—, Irishwoman, æt. 40, had a child about eight years since, but has no knowledge how the present impediment arose, of which, indeed, she was not aware till the present time, as it did not seem to have impeded coition to any great extent.

She had been in labour twelve hours on January 18th, 1861, when Dr. Downing, of Deptford, was sent for, and, having detected the vaginal obstruction, he sent for me. By the time I arrived her condition had become serious—pulse 115 per minute; tongue dry and brown in centre; patient feeble and exhausted, although the pains were yet strong and forcing.

I found the vagina open for about one inch, beyond which it was closed by cicatrices, except that an opening existed through which only a catheter could be passed. It was found that the canal expanded beyond the first portion of the stricture.

Examination per rectum showed that the fœtal head had not descended down to the stricture, but remained about an inch above it. The constricted portion was firm and rigid.

Finding it was necessary to deliver, the patient was placed in the ordinary obstetric position, and the labia being separated, incisions were made through the more marked cicatrices by a blunt-pointed bistoury, guarded to within a short distance of the end. By these and by dilatation with the finger the canal was enlarged sufficiently to allow the forefinger to pass up to the head of the fœtus. I found that bands of cicatrices, of irregular form and length, passed round the vagina to the extent of an inch upwards. These were divided by slightly pressing the bistoury against them during the pains. The divisions were effected in numerous directions, and after a short time three fingers were enabled to pass. The bleeding consequent on the incisions was rather free, but easily controlled by application of ice.

As it was apparent from the putrid discharges, absence of the fœtal sounds, &c., that the child was dead, and as the head was found to be firmly impacted in the brim, I perforated, and after much trouble succeeded in drawing the head through, and it passed the narrow part of the vagina without any marked impediment.

The placenta came away shortly; but after some little time the uterus relaxed, and much hæmorrhage ensued. It was only by the assistance of a lump of ice smeared over the interior of the uterus that it could be brought to contract. It was remarkable, when the hand was passed into the uterus, how little constriction of the vagina remained. She recovered quickly, being about at the end of six days.

She would not allow a bougie to be used, but I heard that she was delivered two years after of a dead child without any trouble.

In this case the more rigid portion of the contraction was towards the vulva, the contrary of the preceding one.

The question which was asked by Trask, and answered by his appeal to the results of the cases he had collected, namely, "Is it best to leave the dilatation to be effected by the child's head, or should it be released by incisions?" did not arise in the last two cases, for the reasons stated in the report of each; but the last three cases show that incisions can be made safely and efficiently, and without risk of deep laceration, when free from downward pressure of the fœtal head.

Dr. Graily Hewitt wished to call the attention of the Society to an important point in the treatment of that class of cases in which there is retention of menstrual fluid within the uterus, whether from imperforate hymen, or congenital closure of the os uteri. It was the fact that, in a certain proportion of the cases in which the fluid had been evacuated from the uterus by puncture or otherwise, death had occurred a short time subsequently from escape of the menstrual fluid into the peritoneal cavity, causing severe and rapidly fatal peritonitis. It was a remarkable fact that, whereas such escape of menstrual fluid into the peritoneal cavity hardly ever occurred when these cases were left alone, yet that this should happen after operation, and when an outlet by the natural way had been prepared; but the fact was undoubted. The probable explanation of this curious circumstance was, he believed, that uterine contractions are set up consequent on the artificial opening into the uterus; that these contractions continue after the first evacuation of the fluid, and when, in all probability, the artificial opening had become occluded or insufficient; and that these contractions have the effect of expelling the remainder of the retained blood through the Fallopian tubes, and so into the peritoneum. In laying down rules, therefore, for the management of these cases, this source of danger should be anticipated, and if possible guarded against. Dr. Hicks had very properly guarded against the admission of air into the uterus during the operation by the procedures recommended, but the danger now alluded to was even greater. The best plan to be followed, in order to avert this danger, would, he believed, be to make a very small aperture in the obstructing tissue, whatever that might be, and to allow the retained menstrual fluid to escape very slowly and gradually, almost *guttatim*. In this way the excitation of strong and forcible contractions of the uterus would, he considered, be avoided.

After some further observations by Dr. Palfrey, Dr. Druitt, Dr. Tyler Smith, and Mr. Walter Chapman, Dr. Hicks replied, and the meeting adjourned.

DECEMBER 3RD, 1862.

DR. TYLER SMITH, President, in the Chair.

Present—41 Fellows, and 1 Visitor.

The following gentlemen were elected Fellows of the Society:—Charles Campbell, M.D. Edin., L.R.C.S. Edin., Kingston, Jamaica; Walter Chapman, F.R.C.S., &c., Lower Tooting, Surrey; Edward Ellis, M.D., 8, Fitzroy Street, W.; Joseph Train, M.D. St. Andrews, L.R.C.P. Edin., Frederick Street, South Shields; Charles Christopher Hayman, M.D., M.R.C.S., Eastbourne, Sussex; John Rutherford Kirkpatrick, M.B.T.C.D., Lic. K. & Q.C.P.I., &c., Lying-in Hospital, Dublin; Frederick Prince, M.R.C.S., and L.S.A., Sawston, Cambridgeshire; Isaac Shortland Shillingford, M.R.C.S., & L.S.A., 1, Hill Street, Peckham; George Frederick Spry, M.R.C.S,, L.M., and L.S.A., Staff-Assistant Surgeon, Fort Gomer, Alverstoke, Hants; Thomas Taylor, F.R.C.S., and L.S.A., 19, Bennett's Hill, Birmingham.

A CASE OF MULTIPLE MEDULLARY CANCER, COMPLICATED WITH PREGNANCY.

By THOMAS HAWKES TANNER, M.D.,

ASSISTANT-PHYSICIAN FOR THE DISEASES OF WOMEN AND CHILDREN TO KING'S COLLEGE HOSPITAL.

I SHOULD hardly have ventured to bring the details of the following solitary case before the Obstetrical Society of London, were it not that examples of multiple cancer, complicated with pregnancy, are very far from common. It seems, therefore, the obvious duty of every physician to record even one instance of this disease, when he has the opportunity; so as to add to that gradually accumulating store of knowledge which is the property of the whole profession. In managing such exceptional cases, no practitioner can venture to trust to his own experience as a guide for treatment; but rather, while acting on sound general principles, it is incumbent upon him to remember and to draw inferences from the examples which have been recorded on various occasions by others.

Without further preface I beg to draw attention to the following narrative:—

On July 29th, 1862, I was requested by Dr. Thane, of Hart Street, Bloomsbury, to see with him, Mrs. C. L—, æt. 39, residing in Drury Lane. The poor woman was the wife of a very respectable working man, and was in comfortable circumstances for her station in life. She had always enjoyed remarkably good health. None of her relatives had ever suffered from cancer; but there was probably a slight family tendency to phthisis—that is to say, all her half-brother's children died from pulmonary consumption. She had been married ten years; and was about five calendar months advanced in her third pregnancy. The first child had been born on October 12th, 1854. While suckling this infant, pregnancy again took place; and on weaning the child, at the beginning of 1856, she aborted, being three months advanced in gestation. After this accident the general health continued very good until May 2nd, 1861, when her child died from an attack of croup, and she was rendered so very miserable by the loss, that she may be said to have been neither happy nor well since the unfortunate event. The catamenia had been quite regular until February 25th, 1862; but this was the last day of their appearance.

At the commencement of the present year (1862), a small swelling, about the size of a hasel nut, was first discovered in the abdominal walls, just to the right of the umbilicus. There was no other symptom of disease appreciable to herself or her husband at this time. The growth gave rise to no annoyance until a few weeks ago, when it began to enlarge, and to be the seat of lancinating pains. Similar swellings, also, then commenced forming in other parts of the body.

On July 29th, at my first visit, I found her much reduced in flesh and strength. The appetite was good; but as she suffered much from indigestion and flatulence, she was afraid to eat, although the remedies prescribed by Dr. Thane had given much relief. The sleep at night was very disturbed. In the abdominal parietes, just to the right of the umbilicus, there was a well-defined tumour, about the size of a large walnut. Adjoining the lower part of the ensiform cartilage of the sternum, there was a more extensive mass, also seated in the abdominal wall. In the left groin there was likewise a flattened growth, about two inches and a half in diameter. On examining per vaginam, a very firm substance was discovered projecting into the canal; feeling as if it had its origin from the lower part of the sacrum, though in reality it was entirely seated in the recto-vaginal septum. It was clear that this mass would soon block up the vagina, and Dr. Thane assured me that it had increased much in size during the last fortnight. As before mentioned, she was five months advanced in pregnancy; and both the uterine souffle and the fœtal heart could be plainly distinguished. The liver was much enlarged; and this enlargement, combined with the size of the uterus, occasioned a wearying feeling of distension, as well as some dyspnœa.

Taking all the foregoing circumstances fairly into consideration, it seemed certain that the poor woman's comfort would be increased, even if her life were not prolonged, by inducing premature labour; a proceeding which did not appear contraindicated by any feeling for the child, as it was certain that a live infant could never be given birth to through the natural passages. The propriety of waiting, and ultimately effecting delivery by the Cæsarean section was discussed; but, for reasons which will afterwards appear, such a plan of treatment was regarded as not applicable in the present instance.

Consequently, on July 30th, the membranes were punctured, and about half a pint of liquor amnii withdrawn. On August 1st, labour pains, of fair severity, set in; and Dr. Thane remained with the patient during the night, expecting delivery. On the following afternoon, however, the os uteri was still very rigid; and as the patient was getting tired and exhausted, and, moreover, as the mass of cancer in the recto-vaginal septum reached to within almost an inch of the pubes, it was evident that nothing would be gained by further delay. I therefore slowly tried to dilate the os uteri, and this being partially effected, the fœtus was broken up with a pair of forceps, and removed piecemeal. No difficulty was experienced with the placenta; the discharge of blood was very slight; no injury was done to the uterus or vaginal walls; and the poor woman was left in a tolerably comfortable condition.

For some few days she continued to progress favorably; but on August 10th, a severe attack of diarrhœa set in, aphthæ formed on the tongue and gums, and for the first time in her life she became jaundiced. It would only be tedious to give an account of the way in which she daily lost ground. Suffice it to say, that matters gradually progressed from bad to worse, until the morning of August 26th, when death took place from exhaustion.

At the *autopsy*, fourteen hours afterwards, made by Dr. Thane and myself, the body was found greatly emaciated. In the abdominal parietes, to the right of the umbilicus, there was a deposit of firm medullary cancer, the size of a walnut; together with a larger growth just below the ensiform cartilage. These were separate tumours, and not infiltrations. The liver was enlarged to about three times its natural size, and studded with medullary masses, varying in size from a pea to a small orange. There were, likewise, several deposits of cancer in the great omentum, in the spleen, in the walls of the colon, and one large mass binding the sigmoid flexure of the colon to the tissues of the pelvis.

In the pelvic cavity there was a separate deposit, extending chiefly down the recto-vaginal septum, and completely blocking up the vagina. The inguinal glands, on both sides, were enlarged and infiltrated with medullary cancer. The uterus, considering the time which had elapsed since delivery, was of its normal size and healthy.

At the apex of the left lung there was a slight deposit of tubercle, which had undergone calcareous degeneration; while at the same part of the right lung there were several small tubercles. The heart was healthy, but its walls were flabby. The kidneys were healthy.

In considering the foregoing particulars, there are two or three points which appear deserving of attention. And, first, this history confirms the general opinion, that the existence of cancer does not interfere with a woman's fertility; pregnancy occurring just as if she were in sound health. In this respect, however, the case is less remarkable than many instances which are recorded, where impregnation has taken place in spite of the presence of ulcerated carcinoma of the cervix uteri.

In the second place the progress of the disease was rapid. It seems quite certain that in May, 1861, the patient was in good health. Mental disquietude (to which she, herself, attributed the malignant affection) did not in the beginning tell upon her system. It is probable that, when the first tumour was discovered, at the commencement of 1862, it had not long been present; and it may, therefore, be inferred that the disorder ran its whole course in less than nine months. The fact is worthy of note, moreover, that the medullary disease existed in various parts of the body in two forms, viz., as separable tumours, and as infiltrations; and that while the rate of growth was comparatively slow in the former, it was very quick in the latter. There are so very few cases of multiple cancer on record, that it is not possible to state the average duration of life in patients afflicted with it. In a very remarkable example, which was in University College Hospital, under the care of Dr. Walshe, in April, 1852, the disease ran its course in twelve weeks from the time of its first external manifestation.

Thirdly, it may fairly be asked whether it would not have been better to have allowed the pregnancy to have gone on without interruption; to have kept the patient alive, if possible, until the end of gestation; and then, on labour supervening, to have resorted to the Cæsarean section, so as to save the infant's life? In reply to this, it is to be urged, that having taken all the circumstances into consideration at the time, there appeared no sufficient reason for departing from that excellent rule of British midwifery, which prohibits the Cæsarean operation except in cases where delivery by other means is impossible. Now, here, the induction of premature labour, though it destroyed the offspring, afforded a safe mode of treatment for the mother. And then, owing to the enlarged state of the liver, it is very doubtful if the woman could have survived when the uterus had further increased in size. As it was, there were troublesome attacks of dyspnœa; and the feeling of abdominal distension was in itself the cause of much suffering. The only physicians, as far as I know, who have successfully resorted to the Cæsarean section for the delivery of women afflicted with cancer of the uterus, are Dr. Oldham,[1] and Dr. James Edmunds;[2] and it is remarkable that these are almost the only instances which have occurred in this country of late years in which the operation has not proved fatal to the mother.

The history of these cases is so instructive, that it may be allowable to give an epitome of them here. The chief features in the patient of Dr. Oldham are these:—Sarah L—, ætat 28, was admitted into Guy's Hospital, under the care of Dr. Oldham, on June 4th, 1851. She had had five children, after favorable labours; the last, two years previously. At the time of her admission she was seven months advanced in her sixth pregnancy. She had suffered

[1] 'Guy's Hospital Reports,' Second Series, vol. vii, p. 426. London, 1851.

[2] 'Lancet,' p. 4. London, 5th January, 1862.

great pain, increased after quickening, in the uterus, loins, hips, and thighs; together with occasional hæmorrhages, and a discharge, sometimes thin and sanious, sometimes thick and yellow. The appetite was good, the pulse 80, and she was neither emaciated nor anæmic. On July 3rd, at 2 a.m., after labour had been on for some hours, Dr. Oldham made a careful examination; and found the vagina filled with a solid, lobulated structure, which resembled lumps of hardened mortar, and presented an insuperable difficulty to delivery. The diseased mass was full of deep clefts; one being more patent than the others, and allowing the finger to penetrate it to its full length. This was supposed to be the os uteri, but the presenting part of the fœtus could not be felt. It was, therefore, determined to resort to the Cæsarean section; and the operation was at once performed by Mr. Poland, while the patient was under the influence of chloroform. A strong female child, which was alive and did well, was extracted from the uterus. On August 11th, more than five weeks after the operation, the woman had recovered from her labour, although the wound was not entirely healed. The original disease of course progressed, and proved fatal about six months after the operation.

With regard to Dr. Edmunds' patient, the principal facts are as follow:—Emma L—, æt. 38, of healthy family, was taken in labour with her third child on December 4th, 1860. Pregnancy had advanced to nearly the full term. Projecting into the vagina, was a hard, tuberculated mass, about two inches in diameter. It was superficially ulcerated. There was much difficulty in making out the os uteri; but after a persevering attempt the left index finger was passed through the mass, when the head could just be felt. After continuing nearly six days in labour, the uterine orifice still remained hard and unyielding; and as no part of it was found healthy or dilatable, abdominal hysterotomy was determined upon. The operation was performed in the usual manner, but the proceeding was complicated, owing to the placenta being wounded. Dr. Edmunds, however, rapidly cut through this organ, and then hooked out the two portions before withdrawing the child. The latter was living and healthy. On the fourth day afterwards there was severe general peritonitis and constant vomiting. Ice, and nothing else, was taken by the mouth; while beef tea and an anodyne were administered in enemata. On the sixth day the peritonitis subsided; and on the twelfth day the patient sat up for a few hours on the sofa. By the fourteenth day from operation she was convalescent; and from that time she gained strength rapidly, suckled the baby until its death on January 7th, 1861, and in all respects did remarkably well. Dr. Edmunds has since informed me that his patient died in the Cancer Hospital on 31st October, 1861; this event having been hastened by large and frequent hæmorrhages from the diseased uterus.

And, lastly, to return to the subject of this communication, there was one other line of practice open to us, and it was this:—To allow the pregnancy to continue, and to endeavour to lengthen the patient's life, so that death might be deferred until the fœtus was sufficiently advanced in growth to be able to maintain a separate existence. Then, as soon as the poor woman succumbed, to open the abdomen and uterus, so as to remove the infant. The only argument against this proceeding was the fact, already alluded to, of the suffering increasing, *pari passu*, with the uterine development; and, therefore, though it is very probable that this practice might in some instances be available to save fœtal life, yet it appeared cruel to resort to it in the case under observation. In short, the treatment had recourse to by Dr. Thane and myself, was based upon these two considerations:—that while it presented the best chance for the mother as regarded the prolongation of her life, it was clearly that which would ensure her the greatest amount of ease until death completely relieved her.

CASE OF RETENTION OF THE CATAMENIA, FOR MORE THAN TWO YEARS, IN A MARRIED WOMAN.

By Walter Chapman, F.R.C.S. Eng.

In order to give a full account of this important case, I must state that the antecedent part of its history is reported in 'The Lancet' for November 24th, 1860, as "Case 5," being one of "Eleven Cases of Vesico-Vaginal Fistula," by I. Baker Brown, Esq., F.R.C.S., "of two months' duration; two operations; cure." Its history is as follows:—"With her first child she was in labour for a week, and was ultimately delivered with instruments. Her second labour was not nearly so severe. Her third labour occurred in March last, 1860. The pains began on the 7th, and were regular, as well as severe, until the 9th, when the child's movements ceased. The pains continued very severe, and on the evening of the 11th instruments were applied. After some hours' exertions, she was delivered of a female child (stillborn), which weighed over twelve pounds. She was not conscious of passing her urine after the labour was over; and when, a few days afterwards, she arose with the intention of doing so, she found that it all passed involuntarily. A slough came away about the tenth day. She has recovered her general health, but has no control over the bladder in any position."

The last operation for the fistula was in the middle of June, 1860.

I first saw this lady professionally on September 26th, 1862. She was sitting up, able to superintend her domestic affairs, to walk out, attend church, and, to a casual observer, presented the aspect of health. She was of robust stature, rather short, with a superabundance of fat, and forty years old. Having related the previous history of her case, as detailed by Mr. T. B. Brown, she complained of great irritability of the bladder and stomach, and frequent vomiting; also of pain in the lumbar and sacral regions.

She could take at times only a little biscuit, and brandy and water throughout the day.

Having a very important engagement in London the following day—which she was most anxious to keep—I simply prescribed with a view to relieve the more urgent symptoms, some henbane, potash, hydrocyanic acid, and an opiate suppository at night—requesting the earliest opportunity of examining her in bed. This I did the next day. On external examination of the abdomen, I had no difficulty in determining the existence of a large tumour, resembling the pregnant uterus at about the sixth month. On questioning her regarding pregnancy, she said she had no reason whatever for supposing it; but told me she had not menstruated since the operation. I then made a vaginal examination, and found the cervix uteri lost in a general enlargement of the uterus, whose mouth I could not discover, but the finger detected a thin membrane in place of the os. The speculum disclosed the spot where the os uteri had existed, and now was hermetically sealed. It bled very slightly from the irritation of the finger. Reflecting on the preceding facts, I stated my opinion that the symptoms resulted from a retention of the catamenia.

She informed me that a few months after the operation feeling uneasy at not being "regular," she consulted a medical gentleman acquainted with her case, who prescribed for her without benefit. She also applied to an eminent surgeon in London, who knew her history; he hoped the menses would recur when she regained her usual strength. Three or four weeks prior to my first visit, remaining uneasy and anxious about herself, and "feeling quite sure that something was wrong in her inside," and perhaps a cancer existed, she again consulted a former medical attendant. He examined her with the speculum, said "there was no cancer," and prescribed some palliative medicines. For my own, not less than for the satisfaction of herself and husband, I requested the opinion of the President, Dr. Tyler Smith. He examined her very carefully. and confirmed my diagnosis. It was strengthened by considering that for two years or more, within a few months after the operation, she had suffered more or less distress, which was augmented to severe pain and spasms at every monthly period, so as to make the application of leeches to the side, belladonna plasters to the back, &c., &c., seem advisable—and to call forth from an old and faithful servant the remark, that every month her mistress "appeared to be in labour." On these occasions she sometimes had a copious whitish discharge, which was not offensive. She experienced much mental relief through my consultation with Dr. Tyler Smith, the result of which was, that an opening should be made into the uterus for the evacuation of the fluid. Having explained to my patient the nature of the proceeding; kindly assisted by my friend, Mr. Thomas Harvey Trent, on October 5th, 1862, whilst the patient was lying on her left side in bed, I introduced the index finger of my right hand to the spot which could be detected by the touch, as having been the site of the os uteri, and scratched through it with the nail, so as to admit the tip of the finger. Its withdrawal was instantly followed by a copious flow of treacly looking fluid, of a dark claret colour, perfectly free from all unpleasant odour. About ten or twelve ounces escaped. Much more gradually flowed away. She bore all well, and we were delighted with our success. She was kept perfectly at rest in bed. The next day, I again inserted my finger into the uterus, and gave exit to more fluid, which was much thinner. At ten o'clock at night, of the same day, she was progressing most satisfactorily.

At four o'clock a.m. of the third day, I was summoned, and found that after my visit of the previous night, she was attacked with great pain over the abdomen, sickness, tympanites, small and rapid pulse, and was very ill. All this she considered to be due to an attack of the spasms, to which she had so long been subject. She informed me now, however, that the evening before, feeling perfectly well able to do so, she got out of bed, walked twice across her large bedroom to procure some articles, and then sat upon the edge of her bed, with her legs hanging down, and sang very loudly, some songs, for the amusement of a little girl, who was under her charge. Her servants were fomenting her abdomen with flannels wrung out of hot water, and I gave her directly five grains of calomel and two of opium, and in a few hours some more. The attack quickly subsided, and the next day her bowels were freely relieved. During the next week I daily (with one or two exceptions, in consequence of her own urgent request) passed a full-sized elastic male catheter into the uterus, and syringed it out with tepid water—for although the discharge escaped for a few days spontaneously, it became thin and offensive. The great indication in the general treatment appeared to be that of supporting her powers of life and soothing her, and she was able to take a very considerable amount of nourishment. Her abdomen became soft and flaccid, and she could bear great pressure over it without pain. One day she sat up for some hours in an easy chair, and all seemed to be doing well.

On October 15th, ten days after the first opening of the uterus, she took a dose of castor-oil, which acted. In the evening of this day, I gave her an opiate enema, as she appeared to be restless and in pain.

The next morning, October 16th, at ten, a.m., she was perfectly sensible, told me she "could give a good report of herself this morning." But I was soon told that she had been very sick in the night, and could not retain any nourishments. Her countenance was pale and sunken, her hands cold and damp, and no pulse could be felt at either wrist.

Brandy and water was constantly administered; she recognised her friends around her, and spoke to them; but continued to sink, and died at two, p.m., the same day, the 16th, remaining sensible till an hour before death.

I requested permission for a post-mortem examination, but the relatives objected.

Mr. Owen felt some hesitation in expressing an opinion contrary to that of their President, but thought that the cause of death might be more directly attributed to the admission of air into the uterus, in its relaxed and enlarged condition. After the gravid uterus is emptied of the fœtus and secundines it immediately contracts to nearly its natural size; but here that reaction was not likely to follow, whilst the daily injection of water which had been employed exposed the organ afresh to contact with the air through the artificial opening, which latter presented no obstruction like that of the os and cervix uteri.

Dr. Graily Hewitt remarked that the chief question to be determined was the cause of the fatal result in this interesting case. He considered that it was probably due, as suggested by Mr. Owen, to pyæmia. At the last meeting of the Society he had alluded to the occasional circumstance of a fatal result following the evacuation of the uterine contents in cases of menstrual retention by subsequent passage of some of the blood into the peritoneal cavity. The explanation of this curious circumstance he had then attempted he still thought the most probable one, and that it was due to the contractions of the uterus becoming more forcible as its bulk diminished. However that might be, it did not seem that in the case now before the Society any such occurrence had taken place. He considered that the best course to adopt in treating such cases would be to make a minute opening, and to allow the fluid to escape as it had collected—gradually; further, that it was decidedly expedient to avoid anything, such as the use of injections of water into the uterus, likely to be the means of conveying air into the cavity of that organ.

CASE OF MONSTROSITY.

By Alfred Meadows, M.D., M.R.C.P.

The following case which occurred some time since in my practice, appears to me to possess sufficient interest to be worth recording, especially as I had the opportunity of making a careful dissection of the parts concerned, and of taking some drawings which I am enabled to show to the Fellows of this Society.

On the 16th March, I was sent for to see Mrs. R—, æt. 36, who had been suddenly taken in labour, accompanied with rather severe flooding. She had had twelve children, all of whom were born at the seventh month; but only three were living, none of them had been the subject of any malformation. She had had dropsy of the feet and legs in several successive pregnancies; in the last of these I attended her and found a considerable quantity of albumen in the urine; this was at the fifth month. The dropsy was greatly relieved by treatment, and labour came on and terminated successfully, the child being born alive at the seventh month. The only remarkable feature occurring in the course of the present pregnancy was that, though tolerably certain from the first of her condition, she never remarked the period of quickening; and up to within a few days of her confinement, which began as usual at the seventh month, she never experienced any movement whatever of the fœtus. During the last few days, she had felt a slight quivering, but no distinct movement such as she had noticed in previous pregnancies.

On examination I found the os was well dilated and soft, the head presenting, pains frequent and strong, fœtal pulsations were audible, but very feeble. The labour progressed very rapidly, and terminated with the birth of the little monster who is the subject of this communication; it was alive when born, and lived about three quarters of an hour, making feeble efforts at crying.

On examining the child which appeared to have arrived at the seventh month, I found that, instead of possessing the usual organs of locomotion, its body terminated in a pointed caudal appendage measuring about five and a half inches from the extremity of the spine. Near this point there was a kind of ball and socket joint, which allowed the tail, if I may so call it, to move backwards and forwards, and slightly from side to side. The movement backwards was limited to a straight line with the spine, while that forwards was sufficient to form an acute angle with the abdomen. Within about an inch and a half of the extreme point was a sort of hinge joint, having the same range of motion from before backwards as the preceding. During life this caudal appendage was several times wagged backwards and forwards, but no other movement was effected by it.

On opening the abdominal cavity, the following appearances were presented:—The liver was very large; the stomach and small intestines were normal; the ascending and transverse colon were very much distended by a considerable accumulation of meconium, the descending colon was much smaller, and ended very abruptly at the sigmoid flexure; the rectum being represented by a small tube about two inches long, and just large enough to admit the passage of an ordinary probe; it was closed at its lower end, which was lying free in the left iliac region. The spleen was normal; supra-renal capsules very large, but with little or no proper structure, being in fact merely two membranous pouches. There was complete absence of all urinary apparatus, both kidneys and bladder. An ovary, or what appeared to be an ovary, and a sort of convoluted Fallopian tube were lying on either side the pelvis, but there was no trace of either vagina or uterus, or any external generative organs; nor was there any anal orifice. The abdominal aorta bifurcated at its usual situation, and each common iliac again divided into two branches, one of which went through a small aperture in the pelvis to the muscles at the back of the caudal appendage; the other went to supply those on the front. There were no branches to the interior of the pelvis because there were no viscera requiring it. The anterior crural and sciatic nerves were both represented

The cavity of the pelvis, if such it could be called, had no proper outlet, indeed it was but a very shallow depression, and except the alæ ilii, was entirely cartilaginous. On the under surface of the floor of the pelvis was a sort of cotyloid cavity, where the head of the bone which represented the two amalgamated femurs was placed. This bone formed three-fourths of the whole lower extremity; at its lower end it presented very much the appearance of an ordinary femur, having its anterior and posterior surfaces reversed, to suit the reversed movements of the joint; flexion being in this case forward instead of backward. There were two patellæ which were situate on the posterior aspect. The rest of the extremity was composed of a short pointed bone about an inch and a quarter long, and was slightly curved forwards. There were well-developed flexor and extensor muscles, and others which might have moved the limb from side to side; these were all well supplied with vessels and nerves. All the other organs of the body, in the head and thorax, presented nothing remarkable.

I ought perhaps to say that when the mother was questioned as to the cause of this strange deformity, she, without expressing much surprise at the result, informed me that throughout the whole of the period of gestation she had experienced a very great affection for the celebrated "talking fish" which just then was creating some sensation in London, and she confessed to such an admiration of it, that she had often taken a walk into Piccadilly for the sole purpose of seeing its painted picture which was placed over the doorway where it was being exhibited, and there she stood often for many minutes together. I do not of course attach any importance to this circumstance, but the coincidence is remarkable, and deserves mention; it would require, however, a very liberal use of imagination to see any resemblance between the talking fish, and this its supposed human representative; nor is fancy likely to risk so severe a shock as she would sustain by attempting to trace a resemblance between the monster and the mermaid. If we look to the internal arrangements, the dissimilarity is found to be still more striking.

There is one fact to which I may perhaps allude as it is interesting in a physiological point of view, namely, the total absence, in this case, of all urinary apparatus; it seems to show clearly that during intra-uterine life, at least, no harm results from the non-elimination of urine; whether the intestine performed the function of the kidney I cannot say, though it does not seem improbable. But when we consider that the urinary secretion is specially destined for the elimination of those products of the disintegration of the tissues, and of the metamorphoses which take place in the living

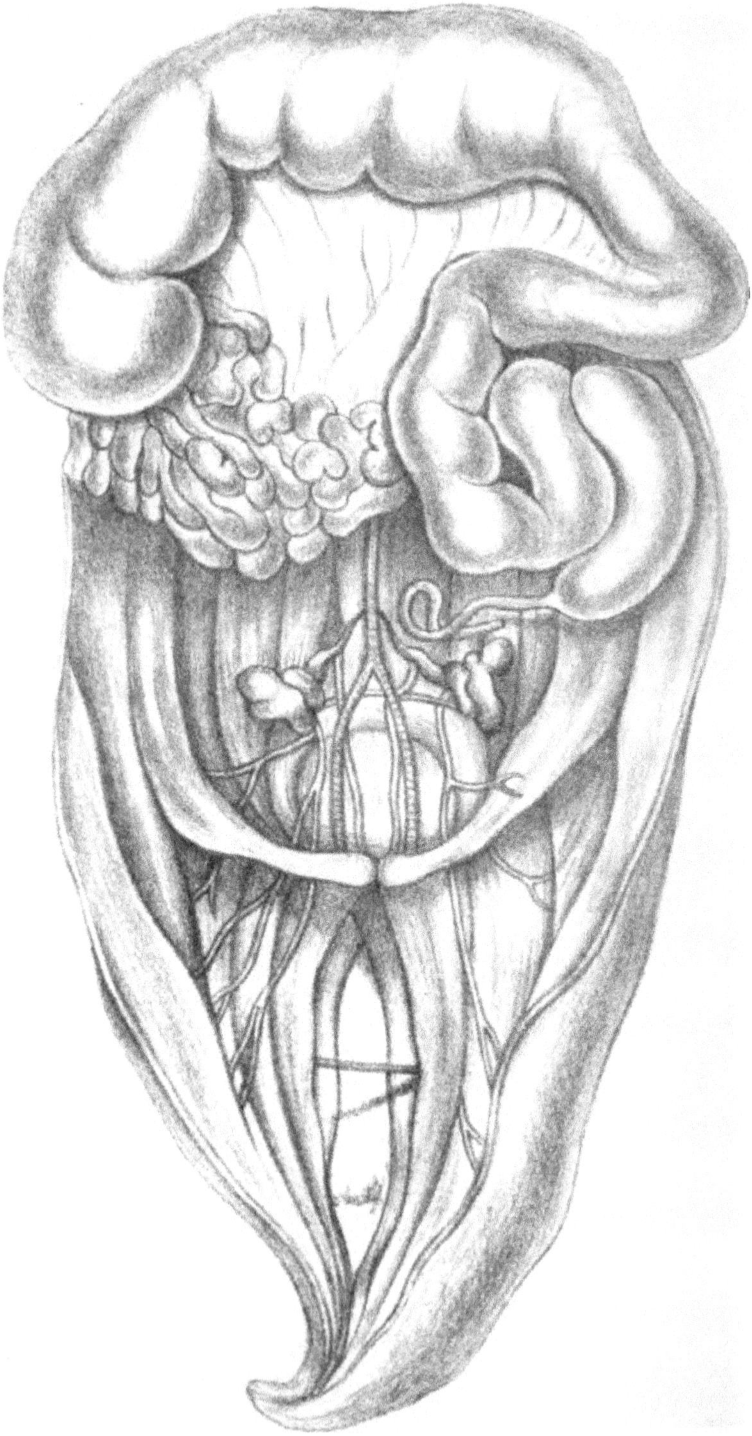

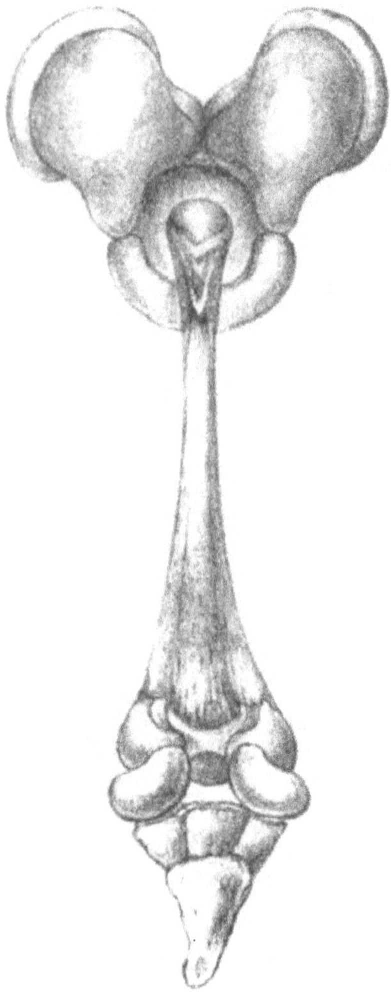

back view

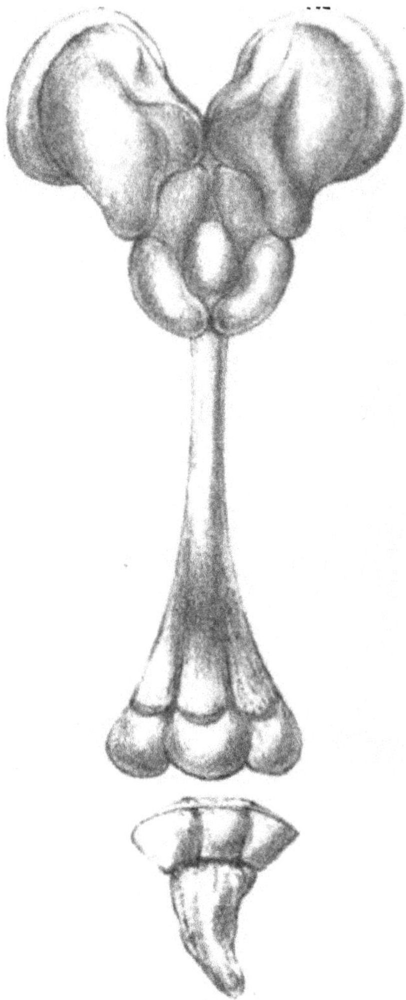

front view.

W. Searson lith. Dr Westmacott dirxt

W. W[illegible] imp.

organism, which are of a highly azotized nature; as well as of those elements which are supplied in excess of the nutrition of the body; we can easily see that during fœtal life, these products would be at a minimum, in consequence of the very limited exercise enjoyed by the fœtus. Possibly the unusually feeble movements which this little monster performed before birth, may have been in consequence of a state of torpor kept up by the renal suppression.

The drawings and preparation will show the chief points detailed in this paper.

EXPLANATION OF PLATES VI, VII, VIII.

Plate VI represents the monster as it appeared at birth.

Plate VII represents the arrangement of the abdominal and pelvic organs as shown by dissection, the parts having been laid open. It will be seen that the large intestine is greatly distended in its ascending and transverse portions, and that it ends at the sigmoid flexure; the rectum being represented by a cord-like process. No kidneys or bladder are visible, but a small body resembling an ovary with a convoluted Fallopian tube (?) is seen on either side the pelvis. The caudal extremity is dissected to show the arrangement of the muscles.

Plate VIII gives two views, front and back, of the bones concerned in the malformation. It will be noticed in the former, that there is no proper pelvic cavity and no outlet, the floor of the pelvis being occupied by the ball-and-socket joint, which is represented in the back view. The lower joint very much resembles the normal knee-joint, with this difference, that there are two patellæ which are situated one on either side of the *posterior* aspect of the joint, as is represented in the drawing.

THE INFLUENCE OF THE MOTHER'S HEALTH IN THE PRODUCTION OF RICKETS.

By W. Tilbury Fox, M.D. Lond.,
UNIVERSITY MEDICAL SCHOLAR.

I propose to give in the briefest possible space such a summary of the pathological characters as will allow me to draw an inference as to the nature of rickets, and then proceed to show that certain unrecognised conditions of the mother's health during lactation, may conduce to the production of the disease.

The symptoms and signs of rickets are, A, General; B, Local

A, *General.*— A want of development, evidenced by stunted growth, and a deficiency of mental power.

B, *Local.*—Abnormal infiltration of organs with albuminous material; enlargement, thickening, softening, arrest of growth, and deformity of the bones, with a corresponding deficient development of the vessels, nerves, and lymphatics; softening of internal viscera. The most striking feature is a non-completion of the intimate process of ossification. The stunted growth of the bones is relative; for example, the pelvis is affected not in part but as a whole. It is not merely deformed but smaller than natural; if the bones are examined by the unaided eye the line of cartilage which is about to be ossified, or rather in which ossification is about to take place, is very considerably broader than that of the normal ossifying bone, it is half an inch, or nearly so, as compared with the normal breadth of half a line; in consequence of epiphyses being soft, the ends of the bones get flattened out to a certain extent.

Microscopic examination.—The "pointed processes" of commencing calcification, are absent in the rickety bone, and the deposit of earthy matter takes place in an irregular form,—here there is a goodly amount between the rows of cartilage cells, there only a dot, or a broken line, or none at all—hence the line of ossification is uneven and broken The cells which antecede the formation of true bone are well and properly developed, and it is very evident that the attempt at the formation of the latter is unsuccessful, simply from the want of calcareous matter. The cartilage cells now and again ossify before the surrounding matrix, and thus an appearance is presented which has been described (according to some, incorrectly) by Kölliker and Virchow, as the formation of lacunæ. The vascular supply is abundant to all parts; there is 21 instead of 63 per cent. of salts in the bones; true bone is really produced if a supply of earthy matter be forthcoming, in which case, the original matrix hardens.

The intimate changes in the rickety bone, it is most essential to remember, do not consist in "a process of softening of the old bone," but an incomplete carrying out of the process of ossification in consequence of a deficiency of calcareous salt, and there is necessarily under these circumstances a relative increase of the cellular structures which precede the formation of bone. My starting point is then, the proposition *that the immediate pathology of rickets is a deficient supply of earthy material in the early nutrition of the child.* Now, how is this brought about? The causes usually held to account for the occurrence of the disease are such as act, not *indirectly* through the mother or nurse, but *directly* upon the child, and comprise bad ventilation, damp dwelling places, want of cleanliness, insufficiency of food, light, and air, &c.; and accordingly in conducting the treatment it is the almost universal practice to treat the rickety child *directly* and not *indirectly* (which is oftentimes possible) through the agency of the nurse, but this is probably a therapeutical error based upon insufficient observation, and, as will presently appear, very likely to mislead *in determining the prophylaxis.* Now, the hygienic malconditions mentioned a moment since are said to be in an equal measure the cause of other maladies, such as scrofula, phthisis, &c.; it must be admitted, consequently, that the ætiology of rickets is not sufficiently understood and appreciated, *quoad* the details which are necessary to give us definite and certain grounds upon which to found a sure mode of prevention and cure. There is fair warrant for adopting a somewhat different view of the matter from that ordinarily taught, and regarding the special causation of rickets, as an abnormal condition of some of the material functions giving rise to a definite and serious alteration of the milk, viz., a deficiency of phosphatic salt, and this view is rendered more probable if we call to mind the fact, that rickets may attack children who have felt all the advantages of perfect hygiene. Writers of late years have noted that the *general* condition of the nurse has some influence—for instance, Dr. Jenner, our highest authority, remarks, "The health of the mother has a decided influence on the development of rickets in the offspring; of this much I am sure, that when the mother is in delicate health, in a state, of which anæmia and general want of power form the prominent features, without being the subject of disease usually so called, there the children are often in a very decided degree rickety, although the father is in robust health, and the hygienic conditions in which children are placed are most favorable." Dr. Jenner's remarks suggest to one, at once, the idea that some *special* state of the mother must determine the result; but no writer, so far as I know, has drawn attention to the relation of any one particular condition of the mother, and the occurrence of rickets, with the exception of Cazeaux, who merely observes, "Nor were it unreasonable to trace some relation of causality between the rachitis of children, and the frequent occurrence of menses during the greater part of lactation;" a view that I had long believed before meeting with Cazeaux's remarks, and a view which has apparently never been entertained, because of the existence on record of certain analyses of Becquerel and Vernois, which appear to prove that menstruation does not materially alter the composition of the lacteal secretion.

I have carefully criticised the condition of a large number of mothers of rickety children, and have as yet met with only two exceptions to the rule (which exceptions, however, can be explained), that wherever the rachitic child is *entirely* dependant upon the mother's milk, the mother will be found to have menstruated during lactation regularly for several months, and the degree of rachitis to be in direct ratio to the frequency, duration, and amount of the menstrual flow. If the child is partly fed upon food other than the nurse's milk, the disease is lessened in degree or altogether prevented, a most important essential to notice in the inquiry, for many cases have been pointed out to me as (apparently) contravening the proposition advanced, but which have been accounted for by eliciting the presence of the overlooked counteracting agency, viz., the supply of artificial food.

The following table exhibits a few of the cases in my note book, which illustrate the influence of menstruation during lactation, with the modifying concomitants, in laying the foundation of rickets.

Table illustrating the influence of Menstruation during

Number.	Name.	Age.	Born in town or country.	Condition of parents.	Menstruation during pregnancy.	How long did lochia last?	Miscarriages.
1	George B—	—	—	Mother and her family healthy. Father's family, maleside, healthy	No	On an average, coloured discharge lasted about a month, often six weeks	—
2	Euphemia B—	—	—	ditto	No	ditto	—
3	Mary B—	—	—	ditto	No	ditto	—
4	Edward B—	—	—	ditto	No	ditto	—
5	Emily B—	—	—	ditto	No	ditto	—
6	Rose B—	—	—	ditto	No	ditto	—
7	James B—	—	—	ditto	No	ditto	—
8	Amy B—	—	—	ditto	No	ditto	—
9	Charles B—	—	—	ditto	No	ditto	—
10	The baby	10 months	—	ditto	No	ditto	—
11	Thurnham	—	—	ditto	No	—	—
12	Wm. F. B—	1 and 8 months	Caledonian Road	Delicate; no phthisis	?	?	—
13	Parker	6	London	Delicate, but not phthisical	No	Not long	One
14	Parker	Still-born child	ditto	ditto	No	ditto	—
15	Parker	3	ditto	ditto	No	ditto	—
16	Parker	1	ditto	ditto	No	ditto	—
17	B—	2	Trieste	Delicate	No	Long time	—
18	Parker	2	London	Healthy	No	ditto	—

Lactation in laying the foundation of Rickets.

Unwell during lactation, when and how long.	How were children brought up, how long nursed, wholly or not.	State of child.	Cause and progress.	Date of observation.
Yes; every month	Nursed	Rickety and scrofulous	Had thirteen large abscesses, dropsy, waxy liver, &c.: died	July, 1860.
ditto	ditto	ditto	Died at 8th month of hydrocephalus	ditto.
ditto	ditto	ditto	Walked when 3½, bones bent, used togs, lame and humpbacked	ditto.
ditto	ditto	ditto	Now like No. 1	ditto.
ditto	Partly fed artificially	Not rickety	When baby had abscesses	ditto.
ditto	ditto	ditto	Pale, fat, doughy, bad eyes	ditto.
ditto	ditto	Very little rickety	Three abscesses at elbow, large ends of bones	ditto.
ditto	ditto	ditto	Short, stinted	ditto.
Not so often	ditto	ditto	When baby bones grew out	ditto.
Only unwell once (two months ago)	ditto	Not at all rickety	Quite right at present	ditto.
At 9th month	Nursed entirely till 12th month	Rickety, convulsions	—	Aug., 1860.
All the time	ditto	Rickety	—	Dr. Jenner, 'Med. Times and Gaz.,' Dec., 1860
No; not with this child	Nursed	Healthy	—	July, 1861.
—	—	—	—	ditto.
At and after 3rd month	A little feeding, but nursed till 10th month	Rickety	Teeth late, runs strangely	ditto.
At 3rd month, and every three weeks	A little feeding, but nursed till one year old	ditto	Head very open, teeth late, pigeon-breasted, &c.	ditto.
2nd and 3rd month and after	Nursed entirely	Very rickety	—	Feb., 1861.
At 8th month, nursed till 14th month	Partly fed	Rickety	Chest affected, legs very crooked	—

Number.	Name.	Age.	Born in town or country.	Condition of parents.	Menstruation during pregnancy.	How long did lochia last?	Miscarriages.
19	Parker	10 months	London	Healthy	No	Long time	—
20	Cryer[1]	2	ditto	ditto	No	More loss than with any other	Two
21	C. D—	5	ditto	Husband's family consumptive	No	Long time	None
22	Frederick D—	3	ditto	ditto	No	ditto	ditto
23	Alice D—[2]	1 and 8 months	ditto	ditto	1st and 4th month	ditto	ditto
24	W. C—	2	Country	Healthy	No	—	—
25	Annie D—	1	London	ditto	No	—	—
26	B—[3]	9	India	ditto	No	—	Two or three
27	B—[4]	22	Town	Scrofula on mother's side	—	A very long time	—
28	B—	20	ditto	ditto	—	ditto	—
29	Harriett B—	19	ditto	ditto	—	ditto	—
30	Mary	—	ditto	ditto	—	ditto	—
31	Ellen	16	ditto	ditto	—	ditto	—
32	Caroline	13	ditto	ditto	—	ditto	—
33	Macauley	12	ditto	ditto	—	ditto	—
34	Harry	11	ditto	ditto	—	ditto	—
35	Florence	10	ditto	ditto	—	ditto	—
36	Samuel	Died: teething; convulsions	ditto	ditto	—	ditto	—
37	Frederick	ditto	ditto	ditto	—	ditto	—
38	Philip	2½	ditto	ditto	—	ditto	—
39	Thirteenth	—	ditto	ditto	—	ditto	Miscarriage

[1] The mother of this child has seven more children, none of whom are rickety, and she was not regular during lactation with any of the seven except the eldest, whom she partly fed because she had not sufficient milk.

[2] The medical man who attended this child said "it did not make any bone at all, but was all gristle, and gave it lime till the time of its death."

[3] This child is the only one of the family possessing a tendency to rickets, the spine is slightly curved, and the chest is flattened laterally and bulges in front (pigeon-breasted). He was brought up (unlike the others) by wet nurse, who, it turns out, was "regular" all the time she nursed him. The child was partly fed. There are several younger children, none of whom are at all rickety, indeed all are quite healthy.

Unwell during lactation, when and how long.	How were children brought up, how long nursed, wholly or not.	State of child.	Cause and progress.	Date of observation.
At 10th month	Fed at 10th month	Healthy	At present	—
After 3rd month, but every month	Nursed entirely till one year old	Rickety	Spine, legs, chest	—
Always after 6th or 7th month, usually nursed till 14th month	Partly fed at 5th month	ditto	Legs crooked	Jan., 1862.
ditto	ditto	ditto	Legs, head open	ditto.
ditto	ditto	Very rickety	Head very open, legs crooked: died	ditto.
Every month	Both partly fed after awhile	Rickety at 7th month	Teeth late, legs, arm, chest, back	April, 1862.
ditto	—	—	ditto	—
—	—	Rickety	ditto	ditto.
Always at and after the 6th month	Partly fed	Healthy	—	July, 1862.
ditto	ditto	ditto	—	—
ditto	ditto	Slight scrofula	—	—
ditto	ditto	Healthy	—	—
ditto	ditto	—	—	—
ditto	ditto	—	—	—
ditto	ditto	—	—	—
ditto	ditto	Scrofula and rickety	—	—
ditto	Nursed almost entirely	Rickety	—	—
ditto	ditto	—	—	—
ditto	ditto	—	—	—
ditto	ditto	Rickety	—	—
ditto	ditto	—	—	—

Almost all nursed till 12th month. (bracketed against the entries from "Partly fed" to the last "ditto" in the second column)

* The mother has been in good circumstances, she has menstruated during lactation at six months, always nursed her children for a year, *and always partly fed them, with the exception of the last few.* When Florence was born began to have trouble, and has lived most miserably since. Has always flooded profusely. Children have had very little milk, often living solely upon bread and butter, consequently the mother has almost *entirely* nursed the last few, and these have become rickety.

The examples sustain the following propositions:

1. That in a family of several children, the eldest, or youngest, or an intermediate, may be independently affected.

2. That given a rickety subject in a family it does not *necessarily* follow that the children born subsequently to this one shall be rickety also, in which case, however, either artificial feeding has been adopted or the child subsisting wholly upon the milk of the mother, the latter has not menstruated regularly during lactation, but

3. If the mother or nurse once become "regular" during the greater part of lactation, the same is usually repeated after each succeeding childbirth, and hence—

4. If one child become rickety, as a rule those subsequently born are rickety also, unless the attendant circumstances (such as artificial feeding) vary in the two cases.

5. One only of several may be rickety, in this case the mother will be found to have menstruated during suckling, and not to have done so on other occasions.

The practical bearing of the matter may be summed up as follows:—Whenever a woman regularly and freely menstruates during the greater part of lactation, and suckles her child for a considerable time, that child will be rickety unless artificially fed. As before observed there are undoubted exceptions; two instances I have met with, but these belonged to a very special class, being the subjects of what is termed "constitutional plethora," women of full habit, and free living, whose par of health appears to be kept intact by free menstruation, and in whom, on that account, lactation is not interfered with.

It is necessary then to consider the *modus operandi* of what may be called abnormal menstruation, upon the composition of the milk.

We are told by Cazeaux that nurses who have menstruated during lactation go on as follows:

1. Some become debilitated and marasmatic.

2. In some the milk diminishes, and becomes serous; the child emaciates.

3. The milk of some women does not appear to be altered, nor the nutrition of the child to suffer except during the flow of the menses.

4. Finally, in many cases the child's health does not suffer.

Bouchut after remarking that the premature appearance of the menses is a phenomenon which gives mothers much uneasiness, appearing in about one third of women between the fifth and seventh month of lactation, and indicating aptitude for conception, adds, "the generality of children do not appear to suffer from this state of the nurse," that "some have colic, slight restlessness, or mild diarrhœa, and a few are very ill, and demand a change of nurse." It is a well known fact that, in animals generally, the milk is so altered during "heat," as to produce very decided ill effects upon the suckling offspring. The whole subject demands investigation; and the only observations of moment, so far as my reading goes, made with the view of determining the intimate chemical changes effected by menstruation in the milk, are those of Messrs. Becquerel and Vernois, who examined three out of ten cases which came under their notice; and Bouchut, accepting the data given by these gentlemen, writes, "after the return of the catamenia in a mother who suckles her infant, and during the menstruation, the lacteal secretion is less abundant, and the milk is slightly altered in its composition, it becomes more dense, richer in solid constituents, which may render it unfit for children;" and he quotes the following table:

	Suspense of catamenia.	Reappearance.	Actual presence.
Specific gravity .	1032·24	1031·94	1031·98
Water . .	889·51	886·44	881·42
Solid . .	110·49	113·56	118·58
Sugar . .	43·88	41·68	40·49
Butter . .	26·54	26·98	29·15
Casein . .	38·69	43·58	47·49
Salts . .	1·38	1·32	1·45

The investigators "did not believe that such changes in the composition can induce any mischief beyond some temporary derangement in the digestive organs, and even this might be prevented by causing the child to suck less, and to drink a little sugar and water to replace the like lost during menstruation." This is the exact opinion of modern authorities.

One may very fairly object to the conclusions here drawn from the analyses of three instances, for it does not appear for how long a period the nurses had been menstruating—if once only, or during several monthly periods—in the former case, the milk would scarcely be altered, and the analyses are valueless as helping to solve the question of the ætiology of rickets, inasmuch as it is necessary for this purpose to examine the milk after menstruation has occurred *regularly during several months*, these being the conditions which conduce to the production of the disease. From the present state of our chemical knowledge little can be derived, but there are arguments, nevertheless, of considerable importance which harmonise with, and countenance the view which I have put forward, and which are consonant with sound physiological doctrine. Foremost among these is—

1. The fact that the activity of the mammæ cannot be carried on properly if the uterus is performing its functions in full antagonism. It is only necessary to refer for confirmation to the occurrence of pregnancy during lactation, "which either speedily reduces the quantity of milk secreted, or lessens the proportion of solid and nutritive constituents to such a degree as to render it unfit for the child." (See a paper by Dr. H. S. Davis, of Chicago, in the 'Transactions of the Illinois State Medical Society,' held at Paris, May 8th and 9th, 1860.) A like result must inevitably follow the complete re-establishment of the function of menstruation during lactation. Dr. Barnes ('Lancet,' vol. ii, 1852) has given a summary of the question of the reciprocal influence of menstruation upon conception and lactation, which bears the impress of care and com-

pleteness which characterises his writings, and he shows that in pregnancies occurring during lactation, abortion is especially liable to take place as compared with other pregnancies, in the ratio of 17 to 10 per cent., and discussing the question as to whether women should nurse when menstruating during lactation, supports the negative, because of the liability (among other reasons) to abort, but I do not gather that Dr. Barnes had in view the additional reason, that rickets is likely to result in the sucklings wholly dependent upon the mother's milk.

2. It is to be observed more particularly that many changes going on in the mucous membrane of the uterus are accompanied by a determination thereto of the lime salts, and this is markedly so in the recently impregnated uterus, and also in the process of healing after menstruation, which occupies considerable time.

3. The menstrual flow probably carries off more or less of the lime salts.

Some such conditions as these it would appear alter the composition of the lacteal secretion, so that the protein matter is in excess, while the lime salts are deficient, and this disproportion plays upon the child at the very time the foundation of its nutrition is being laid, and when the integrity of collateral circumstances is demanded to prevent any abnormal deviations, which are likely to ensue on account of the peculiar sensibility of the system at so early an age.

Simon analysed repeatedly the milk of a woman from August 31st to January 4th (indeed, every eight or ten days), and his results indicated that, though the solid constituents as a whole varied considerably with change of diet, the salts steadily increased in amount. In Becquerel and Vernois' cases, where the women were menstruating, there was a deficiency of fixed salts as compared with Simon's. The mean of Simon's fourteen examinations gave 2·25 as compared with Becquerel and Vernois' 1·38 parts in 1000 of milk. Hence, as far as these analyses go, we may very fairly conclude that menstruation has probably some such influence as that claimed for it.

There are some recent experiments of Dr. A. Milne Edwards ('Moniteur des Sciences méd. et pharm.,' July 2nd, 1851), detailed under the head of "the Influence of Lime Salts upon the Nutrition of Bone," which at first sight would appear to militate against the truth of my observations. He "fed three pigeons with wheat, rice, maize, and decorticated millet, so that the lime supplied was much less than what existed in their ordinary food. A fourth pigeon he fed in the usual way. In three months the three had diarrhœa, began to waste, and were then killed. The bones of the three weighed a third less than the other, but the relative proportions of inorganic and organic matter were not changed, the change of diet did not change the composition, but the size of the bones, the removal taking place in all the constituents, and not in the earthy matter of the bone."

These experiments scarcely affect the question of the production of rickets; we can but rarely make a *true bone* rickety by the withdrawal of the salts of lime in the human body, but the case is different in the very young, where the nutrition *is being founded, as it were*, and the character of that nutrition modified and determined in part probably by the peculiar qualities of the food presented. When the nutritive process has been completed *after a normal type*, or, in other words, when the bones have been originally formed out of materials presented in due proportion relatively to each other, that type or habit, as it may be termed, once acquired, is permanented, unless very unusual circumstances play upon it.

We have, I believe, in our hands, the power to prevent the occurrence of rickets in the majority of cases, and it is because no attention is paid to the influence of menstruation during lactation, as leading to the occurrence of rickets, but only in so far as the mother suffers, that I wish to attract the attention of the Society to the subject. In every instance of women menstruating regularly during lactation, nursing should be relinquished, or the child fed by artificial means.

In conclusion, I may be allowed to say a few words upon the subject of artificial food. Where the substitution is desirable, we should be careful to give something that affords not only starch, but gluten or flesh-forming substance, and inorganic matter or salts. These desiderata are little attended to, and it is by no means generally known, even amongst medical men, that the "foods" usually recommended are utterly valueless *per se*, as nutritive agents. "Brown and Poulson's," *some* of the "Oswego," and "Maizena," all largely used, are merely starch, and contain no gluten and no salts; hence their exhibition will most assuredly help out the tendency to rickets (among other diseases), and it is probably owing to the milk which is used in their cooking that ill-results are prevented. It is true there are exceptions, and in some instances you get true "corn flour," but, perhaps, rarely; and suppose you do get it, it has no special recommendation, indeed, rather the reverse, for it contains more fat, more sugar, and *less gluten*, than the more ordinary flours.

Most people have an idea that anything which "thickens" must be highly nutritious, an erroneous opinion which seems to have taken very firm hold upon nurses in general. Hard's food, which is the best wheaten flour baked, is the best form of "infant's food" before the public.

The semola of Bullock and Reynolds has many recommendations; it contains 45 to 50 per cent. of gluten or flesh-forming substance; but, unfortunately, it cannot be so prepared as to pass through the child's bottle, an absolute necessity now that the use of the latter is so universal. Semola contains 7·33 to 8·15 per cent. of nitrogen, as compared with the 7·25 per cent. of ordinary meat (the quantity of nitrogen being a test of the degree of nutritive quality).

We still are in want of an additional source of phosphatic salts in the treatment of rickets, such as would supply *organized*, as distinguished from *chemical*, products. If we play upon the child indirectly through the nurse, some benefit possibly might result from the use of the salt made from ivory turning. I desire more particularly to call the attention of the Society to a preparation, as yet unknown to the profession, the *bran phosphates* of Messrs. Bullock and Reynolds, which is simply the organized products of the outer covering of the wheat-grain, prepared by infusion and subsequent evaporation. It is then mixed with three parts of sugar, and may take the place of the latter in all articles of food. The most desirable food for a rickety child would appear at present to be "Hard's food," made up with a moderate quantity of milk, and sweetened with *bran phosphates.*

Finally, I would ask those who are disposed to reject as untenable that method of the causation of rickets which I have pointed out as in action in the majority of instances, to criticise fully the details of individual cases, and ascertain whether some such tangible agency as artificial feeding does not explain apparent exceptions. It is only right to add that I have introduced the subject to the Society rather as a provocative than as a certainty of opinion.

Dr. Graily Hewitt believed that there was a very general impression amongst the profession, and he thought also amongst the public at large, as to the inadvisability of allowing lactation and menstruation to go on in the same individual. The theory now propounded by Dr. Tilbury Fox would give an explanation as to the reasonableness of this impression. The subject was so novel that it would hardly be expected that the Fellows of the Society could properly discuss the paper so as to do it justice. Each must observe and collect facts on which to decide *pro* or *con* in reference to the matter. He would ask Dr. Fox one question:—How are those cases to be explained where children, the subjects of rickets, do often, after being apparently successfully treated, relapse long after any evil connected with lactation has ceased to be in operation? Such relapses were, he had observed, by no means uncommon.

Dr. Gervis wished to ask the author of the paper how, on his theory, the occurrence of rickets in children wholly brought up by hand, or in children whose mothers did *not* menstruate during lactation, was to be explained? The fact also of the children of mothers who menstruate during lactation in many cases certainly not proving rickety, would appear to militate against Dr. Fox's view. Dr. Gervis was inclined to consider that the occurrence of menstruation during lactation was not *par excellence* the cause of rickets, though possibly influential in its production just so far as it proved injurious to the mother's health.

Dr. Fox, in reply, begged the Society to remember that the matter had been brought before them, not because the observations were conclusive, but for the purpose of courting inquiry. The mode of causation pointed out was not the *sole* one; for, as Dr. Graily Hewitt had observed, rickets might ensue after the weaning of the child. In this case the disease was due to, or the tendency to it worked out by, the use of foods deficient in certain constituents. So far, however, as his (Dr. Fox's) observation went, it appeared that most rickety children belonged to mothers who had menstruated during lactation; and if the paper should appear in print the Fellows would find in the list of cases instances of rickets affecting one member only of a family, all the concomitants of the rearing of the children being the same, with the exception that the mother menstruated regularly and freely when nursing the rickety child, and then only. In reference to Dr. Druitt's remarks, it might be observed that the leading pathologists held that all that is necessary to the production of rickets is a deficiency of lime; and this conclusion seems inevitable, if we glance at the intimate structure of the rickety bone, in which all the cellular components are fully developed, and in which the only unusual condition is an absence of calcareous matter. Dr. Gervis may possibly find in the exceptional cases mentioned by him, where children are not rickety, though nursed by mothers menstruating, that some such cause as artificial feeding explains the apparent contradiction. In reply to a question from the President, as to how rickets occurring during intra-uterine life could be accounted for, Dr. Fox remarked that the worst case he had met with was that of a child whose mother menstruated during pregnancy.

INDEX.

CATALOGUE

OF THE

LIBRARY

OF THE

OBSTETRICAL SOCIETY OF LONDON,

BEING A LIST OF

DONATIONS TO THE SOCIETY

FROM ITS FOUNDATION TO DECEMBER, 1862.

	Presented by
ABERNETHY (John). Surgical observations on the constitutional origin and treatment of Local Diseases, and on Aneurisms; fourth edition. 8vo. Lond. 1817	Dr. Clay
ACCUM (Fredrick). Guide to the Chalybeate Spring of Thetford 12mo. Lond. 1819	Dr. Rigby
ADDISON (Thomas). Observations on the Disorders of Females, connected with Uterine Irritation 8vo. Lond. 1830	Sir Charles Locock.
ALCOCK (Thomas). See *Haden* on Diseases of Children.	
ALEXANDER (William). History of Women from the earliest Antiquity to the present time; third edition 2 vols. 8vo. Lond. 1782	Dr. Clay
Anatomy—System of Anatomy and Physiology from the latest and best authors, arranged in the order of the Lectures of the Professor of Anatomy in the University of Edinburgh; second edition *plates*, 3 vols. 8vo. Edinb. 1787	Do.
ARCHER (William Henry). The Statistical Register of Victoria, from the foundation of the colony, with an Astronomical Calendar for 1855 8vo. Melbourne, 1854	University of Melbourne

Presented by

ARCHER (Wm. Henry). Statistical Notes on the progress of Victoria, from the foundation of the colony, 1835-60. First series, parts 1 and 2. 4to. Melbourne (1861) University of Melbourne

ARETÆUS Cappadox. Libri VIII, et Ruffi Ephesii de hominis partib. li. III, Junio Paulo Crasso interprete 18mo. Paris, 1554 Dr. Clay.

ARMSTONG (George). Essay on the Diseases most fatal to Infants 12mo. Lond. 1767 Do.

——— Account of the Diseases most incident to Children, with an Essay on Nursing, and account of the Dispensary for the Infant Poor 8vo. Lond. 1777 Dr. Rigby

ARMSTRONG (John). Facts and Observations relative to the Fever commonly called Puerperal 8vo. Lond. 1814 Do.

——— ——— Second edition 8vo. Lond. 1819 Do.

——— Practical Illustration of the Scarlet Fever, Measles, and Pulmonary Consumption, with Observations on Sulphureous Waters in Chronic Complaints; second edition 8vo. Lond. 1818 Dr. Clay

ARNETH (F. H.) Die geburts-hilfliche Praxis, erläutert durch Ergebnisse der II. Gebärklinik zu Wien 8vo. Wien, 1851 Dr. Rigby

ARNOTT (James). On the treatment of Cancer by Congelation and an improved mode of Pressure; second edition 8vo. Lond. 1855 Sir Charles Locock.

ASHBURNER (John). On Dentition and some Coincident Disorders 18mo. Lond. 1834 Dr. Clay

——— ——— Another copy 18mo. Lond. 1834 Sir Charles Locock.

ASHWELL (Samuel). Practical Treatise on Parturition; comprising the attendant circumstances and diseases of the pregnant and puerperal states, with two papers on Abdominal Surgery and Transfusion, by Dr. Blundell *plates*, 8vo. Lond. 1828 Dr. Clay

——— Reports on Obstetric Cases, Cases of Hard Tumours of the Uterus, on Premature Labour, on Chlorosis, Diseases of the Uterus, &c. (from Guy's Hospital Reports,' vols. 1 and 2) *plates*, 8vo. Lond. 1836-37 Sir Charles Locock

——— Practical Treatise on the Diseases peculiar to Women; illustrated by cases Part III, 8vo. Lond. 1844 Do.

Presented by

ASTRUC (John). Treatise on all the Diseases incident to Women; translated by J. R——n 8vo. Lond. 1743 Sir Charles Locock

——— Treatise on all the Diseases incident to Children, from their birth to the age of fifteen 8vo. Lond. 1746 Dr. Clay

——— ——— Another copy 8vo. Lond. 1746 Sir Charles Locock

——— Elements of Midwifery, with a short history of the art, and a casuistical letter on the conduct of Adam and Eve at the birth of their first child; translated, with additions, by S. Ryley 8vo. Lond. 1766 Dr. Rigby

AYRE (Joseph). Researches into the nature and treatment of Dropsy in the Brain, Chest, Abdomen, Ovarium and Skin 8vo. Lond. 1825 Dr. Clay

BAGLIVUS (Georgius). Specimen quatuor librorum de Fibra Motrice et Morbosa; editio tertia 12mo. Ultraj, 1703 Dr. Clay

BAINES (M. A.). The Comparative Properties of Human and Animal Milks; a new theory as to "Essenses;" and a new interpretation of some physiological facts 8vo. Lond. 1860 The Author

——— The Practice of Hiring Wet-Nurses, especially those from the "Fallen," considered as it affects public health and public morals 8vo. Lond. 1860 Do.

BALBIRNIE (John). Treatise on the Organic Diseases of the Womb; second edition 8vo. Lond. 1836 Dr. Clay

BALFOUR (Francis). Collection of Treatises on the effects of Sol-lunar influence in Fevers; second edition. 8vo. Cupar, 1811 Do.

BALLARD (Thomas). New and rational explanation of the Diseases peculiar to Infants and Mothers, with suggestions for their prevention or cure 8vo. Lond. 1860 Dr. Rigby

BALY (William). On the pathology and treatment of Dysentery (Gulstonian Lectures, 1847), (from 'Lond. Med. Gazette') 8vo. Do.

——— See *Müller's* Embryology (notes)

BANCROFT (Edward Nathaniel). Essay on Yellow Fever, with Observations concerning Febrile Contagion, Typhus Fever, Dysentery and the Plague. (Gulstonian Lectures) 8vo. Lond. 1811 Dr. Clay

——— Sequel to ditto, intended to prove that Bulam Fever, has no existence as a distinct or a contagious disease 8vo. Lond. 1817 Do.

Presented by

BARCLAY (John). New Anatomical Nomenclature relating to the terms which are expressive of position and aspect in the Animal System *plates*, 8vo. Edinb. 1803 Dr. Clay

BARDSLEY (Samuel Argent). Medical Reports of Cases and Experiments, with Observations from Hospital Practice, and enquiry on Canine Madness. 8vo. Lond. 1807 Do.

BARKER (T. Herbert). Case of Inversion of the Uterus, with observations (from 'Lond. Med. Gazette,') 8vo. 1844 Dr. Rigby

——— On the Hygienic Management of Infants and Children 8vo. Lond. 1859 Sir Charles Locock

BARLOW (James). Essays on Surgery and Midwifery; with practical observations and select cases *plates*, 8vo. Lond. 1822 Dr. Rigby

——— ——— Another copy *plates*, 8vo. Lond. 1822 Dr. Clay

BARTLETT (Elisha). The history, diagnosis, and treatment of Typhoid and of Typhus Fever, with an Essay on the diagnosis of Bilious Remittent, and of Yellow Fever 8vo. Philadelphia, 1842 Do.

BATEMAN (Thomas). Practical Synopsis of Cutaneous Diseases, according to the arrangement of Dr. Willan *plate*, 8vo. Lond. 1813 Do.

——— ——— fifth edition *plate*, 8vo. Lond. 1819 Do.

BAUDELOCQUE (J. L.). L'Art des Accouchemens *plates*, 2 vols. 8vo. Paris, 1781 Do.

——— System of Midwifery; translated by John Heath *plates*, 3 vols. 8vo. Lond. 1790 Do.

——— Two Memoirs on the Cesarean Operation; translated by John Hull *plates*, 8vo. Manchester, 1801 Do.

BEALE (Lionel). The Microscope, and its application to Clinical Medicine *plates*, &c., 8vo. Lond. 1854 Do.

BEANEY (James G,). Original Contributions to the practice of Conservative Surgery 8vo. Melbourne, 1859 The Author

BECK (Theodric Romeyn). Elements of Medical Jurisprudence; third edition, by John Darwall 8vo. Lond. 1829 Dr. Clay

BELL (Benjamin). Treatise on the theory and management of Ulcers, with a dissertation on White Swellings of the Joints, and the Chirurgical treatment of Inflammation; second edition 8vo Edinb. 1779 Do.

Presented by

BELL (Benjamin). System of Surgery; third edition *plates*, 6 vols. 8vo. Edinb. 1787-8 Dr. Clay

BELL (George). Treatise on the Cowpox *plates*, 12mo. Edinb. 1802 Do.

BENNET (James Henry). Practical Treatise on Inflammation, Ulceration, and Induration of the Neck of the Uterus 8vo. Lond. 1845 Do.

——— ——— second edition 8vo. Lond. 1849 Do.

——— Review of the present state of Uterine Pathology 8vo. Lond. 1856 Sir Charles Locock

BENNETT (James Risdon). The causes, nature, diagnosis and treatment of Acute Hydrocephalus, or Water in the Head. (Fothergillian Prize Essay) 8vo. Lond. 1843 Dr. Clay

BIENVILLE (D. T. de). Nymphomania; or, a Dissertation concerning the Furor Uterinus; translated by Edward Sloane Wilmot 8vo. Lond. 1775 Do.

BILLETER (Fritz). Ein neuer Fall von hochgradiger Spondylolisthesis des Beckens, Inaugural Dissertation 4to. Zürich, 1862 The Author

BILLING (Archibald). First Principles of Medicine 8vo. Lond. 1831 Dr. Clay

BIRD (Frederic). Case of the successful removal of a large Ovarian Tumor. 8vo. Lond. 1844 Dr. Rigby

BISCHOFF (Th. L. W.). The Periodical Maturation and Extrusion of Ova, independently of Coitus in mammalia and man, proved to be the primary condition to their propagation; translated by Henry [Spencer] Smith 8vo. Lond. 1845 Do.

BLACK (William T.). Remarks on the Diseases at North Victoria, South Africa, 1851-2 8vo. 1853 Dr. Clay

BLACKBURNE (William). Facts and Observations concerning the prevention and cure of Scarlet Fever, with remarks on acute contagions in general 8vo. Lond. 1803 Dr. Clay

BLAND (R.). Observations on Human and on Comparative Parturition 8vo. Lond. 1794 Dr. Rigby

——— ——— Another copy 8vo. Lond. 1794 Dr. Clay

——— ——— Another copy 8vo. Lond. 1794 Do.

BLASIUS (Gerard). Observationes Medicæ rariores, accedit Monstri Triplicis historia *plates*, 12mo. Amstel. 1677 Do.

BLUNDELL (James). Researches physiological and pathological, with a view to the improvement of Medical and Surgical practice *plates*, 8vo. Lond. 1825 Do.

——— ——— Another copy 8vo. Lond. 1825 Do.

Presented by

Blundell (James) On Abdominal Surgery and Transfusion, see *Ashwell* on Parturition. Dr. Clay

Boeck (W.). Recherches sur la Syphilis, appuyées de Tableaux de Statistique tirés des Archives des Hôpitaux de Christiania 4to. Christiania, 1862 The Author

Boër (Lukas Johann). Natürliche Geburtshülfe und Behandlung der Schwangern, Wöchnerinnen und neugebornen Kinder 3 vols. in 1, 8vo. Wien, 1817 Dr. Rigby

Boivin (Mme. Veuve). Mémorial de l'Art des Accouchemens; deuxième edition *plates*, 8vo. Paris, 1817 Dr. Clay

—— and A. Duges. Practical Treatise on the Diseases of the Uterus and its appendages; translated with notes by G. O. Heming 8vo. Lond. 1834 Dr. Rigby

—— —— Another copy 8vo. Lond. 1834 Sir Charles Locock

—— —— Another copy *plates*, 2 vols. 8vo. Lond. 1834 Dr. Clay

Bostock (John). Elementary System of Physiology; second edition 3 vols. 8vo. Lond. 1828 Do.

Bourgery (J. M.). Treatise on Lesser Surgery, or the Minor Surgical Operations; translated by Wm. C. Roberts and Jas. B. Kissam 8vo. New York, 1834 Do.

Bracken (Henry). The Midwife's Companion, or a Treatise of Midwifery 12mo. Lond. 1737 Dr. Rigby

Braun (Carl R.). The Uræmic Convulsions of Pregnancy, Parturition and Childbed; translated with notes by J. Matthews Duncan 8vo. Edinb. 1857 Sir Charles Locock

Bremner (John). Observations on Diseased States of the Placenta, as influencing the process of Parturition (from 'Edinb. Med. and Surg. Journal') 8vo. Edinb. 1849 Dr. Rigby

—— Hints on Obstetric Practice, with illustrations (Use of venesection and opium) Part I. 8vo. Edinb. 1849 Do

Breslau (Professor). Jahresbericht über die Ereignisse in der Zürcher Gebäranstalt in 1861 8vo. Zürich, 1862 The Author

Bromfeild (William). Chirurgical Observations and Cases *plates*, 2 vols. 8vo. Lond. 1773 Dr. Clay

Brown (I. Baker). On Scarlatina, its nature and treatment; second edition. 12mo. Lond. 1857 The Author

—— On Vesico-Vaginal Fistula and its successful treatment 8vo. Lond. 1858 Dr. Clay

Presented by

BROWN (I. Baker). On Surgical Diseases of Women; second edition *plates*, 8vo. Lond. 1861 The Author

——— ——— Another copy 8vo. Lond. 1861 Do.

——— On Ovarian Dropsy, its nature, diagnosis, and treatment 8vo. Lond. 1862 Do.

BRUCE (Archibald). Diss. Inaug. de Vaccina. 8vo. Edinb. 1801 Dr. Clay

With autograph note of the author to Dr. Lettsom.

BRUIER D'ABLAINCOURT (J. J.). See *Deventer*, Accouchemens (traduits)

BURK (Gustavus). De Vernice Caseosa, dissertatio inauguralis 8vo. Halis, 1844 Dr. Rigby

BURKE (Thomas Travers). The Accoucheur's Vade-mecum, or Modern Guide to the Practice of Midwifery 12mo. Lond. 1840 Do.

With autograph letter of the author.

BURNS (John). Anatomy of the Gravid Uterus, with practical inferences relative to pregnancy and labour 8vo. Glasgow, 1799 Do.

——— ——— Another copy 8vo. Glasgow, 1799 Sir Charles Locock

——— Observations on Abortion 8vo. Lond. 1806 Dr. Clay

——— Practical observations on the Uterine Hemorrhage, with remarks on the management of the Placenta 8vo. Lond. 1807 Dr. Rigby

——— Principles of Midwifery, including the Diseases of Women and Children; fourth edition 8vo. Lond. 1817 Dr. Clay

——— ——— fifth edition 8vo. Lond. 1820 Sir Charles Locock

——— ——— ninth edition 8vo. Lond. 1837 Dr. Rigby

BURTON (John). Essay towards a complete new system of Midwifery, theoretical and practical *plates*, 8vo. Lond. 1751 Dr. Rigby

——— Letter to William Smellie, containing critical and practical remarks upon his Treatise on Midwifery *plate*, 8vo. Lond. 1753 Do.

BUTTER (William). Account of Puerperal Fevers, as they appear in Derbyshire, &c. 8vo. Lond. 1775 Do.

CABANIS (P. J. G.). Sketch of the Revolutions of Medical Science, and Views relating to its reform; translated with notes by A. Henderson 8vo. Lond. 1806 Dr. Cl

Presented by

CAMPBELL (Alex. D.). Probationary Essay on the Viability of the Fœtus 8vo. Edinb. 1842 Dr. Rigby

CAMPBELL (William). Treatise on the Epidemic Puerperal Fever as it prevailed in Edinburgh in 1821-2, with Gordon's Essay on the Puerperal Fever of Aberdeen in 1789-92 8vo. Edinb. 1822 Dr. Clay

——— Introduction to the study and practice of Midwifery, and the Diseases of Women and Children *plates*, 8vo. Edinb. 1833 Dr. Rigby

With an autograph letter of the author relative to Prof. Naegele, &c.

——— Case of Transposition of the Abdominal Viscera (from 'Med. and Surg. Journ') *plate*, 8vo Do.

CAMPER (Petrus). *Demonstrationum* Anatomico-Pathologicarum, Libri II, Brachium et Pelvis Humani 2 parts folio, Amst., 1760-2 Dr. Clay

CAPURON (J.). Cours théorique et pratique d'Accouchemens 8vo. Paris, 1811 Sir Charles Locock

CARMICHAEL (Richard). Essay on Venereal Diseases, and the uses and abuses of Mercury in their treatment; second edition *plates*, 8vo. Lond. 1825 Dr. Clay

CARPENTER (William B.). Principles of Human Physiology with their chief applications to pathology, hygiene, and forensic medicine 8vo. Lond. 1842 Do.

CASTRO (Rodericus A.). De Universa Muliebrium Morborum Medicina Opus, Partes duæ; Theorica et Praxis; altera editio 2 vols in one—4to. Hamburgi, 1617 Dr. Clay

——— ——— Pars prima Theorica; tertia editio 4to. Hamburgi, 1628 Do.

Catalogue of the Melbourne Public Library roy. 8vo. Melbourne, 1861 University of Melbourne

CHAMBERLEN (Hugh). See *Mauriceau*, on Diseases of Women (translated).

CHAMBERS (Thomas King). Corpulence or Excess of Fat during Pregnancy 8vo. Lond. 1852 Dr. Rigby

CHANNING (Walter). Treatise on Etherization in Childbirth, illustrated by five hundred and eighty-one cases 8vo. Boston, U.S. 1848 Do.

CHAPMAN (Edmund). Essay on the Improvement of Midwifery, chiefly with regard to the operation 8vo. Lond. 1733 Sir Charles Locock

——— ——— second edition *plates*, 8vo. Lond. 1735 Dr. Clay

——— ——— second edition 8vo. Lond. 1735 Dr. Rigby

——— ——— third edition *plates*, 8vo. Lond. 1753 Do.

Presented by

CHEREAU (Achille). Mémoires pour servir à l'étude des Maladies des Ovaires, premièr Mémoire 8vo. Paris, 1844 Dr. Rigby

CHEYNE (John). Essays on the Diseases of Children; Essay III, On Hydrocephalus Acutus vol. 2, 4to. Edinb. 1808 Sir Charles Locock

Children. Full View of all the Diseases incident to Children, containing Harris on Acute Diseases, Boerhaave's Treatise, &c. 12mo. Lond. 1742 Dr. Clay

CHURCHILL (Fleetwood). Outlines of the Principal Diseases of Females 8vo. Dublin, 1838 Dr. Rigby

With MS. Memoranda by Dr. Rigby.

——— On the Principal Diseases of Females; second edition 12mo. Dublin, 1844 Dr. Clay

——— On the Diseases of Women, including those of Pregnancy and Childbed; fourth edition 12mo. Dublin, 1857 Sir Charles Locock

——— Observations on the Diseases incident to Pregnancy and Childbed 8vo. Dublin, 1840 Dr. Rigby

——— Researches on Operative Midwifery *plates*, 8vo. Dublin, 1841 Dr. Clay

——— On the Theory and Practice of Midwifery; third edition 12mo. Lond. 1855 Do.

——— On the Theory and Practice of Midwifery; fourth edition 12mo. Lond. 1860 The Author

——— Manual for Midwives and Monthly Nurses 12mo. Dublin Sir Charles Locock

CLARK Thomas). New Process for Purifying the Waters supplied to the Metropolis by the existing Water Companies 8vo. Lond. 1841 Dr. Rigby

CLARKE (Sir Charles Mansfield). Observations on those Diseases of Females, which are attended by Discharges *plates*, 2 vols., royol 8vo. Lond. 1814-21 Dr. Clay

——— ——— third edition 2 vols., royal 8vo. London. 1831 Dr. Rigby

CLARKE (John). Practical Essays on the Management of Pregnancy and Labour, and on the Febrile Diseases of Lying-in Women 8vo. Lond. 1793 Dr. Clay

——— ——— another copy 8vo. Lond. 1793 Do.

——— ——— another copy 8vo. Lond. 1793 Sir Charles Locock

——— ——— second edition 8vo. Lond. 1806 Dr. Clay

——— ——— another copy 8vo. Lond. 1806 Dr. Rigby

Presented by

CLARKE (John). Commentaries on some of the most important Diseases of Children Part I, royal 8vo. Lond. 1815 Dr. Rigby

——— ——— Another copy Part I, royal 8vo. 1815 Sir Charles Locock

CLARKE (Joseph). On his life and writings, see *Collins* (R.)

CLARKE (R.). Remarks on the Topography and Diseases of the Gold Coast *map and plate*, 8vo. —— 1860 The Author

With MS. additions by the author, those at pages 46-7 relating to Diseases of Women, &c.

CLAUSIUS (Georgius Godofredus). Commentatio inauguralis medica sistens casum rarissimum Mogostociæ Pelvinæ *plates*, 4to. Francof. 1834 Dr. Rigby

CLAY (Charles). Observations on the Term of Utero-Gestation, with a view of correcting the opinions generally entertained in respect to Protracted Gestation 8vo. Lond. 1855 Sir Charles Locock

——— The Complete Handbook of Obstetric Surgery 12mo. Lond. 1856 Do.

——— Case of Cæsarian Section 8vo. Lond. 1857 Dr. Clay

——— British Record of Obstetric Medicine and Surgery vol. 1, 8vo. Manchester, 1848 Do.

——— Obstetric Monographs from the "Obstetric Record" 8vo. Manchester, 1848 Do.

1. Crantz (M. H. N.) on Ruptures of the Uterus.
2. Harvey (W.) on Birth and Conception.
3. Hippocrates, Obstetric Aphorisms.
4. Naegele (F. C.) the Obliquely Contracted Female Pelvis.
5. Goodman (J.) Successful Case of Cæsarian Operation.
6. Christie (J.) Hæmorrhage in Pregnant Women.
7. Newnham (W.) on Eclampsia Nutans.
8. De Graaf, on the Ovaria.
9. Fischer, on the Pelvis of the Mammalia.
10. Dzondi (C. H.) on Congenital Fistulæ.
11. Ascherson on Congenital Fistulæ of the Neck.
12. Newnham, Unusual Case of Utero-Gestation.
13. Naegele (H. F.) Mechanism of Labour.

CLAY (John). Appendix on the Operation of Ovariotomy. [Tables of Cases] 12mo. Birmingham, 1860 Sir Charles Locock

CLENDON (J. C.). On some Severe Forms of Disease arising from the Retention of Decayed Teeth 8vo. Lond. 1858 Dr. Clay

CLOQUET (Jules). Surgical Pathology, a thesis; translated by J. W. Garlick, and W. C. Copperthwaite *plates*, 12mo, Lond. 1832 Do.

COCKLE (John). On Laceration of the Perineum during Labour 8vo. —— —— Dr. Rigby

Presented by

COLLINS (Robert). Practical Treatise on Midwifery, containing the result of 16,654 births at the Dublin Lying-in Hospital during seven years, commencing Nov., 1826 8vo. Lond. 1835 Dr. Rigby

—— —— Another copy 8vo. Lond. 1835 Sir Charles Locock

—— —— Another copy 8vo. Lond. 1835 Dr. Clay

—— Observations on Professor [James] Hamilton's deviations from the ordinary mode of stating practical results 8vo. Dublin, 1838 Dr. Rigby

—— —— Another copy 8vo. —— —— Do.

With autograph letter from Robert Collins, —, 1839.

—— Observations on the Artificial Dilatation of the Mouth of the Womb during Labour, &c. (from 'Dublin Quarterly Review') 8vo. —— —— Do.

COLLINS (Robert). Sketch of the Life and Writings of the late Joseph Clarke, containing the results of his private practice, extending over forty-four years, including 3878 births 8vo. Lond. 1849 Do.

COLOMBAT DE L'ISERE. Treatise on the Diseases and Special Hygiène of Females; translated with additions by Charles D. Meigs 8vo. Philadelphia, 1845 Do.

COMBE (Andrew). Treatise on the Physiological and Moral Management of Infancy 12mo. Edinburgh, 1840 Do.

CONQUEST (J. T.). Oration before the Hunterian Society, Feb., 1830 8vo. Lond. 1830 Do.

—— Outlines of Midwifery, developing its principles and practice; sixth edition *plates*, 12mo. Lond. 1837 Do.

COOKE (John Charles). Case of Loss of the Uterus and its appendages soon after Delivery 8vo. Coventry, 1835 Do.

COOPER (Samuel). First Lines of the Practice of Surgery; third edition *plates* (title wanting), 8vo. Lond. 1813 Dr. Clay

COOPER (Thomas). Tracts on Medical Jurisprudence, with a preface, notes, and a digest of the law relating to Insanity and Nuisance 8vo. Philadelphia, 1819 Do.

Including—Farr's Medical Jurisprudence.
Dease's Medical Jurisprudence.
Male's Epitome of Juridical Medicine.
Haslam's Treatise on Insanity.

COPEMAN (Edward). See *Crosse*, Cases in Midwifery (Introduction)

Presented by

COPLAND (James). Dictionary of Practical Medicine
Part I. 8vo. Lond. 1882 Dr. Clay

CRAIG (John). The Accoucheur, a Treatise on Protracted Natural Labours, Suspended Animation in New-born Infants, and Uterine Hæmorrhage after the birth of the Child, with illustrative cases
12mo. Glasgow, 1839 Do.

CRÈVE (Fridericus D.). De Calvariæ Osteogenia et Fontanellarum ante partum aphanismo, dissertatio inauguralis *plate*, 8vo. Francof. 1841 Dr. Rigby

CROSKERY (Hugh). See JOURNALS (*West India Magazine*)

CROSS (John). See *Rigby* on Uterine Hæmorrhage (memoir)

CROSSE (John Green). Cases in Midwifery; arranged with an introduction and remarks by Edward Copeman
8vo. Lond. and Norwich, 1851 Do.

CULLEN (William). First Lines of the Practice of Physic
4 vols. 8vo. Edinb. 1786 Dr. Clay

——— ——— vol. II. 8vo. Edinb. 1786 Do.

CULPEPER (Nicholas). Treatise of Aurum Potabile, containing the knowledge necessary to the study of Hermetick Philosophy; with Mr. Culpepper's Ghost giving advice to all the lovers of his writings.
12mo. Lond. 1656 Do.

CURCHOD (Henricus). De Cephalotripsia, dissertatio inauguralis 8vo. Berolini, 1842 Dr. Rigby

Cyclopœdia of Practical Medicine, by John Forbes, &c.
Parts I—IV. 8vo. 1832 Dr. Clay

DALE (Thomas). See *Freind* (Emmenologia)

DANYAU (A. C.). See *Naegele*, Vices et Conformation du Bassin

DARWALL (John). Plain Instructions for the Management of Infants 12mo. Lond. 1830 Do.

DARWIN (Erasmus). Zoonomia, or the Laws of Organic Life 2 vols. 8vo. Dublin, 1794 Do.

DAVENTER (Henry à). The Art of Midwifery Improved, made English: the third edition
plates, 8vo. Lond. 1728 Sir Charles Locock

DAVIS (David D.). Principles and Practice of Obstetric Medicine, in a series of systematic dissertations on Midwifery, and on the Diseases of Women and Children Nos. 1—7, *plates*, 4to, Lond, 1832-36 Dr. Clay

——— Elements of Obstetric Medicine, with the description and treatment of some of the principal diseases of Children; second edition 8vo. Lond. 1841 Do.

Presented by

DAWSON (R.). Essay on Marriage, being a microscopic investigation into its physiological and physical relations, with Observations on Spermatorrhœa
8vo. Lond. 1845 Dr. Clay

DEASE (William). Observations in Midwifery, with observations on the principal disorders incident to women and children *plate*, 8vo. Dublin, 1783 Do.

——— Medical Jurisprudence. See *Cooper* (*T.*)

DENMAN (Thomas). Essays on the Puerperal Fever and on Puerperal Convulsions 8vo. Lond. 1768 Dr. Rigby

——— Introduction to the Practice of Midwifery Part I, 8vo. Lond. 1782 Sir Charles Locock

——— ——— Another copy Part I, 8vo. Lond. 1782 Dr. Rigby

——— Essay on Uterine Hæmorrhages depending on Pregnancy and Parturition 8vo. Lond. 1785 Do.

——— Essay on Natural Labours 8vo. Lond. 1786 Do.

——— Essay on Preternatural Labours 8vo. Lond. 1786 Do.

——— Essay on Difficult Labours 8vo. Lond. 1787 Do.

——— Essay on Uterine Hæmorrhages depending on Pregnancy and Parturition 8vo. Lond. 1785 Do.

——— Introduction to the Practice of Midwifery
2 vols. 8vo. Lond. 1794 Dr. Clay

——— ——— *Plates*: Descriptions of the Engravings to the Introduction to Midwifery 8vo. Lond. 1832 Do.

——— ——— Sixth edition 8vo. Lond. 1824 Sir Charles Locock

DEVENTER (Henry de). Observations importantes sur le Manuel des Accouchemens; traduites par Jacques J. Bruier d'Ablaincourt
plates, 2 vols. in 1, 4to. Paris, 1734 Dr. Rigby

DEWEES (Wm. P.). Compendious System of Midwifery, illustrated by occasional cases
plates, 8vo. Lond. 1825 Do.

——— ——— Another copy *plates*, 8vo. Lond. 1825 Dr. Clay

——— Treatise on the Physical and Medical Treatment of Children 8vo. Lond. 1826 Dr. Rigby

——— ——— Another copy 8vo. Lond. 1826 Dr. Clay

——— Treatise on the Diseases of Females; fourth edition *plates*, 8vo. Philadelphia, 1833 Dr. Rigby

DICKINSON (Wm. B.). See *Rayer* on Diseases of the Skin (translated)

DIEL (F. A). See *Rigby*, Thierische Wärme (uebersetzt)

Presented by

DIMSDALE (Baron). The present method of Inoculating for the Smallpox; sixth edition 8vo. Lond. 1772 Dr. Clay

DIONIS (Pierre). General Treatise of Midwifery; translated from the French *plates*, 8vo. Lond. 1719 Dr. Rigby

——— ——— Another copy *plates*, 8vo. Lond. 1719 Dr. Clay

DOUGLAS (Andrew). Observations on an extraordinary case of Ruptured Uterus 8vo. Lond. 1785 Dr. Rigby

——— ——— Another copy 8vo. Lond. 1785 Sir Charles Locock

DOUGLAS (James). On his statement on Cheselden's Lateral Operation: see *Yelloly*

DOUGLAS (John C.). Disputatio Inauguralis de Dysenteria 8vo. Dublin, 1810 Dr. Rigby

——— Explanation of the process of the Spontaneous Evolution of the Fœtus 8vo. Dublin, 1811 Do.

——— ——— second edition 8vo. Dublin, 1819 Do.

——— Explanation of the real process of "Spontaneous Evolution of the Fœtus;" third edition 8vo. Dublin, 1844 Do.

With autograph letter of the author.

——— ——— third edition 8vo. Dublin, 1844 Sir Charles Locock

DOUGLAS (William). Letter to Dr. Smell[i]e, showing the impropriety of his new invented Wooden Forceps, and absurdity of his Method of teaching and practising Midwifery 8vo. Lond. 1748 Dr. Rigby

——— Second Letter to Dr. Smell[i]e, and an Answer to his Pupil 8vo. Lond.—— Do.

DRUITT (Robert). Memoranda on difficult subjects in Anatomy and Surgery 24mo. Lond. 1837 Do.

DU COUDRAY (Madame Angelique M. Le Boursier). Abrégé de l'Art des Accouchemens *plates*, 8vo. Paris, 1785 Dr. Clay

DUGÈS (Ant.). Manuel d'Obstetrique 18mo. Paris, 1826 Do.

——— See *Boivin* on Diseases of the Uterus

——— See *Lachapelle*

DUNCAN (J. Matthews). On the Mode of Presentation of Dead Children in Labour 12mo. 1855 Do.

——— On a hitherto undescribed Disease of the Uterus, namely, Unnatural Patency of the inner extremity of a Fallopian Tube 8vo. 1856 Do.

——— The Internal Surface of the Uterus after delivery 8vo. 1857 Do.

Presented by

DUNCAN (J. Matthews). Notes on the History of the Mucous Membrane of the Body of the Uterus 8vo. 1858 Dr. Clay

——— See *Braun*, Uræmic Convulsions (notes)

DUNGLISON (Robley). Commentaries on Diseases of the Stomach and Bowels of Children *plate*, 8vo. Lond. 1824 Dr. Rigby

——— ——— Another copy *plate*, 8vo. Lond. 1824 Dr. Clay

DUPARCQUE (F.). Geschichte der Durchlöcherungen, Einrisse und Zerreissungen des Uterus, der Vagina und des Perinæums; bearbeitet von J. F. W. Nevermann 8vo. Quedlinburg, 1838 Do.

DUPUYTREN (le Baron G.). Leçons Orales de Clinique Chirurgicale, faites à l'Hôtel-Dieu de Paris 2 vols. 8vo. Paris, 1832 Do.

DYCE (Robert). On the Importance of the Pulse in relation to Chloroform 8vo. 1857 Do.

EBBESEN and HÖRBYE (Drs.). The Sulphureous Bath at Sandefjord in Norway 8vo. Christiania, 1862 The Authors

ELLIS (Robert). Disease of the Cervix Uteri, a new method of treatment and cure; second edition 8vo. Lond. 1852 Sir Charles Locock

ELSE (Joseph). Essay on the Cure of the Hydrocele of the Tunica Vaginalis Testis; third edition 8vo. London, 1776 Dr. Clay.

——— Anatomical Lectures by MS. 4to. Do.

FARR's Medical Jurisprudence: see *Cooper* (*T.*)

FAYE (F. C.). Beretning om Födselsstiftelsen i Christiania i 1855-6-7 8vo. ——— ——— The Author

——— Bidrag til den Obstetriciske Pathologie 8vo. Christiania, 1859 Do.

——— Coccyodynie bevirket ved Fractur af den nederste Ende af Rumpebenet 8vo. (1861) Do.

——— Nogle Bemærkninger om Syphilisation eller Curativ Chankerinoculation 8vo. (1861) Do.

——— Uterus duplex bicornis cum Vagina Simplici 8vo. Christiania, 1861 Do.

FEIST (Franz Ludwig). Beurtheilung der Operationslehre für Geburtshelfer (from the 'Zeitschrift für Geburts') 8vo. Berlin, 1834 Dr. Rigby

FERGUSON (Robert). Essays on the most important Diseases of Women, Part 1, Puerperal Fever [with a Lecture on the Method of Induction and its results in Medical Science] 8vo. Lond. 1839 Do.

Presented by

FERGUSSON (William). System of Practical Surgery
12mo. Lond. 1842 Dr. Clay

FERRIAR (John). Medical Histories and Reflections
vol. 3, 8vo. Lond. 1810 Do.

On Rabies Canina, Croup, Hooping Cough—Use of Nitrous Acid in Syphilis, &c.

FLOURENS (P.). Cours sur la Génération, l'Ovologie et l'Embryologie, recueilli par M. Deschamps
plates, 4to. Paris, 1836 Do.

FOOTE (John). Ophthalmic Memoranda
24mo. Lond. 1838 Dr. Rigby

FOSTER (Edward). Principles and Practice of Midwifery; completed by James Sims 8vo. Lond. 1781 Do.

Fothergillian Prize Essays, 1843: see *Bennett* (*J. R.*)

FOX (Samuel). Observations on the Disorder of the general health of Females called Chlorosis 8vo. Lond. 1839 Dr. Clay

FREIND (John). Emmenologia, translated by Thomas Dale
8vo. Lond. 1729 Do.

FRORIEP (Ludw. Fr. v.). Theoretischpraktisches Handbuch der Geburtshülfe; achte Ausgabe
plate, 8vo. Weimar, 1827 Dr. Rigby

FULLER (Thomas). Exanthematologia, or a rational account of Eruptive Fevers, especially of the Measles and Small-pox, with appendix on Inoculation
4to. Lond. 1730 Dr. Clay

GARLICK (J. W.). See *Cloquet*, Surgical Pathology (translation)

GAUTIER (V.). Du Rhumatisme de l'Utérus envisagé specialement pendant lá grossesse et l'accouchement
8vo. Genève, 1858 The Author

——— Observations de deux Epanchements Sanguins dans la cavité pelvienne 8vo. —— 1860 Do.

——— De la Fissure Anale chez les Enfants
8vo. Genève, 1862 Do.

——— Polypes Fibreux Naso-Pharyngien enlevé au moyen du serre-nœud constricteur de Maisonneuve
plate, 8vo. —— —— Do.

GEIL (Joannes B.). De Hydrorrhœa Uteri Gravidarum, commentatio inauguralis 8vo. Heidelbergae, 1822 Dr. Rigby

GENSOUL (J.). Nouveau procédé pour opérer les Polypes de Matrice 8vo. Lyon, 1851 Do.

——— Sur le Mécanisme de la Vision 8vo. Do.

Presented by

GERBER (Fr.). Elements of the General and Minute Anatomy of Man and the Mammalia, with Notes and an Appendix by George Gulliver *plates*, 2 vols. 8vo. Lond., 1842 Dr. Clay

GIBB (George D.). On Diseases of the Throat, Epiglottis and Windpipe, their symptoms, progress and treatment 8vo. Lond. 1860 The Author

——— On the Diseases and Injuries of the Hyoid or Tongue Bone 8vo. Lond. 1862 Do.

GIFFARD (William). Cases in Midwifry; revis'd by Edward Hody *plates*, 8vo. Lond. 1734 Dr. Rigby

——— ——— Another copy *plates*, 8vo. Lond. 1734 Dr. Clay

GLOVER (R. M.). Case of Tubarian Gestation with Rupture of the Cyst containing the Embryo and fatal hæmorrhage into the Peritonæum 8vo. —— 1842 Dr. Clay

GOERTZ (Frieder. Johannes). Diss. Inaug. in qua novum ad Ligaturam Polyporum Uteri instrumentum descriptum *plate*, 8vo. Goettingæ, 1783 Sir Charles Locock

GOLDSON (William). An Extraordinary case of Lacerated Vagina at the full period of Gestation 8vo. Lond. 1787 Sir Charles Locock

GOLIS (Leopold Anthony). Treatise on the Hydrocephalus Acutus, or Inflammatory Water in the Head; translated by Robert Gooch 8vo. Lond. 1821 Dr. Clay

GOOCH (Benjamin). Medical and Chirurgical Observations, as an appendix to a former publication *plates*, 8vo. Lond. 1773 Dr. Rigby

GOOCH (Robert). Observations on Puerperal Insanity (from 'Med. Trans. of Coll. of Phys.') 8vo. Lond. 1820 Do.

——— Contribution towards solving the disputed question, What is the nature of the process called the Spontaneous Evolution of the Fœtus (from 'Med. Trans. of Coll. of Phys.') 8vo. Lond. 1820 Do.

——— Account of some of the most important Diseases peculiar to Women 8vo. Lond. 1829 Do.

——— See *Golis* on Hydrocephalus Acutus (translated)

GORDON, (Alex). On the Puerperal Fever of Aberdeen in 1789-92, see *Campbell* (W.)

GORDON (John). Outlines of Lectures on Human Physiology 8vo. Edinb. 1817 Dr. Clay

Presented by

GRAAF (Regnerus de). De Virorum organis Generationi inservientibus, de Clysteribus et de usu Siphonis in Anatomia — F. S. Haden, Esq.
portrait and plates, 12mo. Lugd. Bat. 1668

——— De Mulierum Organis Generationi inservientibus
portrait and plates, 12mo. Lugd. Bat. 1672 — Do.

——— ——— Another copy
plates, 12mo. Lugd. Bat. 1672 — Dr. Clay

GRANVILLE (Augustus Bozzi). Report of the Practice of Midwifery at the Westminster General Dispensary, during 1818 — 8vo. Lond. 1819 — Do.

——— Graphic *Illustrations* of Abortion and the Diseases of Menstruation, with preliminary observations, explanations, and remarks, anatomical and physiological
coloured plates, 4to. Lond. 1833 — Do.

GRAVES (R. J.). Lectures on Physiology: see JOURNALS (*London* Med. and Surgical Journal)

GREENHILL (William A.). See *Rhazes* on Smallpox (translated)

——— See *Sydenham*, Opera

GRENSER (Woldemar Ludov). De vi Puerperii lactandique temporis medicatrice, dissertatio inauguralis
8vo. Lipsiæ, 1838 — Dr. Rigby

——— See *Naegele* (Lehrbuch der Geburtshülfe)

GRIFFITH (William). Treatise on Hydrocephalus or Water in the Brain, with the most successful modes of treatment; second edition — 12mo. Lond. 1835 — Sir Charles Locock

GUILLIMEAU (James). "The French Kings Chirurgion." Child-birth or the happy Deliverie of Women, wherein is set downe the government of women in the time of their breeding childe, of their Travaile and of their lying in, with their diseases, and a Treatise of the diseases of Infants [translated] — 4to. Lond. 1612 — Dr. Rigby

GULLIVER (George). See *Gerber's* Anatomy (notes, &c.)

Gulstonian Lectures, 1811. See *Bancroft*

Gynæciorum sive de Mulierum affectibus Commentarii, in tres tomos digesti — Tomi I et 2, 4to. Basileæ, 1586 — Dr. Clay

——— ——— Another copy [General title wanting]
Tomus 1, 4to. ib. 1586. — Do.

Gynæciorum sive de Mulierum affectibus et Morbis libri Græcorum, Arabum, Latinorum veterun et recentium quotquot extant, opera Israelis Spachii
folio, Argentinæ, 1597 — Dr. Clay

Presented by

HABER (Elias de). Dissertatio inauguralis medica exhibens Casum Rarissimum Partus qui propter exostosin in Pelvi absolvi non potuit
plates, 4to. Heidelbergæ, 1830 Dr. Rigby

HADEN (Charles Thomas). Practical Observations on the Management and Diseases of Children; with additional observations, and biographical notice of the author, by Thomas Alcock 8vo. Lond. 1827 Dr. Clay

—— —— Another copy 8vo. Lond. 1827 Do.

—— —— Another copy 8vo. Lond. 1827 Do.

—— —— Another copy 8vo. Lond. 1827 Do.

HAHNEMANN (Samuel). See *Rigby*, über den Zucker (Anmerkungen)

HALL (Archibald). Statistics of the University Lying-in Hospital, Montreal (from 'Brit. Amer. Journ')
8vo. Montreal, 1860 The Author

HAMILTON (Alex). Elements of the Practice of Midwifery
8vo. Lond. 1775 Dr. Rigby

—— —— Another copy 8vo. Edinb. 1775 Dr. Clay
With MS. additions. Title wanting.

—— Outlines of the Theory and Practice of Midwifery
8vo. Edinb. 1784 Dr. Rigby

—— —— fifth edition 8vo. Edinb. 1803 Dr. Clay

—— Letters to Dr. William Osborn on certain doctrines in his Essays on the Practice of Midwifery, &c.
8vo. Edinb. 1792 Dr. Rigby

—— Lectures on Midwifery at the Royal College Edinb. M.S. 1801 Do.
MS. notes taken by the late Dr. Henry Reeve of Norwich, author of an Essay on the Torpidity of Animals.

—— Treatise on the Management of Female Complaints; sixth edition, enlarged, with hints on Diseases of Infants and Children, by James Hamilton
8vo. Edinb. 1809 Do.

—— —— eighth edition; with hints for the treatment of diseases of Infants and Children, by James Hamilton 8vo. Edinb. 1821 Sir Charles Locock

HAMILTON (James, junior). Select Cases in Midwifery, from the records of the Edinburgh General Lying-in Hospital 8vo. Edinb. 1795 Do.

—— Collection of *Engravings* designed to facilitate the study of Midwifery, explained and illustrated
8vo. Lond. 1796 Dr. Clay

Presented by

HAMILTON (James, junior). Hints for the Treatment of the Principal Diseases of Infancy and Childhood: third edition 8vo. Edinb. 1821 Dr. Rigby

——— Practical observations on various subjects relating to Midwifery 2 parts 8vo. Edinb. 1836 Sir Charles Locock

——— On Diseases of Infants, see *Hamilton* (Alex.)

——— Reply, see *Collins* (R.)

——— Examination of his Letters in Defence of his Opinions, see *Murphy*

HANNAY (Alex. John). On some important points connected with the Pathology of Puerperal Fever 8vo. Glasgow, 1827 Dr. Rigby

HARRIS (Walter). De Morbis Acutis Infantum; editio secunda, access. Liber de morbis gravioribus et de Luis venereæ origine 8vo. Londini, 1705 Sir Charles Locock

HARRISON (James Bower). Case of Monstrosity 8vo. 1852 Dr. Rigby

HARVEY (William). Exercitationes de Generatione Animalium; acced. de Partu 18mo. Amst. 1651 Dr. Clay

HARVIE (John). Practical Directions shewing a method of preserving the Perinæum in Birth, and delivering the Placenta without violence 8vo. Lond. 1767 Do.

HASLAM (John). On Insanity, see *Cooper* (T.)

HAYGARTH (John). Sketch of a Plan to exterminate the Casual Small-pox from Great Britain, and to introduce General Inoculation, &c. 2 vols. 8vo. Lond. 1793 Dr. Clay

——— Inquiry how to prevent the Smallpox, and Proceedings of a Society for promoting General Inoculation, &c. 8vo. Bath, 1801 Do.

HAYN (Albert). Abhandlungen aus dem Gebiete der Geburtshülfe 8vo. Bonn, 1828 Dr. Rigby

HAYS (Isaac). See *Rigby's* System of Midwifery (Notes)

HEATH (John). See *Baudelocque's* Midwifery (translated)

HEISTER (Laurence). General System of Surgery; translated, fifth edition *plates*, 4to. Lond. 1753 Dr. Clay

HEMING (G. O.). See *Boivin* on Diseases of the Uterus (translated)

HENKE (Adolph). Handbuch zur Erkenntniss und Heilung der Kinderkrankheiten; dritte Ausgabe 2 vols. 8vo. Franfurt, 1821 Dr. Rigby

Presented by

HENRY (Wm. Chas.). Biographical Notice of Edward Holme, M.D. 8vo. 1848 Dr. Clay

HERDER (Wilh. Gottfried v.). Zur Erweiterung der Geburtshülfe *plates*, 12mo. Leipzig, 1803 Dr. Rigby

HEWITT (Graily). On "Supporting the Perinæum" 12mo. Lond. 1861 Sir Charles Locock

HEY (William jun.) Treatise on the Puerperal Fever, illustrated by Cases which occurred in 1809-12 8vo. Lond. 1815 Dr. Rigby

——— ——— Another copy 8vo. Lond. 1815 Dr. Clay

HILDANUS (Guilhelmus Fabricius). Opera quæ extant omnia, ab authore recognita, tum epistolis tum observationibus aucta, add. M. A. Severini Liber de Efficaci Medicina folio, Francof. 1862 Dr. Rigby

Observationes Chirurgicæ; De Conservanda Valetudine; De Dysenteria; De Lithotomia; De Gangræna; De Ichore Celsi; De Affectibus Uterinis, etc.

HIRZEL (Leonardus). Dissertatio inauguralis medica, sistens Nexus nervi sympathetici cum nervis cerebralibus *plate*, 4to. Heidelbergæ, 1824 Do.

HODY (Edward). See *Giffard's* Cases in Midwifery

HOHL (Anton Friedrich). Die Geburtshülfliche Exploration *plate*, 2 vols. 8vo. Halle, 1833 Do.

Theil 1. Das Hören.
—— 2. Das explorative Sehen und Fühlen.

HOLME (Edward). Biographical Notice: see *Henry*

HOME (Sir Everard). Short Tract on the Formation of Tumours, and the peculiarities in the structure of those that have become cancerous with their mode of treatment *plates*, 8vo. Lond. 1830 Dr. Clay

HOPE (J.). Principles and *Illustrations* of Morbid Anatomy Parts I—III, 8vo. 1833 Do.

HULL (John). Observations on Mr. Simmons's Detection, &c., with a defence of the Cæsarean Operation, description of the Female Pelvis, and account of Embryulcia, and Embryotomy 8vo. Manchester, 1799 Do.

——— Essay on Phlegmatia Dolens, including an account of Peritonitis Puerperalis, and Conjunctiva 8vo. Manchester, 1800 Dr. Rigby

——— ——— Another copy 8vo. Manchester, 1800 Do.

——— See *Baudelocque* on the Cæsarean Operation (translated)

Presented by

HULME (Nathaniel). Treatise on the Puerperal Fever, illustrated by dissections, with a rational method of cure 8vo. Lond. 1772 Dr. Rigby

—— —— Another copy 8vo. Lond. 1772 Dr. Clay

HUNTER (William). Anatomy of the Human Gravid Uterus exhibited in *figures* atlas folio, Birmingham, 1774 Do.

—— —— Another copy atlas folio, Birmingham, 1774 Dr. Rigby

Portrait of Hunter inserted, and with MS. memoranda by Dr. Rigby

—— Anatomical Description of the Human Gravid Uterus and its contents 4to. Lond. 1794 Do.

—— —— second edition, by Edward Rigby 8vo. Lond. 1843 Do.

—— —— Another copy *plates*, 8vo. Lond. 1843 Sir Charles Locock

—— [Nos. 12, 13, 16, 1843-4, of the 'Lancet;' and Nos. 15, 36, 1844, of the 'London Medical Gazette,' containing Dr. Lee's attacks on Dr. Rigby's edition, and Dr. Rigby's Replies] Dr. Rigby

HUXHAM (John). Observationes de Aëre et Morbis Epidemicis, 1728—1737 Plymuthi factæ; acced. De morbo Colico Damnoniensi 8vo. Lond. 1739 Dr. Clay

—— Essay on Fevers, as depending on different constitutions of the Blood, with Dissertations on Slow Nervous Fevers, on Putrid Fevers, on the Smallpox, and on Pleurisies and Peripneumonies; second edition 8vo. Lond. 1750 Do.

—— Essay on Fevers, with a Dissertation on the Malignant Ulcerous Sore-throat 8vo. Lond. 1775 Do.

INGLEBY (John T.). Practical treatise on Uterine Hæmorrhage in connexion with Pregnancy and Parturition *plate*, 8vo. Lond. 1832 Do.

—— —— Another copy *plate*, 8vo. Lond. 1832 Sir Charles Locock

With autograph letter of the author to Dr. Rigby.

—— Facts and Cases in Obstetric Medicine, with observations on the most important diseases of Females 8vo. Lond. n. d. Dr. Rigby

—— —— Another copy 8vo. Lond. —— Dr. Clay

—— —— Another copy 8vo. Lond. —— Sir Charles Locock

—— —— Another copy 8vo. Lond. —— Do.

Presented by

Jacksonian Prize Dissertations. See *Lee* (T. S.)

JANSON (Augustus A.). Dissertatio inauguralis de Atresia vaginæ acquisita *plate*, 8vo. Francof. 1845 Dr. Rigby

JENNER (Edward). Inquiry into the causes and effects of the Variolæ Vaccinæ or Cow-pox; third edition *plates*, 4to. Lond. 1801 Dr. Clay

JEWEL (George). Practical observations on Leucorrhœa, Fluor Albus or weakness, with cases illustrative of a new mode of treatment 8vo. Lond. 1830 Sir Charles Locock

JOHNSON (Christopher). See *Mahon* on Signs of Murder in New-born Children (translated)

JOHNSON (Robert Wallace). System of Midwifery, in four parts, founded on practical observations *plates*, 4to. Lond. 1769 Dr. Rigby

JOHNSTON'S (George) Practical Midwifery. See *Sinclair*

JONES (George). On the Progress of Midwifery and the Diseases of Women, 1857 8vo. —— 1858 Dr. Clay

JONES (Thomas). See *Mauriceau's* Aphorisms (translated)

JONES (Thomas William). Quelques considérations dèduites de l'Anatomie Comparée, relatives à différens points d'Ovologie, au mode de communication de la mère à l'enfant et à la circulation du sang dans le fœtus 4to. Paris, 1834 Dr. Rigby

With MS. notes by Dr. Rigby.

JÖRG (Johann C. G.). Die Zeugung des Menschen und der Thiere *plates*, 8vo. Leipzig, 1815 Do.

KAY (James Phillips). The physiology, pathology, and treatment of Asphyxia 8vo. Lond. 1834 Dr. Clay

KAYSER (C.). De eventu Sectionis Cæsareæ 8vo. Havniæ, 1841 Dr. Rigby

KEATE (T.). Cases of the Hydrocele, with cases of Hernia Vesicæ Urinariæ and Hernia Incarcerata *plate*, 8vo. Lond. 1788 Dr. Clay

KEILLER (Alex.). Case of Thickening and Deep Fissures the Skin, in an infant at birth, [with notes of cases of intra-uterine cutaneous disease analogous to the preceding, by J. Y. Simpson] (from 'Edinb. Monthly') *plate*, 8vo. 1843 Dr. Rigby

KEITH (George S.). Cases of Poisoning by Croton Oil (from 'Edinb. Med. Journal') 8vo. 1843 Do.

KEITH (William). Case of Cancer of the Tongue 8vo. —— 1849 Dr. Clay

Presented by

KEITH (William). Case of Wound of Internal Carotid Artery successfully ligatured 8vo. Edinb. 1851 Dr. Clay

——— Second case of Excision of the Knee-joint successfully treated 8vo. —— 1854 Do.

KENNEDY (Evory). Observations on Obstetric Auscultation, with an analysis of the evidences of Pregnancy, and the proofs of the life and death of the fœtus in utero; with appendix of legal notes by John Smith *plates*, 12mo. Dublin, 1833 Dr. Rigby

——— Observations on Hypertrophy and other affections of the Os Uteri *plate*, 8vo. Dublin, 1838 Do.

——— Introductory Address delivered at the first meeting of the Dublin Obstetrical Society in the Rotunda 8vo. Dublin, 1839 Do.

KENNEDY (James). Instructions to Mothers and Nurses on the Management of Children in Health and Disease 12mo. Glasgow, 1825 Dr. Clay

KIDD (Charles). On Æther and Chloroform as Anæsthetics; second edition 12mo. Lond. 1858 Sir Charles Locock

KIDD (Geo. H.). On Inflammation and Obstruction of the Branches of the Pulmonary Artery 8vo. —— —— Dr. Clay

KILIAN (Hermann Friedrich). Operationslehre für Geburtshelfer 2 vols. in 3, 8vo. Bonn, 1834 Dr. Rigby

Theil 1. Die operative Geburtshülfe, Band 1.
—— 1. Part 2 „ Band 2.
—— 2. Die Rein-Chirurgischen Operationen des Geburtshelfers.

KING (John). Analysis of the subject of Extra-Uterine Fœtation, and of the Retroversion of the Gravid Uterus 8vo. Norwich, 1818 Dr. Clay

KIRKLAND (Thomas). Treatise on Child Bed Fevers; with Dissertations on the Brain and Nerves, and on the sympathy of Nerves and irritability 8vo. Lond. 1774 Dr. Rigby

——— ——— Another copy 8vo. Lond. 1774 Dr. Clay

KRÜGER (Carol. A.). De Febris Puerperalis Epidemia in Lechodochio Heidelbergensi, 1845 8vo. Heidelb. 1846 Dr. Rigby

KUNHARDT (Hermann A.). De Noma, dissertatio inauguralis medica 8vo. Heidelb. 1848 Do.

LACHAPELLE (Mme). Pratique des Accouchemens ou Mémoires et observations choisies sur les points les plus importans de l'art, publiés par Ant. Dugès 8vo. Paris, 1821 Dr. Clay

——— ——— See *Naegele*

Presented by

LAMBE (William). Reports on the effects of a peculiar Regimen [Vegetable] on Scirrhous Tumours and Cancerous Ulcers 8vo. Lond. 1809 Dr. Rigby

LA MOTTE (Mauquest de). Traité complet des Accouchemens naturels, non naturels et contre nature, nouvelle édition 4to. Leiden, 1729 Sir Charles Locock

—— Treatise of Midwifery, illustrated with upwards of four hundred curious observations and reflexions; translated by Thomas Tomkyns 8vo. Lond. 1746 Dr. Rigby

LANE (Butler). Functional Diseases of the Liver, associated with Uterine Derangement 8vo. Lond. 1848 Dr. Clay

LAWRENCE (William). Lectures on Physiology, Zoology, and the Natural History of Man; sixth edition *plates*, 12mo. Lond. 1834 Do.

LEAKE (John). Practical observations on the Childbed Fever, and on Uterine Hæmorrhages, Convulsions, and other acute diseases most fatal to women during Pregnancy 8vo. Lond. 1772 Dr. Rigby

—— —— Another copy 8vo. Lond. 1772 Dr. Clay

—— Lecture introductory to the theory and practice of Midwifery, including the History of that Science; fourth edition 4to. Lond. 1782 Dr. Rigby

—— Syllabus of Lectures on Midwifery 4to Lond. 1782 Do.

—— Description and Use of the New Forceps with three blades 4to. —— —— Do.

—— Vindication of the Forceps described by Dr. Leake 4to. —— —— Do.

LECIEUX, RENARD, &c. Médecine Légale, ou Considérations sur l'Infanticide, sur la manière de procéder à l'ouverture des cadavres, &c., par MM. Lecieux, Renard, Laisné et Rieux 8vo. Paris, 1819 Dr. Clay

Lectures on Medicine and Surgery. MS. Notes of the following Lectures,

Dr. Alison, 1822-23
Dr. Monro on Surgery, 1823
Dr. Monro on Anatomy, &c., 1822
Dr. Duncan, Sen., on the Theory of Medicine
Dr. Campbell on Diseases of Women Dr. Rigby

LEE (Robert). On the Structure of the Human Placenta and its connexion with the Uterus. (From 'Philos. Trans.') *plates*, 4to. Lond. 1832 Do.

—— Memoirs on the Ganglia and Nerves of the Uterus *plates*, 4to. Lond. 1849 Do.

—— —— Another copy *plates*, 4to. Lond. 1849 Sir Charles Locock

Presented by

LEE (Robert). On the Ganglia and Nerves of the Heart *plates*, 4to. Lond. 1849 Dr. Rigby

——— Treatise on the Employment of the Speculum Do.

——— Review of ditto. (From the 'Midland Quarterly Journal') 8vo. 1858 Do.

——— See *Hunter* on the Gravid Uterus, by Rigby

——— ——— Another copy *plates*, 4to. Lond. 1849 Sir Charles Locock

LEE (Thomas Safford). On Tumors of the Uterus and its appendages. (Jacksonian Prize Dissertation) *plate*, 8vo. Lond. 1847 Dr. Rigby

——— ——— Another copy *plate*, 8vo. Lond. 1847 Dr. Clay

LEVER (John C. W.). On some Disorders of the Nervous System associated with Pregnancy and Parturition 8vo. —— 1847 Dr. Rigby

——— Cases of Puerperal Convulsions, with remarks 8vo. —— —— Do.

——— Cases of Hæmorrhage occurring after delivery, and complicated with disease of the spleen and kidneys 8vo. —— —— Do.

——— Observations on Pelvic Tumors obstructing Parturition, with cases. (From 'Guy's Hospital Reports') 2 parts, 8vo. Do.

With autograph note of the author.

——— Cases of Pelvic Inflammation, with abscess, occurring after delivery, with remarks (From ditto) 8vo. Do.

——— Two cases of Labour, protracted by insuperable rigidity of the os uteri. (From ditto.) *plate*, 8vo. Do.

——— Statistical Report of Guy's Hospital Lying-in Charity, 1833-40. (From ditto.) 8vo. Do.

LEVRET (André). Observations sur la cure radicale de plusieurs Polypes de la Matrice, de la Gorge et du Nez; seconde edition 8vo. Paris, 1759 Do.

——— Essai sur l'Abus des Régles générales et contre les préjugés qui s'opposent aux progrés de l'art des Accouchemens *plates*, 8vo. Paris, 1766 Do.

——— L'art des Accouchemens démontré par des principes de physique et de méchanique *portrait and plates*, 8vo. Paris, 1766 Do.

——— Observations sur les causes et les accidens de plusieurs Accouchemens Laborieux 8vo. Paris, 1780 Do.

Presented by

LEVY (C. E. M.). Om Collisionen mellem Perforation og Kaisersnit [de jure vitæ et necis quod competit medico in partu] 8vo. Kiöbenhavn, 1840 Dr. Rigby

—— Beretning om Födselsstiftelserne og den praktiske Accouchementsundervisning i London og Dublin 8vo. Kjobenhavn, 1847 Do.

LEWIS (George). Anatomico-Chirurgical *Views* of the male and Female Pelvis; second edition folio, Lond. 1822 Dr. Clay

LEY (Hugh). Essay on the Laryngismus Stridulus or Croup-like Inspiration of Infants, with illustrations of the Pathology of Nerves, and the functions and diseases of the par vagum *plates*, 8vo. Lond. 1836 Do.

LISTON (Robert). Practical Surgery; third edition *woodcuts*, 8vo. Lond. 1840 Do.

LITZMANN (Carl C. T.). Die Formen des Beckens, insbesondere des engen weiblichen Beckens nebst einem Anhange über die Osteomalacie *plates*, 4to. Berlin, 1861 The Author

LOBB (Theophilus). Treatise of the Smallpox 8vo. Lond. 1731 Dr. Clay

LOMBARD (Henri Clermond). Essai sur les Tubercules 4to. Paris, 1827 Dr. Rigby

LOUIS (A.). Memoire contre la Legitimité des naissames prétendues tardives 8vo. Paris, 1764 Dr. Clay

LOWDER (W.). Abstracts of Lectures on the theory and practice of Midwifery MS. 4to. 1776 Dr. Rigby

MACKALL (Louis). The Action of the Voluntary Muscles 8vo. —— —— The Author

M'KEEVER (Thomas). Practical Remarks on Lacerations of the Uterus and Vagina, with cases 8vo. Lond. 1824 Dr. Rigby

—— —— Another copy 8vo. Lond. 1824 Dr. Clay

M'KENZIE (—). Lectures on the Theory and Practice of Midwifery MS. 4to. 1769 Dr. Rigby

MACKENZIE (F. W.). On the Relations of Uterine to Constitutional Disorder Part I, 8vo. Lond. 1852 Sir Charles Locock

MACLEOD (Roderick). On Rheumatism in its various forms, and on the Affections of Internal Organs, more especially the Heart and Brain, to which it gives rise 8vo. Lond. 1842 Dr. Rigby

M'WHINNIE (A. M.). On the Varieties in the Muscular System of the Human Body (from 'Lond. Med. Gazette) 8vo. Lond. Do.

Presented by

MADDOX (Richard). See *Morley*.

MADGE (Henry). On Diseases of the Fœtus in Utero; second edition 12mo. Lond. 1859 The Author

—— Remarks on the Anatomical Relations between the Mother and the Fœtus 12mo. Lond. 1859 Do.

—— —— Another copy 12mo. Lond. 1859 Sir Charles Locock

MAGENDIE (F.). Elementary Compendium of Physiology; translated with notes and illustrations by E. Milligan 8vo. Edinb. 1823 Dr. Clay

MAHON (P. A. O.) Essay on the Signs of Murder in New-born Children; translated by Christopher Johnson 8vo. Lancaster, 1813 Do.

MALE's Juridical Medicine, see *Cooper* (T.)

MANNING (Henry). Treatise on Female Diseases, comprehending those incident to Pregnant and Child-bed Women 8vo. Lond. 1771 Dr. Rigby

MARLEY (Miles). On the Nature and Treatment of the most frequent Diseases of Children 8vo. Lond. 1830 Dr. Clay

—— —— Another copy 8vo. Lond. 1830 Sir Charles Locock

MARTIN (Eduard). Hand-*atlas* der Gynäkologie und Geburtshülfe 4to. Berlin, 1862 The Author

MAUBRAY (John). The Female Physician, containing all the Diseases incident to that sex, with the whole Art of Midwifery 8vo. Lond. 1724 Dr. Rigby

MAUQUEST de la Motte. See *La Motte*.

MAURICEAU (Francois). Traité des Maladies des Femmes Grosses; dernière edition, corrigée par l'Auteur *plates*, 4to. Paris, 1683 Do.

Autograph of Thomas Martin.

—— Traité des Maladies des Femmes Grosses et de celles qui sont Accouchées; sixième edition 2 vols. 4to. Paris, 1721 Dr. Rigby

—— The Diseases of Women with Child and in Childbed; translated by Hugh Chamberlen; third edition *plates*, 12mo. Lond. 1697 Dr. Clay

—— —— translated by Hugh Chamberlen; sixth edition *plates*, 8vo. Lond. 1727 Sir Charles Locock

—— —— eighth edition, translated by Hugh Chamberlen *plates*, 8vo. Lond. 1752 Dr. Rigby

—— Aphorisms relating to the Pregnancy, Delivery, and Diseases of Women; translated by Thomas Jones 8vo. Lond. 1739 Sir Charles Locock

Presented by

MAURICEAU (Francois). Reponse à ses observations sur la Grossesse. See *Peu*

MAYER (Guilielmus Augustus). De Circumvolutionibus Funiculi Umbilicalis Fœtus vitæ haud raro infestis dissertatio inauguralis 8vo. Heidelb. 1842 Dr. Rigby

MAYNE (R. G.). Expository Lexicon of the Terms, ancient and modern, in Medical and General Science Parts I—VI, 8vo. Lond. 1854 Dr. Clay

MEAD (Richard). Mechanical Account of Poisons, in several Essays *plates*, 8vo. Lond. 1702 Do.

——— Treatise concerning the influence of the Sun and Moon upon Human bodies, and the Diseases thereby produced; translated by Thomas Stack 8vo. Lond. 1748 Do.

MEIER (Dan. Ed.). Geburtshülfliche Beobachtungen und Ergebnisse in der Obstet. Klinik zu Halle, nebst Beschreibung der Niemeyerschen Kopfzange und eines Kephalopelykometer *plates*, 8vo. Bremen, 1838 Do.

MEIGS (Charles). Lecture introductory to the course of Obstetrics in Jefferson Medical College of Philadelphia. 8vo. Philad. 1842 Do.

——— Treatise on Acute and Chronic Diseases of the Neck of the Uterus *plates*, 8vo. Philadelphia, 1854 Do.

——— See *Colombat* on diseases of Females (translated)

Memoirs (Authentic) Biographical, Critical and Literary, of the most eminent Physicians and Surgeons of Great Britain, with collection of their prescriptions, account of the medical charities of the metropolis, &c.; second edition 8vo. Lond. 1818 Do.

MERRIMAN (Samuel). Observations on some late attempts to depreciate the value and efficacy of Vaccine Inoculation 8vo. Lond. 1805 Dr. Rigby

——— Synopsis of the various kinds of Difficult Parturition, with practical remarks on the management of Labours; third edition *plates*, 8vo. Lond. 1820 Dr. Clay

——— ——— Another copy *plates*, 8vo. Lond. 1820 Sir Charles Locock

——— New edition, with observations on Pregnancy *plates*, 8vo. Lond. 1838 Dr. Rigby

MICHELL (Janus Petersen). De Synchondrotomia Pubis commentarius 8vo. Amst. 1783 Do.

MICHELL (W.). On Difficult Cases of Parturition, and the use of Ergot of Rye 8vo. Lond. 1828 Dr. Clay

Presented by

Midwifery—Syllabus of the Lectures on, at Guy's Hospital, and at Dr. Haighton's Theatre 8vo. Lond. 1803 Dr. Rigby

MILLIGAN (E.). See *Magendie's* Physiology (translated)

MONTGOMERY (W. F.). Case of Ovarian Disease of a remarkable character *plates*, 8vo. Dublin, 1830 Do.

—— Catalogue of the Preparations in his Museum 8vo. Dublin, 1834 Do.

—— Practical Observations in Midwifery: on some peculiar forms of Relaxation of the Uterine Tissue (from 'Dublin Journal') 8vo. —— 1835 Do.

With autograph letter of the author.

—— Exposition of the Signs and Symptoms of Pregnancy, the Period of Human Gestation, and the Signs of Delivery *plates*, 8vo. Lond. 1837 Do.

With two autograph letters of the author relative to his notice of Decidual Cotyledons, Dr. Rigby's edition of Hunter on the Gravid Uterus, &c.

—— —— Another copy *plates*, 8vo. Lond. 1837 Dr. Clay

MOORE (James). History and Practice of Vaccination 8vo. Lond. 1817 Do.

MOORE (William). Elements of Midwifery, or the Arcana of Nature in the Formation and Production of the Human Species elucidated 8vo. Lond. 1777 Dr. Rigby

MORLEY (Dr.). Trial of a Cause between Richard Maddox and Dr. M[orle]y, defendant, Physician and Man-midwife, before Sir Michael Foster, 1754; with some extraordinary cases in Midwifery, by Dr. Deventer, of Leyden 8vo. Lond. —— Sir Charles Locock

MORTIMER (W. H.). Observations on the Growth and Irregularities of Children's Teeth, with an Essay on the advantages of Artificial Teeth *plates*, 8vo. Paris, 1836 Dr. Clay

MORTON (Edward). Remarks on the subject of Lactation; Healthy and Diseased conditions of the Breast-milk, disorders produced in Mothers by Suckling, and cases proving that when protracted it is a common cause of Hydrencephalus, &c. 8vo. Lond. 1831 Do.

MOSS (William). Essay on the Management and Nursing of Children in the earlier periods of Infancy 8vo. Lond. 1781 Dr. Rigby

MOXEY (Georgius Todd). Disp. Med. Inaug. de Puerperarum Hysteritide 8vo. Edinb. 1821 Dr. Clay

Presented by

MULDER (Johannes). Historia litteraria et critica Forcipum et Vectium Obstetriciorum *plates*, 8vo. Lugd. Bat. 1794 Dr. Clay

——— Litterärische und kritische Geschichte der Zangen und Hebel in der Geburtshülfe; uebersetzt mit Anmerkungen von Johann W. Schlegel *plates*, 8vo. Leipzig, 1798 Dr. Rigby

MÜLLER (J.). Embryology with the Physiology of Generation; translated with notes by William Baly *plates*, 8vo. Lond. 1848 Dr. Clay

MÜLLER (Joannes C.). Meditationes nonnullæ de Cephalotomia seu perforatione Cranii 8vo. Hauniæ, 1836 Dr. Rigby

MURPHY (Edward William). Report of the Obstetric Practice of University College Hospital *plate*, 8vo. Dublin, 1844 Do.

——— Lectures on Natural and Difficult Parturition 8vo. Lond. 1845 Do.

——— ——— Another copy 8vo. Lond. 1845 Dr. Clay

——— Examination of Dr. Hamilton's Letters in Defence of his Opinions, especially in reference to the Management of the First Stage of Labour (from 'Dublin Journal') 8vo. ——— ——— Dr. Rigby

——— Inquiry into the Management of the First and Second Stages of Labour (Mechanism of Parturition) 8vo. ——— ——— Do.

MURRAY (Adolphus). Description of the Arteries of the Human Body, reduced to Tables; translated by Archibald Scott 8vo. Edinb. 1801 Dr. Clay

NAEGELE (Franz Carl). Erfahrungen und Abhandlungen aus dem Gebiethe der Krankheiten des weiblichen Geschlechtes; nebst Methodenlehre der Geburtshülfe *plates*, 8vo. Mannheim, 1812 Dr. Rigby

——— Ueber den Mechanismus der Geburt 8vo. Heidelberg, 1822 Do.

With autograph of the author.

——— Essay on the Mechanism of Parturition; from the German, by Edward Rigby 12mo. Lond. 1829 Do.

——— ——— Another copy 12mo. Lond. 1829 Sir Charles Locock

——— Ueber der Frau la Chapelle Pratique des Accouchemens 8vo. Heidelberg, 1823 Dr. Rigby

——— Dissertatio de Jure Vitæ et Necis quod competit medico in partu 4to. Heidelbergæ, 1826 Do.

Presented by

NAEGELE (Franz Karl). Lehrbuch der Geburtshülfe für Hebammem; zweite Auflage *plate*, 8vo. Heidelberg, 1833 Dr. Rigby

—— —— Another copy *plate*, 8vo. Heidelberg, 1833 Dr. Clay

—— —— Dritte Auflage 8vo. ib. 1836 Dr. Rigby

—— —— Sechste Auflage 8vo. ib. 1844 Do.

—— —— Siebente Auflage 8vo. ib. 1847 Do.

—— —— Achte Auflage 8vo. ib. 1850 Do.

With an autograph letter from the author.

—— Katechismus der Hebemmankunst als Anhang zu seinem Lehrbuche der Geburtshülfe für die Hebammen; dritte Auflage 8vo. Heidelberg, 1836 Do.

—— Das Schräg Verengte Becken, nebst einem Anhange über die wichtigsten Fehler des Weiblichen Beckens *plates*, 4to. Mainz, 1839 Do.

With autograph letter of the author.

—— Des principaux Vices et Conformation du Bassin, et spécialement du rétrécissement oblique; traduit par A. C. Danyau *plates*, royal 8vo. Paris, 1840 Sir Charles Locock

—— Zur Methodologie der Geburtshülfe; Grundzüge der allgemeinen Pathologie und Therapie der Geburt Lief. 1, 8vo. Heidelberg, 1847 Dr. Rigby

—— Fälle von Blutgeschwülsten der äusseren weiblichen Geschlechtstheile (from Klin. Annalen') 8vo. Do.

—— Ueber das gänzliche Zurückbleiben der Nachgeburt ('Klin. Annalen') 8vo. Do.

—— Ueber eine besondere Art fehlergaft gebildeter weiblichen Becken (from 'Klin. Annalen') *plates*, 8vo Do.

—— Ueber eine besondere Art fehlerhaft gebildeter weiblichen Becken ('Zusatz') 8vo. Do.

—— See *Wigand*, Geburt des Menschen

NAEGELE (Hermann Franz). Die Lehre vom Mechanismus der Geburt, nebst Beiträgen zur Geschichte derselben 8vo. Mainz, 1838 Do.

With autograph of the author.

—— Die Geburtshülfliche Auscultation 8vo. Mainz, 1838 Do.

—— Treatise on Obstetric Auscultation, translated by Charles West 12mo. Lond. 1839 Sir Charles Locock

Presented by

NAEGELE (Hermann Franz). Lehrbuch der Geburtshülfe 2 vols. 8vo. Mainz, 1843—5 Dr. Rigby

Theil 1. Physiologie und Diätetik der Geburt.
—— 2. Pathologie und Therapeutik der Geburt.

—— —— funfte Auflage, bearbeitet von Woldemar Ludwig Grenser 8vo, Mainz, 1863 Dr. Grenser

—— Fall von Verletzung des Unterleibs bei einer im achten Monate Schwangeren (from 'Klin. Annalen') 8vo. —— Dr. Rigby

With autograph letter of the author.

—— Ein Fall von Kaiserschnitt 8vo. —— Do.

—— Ueber die Verklebung des äusseren Muttermundes als Geburtshinderniis (from 'Med. Annalen') 8vo. —— —— Do.

NEEDHAM (Gualter). Disquisitio Anatomica de Formato Fœtu *plates*, 12mo. Londini, 1667 Dr. Clay

—— —— Another copy 12mo. Londini, 1667 Do.

NÉGRIER (C.). Recherches anatomiques et physiologiques sur les Ovaires dans l'espèce humaine, spécialement sous le rapport de leur influence dans la Menstruation *plates*, 8vo. Paris, 1840 Dr. Rigby

—— Recherches et considérations sur la constitution et les fonctions du Col de l'Utérus 8vo. Angers, 1846 Do.

NELSON (James). Essay on the Government of Children: health, manners, and education; second edition 12mo. London, 1756 Dr. Clay

NEWNHAM (William). Essay on the symptoms, causes, and treatment of Inversio Uteri, with a history of the successful extirpation of that organ 8vo. Lond. 1818 Dr. Rigby

—— —— Another copy 8vo. Lond. 1818 Dr. Clay

NIHELL (Elizabeth). Treatise on the Art of Midwifery, setting forth various abuses therein, especially as to the practice with instruments 8vo. Lond. 1760 Dr. Clay

—— —— Another copy 8vo. Lond. 1760 Do.

NISBET (William). Clinical Guide to Midwifery 12mo. London, 1800 Do.

NUNN (Thomas William). Inflammation of the Breast, and Milk Abscess 8vo. Lond. 1853 Sir Charles Locock

OLDHAM (Henry). On Polypus Uteri, and its co-existence with Pregnancy (from 'Guy's Hosp. Reports') *plates*, 8vo. —— —— Dr. Rigby

Presented by

OLDHAM (Henry). On a Follicular Disease of the Vulva (from 'Lond. Med. Gazette') 8vo. —— Dr. Rigby

ORMEROD (Edward Latham). Cases of Diabetes, illustrating the effects of certain modes of treatment on some of the symptoms of the disease (from 'Edinb. Med. and Surg. Journal') 8vo. —— Do.

—— On a Systolic Murmur in the Pulmonary Artery, and its application to the Diagnosis of Functional and Organic Murmurs (from 'Edinb. Med. and Surg. Journal') 8vo. —— Do.

OSBORN (William). Essay on Laborious Parturition, in which the division of the Symphysis Pubis is particularly considered 8vo. Lond. 1783 Do.

—— —— Another copy 8vo. Lond. 1783 Sir Charles Locock

—— Essays on the Practice of Midwifery in Natural and Difficult Labours *plate*, 8vo. Lond. 1792 Dr. Rigby

With three autograph letters of the author.

—— —— Another copy *plate*, 8vo. Lond. 1792 Sir Charles Locock

—— Letters on his Essays on Midwifery, see *Hamilton* (A.)

OSIANDER (Friedrich Benjamin). Lehrbuch der Entbindungskunst 8vo. Göttingen, 1799 Dr. Rigby

Theil 1. Litterärische und pragmatische Geschichte dieser Kunst.

—— Grundriss der Entbindungskunst 2 vols. 12mo. Gottingen, 1802 Do.

Theil 1. Schwangerschafts und Geburts-lehre.
—— 2. Entbindungs und Werkzeuge-Lehre.

OULD (Fielding). Treatise on Midwifery *plates*, 8vo. Dublin, 1742 Do.

—— —— Another copy *plates*, 8vo. Dublin, 1742 Do.

PAGET (James). Report on the Progress of Human Anatomy and Physiology in 1844-5 8vo. Lond. 1846 Do.

—— Ditto, Part 2 8vo. —— —— Do.

PARIS (J. A.). Pharmacologia; edition the seventh vol. 2, 8vo. Lond. 1829 Dr. Clay

PARKES (Samuel). The Chemical Catechism; twelfth edition 8vo. Lond. 1826 Do.

PARR (Bartholomew). London Medical Dictionary including, under distinct heads, every branch of Medicine, with whatever relates to Medicine, in Natural Philosophy, Chemistry and Natural History *plates*, 2 vols. 4to. Lond. 1809 Do.

Presented by

PARRY (Caleb Hillier). Lectures on Midwifery and Diseases of Women, written at Edinburgh, 1777
MS. 2 vols. 8vo. —— Dr. Rigby

Given to Dr. Rigby by the cousin of the author, Charles H. Parry, Dec. 26, 1831.

PEARCE (A. L.). Essay on Children, and that disease designated Mesenteric Obstruction, Atrophy or Marasmus 12mo. Lond. 1838 Dr. Clay

—— —— Another copy 12mo. Lond. 1838 Sir Charles Locock

PERFECT (William). Cases in Midwifery, with references, quotations, and remarks
2 vols. 8vo. Rochester, 1783 Dr. Clay

PETER (Robert). Chemical Examination of the Urinary Calculi in the Museum of Transylvania University, U.S. 8vo.—— —— Dr. Rigby

PETIT (A.). Recueil de Piéces relatives à la question des Naissances Tardives 8vo. Amsterdam, 1766 Dr. Clay

PEU (Philip). La Pratique des Ac[c]ouchemens [avec Reponse aux Observations de M. Mauriceau sur la Grossesse et l'Accouchement]
port. and plates, 8vo. Paris, 1694 Dr. Rigby

PLENCK (Josephus Jacob). Hygrologia Corporis Humani sive Doctrina chemico-physiologica de Humoribus, in Corpore humano contentis 8vo. Viennæ, 1794 Dr. Clay

PLOUCQUET (Guilielmus G.). Initia Bibliothecæ Medico-Practicæ et Chirurgicæ realis sive Repertorii Medicinæ Practicæ et Chirurgiæ, cum Continuatione
10 vols. 4to. Tubingæ, 1793-1800 Do.

PORTAL (Paul). Compleat Practice of Men and Women Midwives; translated *plate*, 8vo. Lond. 1705 Do.

—— Compleat Practice of Men and Women Midwives; translated 8vo. Lond. 1763 Dr. Rigby

POWER (John). Essays on the Female Economy; on the Periodical Discharge of the human female, and on a species of abortion 8vo. Lond. 1821 Dr. Clay

—— Treatise on Midwifery; second edition, with numerous Cases, and observations on Premature Expulsion of the Ovum, and Retention of the Placenta
8vo. Lond. 1823 Dr. Rigby

PRICHARD (Thomas). Statistical Report of Cases of Insanity in Abington Abbey, Northampton, 1854-8
No. 3, 8vo. 1859 Dr. Clay

Presented by

PRIESTLEY (William O.). Lectures on the Development of the Gravid Uterus 8vo. Lond. 1860 Sir Charles Locock

PUCHELT (Benno R.). Quæ fuerint doctrinæ de Tumoribus in Pelvi partum impedientibus fata, dissertatio inauguralis 8vo. Heidelbergæ, 1839 Dr. Rigby

PUGH (Benjamin). Treatise of Midwifery chiefly with regard to the Operation, with Cases, and description of Instruments *plates*, 8vo. Lond. 1754 Do.

QUIN (Charles William). Treatise on the Dropsy of the Brain, illustrated by cases, with observations on the use of the Digitalis Purpurea in Dropsies 8vo. Lond. 1790 Dr. Clay

RADFORD (Thomas). Essays on various subjects connected with Midwifery 8vo. Manchester, 1834-7 Do.

Umbilical Hæmorrhage.
Malposition of Fœtal Head.
Long Forceps.
Turning.
Inversion of Uterus.

—— —— Another copy *plate*, 8vo. Manchester, 1832-7 Do.

—— Two Cases of Impracticable Labour arising from Malacosteon of the Pelvis, in which the Cæsarean Operation was performed (from 'Edinb. Med. and Surg. Journal') 8vo. —— Dr. Rigby

RAMSBOTHAM (Francis H.). Principles and Practice of Obstetric Medicine and Surgery in reference to the process of Parturition *plates*, 8vo. Lond. 1841 Dr. Clay

RAMSBOTHAM (John). Practical observations in Midwifery, with a selection of cases Part 1, 8vo. Lond. 1832 Sir Charles Locock

RAYER (P.). Treatise on Diseases of the Skin, founded on new researches in Pathological Anatomy and Physiology; translated by Wm. B. Dickinson 8vo. Lond. 1833 Dr. Clay

RAYNALDE (Thomas). The Birth of Mankynde, otherwyse named the Woman's Booke, newly set foorth, corrected and augmented *black letter*, 4to. *no date* Dr. Rigby

Some leaves imperfect at the commencement.

—— The Birth of Mankynd otherwyse named the Woman's Booke (*title and last two leaves in MS.*) *black letter, woodcuts*, 4to. 1540 Dr. Clay

READ (William). Placenta Prævia, its history and treatment, (Library of Pract. Med. of Massachusetts Med. Society, vol. 23) 8vo. Philadelphia, 1861 Sir Charles Locock

Presented by

Reeve (Henry) of Norwich, see *Hamilton's* Lectures on Midwifery

Reid (David Boswell).—Extracts from official documents, reports, and papers referring to the Progress of Dr. Reid's Plan for Ventilation 8vo. —— —— Dr. Rigby

Reid (James). Annual Report of Parochial Lying-in Cases during 1837 and 1839-40 (from 'London Med. Gazette') 8vo. —— —— Do.

—— Report of Pathological Lying-in Cases, 1840-42 (from 'London Med. Gazette') 8vo. —— Do.

—— Obstetric Report of Cases occurring in the practice of the Infirmary of St. Giles and St. George, Bloomsbury, and of the Northern Dispensary, during three years ending 1845 (from 'Lond. Med. Gazette') 8vo. 1845 Do.

—— On the symptoms, causes, and treatment of Puerperal Insanity (from 'Journal of Psycholog. Med.') 8vo. —— —— Do.

—— On Infantile Laryngismus, with observations on Artificial Feeding, as a frequent cause of this complaint, and of other convulsive diseases of infants 8vo. Lond. 1849 Sir Charles Locock

Reid (John). Essays on Hypochondriacal and other Nervous Affections 8vo. Lond. 1816 Dr. Clay

Reuter (Carl). Der Kaiserschnitt bei einer Lebenden, verglichen mit dem Kaiserschnitte bei einer an dem Ende ihrer Schwangerschaft plötzlich verstorbenen 8vo. —— —— Dr. Rigby

—— Der Kaiserschnitt bei einer Lebenden 8vo. —— —— Do.

Reuter (Karl Friedrich). Ueber Præcocität der Menstruation in psychologischer und kranioskopischer Hinsicht 8vo. Wiesbaden, 1846 Do.

Rhazes. Treatise on the Smallpox and Measles; translated by William Alex. Greenhill (Sydenham Society) 8vo. Lond. 1848 Dr. Clay

Rhind (William). Treatise on the nature and cure of Intestinal Worms of the human body, arranged according to the classification of Rudolphi and Bremser *plates*, 8vo. Lond. 1829 Do.

Ridge (Benjamin). Physiology of the Uterus, Placenta and Fœtus, with observations on the Membrana Meconii and Rete Vasculare in the fœtus *plate*, 8vo. Lond. 1845 Do.

Presented by

Rigby (Edward, sen.). Essay on the Uterine Hæmorrhage which precedes the delivery of the full grown fœtus, with cases [First edition.] 8vo. Lond. 1775 Dr. Rigby

—— —— Another copy, [with additional cases in MS.] 8vo. ib. 1775 Do.

—— —— Second edition 8vo. ib. 1777 Do.

—— —— Third edition 8vo. ib. 1784 Do.

—— —— ditto, another copy 8vo. ib. 1784 Do.

—— —— Fourth edition 8vo. ib. 1789 Do.

—— —— Another copy 8vo. ib. 1789 Sir Charles Locock

—— —— Fifth edition 8vo. ib. 1811 Dr. Rigby

—— —— Sixth edition, with Memoir by John Cross 8vo. Norwich, 1822 Do.

—— Versuch über die Mutterblutflüsse; übersetzt 12mo. Leipzig, 1786 Do.

—— Essay on the Use of the Red Peruvian Bark in the cure of Intermittents 8vo. Lond. 1783 Do.

—— —— Another copy 8vo. Lond. 1783 Do.

—— Charitable Inoculation of the Poor in Norwich 8vo. Norwich, 1783 Do.

—— Account of Mr. James Deeker's two Aerial Expeditions from the City of Norwich, June, 1785 8vo. Norwich, 1785 Do.

—— Account of the ascent of Major Money (Extract from a Newspaper) 1785 Do.

—— Essay on the theory of the Production of Animal Heat, and its application in the treatment of Cutaneous Eruptions, Inflammations, &c. 8vo. Lond. 1785 Do.

—— Versuch über den Ursprung der thierischen Wärme; mit Anmerkungen übersetzt von August F. A. Diel 8vo. Altenburg, 1789 Do.

—— Reports of the Special Provision Committee at Norwich, with account of the Savings in the Diet of the Workhouses, &c. 8vo. Lond. 1788 Do.

—— Chemical observations on Sugar 8vo. Lond. 1788 Do.

—— Chemische Bemerkungen über den Zucker; aus dem Englischen mit Anmerkungen von Samuel Hahnemann 8vo. Dresden, 1791 Do.

—— Midwifery Book. List of Patients delivered from Sept. 1783 to Dec. 1786 MS. 4to —— Do.

Presented by

RIGBY (Edward, jun.). Memoranda for young practitioners in Midwifery 24mo. Lond. 1837 Dr. Rigby

Interleaved with MS. additions and corrections by the author.

——— ——— ditto. six copies, 24mo. Lond. 1837 Do.

——— ——— second edition two copies, 24mo. Lond. 1848 Do.

——— System of Midwifery (Tweedie's Library of Medicine). 8vo. Do.

Author's proofs, interleaved, with various MS. corrigenda by the late Dr. Rigby.

Inserted also are several letters relative to Difficult Points in Practice from S. Monckton, Th. Green, Henry A. Cleaver, D. R. McNab, and E. Vise.

——— ——— ditto. pp. 201—308 8vo. Do.

——— System of Midwifery; with notes and additional illustrations by Isaac Hays 8vo. Philadelphia, 1841 Do.

——— On Dysmenorrhœa and other Uterine affections, in connection with derangement of the assimilating functions *plates*, 8vo. Lond. 1844 Do.

——— ——— Another copy *plates*, 8vo. Lond. 1844 Dr. Clay

——— ——— Another copy *plates*, 8vo. Lond. 1844 Sir Charles Locock

——— ——— The two plates to the work 100 sets Dr. Rigby

——— On the Constitutional Treatment of Female Diseases [The original MS. of the work], 4to—— Do.

——— On the Constitutional Treatment of Female Diseases 8vo. Lond. 1856 Do.

Author's proof sheets, interleaved, with MS. corrigenda and Memoranda, Draft for Index, &c.

——— ——— Another copy, author's proof sheets 8vo. Lond. 1856 Do.

——— [Collection of his MS. Lectures on Midwifery and Diseases of Women and Children.] 4to. Do.

——— Lectures on Midwifery, see JOURNALS (London Med. and Surg. Journ).

——— See *Hunter* on the Gravid Uterus (second edition).

——— See *Naegele*, Mechanism of Parturition (translated).

——— MS. Memoranda, see *Churchill*, *Hunter*, *Jones* (T. W.), *Smith* (W. Tyler)

RITGEN (Ferdinand August). Beiträge zur Aufhellung der Verbindung der Menschlichen Frucht mit dem Fruchthälter und der Ernährung derselben *plates*, folio, Leipzig, 1835 Dr. Rigby

Presented by

RIVERIUS (Lazarus). Opera Medica Universa; editio ultima *title imperfect*, folio Paris, 1646 Dr. Clay

Institutiones Medicæ.
Praxis Medica.
Observationes Medicæ.

ROBERTON (John). Observations on the Mortality and Physical Management of Children 12mo. Lond. 1827 Do.

ROCHE (Nicolaus). Diss. Med. Inaug. de Peritonitide Puerperarum 8vo. Edinb. 1818 Do.

ROEDERER (Joannes Georgius). Elementa Artis Obstetriciæ *portrait*, 8vo. Gottingæ, 1759 Dr. Rigby

——— Elementa Artis Obstetritiæ; edidit, annotationibus Henricus A. Wrisberg 8vo. Goettingæ, 1766 Do.

ROGER (Henri). De la Température chez les enfants à l'état physiologique et pathologique 8vo. Paris, 1844 Sir Charles Locock

ROOTES (Mr.). Case of. See *Watts*.

ROSEN von ROSENSTEIN (Nicholas). Diseases of Children, and their remedies; translated by Andrew Sparrman 8vo. Lond. 1776 Dr. Rigby

ROUTH (C. H. F.). Infant Feeding, and its influence on Life, or the causes and prevention of Infant Mortality 12mo. Lond. 1860 Do.

RUFFUS Ephesius. De Hominis partibus; see *Aretæus*

RYAN (Michael). Manual of Midwifery, or Compendium of Gynœcology and Paidonosology; third edition 12mo. Lond. 1831 Dr. Clay

RYLEY (S.). See *Astruc's* Midwifery (additions)

SALMON (Frederick). Practical Essay on Stricture of the Rectum, illustrated by cases, with observations on Piles and the Hæmorrhoidal excrescence; third edition 8vo. Lond. 1829 Dr. Rigby

SARELL (Richard). Sur un très grand Polype adhérent de la cavité de la Matrice opéré par excision, et sur l'excision des Polypes dans la cavité même de la Matrice 8vo. Constantinople, 1860 The Author

SAXTORPH (Matthias). Gesammelte Schriften geburtshülflichen, praktischen und physiologischen Inhalts; herausgegeben, mit dessen Biographie von Paul Scheel *plates*, 8vo. Kopenhagen, 1803 Dr. Rigby

SCARPA (Antonio). Memoir on the Congenital Club-feet of Children, and on the mode of correcting that deformity; translated by J. H. Wishart *plates*, 4to. Edinb. 1818 Dr. Clay

Presented by

SCÆVOLA de St. Marthe. Pædotrophia, or the art of Nursing and Rearing Children; a poem, translated with notes, life of the author, &c., by H. W. Tytler 8vo. Lond. 1797 — Dr. Clay

SCHAIBLE (Karl). Ueber Croup und Tracheotomie, Inaugural dissertation 4to. Basel, 1853 — Dr. Rigby

SCHEEL (Paul). See *Saxtorph* (Biographie).

SCHLEGEL (Johann W.). See *Mulder*, Zangen und Hebel in der Geburtshülfe (uebersetzt).

SCHMIDTMÜLLER (Joh. Ant.). Handbuch der medizinischen Geburtshülfe 8vo. Frankfurt, 1809 — Do.

Theil 1. Krankheiten der Schwangeren und Gebärenden.
—— 2. Krankheiten der Wöchnerinnen und Neugebornen.

SCHMITT (Wilhelm Joseph). Sammlung zweifelhafter Schwangerschaftsfälle 8vo. Wien, 1818 — Do.

SCHULTZE (Bernhard Sigmund). Ein Kaiserschnitt *plate*, 4to. Jena, 1862 — The Author

SCOTT (P. N.). Case of a separation of a portion of the Uterus during severe Labour *plate*, 8vo. Lond. 1821 — Dr. Rigby

SEMMELWEIS (Ignaz Philipp). Die Aetiologie, der Begriff, und die Prophylaxis des Kindbettfiebers 8vo. Pest, 1861 — Executors of Dr. Rigby

SEVERINUS (M. A.). Liber de Efficaci Medicina. See *Hildanus*, Opera

SEVERN (Charles). First Lines of the Practice of Midwifery, with remarks on the forensic evidence requisite in cases of fœticide and infanticide *plates*, 8vo. Lond. 1831 — Dr. Clay

SEWELL (Richard Clarke). Treatise on the Law of Coroner, with copious precedents of inquisitions, and practical forms of proceedings interleaved in 2 vols. (with some printed additions) 8vo. Lond. 1843 — Do.

SHAW (Peter). New Practice of Physic; fifth edition Vol. 2, 8vo. Lond. 1738 — Do.

SIMMONS (Foart). See JOURNALS (*Medical* Facts).

SIMON (John). Physiological Essay on the Thymus Gland 4to. Lond. 1845 — Do.

SIMPSON (James Y.). Remarks on the Conduct and Duties of young Physicians 8vo. Edinb. 1842 — Dr. Rigby

—— Memoir on the sex of the Child, as a cause of difficulty and danger in human parturition 8vo. Edinb. 1844 — Do.

Presented by

SIMPSON (James Y.) Some Remarks on the Treatment of Unavoidable Hæmorrhage, by extraction of the Placenta before the child (from 'Lond. Med. Gazette') 8vo. 1845 Dr. Rigby

——— [Correspondence between Dr. Simpson, Dr. Ramsbotham, and Dr. Lee, in relation to ditto] 1845 Do.

——— Observations regarding the influence of Galvanism upon the action of the Uterus during Labour (from 'Edinb. Monthly Journal') 8vo. Edinb. 1846 Do.

——— Suggestions regarding the anatomical source and pathological nature of Post-Partum Hemorrhage (from 'Northern Journal of Med.') 8vo. 1846 Do.

——— Clinical Lectures on Midwifery and the Diseases of Women and Infants during 1845-46 (from 'Northern Journal of Med.') 8vo. 1846 Do.

——— Clinical Lectures on Midwifery, and the Diseases of Women and Children, Lecture I. (from 'Edinb. Monthly Journal') *plate*, 8vo. —— Do.

——— Cases of Excision of the Cervix Uteri for Carcinomatous Disease (from 'Dublin Quarterly') *plates*, 8vo. Dublin, 1846 Do.

——— On the Diagnosis and Treatment of Retroversion of the Unimpregnated Uterus (from 'Dublin Quarterly') 8vo. Dublin, 1848 Do.

——— Anæsthetic Midwifery; Report on its early history and progress (from 'Edinb. Monthly Journal' 8vo. Edinb. 1848 Do.

——— Anæsthesia in Surgery; does it increase or decrease the mortality attendant upon Surgical operations (from 'Edinb. Monthly Journal') 8vo. Edinb. 1848 Do.

——— Anæsthesia, or the employment of Chloroform and Ether in Surgery, Midwifery, &c. 8vo. Philadelphia, 1849 Dr. Clay

——— On the detection and treatment of Intra-Uterine Polypi *plates*, 8vo. Edinb. 1850 Dr. Rigby

——— Contributions to the Pathology and Treatment of Diseases of the Uterus (from 'Edinb. Monthly Journal') 8vo. —— Do.

——— On the Nature of the Membrane occasionally expelled in Dysmenorrhœa (from 'Edinb. Monthly Journal') 8vo. —— Do.

——— Contributions to Intra-Uterine Pathology. Part I Notices of Cases of Peritonitis in the Fœtus in Utero (from 'Edinb. Medical and Surg. Journal') 8vo. —— Do.

Presented by

SIMPSON (James Y.) Contributions to Intra-Uterine Pathology. Part II. On the Inflammatory Origin of some varieties of Hernia and Malformation in the Fœtus (from 'Edinb. Med. and Surg. Journal') 8vo. —— Dr. Rigby

—— Case of amputation of the neck of the Womb, followed by pregnancy; with remarks on the cauliflower excrescence from the Os Uteri (from 'Edinb. Med. and Surg, Journal') *plate*, 8vo. —— Do.

—— See *Keiller*

SIMS (James). See *Foster's* Midwifery

SINCLAIR (Edward B.) and George JOHNSTON. Practical Midwifery, comprising an account of 13,748 Deliveries at the Dublin Lying-in Hospital, during seven years, commencing Nov. 1847 8vo. Lond. 1858 Dr. Rigby

SMEE (Alfred). General Debility and Defective Nutrition, their causes, consequences, and treatment 12mo. Lond. 1859 Sir Charles Locock

SMELLIE (William). Sett of Anatomical *Tables*, with explanations and an abridgement of the Practice of Midwifery atlas folio, Lond. 1754 Dr. Rigby

—— —— Another copy atlas folio, Lond. 1754 F. S. Haden, Esq.

—— Treatise on the Theory and Practice of Midwifery; second edition 8vo. Lond. 1752 Sir Charles Locock

—— —— with a collection of cases and observations; third edition 2 vols. 8vo. Lond. 1756 Sir Charles Locock

—— —— fourth edition 3 vols. 8vo. Lond. 1762 Dr. Rigby

—— —— Another edition *plates*, 3 vols. 8vo. Lond. 1779 Dr. Clay

—— —— Remarks on, see *Burton*

—— Letter on the impropriety of his Wooden Forceps, &c., see *Douglas*

—— Answer to a late Pamphlet "A Letter to Dr. Smellie, showing the Impropriety of his Forceps" [Douglas's] 8vo. Lond. —— Dr. Rigby

SMILES (John Finch). Essay on the Cæsarean Operation 12mo. Edinb. 1853 Dr. Cl a

SMITH (H. Spencer). See *Bischoff* on Periodical Maturation of Ova (translated)

SMITH (John). See *Kennedy* on Obstetric Auscultation (legal notes)

SMITH (Robert). Disput. Med. Inaug. de Febre Infantili Remittente 8vo. Edinb. 1817 Do.

Presented by

SMITH (Wm. Tyler). The Pathology and Treatment of Leucorrhœa 8vo. Lond. 1855 Dr. Rigby
MS. mems. of Dr. Rigby.

SMYTH (James Richard). Miscellaneous contributions to Pathology and Therapeutics, being a series of original and practical papers on Rickets, Hydrocephalus, Impotence and Sterility, Pulmonary Apoplexy, and Hæmoptysis 8vo. Lond. 1844 Dr. Clay

SNOW (John). On the Inhalation of the Vapour of Ether in Surgical Operations 8vo. Lond. 1847 Sir Charles Locock

SOHEGE (Carolus Joan.). De Graviditate Extrauterina, dissertatio inauguralis 8vo. Heidelb. 1841 Dr. Rigby

SOMMER (Franz). Einiges aus dem Bereiche der Geburtshülfe 8vo. —— —— Do.

SONNTAG (Ernestus H.). Dissertatio Inauguralis de Rhachitide congenita · *plate*, 8vo. Heidelbergæ, 1844 Do.

SOUTHAM (George). Removal of a Dropsical Ovarium 8vo. Lond. 1843 Do.
With autograph letter on the subject from the author.

—— Ovariotomy: Removal of an Encysted Tumour of the Left Uterine Appendages 8vo. Salford, 1845 Do.

SPACHIUS (Israel). See *Gynæciorum* libri

SPARRMAN (Andrew). See *Rosen*, Diseases of Children (translated)

SPENCE (David). System of Midwifery, theoretical and practical *plates*, 8vo. Edinb. 1784 Do.

SPENGEL (Henricus G.). Dissertatio inauguralis sistens Dilatationem Pelvis ex osteomalacia coarctatæ in partubus observatam 8vo. Heidelb. 1842 Do.

SPILLAN (D.). Manual of the Practice of Medicine 24mo. Lond. 1838 Do.

—— Collection of Medical Formulæ 24mo. Lond. 1838 Do.

STALPARTIUS vander Wiel (C.). Observationum Rariorum Medic. Anatom. Chirurgicarum Centuria prior et Centuriæ posterioris pars prior, acced. de Unicornu et de Nutritione fœtus 2vols. 12mo. Leidæ, 1727 Dr. Clay

STARK (Johann Christian). Lehrbuch der Geburtshülfe, zum Unterricht für Hebammen 8vo. Jena, 1837 Dr. Rigby

STEINAU (Julius Henry). Pathological and philosophical Essay on Hereditary Diseases, with appendix on Intermarriage, and the inheritance of the tendency to moral depravities and crimes 8vo. Lond. 1843 Do.

STEWART (Duncan). Treatise on Uterine Hæmorrhage 8vo. Lond. 1816 Do.

Presented by

STRUVE (Christian Augustus). Familiar treatise on the Physical Education of Children during the early period of their lives; translated, with three Lectures by A. F. M. Willich. 8vo. Lond. 1801 Dr. Clay

SYDENHAM (Thomas). Opera omnia, edidit Guilielmus Alex. Greenhill (Sydenham Soc.) 8vo. Lond. 1844 Do.

SYER (John). Treatise on the Management of Infants 8vo. Lond. 1812 Do.

TANNER (Thomas Hawkes). On the Signs and Diseases of Pregnancy 8vo. Lond. 1860 Dr. Rigby

——— ——— Another copy 8vo. Lond. 1860 The Author

TATE (George). Treatise on Hysteria 8vo. Lond. 1830 Dr. Clay

TAYLOR (Alfred S.). Elements of Medical Jurisprudence, with a selection of Cases, and Analyses of opinions at Coroners' Inquests 8vo. Lond. 1843 Do.

TAYLOR (Thomas). On some new Species of animal Concretions 8vo. —— Dr. Rigby

THACKRAH (Charles Turner). Lectures on Digestion and Diet royal 8vo. Lond. 1824 Dr. Clay

THEMMEN (Phœbus Hitzerus). Diss Inaug. De Mensibus, ex Materia quadam peculiari, ovariis secreta, oriundis 8vo. Lugd. Batav. 1781 Sir Charles Locock

THOMAS (Robert). The Modern Practice of Physic; fifth edition 8vo. Lond. 1816 Dr. Clay

TIEDEMANN (Friedrich). Von den Duverneyschen, Bartholinschen oder Cowperschen Drüsen des Weibs, und der schiefen Gestaltung und Lage der Gebärmutter *plates*, 4to. Heidelberg, 1840 Dr. Rigby

With autograph letter of the author.

TILT (Edward John). On Diseases of Menstruation and Ovarian Inflammation, in connexion with sterility, pelvic tumours, and affections of the womb 8vo. Lond. 1850 Do.

——— ——— Another copy 8vo. Lond. 1850 Dr. Clay

——— ——— Another copy 8vo. Lond. 1850 Sir Charles Locock

TOLVER (A.). The Present State of Midwifery in Paris, with a theory of the cause and mechanism of Labour 8vo. Lond. 1770 Dr. Rigby

TOMKYNS (Thomas). See *La Motte*, Midwifery (translated)

TURNER (Daniel). Treatise of Diseases incident to the Skin with appendix on Local Remedies; fourth edition *portrait*, 8vo. Lond. 1731 Do.

Presented by

Tytler (H. W.). See *Scevola's* Pædotrophia (notes)

Underwood (Michael). Treatise upon Ulcers of the Legs 8vo. Lond. 1783 — Sir Charles Locock

With MS. additions.

—— Surgical Tracts, containing a Treatise upon Ulcers of the Legs, and Scrofulons Tumours &c.; second edition with observations on Disorders of the Eye and on Gangrene 8vo. Lond. 1788 — Dr. Clay

—— Treatise on the Diseases of Children 2 vols. 12mo. Lond. 1789 — Sir Charles Locock

—— —— fifth edition vol. 1, 8vo. Lond. 1805 — Dr. Rigby

—— —— with directions for the management of Infants from the birth; sixth edition 3 vols. 12mo. Lond. 1811 — Dr. Clay

—— —— eighth edition, with notes by Samuel Merriman 8vo. Lond. 1827 — Sir Charles Locock

Ure (Alexander). On Gouty Concretions, with a new method of treatment (from 'Med.-Chir. Trans.') 8vo. Lond. 1841 — Dr. Rigby

Vaughan (J.). Cases and Observations on the Hydrophobia; with an account of the Cæsarian Section, and on dividing the symphisis of the Ossa Pubis; second edition 8vo. Lond. 1778 — Do.

—— —— Another copy *plates*, 8vo. Lond. 1778 — Sir Charles Locock

Velpeau (Alf.). Traité complet de l'Art des Accouchemens; deuxième édition *plates*, 2 vols. 8vo. Paris, 1835 — Dr. Clay

—— —— troisieme edition roy. 8vo. Bruxelles, 1835 — Sir Charles Locock

—— Eléments de Médecine Opératoire roy. 8vo. Bruxelles, 1835 — Dr. Clay

Victoria. Catalogue of the Victorian Exhibition 1861, with prefatory Essays, indicating the progress, resources, and physical characteristics of the Colony, by W. H. Archer, F. Mueller, R. B. Smyth, Neumayer, &c 8vo. Melbourne, 1861 — University of Melbourne

—— (in French) Essais divers, &c. 8vo. ib. 1861 — Do.

—— (in German) Die Colonie Victoria in Australien, &c. 8vo. ib. 1861 — Do.

—— The Victorian Government Prize Essays, 1860 *map* 8vo. Melbourne, 1861 — Do.

—— See *Archer*

Presented by

VIRCHOW (Rudolf). Das Eierstocks-Colloid *plate*, 8vo. Dr. Rigby

WAGNER (Damian). Beschreibung eines Geburtsfalles bei prolapsus Uteri, verbunden mit einer Geschwulst am Mutterhalse und mit Verwachsung des inneren Muttermundes 8vo. —— Do.

WAGSTAFFE (M. F.). Description of a case of Extra-Uterine Fœtation, which terminated fatally by extravasation of blood into the cavity of the abdomen, from a Rupture of the left Fallopian Tube *plate*, 4to. Lond. 1831 Do.

WALLER (Charles). Practical treatise on the function and diseases of the Unimpregnated Womb, with a chapter on Leucorrhœa *plates*, 8vo. Lond. 1840 Dr. Clay

WALSH (Philip Pitt). Practical Observations on the Puerperal Fever 8vo. Lond. 1787 Do.

WALSHE (Walter Hayle). The Nature and Treatment of Cancer *plate*, 8vo. Lond. 1846 Dr. Rigby

With an autograph letter of the author.

WARD (F. O.). Outlines of Human Osteology 2 parts, 24mo. 1838 Do.

WARDEN (Adam). The Application of Prismatic Reflection to the Investigation of Disease *plate*, 8vo. Edinb. 1844 Do.

—— Sequel to Description of the application of a totally reflecting Prism to the Investigation of Disease in the open cavities of the Body *plates*, 8vo. 1845 Do.

—— Observations on Diseases of the Ear, and on the importance of their minute investigation as tending to their more accurate diagnosis and successful treatment (from 'Edinb. Monthly Journal') 8vo. —— Do.

WARE (John). Contributions to the history, diagnosis, and treatment of Croup 8vo. Boston, U.S. 1850 Do.

WARNER (Joseph). Account of the Testicles, their common coverings and coats, and the diseases to which they are liable 8vo. Lond. 1774 Dr. Clay

WATSON (George C.). Some account of the Epidemic Fever in Liverpool in 1844 8to. Worcester, 1846 Do.

WATT (Robert). Treatise on the history, nature and treatment of Chincough with Inquiry into the relative mortality of the principal diseases of Children 8vo. Glasgow, 1813 Do.

—— —— Another copy 8vo. Glasgow, 1813 Do.

Presented by

WATTS (Giles). Reflections on slow and painful Labours, and other subjects in Midwifery 8vo. Lond. 1755 Dr. Rigby

——— Dissertation on the ancient and noted doctrine of Revulsion and Derivation 8vo. Lond. 1754 Do.

——— Letter to Dr. Frewen on his behaviour to the author, in the unhappy case of Mr. Rootes, surgeon (Suppl. to Diss. on Revulsion and Derivation) 8vo. Lond. 1755 Do.

WEATHERHEAD (George Hume). Treatment on Infantile and Adult Rickets, with remarks on nursing, and on a reclining couch for the distorted 12mo. Lond. 1820 Dr. Clay

WEST (Charles). De Pelvi Muliebri ejusque in partu vi et dignitate, dissertatio inauguralis 4to. Berolini, 1837 Dr. Rigby

——— ——— Another copy 4to. Berolini, 1837 Sir Charles Locock

——— Clinical and pathological Report on the Pneumonia of Children, as it prevails among the Poor in London (from 'Brit. and For. Med. Rev.') 8vo. Lond. 1843 Dr. Rigby

——— Report on the Progress of Practical Medicine in the departments of Midwifery, and the diseases of women and children during 1842-3 8vo. Lond. 1844 Do.

——— ditto, during 1844-5 8vo. Lond. 1845 Do.

——— ——— Another copy 8vo. Lond. 1845 Sir Charles Locock

——— ditto, in 1845-6 8vo. Lond. 1847 Dr. Rigby

——— Lectures on the Diseases of Infancy and Childhood 8vo. Lond. 1848 Sir Charles Locock

——— Observations on some of the more important Diseases of Childhood (from 'Lond. Med. Gazette') 8vo. Dr. Rigby

——— Sketch of the more important fluctuations in opinion with reference to the performance of Turning 8vo. Lond. 1850 Do.

——— Enquiry into the pathological Importance of Ulceration of the Os Uteri (Croonian Lectures for 1854) 8vo. Lond. 1854 Sir Charles Locock

——— Lectures on the Diseases of Women 2 vols. 8vo. Lond. 1856 Dr. Rigby

Part 1. Diseases of the Uterus.
— 2. Diseases of the Ovaries, &c.

Presented by

WEST (Charles). Lectures on Diseases of Women, Part I, Diseases of the Uterus 8vo. Lond. 1856 Sir Charles Locock

—— See *Naegele* (H. F.) on Obstetric Auscultation (translation)

WHITE (Charles). Treatise on the management of Pregnant and Lying-in Women; second edition *plates*, 8vo. Lond. 1777 Dr. Rigby

With autograph letter of the author.

—— —— Another copy 8vo. Lond. 1777 Dr. Clay

—— —— third edition *plate*, 8vo. Lond. 1785 Sir Charles Locock

—— Observations on Gangrenes and Mortifications, accompanied with Convulsive Spasms, or arising from local injury 8vo. Warrington, 1790 Dr. Clay

—— Inquiry into the nature and cause of Swelling of the lower extremities in Lying-in Women *plates*, 2 parts, 8vo. Warrington, 1784 Manchester, 1801 Do

—— —— Another copy *plates*, 2 parts in 1, 8vo. Lond. 1792, Manchester, 1801 Do.

WHITEHEAD (James). On the causes and treatment of Abortion and Sterility, the result of an inquiry into the physiological and morbid conditions of the Uterus, with reference to Leucorrhœal affections, and the diseases of Menstruation *plate* 8vo. Lond. 1847 Dr. Rigby

—— —— Another copy *plate*, 8vo. Lond. 1847 Dr. Clay

—— On the Transmission, from Parent to Offspring of some forms of disease and of morbid taints and tendencies 8vo. Lond. 1851 Do.

WIEL (Vander) see *Stalpartius*

WIGAND (Justus Heinrich). Die Geburt des Menschen; herausgegeben von Dr. Franz Carl Naegele *plates*, 2 vols. 8vo. Berlin, 1820 Dr. Rigby

WILHELMI (Carolus F.). De Perityphlitide, dissertatio inauguralis 8vo. Heidelbergæ, 1837 Do.

WILKIE (James). Remarks on Vaccination 12mo. Newcastle, 1833 Dr. Clay

WILLAN (Robert). On Vaccine Inoculation *plates*, 4to. Lond. 1806 Dr. Rigby

WILLICH (A. F. M.) See *Struve* on Children

Presented by

WILLIS (R.) On the Signification and ends of the Portal Circulation (from 'Edinb. Monthly Journal') 8vo. —— Dr. Rigby

WILMER (B.) Cases and Remarks in Surgery, with Appendix containing the method of curing the Bronchocele in Coventry 8vo. London, 1779 Sir Charles Locock

WILMOT (E. S.). See *Bienville* on Nymphomania (translated)

WILSON (Erasmus). On Eczema Infantile 12mo. Lond. 1856 Dr. Clay

WILSON (J. G.). Two Cases illustrative of the advantages of Turning as an alternative or substitute for Craniotomy and the Long Forceps in Pelvic Contraction 8vo. Glasgow, 1857 Do.

WISHART (J. H.). See *Scarpa* on Club Feet (translated)

WRISBERG (Henricus A.). See *Roederer*, Ars Obstetricia (annotationes)

YELLOWLY (John). Observations on the statement made by Dr. Douglass of Cheselden's Improved Lateral Operation of Lithotomy (from 'Med.-Chir. Trans.') 8vo. Lond. 1829 Dr. Rigby

YOUNG (Samuel). Inquiry into the Nature and Action of Cancer, with a mode of cure by natural separation 8vo. Lond. 1805 Do.

—— —— Ditto, *reprinted* 8vo. Lond. —— Do.

—— Minutes of Cases of Cancer, Part II, being further Reports of Cancerous cases successfully treated by Pressure 8vo. Lond. 1818 Do.

TRANSACTIONS, REPORTS, ETC.

Presented by

DUBLIN MEDICAL TRANSACTIONS of the Association of Fellows and Licentiates of the King and Queen's College of Physicians in Ireland; new series, vol. i, Part I. 8vo. Dublin, 1830 Dr. Rigby

DUBLIN HOSPITAL REPORTS and Communications in Medicine and Surgery vol. 4, 8vo. Dublin, 1827 Dr. Clay

GESELLSCHAFT FÜR GEBURTSHÜLFE IN BERLIN, Verhandlungen, Parts III. to VIII. 8vo. Berlin, 1848-55 Dr. Rigby

GUY'S HOSPITAL REPORTS, Nos. 1, 2, 3, and 5, 8vo. 1836-7 Dr. Clay

Medical Communications [by a SOCIETY for PROMOTING MEDICAL KNOWLEDGE] *plates*, 2 vols. 8vo. Lond. 1784-90 Do.

Medical Observations and Inquiries, by a SOCIETY OF PHYSICIANS in London; fourth edition 6 vols. 8vo. Lond. 1771-84 Do.

Medical Records and Researches selected from the papers of a private Medical Association *plates*, 8vo. Lond. 1813 Do.

MEDICAL SOCIETY OF LONDON—
Transactions vols. 1 and 2, 8vo. Lond. 1861 The Society

SOCIETY for the Improvement of MEDICAL and CHIRURGICAL KNOWLEDGE—
Transactions vol. 3, 8vo. Lond. 1812 Dr. Clay

MEDICAL AND CHIRURGICAL SOCIETY (Royal)—
Medico-Chirurgical Transactions vols. 1 and 2, 8vo. Lond. 1809-11 Do.

——— Medico-Chirurgical Transactions vol. 45, 8vo. Lond. 1862 The Society

Presented by

MEDICAL SOCIETY of the State of New York— Dr. N. C.
Transactions for 1862 8vo. Albany, 1862 Husted

OBSTETRICAL SOCIETY OF LONDON—
Transactions [from the commencement in 1859] (2 sets) 8vo. ——

OBSTETRIC SOCIETY OF EDINBURGH—
Abstract of Proceedings for 1846-8; series VI. and VII 8vo. Edinb. 1847-8 Dr. Rigby

PROVINCIAL MEDICAL AND SURGICAL ASSOCIATION—
Transactions
vols. 2 to 8 and vol. 16, part II. 8vo. Lond. 1834-49 Dr. Clay

ROYAL SOCIETY—
Philosophical Transactions, 1806-7-9-10; portions of volumes 4to. —— Do.

Knight, on Alburnous Vessels of Trees.
——— on the Bark of Trees.
Wollaston, on Fairy Rings.
Knight, on the Influence of Male and Female Parents on their Offspring.
——— on Parts of Trees impaired by Age.
——— on the Motion of the Tendrils of Plants.

——— Philosophical Transactions; portions of the volumes for 1807-9-10 4to. —— Do.

Allen and Pepys, on Carbonic Acid.
Marcet, on the Waters of the Dead Sea.
Wollaston, on a Reflective Goniometer.
Pearson, on Expectorated Matter.
Brande, on Albumen.
Allen and Pepys, on Respiration.
Pearson, on Pus.
Pepys, on a Eudiometer.

JOURNALS.

Presented by

American Journal of the Medical Sciences, edited by Isaac Hays, M.D. (July and October, 1862) 8vo. The Editor

Annales de Chemie parts of vols. 12 to 16. 8vo. Paris, 1792-3 Dr. Rigby

Archives Générales de Médecine tome 3, 8vo. Paris, 1823 Dr. Clay

Braithwaite (W.) Retrospect of Practical Medicine and Surgery Vol. 1 to 22. 12mo. Lond. 1840-51 Do.

British and Foreign Medical Review, edited by J. Forbes and J. Conolly [with general index] 25 vols. 8vo Lond. 1836-48 Sir Charles Locock

——— See *Medico-Chirurgical Review*

British and Foreign Medico-Chirurgical Review [from 1848 to the present time] vols. 1 to 6 bound, the rest in Nos. 8vo. Lond. 1848— Do.

Dublin Medical Press Vol. 2. 4to. 1839 Dr. Clay

London Medical and Surgical Journal vols. 6 and 7. 8vo. 1835 Dr. Rigby

Containing the lectures on Physiology of Dr. Graves, and those on Midwifery of Dr. Rigby.

London Medical Gazette, a weekly Journal of Medicine and the Collateral Sciences [from the commencement, in 1827] 20 vols. 8vo. Lond. 1827-37 Sir Charles Locock

——— New series, vols. 21 to 32 8vo. Lond. 1838-48 Do.

London Medical Gazette—Various numbers between 1829 and 1837, containing Papers on Obstetrical subjects, by Dr. Rigby, Dr. R. Lee, Dr. Ramsbotham, &c. 2 vols. 8vo. Dr. Rigby

London Medical Review, Nos. 8 to 10 and vol. ii. No. 2 8vo. 1860-1 Dr. Clay

Medical and Physical Journal, conducted by T. Bradley and A. F. M. Willich, vols. 1, 2 8vo. Lond. 1799 Do.

——— ——— vols. 20, 21, and 23 to 28 8vo. Lond. 1808— Do.

Presented by

Medical Facts and Observations [edited by Dr. Foart Simmons] 8 vols. 8vo. Lond. 1791-1800 Dr. Clay

Sequel to London Medical Journal.

Medical Times
vol. 3 to 10, 12, and 14 to 16, in 9 vols. 4to. Lond. 1840-47 Do.

Medico-Chirurgical Journal, or Quarterly Register of Medical and Surgical Science (or London Medical and Surgical Review) [1818-20], by James Johnson 2 vols. 8vo. Lond. 1819-20 Sir Charles Locock

——— Medico-Chirurgical Review, and Journal of Medical Science, analytical series, edited by James Johnson 4 vols. 8vo. Lond. 1821-4 Do.

——— Medico-Chirurgical Review, new series, by James Johnson [Vol. 41, 1844, wanting] vols. 1 to 40, 8vo. Lond. 1824-44 Do.

——— Medico-Chirurgical Review and Journal of Practical Medicine, new series vols. 1 to 6, 8vo. Lond. 1845-7 Do.

——— See *British and Foreign Med.-Chir. Review*

Midland Quarterly Journal of the Medical Sciences vol. i and vol. ii, part i, 8vo. Birmingham, 1857-8 Dr. Clay

Monatsschrift für Geburtskunde und Frauenkrankheiten vol. 15 —— Dr. E. Martin

Ranking (W. H.) Half-yearly Abstract of the Medical Sciences vols. 1 to 8 [wanting vol. 4]. 12mo. Lond. 1845-8 Dr. Clay

Recueil général de Médecine, par J. Sedillot tome 58, 8vo. Paris, 1816 Do.

West India Quarterly Magazine, containing original communications, reviews, &c. in Medicine, Surgery, &c., edited by Hugh Croskery, Nos. 1 to 4 8vo. 1861-2 The Editor

Wonderful Magazine (The), or Marvellous Chronicle vol. i, 8vo. Lond. 1764 Sir Charles Locock

---

Portfolio containing various Obstetrical Drawings, Prints, Diagrams, &c. Dr. Rigby

---

CPSIA information can be obtained
at www.ICGtesting.com
Printed in the USA
LVHW101648140522
718424LV00010B/114

9 783375 003333